Praise for the Aubrey/Maturin Series
and Patrick O'Brian

"The best historical novels ever written."
— Richard Snow, *New York Times Book Review*

"I love these books. . . . [They offer] the same sense of lived experience as Hilary Mantel. . . . They will sweep you away and return you delighted, increased and stunned. If the phrase 'Napoleonic war fiction' fills you with anticipation, then you don't need me to convince you to read [Patrick] O'Brian. But for the rest of you. . . . [P]lease, just trust me."
— Nicola Griffith, NPR

"A few books work their way . . . onto [bestseller] lists by genuine, lasting excellence—witness *The Lord of the Rings*, or Patrick O'Brian's sea stories."
— Ursula K. Le Guin

"Like John LeCarré, [O'Brian] has erased the boundary separating a debased genre from 'serious' fiction. O'Brian is a novelist, pure and simple, one of the best we have."
— Mark Horowitz, *Los Angeles Times Book Review*

"[Patrick O'Brian has] the power of bringing near to the reader . . . savagery and tenderness, beauty and mystery and boldness and dignity."
— Eudora Welty

"O'Brian's eloquent admirers include not merely distinguished critics and reviewers but . . . thousands upon thousands of fervent readers who thank the gods for him. . . . [H]is work accomplishes nobly the three grand purposes of art: to entertain, to edify, and to awe."
— Stephen Becker, *Paris Review*

"For escapist reading, I especially like the sea novels of Patrick O'Brian."
— Bill Bryson

T0026211

"O'Brian's narrative... provides endlessly varying shocks and surprises—comic, grim, farcical and tragic. An essential of the truly gripping book for the narrative addict is the creation of a whole, solidly living world for the imagination to inhabit, and O'Brian does this with prodigal specificity and generosity."

—A. S. Byatt

"I prefer the Aubrey-Maturin series to all others. . . . Every book is packed to absolute straining with erudition, wit, history, and thunderous action."

—Joe Hill

"All of the Aubrey-Maturin series by Patrick O'Brian [is on my shelves]."

—Mindy Kaling, *New York Times*

"Although O'Brian is ingenious at devising new adventures, it is the richness of his characters which justifies his reader's continuing enthusiasm. . . . O'Brian acknowledges Jane Austen as one of his inspirations, and she need not be ashamed of the affiliation."

—*The New Yorker*

"I fell in love with [O'Brian's] writing straightaway, at first with *Master and Commander*. . . . Jack Aubrey and Stephen Maturin always remind me a bit of Mick and me."

—Keith Richards

"Aubrey and Maturin have been described as better than Holmes and Watson, the equal of Quixote and Panza. . . . All this is true. And the marvel is, it hardly says enough."

—John Balzar, *Los Angeles Times*

"The high seas are his home place—as they were for Melville and Conrad. And his time, the age and era of the great Nelson, is the altogether gracefully resurrected past. . . . But Patrick O'Brian is a novelist for here and now, someone who shares his splendid vision, his wonderful sense of character, with a growing number of lucky contemporary readers."

—George Garrett

"There are two types of people in the world: Patrick O'Brian fans, and people who haven't read him yet."

—Lucy Eyre, *Guardian*

Desolation
Island

THE WORKS OF PATRICK O'BRIAN

The sails of a square-rigged ship, hung out to dry in a calm.

1. Flying jib
2. Jib
3. Fore topmast staysail
4. Fore staysail
5. Foresail, or course
6. Fore topsail
7. Fore topgallant
8. Mainstaysail
9. Maintopmast staysail
10. Middle staysail
11. Main topgallant staysail
12. Mainsail, or course
13. Maintopsail
14. Main topgallant
15. Mizzen staysail
16. Mizzen topmast staysail
17. Mizzen topgallant staysail
18. Mizzen sail
19. Spanker
20. Mizzen topsail
21. Mizzen topgallant

PATRICK O'BRIAN

Desolation Island

THE AUBREY/MATURIN SERIES

W. W. NORTON & COMPANY
Independent Publishers Since 1923

For information about permission to reproduce selections from this book, write to
Permissions, W. W. Norton & Company, Inc., 500 Fifth Avenue, New York, NY 10110

For information about special discounts for bulk purchases, please contact
W. W. Norton Special Sales at specialsales@wwnorton.com or 800-233-4830

Manufacturing by LSC Harrisonburg
Book design by Chris Welch
Production manager: Delaney Adams

Library of Congress Cataloging-in-Publication Data

Names: O'Brian, Patrick, 1914–2000, author.
Title: Desolation island / Patrick O'Brian.
Description: New York, NY : W. W. Norton & Company, 2021. |
Series: The Aubrey/Maturin series |
"First published in 1978 by William Collins Sons & Co. Ltd."—
Title page verso.
Identifiers: LCCN 2021026537 | ISBN 9780393541625 (paperback)
Subjects: GSAFD: War stories. | Historical fiction.
Classification: LCC PR6029.B55 D47 2021 | DDC 823/.914—dc23
LC record available at https://lccn.loc.gov/2021026537

W. W. Norton & Company, Inc., 500 Fifth Avenue, New York, N.Y. 10110
www.wwnorton.com

W. W. Norton & Company Ltd., 15 Carlisle Street, London W1D 3BS

1 2 3 4 5 6 7 8 9 0

FOR MARY, WITH LOVE

CHAPTER ONE

The breakfast-parlour was the most cheerful room in Ashgrove Cottage, and although the builders had ruined the garden with heaps of sand and unslaked lime and bricks, and although the damp walls of the new wing in which this parlour stood still smelt of plaster, the sun poured in, blazing on the covered silver dishes and lighting the face of Sophie Aubrey as she sat there waiting for her husband. A singularly lovely face, with the lines that their earlier poverty had marked upon it quite smoothed away; but it had a somewhat anxious look. She was a sailor's wife, and although the Admiralty in the goodness of its heart had allowed her the company of her husband for a surprising length of time, appointing him (much against his will) to the command of the local Sea-Fencibles in recognition of his services in the Indian Ocean, she knew that this period was coming to an end.

The anxiety changed to unmixed pleasure as she heard his step: the door opened; a ray of sun fell on Captain Aubrey's beaming face, a ruddy face with bright blue eyes; and she knew as certainly as though it had been written on his forehead that he had bought the horse he coveted. 'There you are, sweetheart,' he cried, kissing her and lowering himself into a chair by her side, a broad elbow-chair that creaked beneath his weight.

'Captain Aubrey,' she said, 'I am afraid your bacon will be cold.'

'A cup of coffee first,' said he, 'and then all the bacon in the world – Lord, Sophie –' lifting the covers with his free hand – 'here's Fiddler's Green – eggs, bacon, chops, kippered herrings, kidneys, soft tack . . . How is the tooth?' Here he was referring to his son George, whose howls had made the household uneasy for some time past.

'It is through!' cried Mrs Aubrey. 'He cut it in the night, and now he is as good as gold, poor lamb. You shall see him after breakfast, Jack.'

Jack laughed with pleasure; but after a pause, and in a slightly conscious tone, he said, 'I rode over to Horridge's this morning to stir them up. Horridge was not in the way, but his foreman said they had no notion of coming to us this month – the lime ain't thoroughly slaked, it appears – and even then they will be at a stand, with their carpenter laid up, and the pipes not yet delivered.'

'What nonsense,' said Sophie. 'There was a whole gang of them laying pipes at Admiral Hare's only yesterday. Mama saw them as she was driving by; and she would have spoken to Horridge, but he dodged behind a tree. Builders are strange, unaccountable creatures. I am afraid you were very disappointed, my dear?'

'Why, I was a little put out, I must confess: and on an empty belly, too. But, however, seeing I was there, I stepped into Carroll's yard, and bought the filly. I bated him forty guineas of her, too; and, do you see, quite apart from the foals she will bring, it will be a remarkable saving, since she will train with Hautboy and Whiskers – with her to bring out their metal, I will lay fifty to one on placing Hautboy in the Worral Stakes.'

'I long to see her,' said Sophie, with a sinking heart: she disliked most horses, except those of the very gentle kind, and she particularly disliked these running horses, even though they descended, through Old Bald Peg, from Flying Childers and the Darley Arabian himself. She disliked them for many reasons, but she was better at disguising her feelings than her husband, and with a happy, eager look he ran on unchecked, 'She will be up some time in the forenoon: the only thing I am not quite pleased about is the new stable floor. If only we could have had some sun, and a good brisk north-easter, it would have dried out completely . . . nothing so bad for a horse's hoofs as remaining damp. How is your mama this morning?'

'She seems quite well, I thank you, Jack: a little remaining head-ache, but she ate a couple of eggs and a bowl of gruel, and she will come down with the children. She is quite excited about seeing the doctors, and she has dressed earlier than usual.'

'What can be keeping Bonden?' said Jack, glancing at the stern regulator, his astronomical clock.

'Perhaps he fell off again,' said Sophie.

'Killick was there to prop him up: no, no, 'tis ten to one they are prating about their horsemanship in the Brown Bear tap, the infernal lubbers.' Bonden was Captain Aubrey's coxswain, Killick his steward; and whenever it could be managed they moved with him from one command to the next: both had been bred to the sea from their earliest years – Bonden, indeed, had been born between two of the *Indefatigable*'s lower-deck guns – and while both were prime man-of-war's men, neither was a great hand with a horse. Yet it was clear to all that in common decency the mail addressed to the Commanding Officer of the Sea-Fencibles had to be fetched by a mounted man; and daily the two traversed the Downs on a powerful, thickset cob, conveniently low to the ground.

A powerful, thickset woman, Mrs Williams, Captain Aubrey's mother-in-law, walked in, followed by a nurse with the baby and a one-legged seaman shepherding the two little girls. Most of the servants in Ashgrove Cottage were sailors, partly because of the extreme difficulty of inducing maids to stay within reach of Mrs Williams's tongue: upon seamen, however, long inured to the admonition of the bosun and his mates, its lash fell unregarded; and in any case its virulence was much diminished, since they were men, and since in fact they kept the place as trim as a royal yacht. The rigid lines of the garden and shrubbery might not be to everyone's taste, nor the white-painted stones that bordered every path; but no housekeeper could fail to be impressed by the gleaming floors, sanded, swabbed, and flogged dry every day before sunrise, nor by the blaze of copper in the spotless kitchen, the gleaming windowpanes, the paint perpetually renewed.

'Good morning to you ma'am,' said Jack, rising. 'I trust I see you well?'

'Good morning, Commodore – that is to say Captain – you know I never complain. But I have a list here –' waving a paper with her symptoms written upon it – 'that will make the doctors stare. Will the hairdresser be here before them, I wonder? We are not to be talk-

ing about me, however: here is your son, Commodore, that is to say
Captain. He has cut his first tooth.' She led the nurse forward by the
elbow, and Jack gazed into the little pink, jolly, surprisingly human
face among all the wool. George smiled at him, chuckled, and displayed his tooth: Jack thrust his forefinger into the wrapping and said,
'How are you coming along, eh? Prime, I dare say. Capital, ha, ha.'
The baby looked startled, even stunned – the nurse backed away –
Mrs Williams said, 'How can you call out so loud, Mr Aubrey?' with
a reproachful look, and Sophie took the child into her arms, whispering, 'There, there, my precious lamb.' The women gathered round
young George, telling one another that babies had sensitive ears – a
thunder-clap might throw them into fits – little boys far more delicate than girls.

Jack felt a momentary and quite ignoble pang of jealousy at the
sight of the women – particularly Sophie – concentrating their idiot
love and devotion upon the little creature, but he had barely time to
be ashamed of it, he had barely time to reflect 'I have been Queen of
the May too long', before Amos Dray, formerly bosun's mate in HMS
Surprise and, in the line of duty, the most conscientious, impartial
flogger in the fleet before he lost his leg, shaded his mouth with his
hand and in a deep rumble whispered, 'Toe the line, my dears.'

The two little pudding-faced twin girls in clean pinafores stepped
forward to a particular mark on the carpet, and together, piping high
and shrill, they cried, 'Good morning, sir.'

'Good morning, Charlotte. Good morning, Fanny,' said their
father, bending down until his breeches creaked to kiss them. 'Why,
Fanny, you have a lump on your forehead.'

'I'm not Fanny,' said Charlotte, scowling. 'I'm Charlotte.'

'But you are wearing a blue pinafore,' said Jack.

'Because Fanny put on mine; and she fetched me a swipe with her
slipper, the — swab,' said Charlotte, with barely contained passion.

Jack cast an apprehensive look at Mrs Williams and Sophie, but
they were still cooing over the baby, and almost at the same moment
Bonden brought in the post. He put it down, a leather bag with Ash-

grove Cottage engraved on its brass plate; and the children, their grandmother and their attendants leaving the room at this point, he begged pardon for being late: the fact of the matter was, it was market-day down there. Horses and cattle.

'Crowded, I dare say?'

'Uncommon, sir. But I found Mr Meiklejohn and told him you was not attending at the office till Saturday.' Bonden hesitated: Jack gave him a questioning look, and he went on, 'The fact of the matter is, Killick made a purchase, a legal purchase. Which he asked me to tell you first, your honour.'

'Aye?' said Jack, unlocking the bag. 'A nag, I suppose: well, I wish him joy of it. He may put it in the old byre.'

'Not exactly a nag, sir, though it was in a halter: two legs and a skirt, if I may say so. A wife, sir.'

'What in God's name does he want with a wife?' cried Jack, staring.

'Why, sir,' said Bonden, blushing and looking quickly away from Sophie, 'I can't rightly say. But he bought one, legal. It seems her husband and she did not agree, so he brought her to market in a halter; and Killick, he bought her, legal – laid down the pewter in sight of one and all, and shook hands on it. There was three to choose on.'

'But you cannot possibly sell your wife – treat women like cattle,' cried Sophie. 'Oh fie, Jack; it is perfectly barbarous.'

'It does seem a little strange, but it is the custom, you know, a very old custom.'

'Surely you will never countenance such a wicked thing, Captain Aubrey?'

'Why, as to that, I should not like to go against custom: common law too, for all I know. Not unless there was any constraint – undue influence, as they say. Where would the Navy be without we followed our customs? Let him come in.'

'Well, Killick,' he said, when the pair stood before him, his steward an ugly slab-sided middle-aged man rendered more awkward than usual by his present bashfulness, the young woman a snapping black-eyed piece, a perfect sailor's delight. 'Well, Killick, I trust you are not rushing into matrimony without due consideration? Matrimony is a very serious thing.'

'Oh no, sir. I considered of it: I considered of it, why, the best part of twenty minutes. There was three to choose on, and this here –' looking fondly at his purchase – 'was the pick of the bunch.'

'But, Killick, now I come to think of it, you had a wife in Mahon. She washed my shirts. You must not commit bigamy you know: it is against the law. You certainly had a wife in Mahon.'

'Which I had two, your honour, t'other in Wapping Dock; but they was more in the roving, uncertificated line, if you follow me, sir, not bought legal, the halter put into my hand.'

'Well,' said Jack, 'so I suppose you want to add her to the establishment. You will have to go in front of the parson first, however: cut along to the Rectory.'

'Aye aye, sir,' said Killick. 'Rectory it is.'

'Lord, Sophie,' said Jack when they were alone once more. 'What a coil!' He opened the bag. 'One from the Admiralty, another from the Sick and Hurt Board, and one that looks as though it must be from Charles Yorke – yes, that is his seal – for me; and two for Stephen, care of you.'

'I wish I *could* take care of him, poor dear,' said Sophie, looking at them. 'These are from Diana, too.' She laid them on a side table, to wait with another, addressed in the same bold determined hand to Stephen Maturin, Esqr., MD, and gazed at them in silence.

Diana Villiers was Sophie's cousin, a slightly younger woman, one with a far more dashing style and a black-haired, dark-blue-eyed beauty that some preferred to Mrs Aubrey's: at a time when Sophie and Jack had been separated, long before their marriage, both Jack and Stephen Maturin had done all they could to win Diana's favours; and in the result Jack very nearly wrecked both his career and his marriage, while Stephen, who had supposed she would marry him at last, had been most cruelly wounded by her departure for America under the protection of a Mr Johnson – so wounded that he had lost much of his taste for life. He had supposed she would marry him, for although his reason told him that a woman of her connections, beauty, pride and ambition could not be an equal match for the illegitimate son of an Irish officer in the service of His Most Catholic Majesty and a Catalan lady, a short, disagreeably plain man whose ostensible status was that of a naval surgeon, no more, his heart was entirely lost to her, and to his infinite cost it had overruled his head.

'Even before we heard she was in England, I knew that something was working on his mind, poor dear Stephen,' said Sophie. She would have added her ludicrous proof – a new wig, new coats, a dozen of the finest cambric shirts – but since she loved Stephen as few brothers are ever loved, she could not bear any ridicule to touch him. She said, 'Jack, why do you not find him a decent servant? At the worst of times Killick would never have allowed you to go out in a shirt a fortnight old, odd stockings, and that dreadful old coat. Why has he never had a steady, reliable man?'

Jack knew very well why Stephen had never kept a servant for any length of time, never a man who could grow used to his ways, but had contented himself with casual and preferably illiterate Marines or ship's boys or a half-witted member of the after-guard: for Dr Maturin, as well as being a naval surgeon, was one of the Admiralty's most highly-valued intelligence agents, and secrecy was essential to the preservation of his life and the lives of his many contacts in the vast area controlled by Buonaparte, to say nothing of the prosecution of his work. This had necessarily come to Jack's knowledge in the course of their service together, but he did not intend to pass it on, even to Sophie, and now he made a reply to the effect that whereas by steady application you might hope to persuade a parcel of pig-headed mules, nothing, no not purchase-upon-purchase, would ever shift Stephen from his chosen path.

'Diana could, by waving her fan,' said Sophie: her face was not well-suited for crossness, but now it expressed a variety of cross emotions – indignation for Stephen, displeasure at this renewed complication, and something of the disapproval or even jealousy of a woman with a very modest sexual impulse for one in whom it was quite the reverse – the whole tempered by an unwillingness to think or speak unkindly.

'I dare say she could,' said Jack. 'And if she could make him happy again by doing so, I should bless the day. There was a time, you know,' he went on, staring out of the window, 'when I thought it was my duty as a friend – when I thought I was doing the right thing by him to keep them apart. I thought that she was just plain wicked – devilish – wholly destructive – and that she would be the end of him. But now I don't know: perhaps you should never interfere in such things: too delicate. Yet if you see a fellow walking blindfold into a pit . . . I acted for the best, according to my lights; but it may be that my lights were not of the very brightest kind.'

'I am sure you were right,' said Sophie, touching his shoulder to comfort him. 'After all, she had shown herself to be – well, to be, what shall I say? – a light woman.'

'Why, as to that,' said Jack, 'the older I grow, the less I think of capers of that kind. People differ so, even if they are women. There may be women for whom these things are much as they might be for a man – women for whom going to bed to a man doesn't necessarily signify, don't affect them in the essence, as I might say, and don't make whores of 'em. I beg your pardon, my dear, for using such a word.'

'Do you mean,' asked his wife, taking no notice of his last remark, 'that there are men to whom breaking the commandment does not signify?'

'I am got on to dangerous ground, I find,' said Jack. 'What I mean is . . . I know very well what I mean, but I am not clever at putting it into words. Stephen could explain it far better – could make it clear.'

'I hope that neither Stephen nor any other man could make it clear to me that breaking marriage vows did not signify.'

At this juncture a terrible animal appeared among the builders' rubble, a low dull-blue creature that might have been a pony if it had had any ears; it carried a small man on its back and a large square box. 'Here is the hairdresser,' cried Jack. 'He is hellfire – he is extremely late. Your mother will have to be frizzed after the consultation: the doctors are due in ten minutes, and Sir James is as regular as a clock.'

'The house on fire would not induce Mama to appear with her head undressed,' said Sophie. 'They will have to be shown the garden; and in any case Stephen will certainly be late.'

'She could put on a cap,' said Jack.

'Of course she will put on a cap,' said Sophie, with a pitying look. 'How could she possibly receive strange gentlemen without a cap? But her hair must be dressed under it.'

The consultation for which these gentlemen were converging upon Ashgrove Cottage had to do with Mrs Williams's health. At an earlier period she had undergone an operation for the removal of a benign tumour with a fortitude that astonished Dr Maturin, accustomed though he was to the uncomplaining courage of his seamen; but since then her spirits had been much oppressed by vapours, and it was hoped that the high authority of these eminent physicians would persuade her to take the waters at Bath, at Matlock Wells, or even farther north.

Sir James had travelled in Dr Lettsome's chariot: they arrived together, and together they absolutely declined Captain Aubrey's suggestion of viewing the garden; so Jack, called away to receive the horse-coper and his new filly, left them with the decanter.

The physicians had taken note of the new wings being added to Ashgrove Cottage, of the double coach-house, the long line of stables, the gleaming observatory-dome on its tower at a distance: now their practiced eyes assessed the evident wealth of the morning-room, its new and massive furniture, the pictures of ships and naval engagements by Pocock and other eminent hands, of Captain Aubrey himself by Beechey in the full-dress uniform of a senior post-captain, with the red ribbon of the Bath across his broad chest, looking cheerfully at a bursting mortar-shell in which were to be seen the Aubrey arms with the honourable augmentation of two Moors' heads, proper – Jack had recently added Mauritius and La Réunion to his grateful sovereign's crown, and although the Heralds' College had but a hazy notion of these possessions, they had felt that Moors would suit the case. The physicians looked about them as they sipped their wine, and with a visible satisfaction they gauged their fees.

'Allow me to pour you another glass, my dear colleague,' said Sir James.

'You are very good,' said Dr Lettsome. 'It really is a most capital Madeira. The Captain has been fortunate in the article of prize-money, I believe?'

'They tell me that he recaptured two or three of our Indiamen at La Réunion.'

'Where is La Réunion?'

'Why, it is what they used to call the Ile Bourbon – in the neighbourhood of the Mauritius, you know.'

'Ah? Indeed?' said Dr Lettsome; and they turned to the subject of their patient. The tonic effects of steel commended; the surprising side-effects of colchicum, when exhibited in heroic doses; valerian quite exploded; the great value of a pregnancy in these and indeed in almost all other cases; leeches behind the ears always worth a trial; lenitives considered, and their effect upon the spleen; hop-pillows; cold-sponging, with a pint of water on an empty stomach; low diet, black draughts; and Dr Lettsome mentioned his success with opium in certain not dissimilar cases. 'The poppy,' he said, 'can make a rose of a termagant.' He was pleased with his expression: in a louder, rounder voice he said, 'Of a termagant, the poppy can make a rose.' But Sir James's face clouded over, and he replied, 'Your poppy is very well, in its proper place; but when I consider its abuse, the danger of habituation, the risk of the patient's becoming a mere slave, I am sometimes inclined to think that its proper place is the garden-plot. I know a very able man who did so abuse it, in the form of the tincture of laudanum, that he accustomed himself to a dose of no less than eighteen thousand drops a day – a decanter half the size of this. He broke himself of the habit; but in a recent crisis of his affairs he had recourse to his balm once more, and although he was never as who should say opium-drunk, I am credibly informed that he was not sober either, not for a fortnight on end, and that – Oh, Dr Maturin, how do you do?' he cried as the door opened. 'You know our colleague Lettsome, I believe?'

'Your servant, gentlemen,' said Stephen. 'I trust you have not been waiting on me?'

Not at all, they said; their patient was not yet ready for them; might they tempt Dr Maturin to a glass of this capital Madeira? They might, said Dr Maturin, and as he drank he observed that it was shocking how corpses had risen: he had been cheapening one that very morning, and the villains had had the face to ask him four guineas – the London price for a provincial cadaver! He had represented to them that their greed must stifle science, and with it their own trade, but in vain: four guineas he had had to pay. In fact he was quite pleased with it: one of the few female corpses he had seen with that curious quasicalcification of the palmar aponeuroses – fresh, too – but since it was only the hands that interested him at the moment, would either of his colleagues choose to go snacks?

'I am always happy to have a good fresh liver for my young men,' said Sir James. 'We will stuff it into the boot.' With this he rose, for the door had opened, and Mrs Williams came in, together with a strong smell of singed hair.

The consultation ran its weary course, and Stephen, sitting a little apart, felt that the grave attentive physicians were earning their fee, however exorbitant it might prove. They both had a natural gift for the histrionic side of medicine, which he did not possess to any degree: he also wondered at the skill with which they managed the lady's flow. He wondered, too, that Mrs Williams should tell such lies, he being in the room: 'she was a homeless widow, and since her son-in-law's degradation she had been unwilling to appear in public.' She was not homeless. The mortgage on Mapes, her large and spreading house, had been paid off with the spoils of Mauritius; but she preferred letting it. Her son-in-law, when in command of a squadron in the Indian Ocean, had held the temporary post of commodore, and as soon as the campaign was over, as soon as the squadron was dispersed, he had in the natural course of events reverted to the rank of captain: there was no degradation. This had been explained to Mrs Williams time and again; she had certainly understood the simple facts; and it was no doubt a measure of the strong, stupid, domineering woman's craving for pity, if not approval, that she could now bring it all out again in his presence, knowing that he knew the falsity of her words.

Yet in time even Mrs Williams's voice grew hoarse and Sir James's manner more authoritative; the imminence of dinner became unmistakable; Sophie popped in and out; and at last the consultation came to an end.

Stephen went out to fetch Jack from the stables, and they met half way, among the steaming heaps of lime. 'Stephen! How very glad I am to see you,' cried Jack, clapping both hands on Stephen's shoulders and looking down into his face with great affection. 'How do you do?'

'We have brought it off,' said Stephen. 'Sir James is absolute: Scarborough, or we cannot answer for the consequences; and the patient is to travel under the care of an attendant belonging to Dr Lettsome.'

'Well, I am happy the old lady is to be looked after so well,' said Jack, chuckling. 'Come and look at my latest purchase.'

'She is a fine creature, to be sure,' said Stephen, as they watched the filly being led up and down. A fine creature, perhaps a shine too fine, even flashy; slightly ewe-hocked; and surely that want of barrel would denote a lack of bottom? An evil-tempered ear and eye. 'Will I get on her back?' he asked.

'There will never be time,' said Jack, looking at his watch. 'The dinner-bell will go directly. But –' casting an admiring backward eye as he hurried Stephen away – 'is she not a magnificent animal? Just made to win the Oaks.'

'I am no great judge of horseflesh,' said Stephen, 'yet I do beg, Jack, that you will not lay money on the creature till you have watched her six months and more.'

'Bless you,' said Jack, 'I shall be at sea long before that, and so will you, I hope, if your occasions allow it – we must run like hares – I

have great news – will tell you the moment the medicoes are away.'
The hares blundered on, gasping. Jack cried, 'Your dunnage is in your
old room, of course,' and plunged up the stairs to shift his coat, reappearing to wave his guests to the dining-table as the clock struck the
first stroke of the hour.

'One of the many things I like about the Navy,' said Sir James, half
way through the first remove, 'is that it teaches a proper respect for
time. With sailors a man always knows when he is going to sit down
to table; and his digestive organs are grateful for this punctuality.'

'I could wish a man also knew when he was going to rise from
table,' observed Jack within, some two hours later, when Sir James's
organs were still showing gratitude to the port and walnuts. He
was boiling with impatience to tell Stephen of his new command,
to engage him, if possible, to sail with him once more on this voyage, to admit him to the secret of becoming enormously rich, and to
hear what his friend might have to say about his own affairs – not
those which had filled his recent absence, for there Stephen was no
more loquacious than the quieter sort of tomb, but those which were
connected with Diana Villiers and the letters that had so lately been
carried up to his room. Yet aloud he said, 'Come, Stephen, this will
never do. The bottle is at a stand.' Although Jack's voice was loud and
clear, Stephen did not move until the words were repeated, when he
started from his reflections, gazed about, and pushed the decanter
on: the two physicians looked at him attentively, their heads on one
side. Jack's more familiar eye could not make out any marked change:
Stephen was pale and withdrawn, but not much more so than usual;
perhaps a little dreamier; yet even so Jack was heartily glad when the
doctors excused themselves from taking tea, called for their footman,
were led into the coach-house by Stephen for a grisly interval with a
saw, bundled a shrouded object into the back of the chariot (it had
carried many another – the footman and the horses were old hands
in the resurrection line), reappeared, pocketed their fees, took their
leave, and rolled away.

Sophie was alone in the drawing-room with the tea-urn and the coffee-pot when at last Jack and Stephen joined her. 'Have you told Stephen about the ship?' she asked.

'Not yet, sweetheart,' said Jack, 'but am on the very point of doing so. Do you remember the *Leopard*, Stephen?'

'The horrible old *Leopard*?'

'What a fellow you are, to be sure. First you crab my new filly, the finest prospect for the Oaks I have ever seen – and let me tell you, old Stephen, with all due modesty, that I am the best judge of a horse in the Navy.'

'I make no doubt of it, my dear: I have seen several naval horses, ha, ha. For horses they must be called, since they generally have the best part of four legs, and no other member of the animal kingdom can call them kin.' Stephen relished his own wit, and for some little time he uttered the creaking sound that was his nearest approach to laughter, and said, 'The Oaks, forsooth!'

'Well,' said Jack, 'and now you say "the horrible old *Leopard*". To be sure, she was something of a slug, and a ramshackle old slug, when Tom Andrews had her. But the Dockyard has taken her in hand – a most thoroughgoing overhaul – Snodgrass's diagonal braces – new spirketting – Roberts's iron-plate knees throughout – I spare you the details – and now she is the finest fifty-gun ship afloat, not excepting *Grampus*. Certainly the finest fourth-rate in the service!' The finest fourth-rate in the service: perhaps. But as Jack knew very well, the fourth-rates were a poor and declining class; they had been excluded from the line of battle this last half-century and more; the *Leopard* had never been a shining example of them at any time. Jack knew her faults as well as any man; he knew that she was laid down and half built in 1776; that she had remained in that unsatisfactory state, quietly rotting in the open, for ten years or so; and that she had then been taken to Sheerness, where they eventually launched her on her undistinguished career in 1790. But he had watched her overhaul with a very attentive, professional eye, and although he knew she would never be an outstanding performer he was sure she was seaworthy:

and above all he wanted her not for herself but for her destination: he longed for unknown seas, and the Spice Islands.

'The *Leopard* had quite a number of decks, as I recall,' said Stephen.

'Why, yes: she is a fourth-rate, so she is a two-decker – roomy, almost as roomy as a ship of the line. You will have all the room in the world, Stephen; it will not be like being crammed up tight in a frigate. I must say that the Admiralty has done the handsome thing by me, for once.'

'I think you should have had a first-rate,' said Sophie. 'And a peerage.'

Jack gave her a very loving smile and went on, 'They offered me the choice between *Ajax*, a new seventy-four on the stocks, or the *Leopard*. The seventy-four will be a very fine ship, as good a seventy-four as you could wish; but she would mean the Mediterranean, under Harte; and there's no distinction in the Mediterranean nowa-days. Nor no fortune, either.' Here again Jack was a little devious, for although it was quite true that at this stage of the war there was little for a sailor in the Mediterranean the presence of Admiral Harte had more importance than he chose to explain. In former days Jack had cuckolded the Admiral, an unscrupulous, revengeful man who would not hesitate to break him if he could. During his naval career, Jack had made a great many friends in the service, but he had also made a surprising number of enemies for so amiable a man: some had been jealous of his success; some (and these were his seniors) had found him too independent, even insubordinate in his youth; some disliked his politics (he hated a Whig); and some had the same grudge as Admiral Harte, or fancied they did.

'You have all the distinction a man could wish, Jack,' said Sophie. 'Such dreadful wounds: and quite enough money.'

'If Nelson had been of your mind, sweetheart, he would have cried quits after St Vincent. We should have had no Nile, and where would Jack Aubrey have been then? A mere lieutenant to the end of his days. No, no: a man can't have enough distinction in his line of service.

And I don't know he can ever have enough money either, if it comes to that. But, however, *Leopard* is bound for the East Indies – not that there is likely to be much fighting there,' he added with a glance at Sophie, 'and the charming point about it is that a curious situation has arisen at Botany Bay. *Leopard* is to go south about, deal with the state of affairs in those parts, and then join Admiral Drury somewhere in the neighbourhood of Penang, making observations on her way. Think of the opportunities, Stephen – thousands of miles of almost unknown sea and coastline – wombats on shore for those that like them, because although this is not one of your leisurely exploring voyages, I am sure there would be time for a wombat or a kangaroo, when some important anchorage is to be surveyed – islands never seen, for sure, and their positions to be laid down – and in about a hundred and fifty east, twenty south, we should be in the full path of the eclipse, if only our times coincide – think of the birds, Stephen, think of the beetles and cassowaries, to say nothing of the Tasmanian Devil! There has not been such an opportunity for a philosophical chap since the days of Cook and Sir Joseph Banks.'

'It sounds the sweetest voyage,' said Stephen, 'and I have always longed to see New Holland. Such a fauna – mono-tremes, marsupials . . . But tell me, what is this curious situation to which you advert – what is the state of affairs at Botany Bay?'

'You remember Breadfruit Bligh?'

'I do not.'

'Of course you do, Stephen. Bligh, that was sent to Tahiti in the *Bounty* before the war, to collect breadfruit-trees for the West Indies.'

'Yes, yes! He had an excellent botanist with him, David Nelson: a most promising young man, alas. I was looking into his work on the bromeliads only the other day.'

'Then you will remember that his people mutinied on him, and took his ship away?'

'Sure, I have some hazy recollection of it. They preferred the charms of the Tahitian women to their duty. He survived, did he not?'

'Yes, but only because he was a most prodigious seaman. They turned him adrift with precious little food in a six-oared boat, loaded to the gunwales with nineteen men, and he navigated her close on four thousand miles to Timor. A most astonishing feat! But perhaps he is not quite so lucky with his subordinates: some time ago he was made Governor of New South Wales and the news is that his officers have mutinied on him again – they have deposed him and shut him up. Army people for the most part, I believe. The Admiralty don't like it, as you may imagine, and they are sending out an officer of sufficient seniority to deal with the situation and set Bligh up again or bring him home, according to his judgment.'

'What kind of man is Mr Bligh?'

'I have never met him, but I know he sailed with Cook as master. Then he was given a commission, one of those rare promotions from warrant-rank: a reward, I dare say, for his uncommon seamanship. Then he did well at Camperdown, taking the *Director*, sixty-four, right in among the Dutch ships of the line and then lying alongside their admiral – as bloody a fight as ever you could wish. And he did well at Copenhagen too: Nelson mentioned him particularly.'

'Perhaps it is still another instance of a man's being corrupted by authority.'

'It may be so. But although I cannot tell you much about him, I know a man who can. Do you remember Peter Heywood?'

'Peter Heywood? A post-captain who dined with us aboard the *Lively*? The gentleman upon whom Killick poured the boiling jam sauce, and whom I treated for a not inconsiderable burn?'

'That's the man,' said Jack.

'How did the sauce come to be boiling?' asked Sophie.

'The Port-Admiral was with us, and he always says, jam sauce ain't worth eating if it don't boil; so we shipped a little stove just abaft the scuttle of the coach. Yes, that's the man: the only post-captain in the Navy who was ever condemned to death for mutiny. He was one of Bligh's midshipmen in the *Bounty*, and one of the few men or boys to be taken.'

'How did he come to commit so rash an act?' asked Stephen. 'He seemed to me a mild, peaceable gentleman; he bore the Admiral's strictures on his flinging the jam about with becoming modesty; and he bore the jam itself with so Spartan a fortitude that I should have conceived him incapable of acting in such an inconsiderate manner. Was it the petulance of youth, or a sudden disgust, or a dusky amour?'

'I never asked,' said Jack. 'All I know is that he and four others were ordered to be hanged, and I saw three of them run up to the yard-arm of the *Brunswick* with a nightcap over their eyes when I was a youngster in the *Tonnant*. But the King said it was all stuff to hang young Peter Heywood. So he was pardoned, and presently Black Dick Howe, who had always been fond of him, gave him his commission. I never did learn the ins and outs of it, although Heywood and I were shipmates in the *Fox*: it is a delicate thing to touch upon, a court-martial – and such a court-martial! But we can certainly ask him about Bligh when he comes to the house on Thursday: it is important to know what kind of a man we have to deal with. In any case, I want to ask him about those waters. He knows them well, because he was wrecked in the Endeavour Straits. And even more than that, I want him to tell me about *Leopard*'s little ways: he commanded her in the year five. Or was it six?'

Sophie's attentive ear caught a remote howl, a howl far fainter than it would have been before Ashgrove Cottage burst its seams, but still a howl. 'Jack,' said she, as she hurried from the room, 'you must show Stephen the plans of the orangery. Stephen knows all about oranges.'

'So I shall,' said Jack. 'But first, Stephen – a little more coffee? There is plenty in the pot – first let me tell you about an even more interesting plan. Turn your mind to the wood where the honey-buzzards are nesting.'

'Yes, yes. The honey-buzzards,' cried Stephen, brightening at once. 'I have brought a jointed booth for them.'

'What do they want with a jointed booth? They have a perfectly respectable nest.'

'It is a portable booth. I mean to set it up at the edge of the wood, and advance it by degrees to the rise that dominates their tree. There I shall sit at my ease, unseen, protected from the vicissitudes of the weather, watching the progress of their domestic economy. It is supplied with flaps, and every convenience for making observations.'

'Well, I showed you the Roman mine-shafts, I remember – miles of 'em, and mortal dangerous – but do you know what the Romans mined there?'

'Lead.'

'And do you know what all those lumpy hills are? One of them is the very place where you mean to set up your booth.'

'Dross.'

'Well, Stephen,' said Jack, leaning forward with a very knowing look indeed, 'now I shall tell you something you do not know, for once. That dross is full of lead; and what is more, that lead contains silver. The Romans' way of smelting did not extract it all, no, not by a chalk as long as your arm, and there it lies, thousands and thousands of tons of valuable dross just waiting to be treated by Kimber's new process.'

'Kimber's new process?'

'Yes. I dare say you have heard of him – a very brilliant fellow. He proceeds by lixiviation with some particular chemicals and then by cupellation according to principles discovered by himself. The lead pays for the working, and the silver is pure profit. The scheme would answer even if there were only one part of lead in one hundred and thirty-seven of dross, and one part of silver in over ten thousand; and on the average of close on a hundred random samples, our dross contains more than seventeen times as much!'

'I am amazed. I did not know the Romans ever mined silver in Britain.'

'Nor did I. But here's the proof.' He unlocked the door of a cupboard under the window-seat and came staggering back with a pig of lead upon which there lay a little silver ingot, four inches long. 'That was the result of no more than a first rough trial,' he said. 'No more than a few cart-loads of dross. Kimber set up a little furnace in the old linhay, and I saw the stuff pour out with my own eyes. I wish you had been there.'

'So do I,' said Stephen.

'Of course, it will call for quite a considerable capital outlay – roads, buildings, proper furnaces and so on – and I had thought of using the girls' portions; but it seems that they can't be touched by reason of the trust – that they have to remain in Consols and Navy five per cents, although I proved that it was mathematically impossible for them to yield a seventh part as much, even going by the poorest sample. I do not mean to set it going full-blast until I am likely to be on shore for some years on end –'

'You foresee this eventuality?'

'Oh yes. Unless I am knocked on the head, or unless I am caught doing something very wicked, I should get my flag in the next five years or so – sooner, if those old fellows at the head of the list did not cling to life so – and since it is harder for an admiral to find employment than a captain, I shall have plenty of time to build up my stud and work my mine. But I do mean to make a start, in a modest way, just to get things running and to lay by a fair amount of treasure. Fortunately Kimber is very moderate in his demands: he leases me the use of his patent, and he will supervise the working of the stuff.'

'For a salary?'

'Yes, and a quarter share. A really modest salary, which I think particularly handsome of him, because there is a Prince Kaunitz begging and praying him to attend to his mines in Transylvania, proposing ten guineas a day and a third share; he showed me all sorts of letters from great men in Germany and Austria. But do not run away with the idea that he is one of your enthusiastic vapouring projectors, promising Peru tomorrow: no, no, he is a very honest fellow, scrupulous to a fault, and he gave me fair warning – we may have to operate at a loss for as much as a year. I quite see that, but I can't wait to begin.'

'Surely you do not mean that you will disturb my buzzards, Jack?'

'Never you fear for them. There's a long way to go yet: Kimber still needs time and money to make his patents watertight, and for certain experiments; they will have hatched and flown before we have even lit our furnaces, I dare say. And what is more, Stephen, what is more, you will be well on your way to wealth; because although Kimber is unwilling to admit many venturers, I made him promise to let you in on the ground floor, as he puts it.'

'Alas, Jack. What I have is all bespoke, locked up in Spain. Indeed, I am so short in England that it is my intention to beg you to lend me, let us see – ' consulting a paper, 'seven hundred and eighty pounds.'

'Thank you,' he said, when Jack came back with a draft on his banker. 'I am obliged to you, Jack.'

'I beg you will not speak nor think of obligation,' said Jack. 'Between you and me, it would be precious strange to speak of obligation. By the way, that is drawn on London, but for these coming days, there is plenty of gold in the house.'

'No, no, my dear: this is for a particular purpose. For myself, I am as comfortable as my best friend could wish.'

His best friend gazed at him doubtfully: Stephen did not look comfortable in his mind, and he seemed ill at ease in his body too, weary, sad, constrained.

'What do you say to a ride?' he said. 'I am half engaged to meet some men at Craddock's: they promised me my revenge.'

'With all my heart,' said Stephen, but with so melancholy an attempt at heartiness that Jack could not refrain from saying, 'Stephen, if anything is amiss, and if I can be of any kind of use, you know . . .'

'No, no, Jack: you are very good, however. I am a little low in my spirits, to be sure; but I am ashamed that it should be so apparent. I lost a patient in London, and I am by no means sure that I did not lose him through my own fault. My conscience troubles me: and I grieve for him extremely, a young man full of promise. And then again, in London I met Diana Villiers.'

'Ah,' said Jack awkwardly. 'Just so.' And after a pause in which the horses were led to the door and in which Stephen Maturin reflected upon a third factor of his distress – the hare-brained leaving of a folder containing highly confidential papers in a hackney-coach – Jack added, 'You said Villiers, not Johnson?'

'Yes,' said Stephen, mounting. 'It seems that the gentleman already had a wife in America, and that the decree of nullity or whatever they have in those parts was not to be obtained.'

Diana Villiers was an uncomfortable subject between the two, and after they had ridden for some way, Jack, to change the current of his mind, remarked, 'You would not think there was any skill in a game like Van John, would you? No. Yet these fellows strip me bare almost every time we sit down together. You used to do the same at picquet, but that is another pair of drawers.'

Stephen made no reply: he pushed his horse on faster and faster over the bare down, sitting forward with a set, urgent expression on his face, as though he were making an escape; and so they cantered and galloped over the firm turf until they came to the brow of Portsdown Hill, where Stephen reined in for the steep descent. They stood for a while, surrounded by the smell of hot horse and leather, looking down at the vast sweep of the harbour, Spithead, the Island, and the Channel beyond: men-of-war at their moorings, men-of-war moving in and out, a huge convoy tiding it down off Selsey Bill.

They smiled at one another, and Jack had a premonition that Stephen was about to say something of great importance: a false premonition. Stephen spoke only to remind him that Sophie had desired them to pick up some fish at Holland's, and to add three dabs for the children.

Craddock's was already lighting up when they left their horses with the ostler, and Jack led Stephen under a series of noble chandeliers to the card-room, where he gave a man at a little table inside the door eighteen-pence. 'Let us hope the game will be worth the candle,' he said, looking round. Craddock's was frequented by the wealthier officers, country gentlemen, lawyers, officials in Government employ, and other civilians; and it was among these that Jack saw the men he was looking for. 'There they are,' he said, 'talking to Admiral Snape.

The one in the bag wig is Judge Wray, and the other is his cousin, Andrew Wray, pretty eminent in Whitehall – spends most of his time down here on Navy Office business. I dare say they have made up our table already: I see Carroll standing by until they have finished with the Admiral – the tall fellow in a sky-blue coat and white pantaloons. Now there's a man who understands horses for you. His stables are over behind Horndean.'

'Running horses?'

'Oh yes, indeed. His grandfather owned Potooooooooo, so it's in the blood. Do you choose to take a hand? We play the French game here.'

'I believe not; but I will sit by you, if I may.'

'I should be very happy; you will bring me some of your luck. You was always lucky at cards. Now I must step over to the desk and buy some counters.'

While Jack was gone, Stephen paced about the room. Many of the tables were already occupied, and some quiet, intense, scientific whist was going on; but he had a feeling that the evening had not really begun. He met some naval acquaintances, and one of these, Captain Dundas, said, 'I hope he will prove to be Lucky Jack Aubrey again this evening: last time I was here . . .'

'There you are, Heneage,' cried Jack, bearing down on them. 'Will you join us? We have a table of Van John.'

'Not I, Jack. We half-pay paupers can't stand in the line with nabobs like you.'

'Come along then, Stephen. They are just going to sit down.' He led Stephen to the far end of the room. 'Judge Wray,' he said, 'allow me to name Dr Maturin, my particular friend. Mr Wray. Mr Carroll. Mr Jenyns.' They bowed to one another, uttered civil expressions, and settled down to the broad green baize. The judge carried judicial impenetrability into his social life to such a pitch that Stephen received little impression but that of self-consequence. Andrew Wray, his cousin, was a somewhat younger and obviously far more intelligent man; he had served under the political heads of the Admiralty, and Stephen had heard of him in connection with the Patronage Office and the

Treasury. Jenyns was neither here nor there, a man who had inherited a vast brewery and a broad, pale, unmeaning countenance; but Carroll was a more interesting creature by far, as tall as Jack though less burly, with a long face very like that of a horse, but of a horse endowed with a high degree of life and wit. As he shuffled, his jovial eye, as blue as Jack's, fell upon Stephen, and he smiled, a singularly winning smile that compelled a return: the cards flowed through his hands in an obedient stream.

Each drew in turn, and the deal fell to Mr Wray. Stephen was not familiar with their version of the game, although its childish basis was clear enough; and for a while their cries of 'imaginary tens', 'rouge et noir', 'sympathy and antipathy', 'self and company', and 'clock' were amusing enough. He also took some pleasure in watching their faces – the judge's pomp yielding to a sly satisfaction, and that succeeded by a sourness and an evil-tempered jerk of his mouth; the deliberate nonchalance of his cousin, betrayed now and then by a sudden blaze in his eye; Carroll's intense eagerness, his whole person vividly alive with a look that reminded Stephen of Jack's when he was taking his ship into action. Jack seemed very well with them all, even with the phlegmatic Jenyns, as though he had known them these many years; but that did not mean a great deal. With his open, friendly character, Jack was always well with his company, and Stephen had known him get along famously with country gentlemen whose talk was all of bullocks. There was no money on the table, only counters: these moved from one place to another, though with no determined tide as yet, and as Stephen did not know what they represented his interest in the matter faded quickly. Reminded by the shape of some of the tokens, he thought of Sophie's fish, silently withdrew, and made his way along the busy High Street, past the George, to Holland's, where he bought a couple of fine plump lampreys (his favourite dish) and the dabs: these he carried with him down to the Hard, where the *Mentor*'s crew, just paid off, were bawling and hallooing round a bonfire, together with a growing crowd of the thick, powerful young women known as brutes and a large number of pimps, idle apprentices, and pickpockets. The bonfire sent a ruddy glow far up into the night air, accentuating the darkness: disturbed gulls could be seen far above, their wings a reflected pink; and in the midst of the flames hung the effigy of the *Mentor*'s first lieutenant. 'Shipmate,' said Stephen into the ear of a bemused sailor whose brute was openly robbing him, 'mind your poke.' But even as he spoke he felt a violent twitch at the parcel under his arm. His lampreys and his dabs were gone – a wicked flying boy, not three foot tall, vanished in the milling crowd – and Stephen walked back to the shop, which could now afford him no more than a salmon of enormous price, and a pair of wizened plaice.

Their smell grew more apparent as they warmed against his bosom, and he left them with the horses before returning to his seat. Everything seemed much as it had been, except that Jack's store of counters had grown thin and sparse; they still called 'pay the difference' and 'antipathy'; but there was certainly a new tension. Jenyns' pale expanse of face was sweating more profusely; Carroll's whole being was electric with excitement; the two Wrays were even colder and more guarded. As he was drawing a card, Jack brushed one of his remaining counters, a mother-of-pearl fish, off the table: Stephen picked it up, and Jack said, 'Thankee, Stephen, that's a pony.'

'It looks more like a fish,' said Stephen.

'That is our slang term for five and twenty pound,' said Carroll, smiling at him.

'Indeed?' said Stephen, realizing that they were playing for far, far higher stakes than he had ever imagined. He watched the silly game with much keener attention, and presently he began to think it strange that Jack should lose so much, so often, so regularly. Andrew Wray and Carroll were the principal winners; the judge seemed to be more or less where he had begun; Jack and Jenyns had lost heavily, and they both called for fresh counters before Stephen had been back half an hour. During this half hour he had made up his mind that something was amiss. Something was holding the law of probabilities in abeyance. Just what it was he could not tell, but he was sure that if only he could as it were break the code he should find evidence for the collusion that he sensed. A dropped handkerchief allowed him to inspect their feet, a usual means of communication; but their feet told him nothing. And where did the collusion lie? Between whom? Was Jenyns in fact losing as much as he appeared to be losing, or was he a deeper man than he seemed? It was easy to be too clever by half, and to over-reach oneself, in matters of this kind: in natural philosophy and in political intelligence a good rule was to look into the obvious first, and to solve the easy parts of the problem. The judge had a trick of drumming his fingers on the table; so did his cousin. Natural enough: but was not Andrew Wray's drumming of a some-what particular kind? Not so much the ordinary rhythmic roll as the motion of a man picking out a tune with variations: was he mistaken in thinking that Carroll's lively, piratical eye dwelt upon those move-ments? Unable to decide, he moved round the table and stood behind Wray and Carroll, to establish a possible relationship between the drumming and the cards they held. His move was not directly useful, however. He had not been there for any length of time before Wray called for sandwiches and half a pint of sherry, and the drumming stopped — a hand holding a sandwich is naturally immobilized. Yet with the coming of the wine, the law of probabilities reasserted itself: Jack's luck changed; fish returned to him in a modest shoal; and he stood up somewhat richer than he had sat down.

He displayed no indecent self-complacency; indeed, all the gen-tlemen present might have been playing for love, from their lack of apparent emotion; but Stephen knew that secretly he was delighted. 'You brought me luck, Stephen,' he said, when they had mounted. 'You broke the damnedest sequence of cards I have ever seen in my life, week after goddam week.'

'I have also brought you a salmon, and a pair of plaice.'

'Sophie's fish!' cried Jack. 'God's my life, they had gone completely out of my mind. Thank you, Stephen: you are a friend in a thousand.'

They rode through Cosham in silence, avoiding drunken seamen, drunken soldiers, and drunken women. Stephen knew that Jack had repaired his fortunes in the Mauritius campaign: even with the admiral's share, the proctors' fees, and the civilians' jobbery deducted, the recaptured Indiamen alone must have set him quite high in the list of captains who had done well out of prize-money. But even so . . . When they were clear of the houses he said, 'As such I should tell you some of the disagreeable things that are said to fall to friends; yet since I have so lately borrowed a large sum of money from you, I can scarcely cry up thrift, nor even common prudence, with much decency or conviction. I am struck dumb; and must content myself with observing that Lord Anson, whose wealth had the same source as yours, was said to have gone *round* the world, but never *into* the world.'

'I take your meaning,' said Jack. 'You think they are sharps and I am a flat?'

'I assert nothing: only that in your place I should not play with those men again.'

'Oh come, Stephen, a judge, for all love? And a man so high in Government service?'

'I make no accusation. Though if I had a certainty where in fact I have only a suspicion, a man's being a judge would not weigh heavily. Sure, it is weak and illiberal to speak slightingly of any considerable body of men; yet it so happens that the only judges I have known have been froward companions, and it occurs to me that not only are they subjected to the evil influence of authority but also to that of righteous indignation, which is even more deleterious. Those who judge and sentence criminals address them with an unbridled, vindictive righteousness that would be excessive in an archangel and that is indecent to the highest degree in one sinner speaking to another, and he defenceless. Righteous indignation every day, and publicly applauded! I remember an acquaintance of mine literally foaming – there was a line of white between his lips – as he condemned a wretched youth to transportation for carnal knowledge of a fine bold up-standing wench: yet this same man was himself a smell-smock, a cold, determined lecher, a voluptuary, a libertine, a discreet frequenter of Mother Abbot's establishment in Dover Street; while another, in whose house I have drunk uncustomed wine, tea, and brandy, told a smuggler, with great vehemence, that society must be protected from such wicked men as he and his accomplices. Do not suppose, however, that I am calling this judge of yours a sharper: his respectability may be no more than a useful screen.'

'Well, I shall take care of them,' said Jack. 'I have given them another meeting next week, but I shall keep a weather-eye wide open. A delicate business . . . it would never do to offend Andrew Wray . . .'

They walked their horses up the hill, and over on the right a night-jar churred, perched lengthways on the gibbet at the crest. After half a mile Jack said, 'I cannot believe it of him. He is a great man in the City, apart from anything else. He understands the movement of the Funds, and once he told me that if I put money into Bank Stock, I should certainly make a handsome profit before the month was out. And sure enough, Mr Perceval made a statement, and some people cleared thousands. But I am not such a flat as that, Stephen; stocks and shares is gambling, and I stick to what I understand: ships and horses.'

'And silver-mining.'

'That is entirely different,' cried Jack. 'As I keep telling Sophie, the Lowthers did not have to understand coal when it was found on their land: all they had to do was to listen to experts, see that proper mea-sures were taken, and then set up a coach and six, become the richest family in the north, with God knows how many members in Par-liament and one of them now a lord of the Admiralty at this very minute – but no, she cannot abide poor Kimber, though he is a very civil, obliging little man: calls him a projector. We went to the play last time we were in town, and there was a fellow there, on the stage, that said he could not tell how it was, but every time he and his wife disagreed, it so happened that she was invariably in the wrong: and although everybody simpered and clapped, I thought he put it very well, and I whispered "Coal" in Sophie's ear; but she was laughing so hearty she did not catch it.' He sighed: and then, in a different tone, he said, 'Lord, Stephen, how Arcturus blazes! The orange star up there. We shall have such a blow from the south-west tomorrow, or I'm a Dutchman: still, 'tis an ill wind that spoils the broth, you know.'

Their broth was waiting for them at the cottage, with Sophie, pink and sleepy, the very type of dutiful wife, to ladle it out for them. While Stephen was supping his, Jack left the room and came back with a beautiful model of a ship. 'There,' he said, 'that's Moses Jenkins's work, the Dockyard sculptor. Now that's what I call art – Pheidias ain't in the running. You recognize her, of course?'

Stephen bent low to see the ship as she would appear from the waterline. The figurehead, a lady in a flowing gown, mysteriously opening a covered dish, or perhaps playing cymbals, was vaguely familiar, but he could not put a name to her until his eye caught a bulbous yellow spotted dog in the sweep of the head just behind. 'The horrible old – that is to say, the *Leopard*,' he said.

'Exactly so,' said Jack, with an affectionate, approving look. 'I was afraid her altered stern-transom might have thrown you out, but you smoked her right away. The new-built *Leopard*. Here is her diagonal bracing, do you see? Roberts's iron-plate knees. Everything abaft the clamps of the quarterdeck refashioned. The only thing I do not quite care for is the new-fangled stern-post. It is all exactly to scale, and her measurements are, gun-deck one hundred and forty-six foot five inches, keel one hundred and twenty foot and three-quarters of an inch, beam forty foot eight, and tonnage by our measurement, one thousand and fifty-six. The very thing for a really distant voyage! She only draws fifteen foot eight abaft, light, yet she has seventeen foot six depth of hold! You remember how we cried out for tenpenny nails in the dear old *Surprise*? *Leopard*'s maw will be stuffed with tenpenny nails, and with all kinds of other stores too, such quantities of 'em. And she has plenty of teeth, as you see: twenty-two twenty-four-pounders on the lower deck, twenty-two twelve-pounders on the upper deck, a couple of six-pounders on her forecastle, and four five-pounders on the quarterdeck; and I shall take my brass nines as stern-chasers. A broadside weight of metal of four hundred and forty-eight pound, more than enough to blow any Dutch or French frigate out of the water: for they have no ship of the line in the Spice Islands, so far away.'

'The Spice Islands,' murmured Stephen; and then, feeling that something more was called for, 'What would her complement be, now?'

'Three hundred and forty-three. Four lieutenants, three Marine officers, ten midshipmen: and even the surgeon has two mates, Stephen. No want of company, nor no want of room. And another charming thing about this commission is that at last I have time to prepare for it, and have people after my own heart. Tom Pullings is to be my first lieutenant, Babbington is on his way back from the West Indies, and I hope to pick up Mowett at the Cape. You will see Pullings on Thursday, along with Heywood. And Tom will be as eager as we are to hear about those waters and about Bligh, because obviously he takes over if – I mean, he would be in command if I were on shore.'

Thursday brought Mr Pullings, and in his candid pleasure at seeing Jack and Stephen again he seemed scarcely to have changed from the long-legged, long-armed, shy, friendly, tubular youth Stephen had first met as a midshipman so many years ago; but in fact he was a man of far greater weight, more burly both in character and person. It was apparent, from his competent handling of young George, produced for his inspection, and from his behaviour to Captain Heywood, that he was now in the full tide of his life, and swimming well. His behaviour was of course perfectly deferential, but it was that of a man who had seen a great deal of service, and who thoroughly understood his profession.

Yet in spite of their eagerness, they learnt little about Bligh. 'He did not wish to say anything against Captain Bligh – a capital navigator – very touchy himself, but had no notion of how he offended others – would give you the lie in front of all hands one day and invite you to dinner the next – you never knew where you were with him – led Christian, the master's mate, a sad life of it, yet probably liked him in his own strange way – never knew where he was with *Bounty*'s people – no idea at all – was amazed when they turned on him – an odd, whimsical man: had gone to great pains to teach Heywood how to work his lunar observations, yet had sworn his life away with a most inveterate malice – had also brought his carpenter to court-martial for insolence, and that after they had survived the voyage in the launch together – four thousand miles in an open boat, and you bring a man to trial at Spithead!'

A silence followed this, broken only by the cracking of nuts. Heywood had been a boy at the time: waking from a deep sleep, he found the ship in the hands of armed, angry, determined mutineers, the captain a prisoner, the launch going over the side; he hesitated, lost his head, and went below. It was not very criminal, but it was not very heroic either: he did not like to dwell upon it.

Jack, aware of his feelings, sent the bottle round; and after some time Stephen asked Captain Heywood what he could tell him about the birds of Tahiti. Precious little, it appeared: there were parrots of different sorts, he recalled, and some doves, and gulls 'of the usual kind.'

Stephen lapsed into a reverie while they discussed the *Leopard*'s little ways, and he did not emerge from it until Heywood cried, 'Edwards! There's a man I don't mind telling you my opinion of. He was a blackguard, and no seaman neither; and I hope he rots in hell.' Captain Edwards had commanded the *Pandora*, which was sent to capture the mutineers, and which found those who had remained on Tahiti. Heywood looked back to the boy he had been, putting off from the shore as soon as the ship was seen, delighted, and sure of a welcome: he emptied his glass, and with bitter resentment he said, 'That damned villain of a man put us in irons, built a thing he called Pandora's Box on the quarterdeck, four yards by six, and crammed us into it, fourteen men, innocent and guilty all together – kept us in it four months and more while he looked for Christian and the others – never found them, of course, the lubber – in irons all the time, never allowed out, even to go to the head. And we were still in the box and still in irons when the infernal bugger ran his ship on to a reef at the entrance to the Endeavour Straits. And what do you think he did for us when she went down? Nothing whatsoever. Never had our irons

taken off, never unlocked the box, though it was hours before she settled. If the ship's corporal had not tossed the keys through the scuttle
at the last moment, we must all have been drowned: as it was, four
men were trodden under and smothered in the wicked scuffle – water
up to our necks . . . Then, although the wretched fellow had four boats
out, he had not the wit to provision them: a little biscuit and two or
three beakers of water were all we had until we reached the Dutchmen at Coupang, a thousand miles away and more: not that he would
ever have found Coupang, either, but for the master. The scoundrel. If
it were not uncharitable, I should drink to his damnation for ever and
a day.' Heywood drank, in any case, but silently; and then, his mood
changing abruptly, he told them about the East Indian waters, the
wonders of Timor, Ceram, and the tame cassowaries stalking among
the bales of spice, the astonishing butterflies of Celebes, the Java rhi-
noceros, the torrid girls of Surabaya, the tides in the Allus Strait. It
was a fascinating account, and in spite of messages from the drawing-
room, where the coffee was growing cold, they would have listened
for ever; but while he was speaking of the pilgrim dhows bound for
Arabia, Heywood's voice faltered. He repeated himself once or twice,
looking anxiously from side to side, took a good hold on the table and
rose to his feet, where he stood swaying, speechless, until Killick and
Pullings led him out.

'It would be the voyage of the world,' said Stephen. 'How I wish I
could make it, alas.'

'Oh, Stephen,' cried Jack. 'I had counted on you.'

'You know something of my affairs, Jack: I am not my own master,
and I am afraid that when I return from London – for I must go up on
Tuesday, I find – I shall have to decline. It is scarcely possible at all.
But at least I can promise you will have an excellent surgeon. I know
a very able young man, a brilliant operator, a profound naturalist – an
authority on corals – who would give his eye-teeth to go with you.'

'The Mr Deering, to whom you sent all our Rodriguez coral?'

'No. John Deering was the man I spoke of this afternoon. He died
under my knife.'

When his post-chaise reached the outskirts of Petersfield, Stephen Maturin opened his bag and drew out a square bottle: he looked at it with an anxious longing, but reflecting that in spite of his present craving, by his own rules the crisis itself was to be faced without allies of any kind, he lowered the glass and flung it out of the window.

The bottle struck a stone rather than the grassy bank, exploding like a small grenade and covering the road with tincture of laudanum: the post-boy turned at the sound, but meeting his passenger's pale eyes, fixed upon him in a cold, inimical stare, he feigned interest in a passing tilbury, calling out to its driver 'that the knacker's yard was only a quarter of a mile along the road, first turning on the left, if he wanted to get rid of his cattle.' At Godalming, however, where the horses were changed, he told his colleague to look out for the cove in the shay: a rum cove that might have a fit on you, or throw up quantities of blood, like the gent at Kingston; and then who would have to clean up the mess? The new post-boy said in that case he would certainly keep an eye on the party; no move should escape him. Yet as they drove along it came to the post-boy that all the vigilance in the world could not prevent the gentleman from throwing up quantities of blood, if so inclined; and he was pleased when Stephen bade him stop at an apothecary's shop in Guildford – the gentleman was no doubt laying in some physic that would set him up for the rest of the journey.

In fact the gentleman and the apothecary were searching the shelves for a jar with a neck wide enough to admit the hands that Stephen carried in his handkerchief: it was found at last, filled, and topped up with the best rectified spirits of wine; and then Stephen said, 'While I am here, I might as well take a pint of the alcoholic tincture of laudanum.' This bottle he slipped into his greatcoat pocket, carrying the jar naked back to the chaise, so that all the post-boy saw was the grey hands with their bluish nails, brilliantly clear in the fine new spirits. He mounted without a word, and his emotion communicating itself to the horses, they flew along the London Road, through Ripley and Kingston, across Putney Heath, through the Vauxhall turnpike, across London Bridge and so to an inn called the Grapes in the liberty of the Savoy, where Stephen always kept a room, at such a pace that the landlady cried out, 'Oh, Doctor, I never looked for you this hour and more. Your supper is not even put down to the fire! Will you take a bowl of soup, sir, to stay you after your journey? A nice bowl of soup, and then the veal the moment it is enough?'

'No, Mrs Broad,' said Stephen. 'I shall just shift my clothes, and then I must go out again. Lucy, my dear, be so good as to take the small little bag upstairs: I shall carry the jar. Post-boy, here is for your trouble.'

The Grapes were used to Dr Maturin and his ways: one more jar was neither here nor there – indeed it was rather welcome than not, a hanged man's thumb being one of the luckiest things a house can hold, ten times luckier than the rope itself; and in this case there were two of them. The jar, then, caused no surprise; but Stephen's reappearance in a fashionable bottle-green coat and powdered hair left them speechless. They looked at him shyly, staring, yet not wishing to stare: he was perfectly unconscious of their gaze, however, and stepped into his hackney-coach without a word.

'You would not say he was the same gentleman,' said Mrs Broad.

'Perhaps he is going to a wedding,' said Lucy, clutching her bosom. 'One of them weddings by licence, in a drawing-room.'

'No doubt there is a lady in the case,' said Mrs Broad. 'Who ever saw such a dusty gentleman come out so fine, without there was a lady in the case? Still, I wish I had taken the price-ticket off his cravat. But I did not dare: no, not even after all these years.'

Stephen told the man to set him down in the Haymarket, saying he would walk the rest of the way. He had in fact the best part of an hour to spare, so he walked slowly through St James's market in the general direction of Hyde Park Corner and took half a dozen turns round St

James's Square. At this end of the town his clothes excited no attention, except from the women who shared the streets with him, a great
number of them, in arcades, shop doorways, and porticoes, some of
them fierce, angry, scornful creatures with their bosoms laid out, the
caterers to special tastes, others so young – mere slips – that it was
a wonder they should find customers, even in so huge a city. One
assured him she would give him a good breakfast, with sausages, if
he came with her; and although he civilly declined her offer on the
grounds that he was going to see his sweetheart, the idea of food
so spurred his mind that he walked into one of the alleys haunted
by footmen behind St James's Street and bought a mutton-pie of an
old lady with a glowing brazier, to eat in his hand as he walked. He
moved on, carrying it, until he reached Almack's, where they were
giving a ball: here he paused in the little crowd that was watching
the carriages arrive. He took a bite or two, but his appetite, a purely
theoretical appetite, was gone. He offered the pie to a tall black dog
that belonged to a neighbouring club and that was watching by his
side: the dog sniffed it, looked up into his face with an embarrassed
air, licked its lips, and turned away. A dwarfish boy said, 'I'll eat it for
you, governor, if you like.'

'May it profit you,' said Stephen, walking off. Through to the Green
Park, an expanse lit faintly by the horned moon in which couples
could vaguely be seen, and single, waiting figures among the nearer
trees. Stephen was not ordinarily a timid man, but the park had seen
many murders recently, and tonight he had a greater value for his
life than usual: in fact his heart, though admonished and kept down
by experience on the one side and prudence (or superstition) on the
other, was beating like a boy's. He cut up to Piccadilly and walked
down the hill to Clarges Street.

Number seven was a large house let out in apartments, with a porter common to them all; so when he knocked at the door it opened. 'Is
Mrs Villiers at home?' he asked in a harsh, formal tone that betrayed
the most eager expectation.

'Mrs Villiers? No, sir. She don't live here any more,' said the porter in an absolute, decided, rejecting voice; and he made as though to close the door.

'In that case,' said Stephen, walking quickly in, 'I wish to see the lady of the house.'

The lady of the house was very willing to see him – she had indeed been hovering behind a curtained glass door in the hall, peering through – but she was by no means so inclined to give him any information. She knew nothing about it: such a thing had never happened in her house before: no such person as a Bow Street officer had ever crossed its threshold. She had always taken the greatest pains to ensure that all the inmates of the house were above suspicion, and she had never countenanced the least irregularity. The whole neighbourhood, the whole congregation of St James's, all the tradesmen, could testify that Mrs Moon had never allowed the least irregularity. In the following discourse, which dealt with the difficulties of maintaining the highest reputation, it seemed that there was some question of unpaid bills: Stephen said that any inadvertence in this respect would be remedied directly, and that he would take it upon himself to look into any unsettled account. He was Mrs Villiers's medical adviser – naming himself – and the medical adviser to several members of her family: he was perfectly authorized to do so.

'Dr Maturin!' cried Mrs Moon. 'There is a letter for a gentleman of that name. I will fetch it.' She brought a single sheet, folded, sealed, and addressed in that well-known hand, together with a number of bills from her desk, tied in a roll with a piece of ribbon. Stephen put the letter into his pocket and looked at the accounts: he had never suspected Diana of moderation, had never supposed that she would live within her income nor within any other income, but even so some of the items startled him.

'Ass's milk,' he said. 'Mrs Villiers is not in a consumption, ma'am; and even if she were, which God forbid, here is more ass's milk than a regiment could drink in a month.'

'It is not for drinking, sir,' said Mrs Moon. 'Some ladies like it to bathe in, for their complexions: not that I ever saw a lady less in need of ass's milk than Mrs Villiers.'

'Well, now, ma'am,' said Stephen after a while, writing down the sums and drawing a line under them, 'perhaps you will be so good as to give me a brief account of how Mrs Villiers came to leave so abruptly; for the apartments, I know, were taken until Michaelmas.'

Mrs Moon's account was neither brief nor particularly coherent, but it appeared that a gentleman, accompanied by several strong-looking attendants, had asked for Mrs Villiers; on being told that she could not receive a gentleman unknown to her, he had walked upstairs, ordering the porter to stay where he was in the name of the law – the attendants produced truncheons with little crowns on them, and no one dared move. She would never have known they were Bow Street runners, but for some of them guarding the back-door and coming into the kitchen: they had told the servants what they were, and they said the gentleman was a messenger from the Secretary of State's office, or something like that – something in the government line. High words were heard upstairs, and presently the gentleman and two of the runners led Mrs Villiers and her French waiting-woman down and into a coach; they were very polite, but firm, and they desired Mrs Villiers not to speak to Mrs Moon or any-one else; and they locked her door behind them. Then the gentleman came back with two clerks, and they took away a quantity of papers.

Nobody could tell what to make of it, and then on the Thurs-day Madam Gratipus, the waiting-woman, suddenly came back and packed up their things. She spoke no English, but Mrs Moon thought she could make out something about America. Most unfortunately Mrs Moon was not at home later that afternoon, when Mrs Villiers came in with a gentleman she called Mr Johnson, an American gen-tleman, by his old-fashioned, twangling way of speaking through his nose, though very well dressed. It seemed that she was uncommonly cheerful, laughed a great deal, gave a turn about her apartments to see that everything was packed, took a dish of tea, tipped the ser-

vants handsomely, left this note for Dr Maturin, and so stepped into
a coach and four, never to be seen again. Had said nothing of her destination, and the servants did not like to ask, she being such a high
lady and apt to fly out at the least impertinence or liberty, though
otherwise esteemed by all – a most open-handed lady.

Stephen thanked her and gave her a draft for the total sum, observing that he never carried so considerable an amount in gold.

'No, indeed,' said Mrs Moon. 'That would be the height of impru-
dence. Not three days since, and in this very street, a gentleman was
robbed of fourteen pounds and his watch, not long after sunset. Shall
William call a chair for you, sir, or a coach? It is as black as pitch
outside.'

'I beg your pardon?' said Stephen, whose mind was far away.

'Should you not like a coach, sir? It is as black as pitch outside.'

It was also as black as pitch inside: he knew that the letter in his
pocket contained farewells, his dismission, and the ruin of his hopes.
'I believe not,' he said, 'I have only a few steps to go.'

These steps took him to a coffee-house on the corner of Bolton
Street; a very few steps, as he had said. Yet what a quantity of thoughts
formed in his mind before he pushed the door, sat down, and called
for coffee: thoughts, ideas, recollections forming infinitely faster than
the words that could, however inadequately, have expressed them
and tracing the history of his long connection with Diana Villiers, a
relationship made up of a wide variety of miseries interspersed with
rare intervals of shining happiness, but one that he had hoped, until
tonight, to bring to a successful end. Yet just as his mind had been
too cautious to admit full confidence in his success, so now it was
unwilling to see the proof of total failure. He placed the letter on the
table and stared at it a while: until it was opened, the letter might still
contain a rendezvous; it might still be a letter that fulfilled his hopes.

Eventually he broke the seal. 'Maturin – I am using you abom-
inably once again, although this time it is not altogether my fault.
A most unfortunate thing has happened that I am not at leisure to
explain; but it appears that a friend of mine has behaved most *indis-*

creetly. So much so, that I have been molested by a gang of wretches, of thief-takers, who searched all my few belongings and my papers, and questioned me for hours on end. What crime I am supposed to have committed, I cannot tell; but now that I am at liberty, I am determined to return to America at once. Mr Johnson is here, and he has seen to the arrangements. I was too hasty in my resentment, I see; I should never have flown back to England like a simple passionate headstrong girl – these legal matters – and they are going better – call for patience and deliberation. I shall not see you again, Stephen. Forgive me, but it would not answer. Think of me kindly, for your friendship is very dear to me. D.V.'

In a brief flare of rebellion, anger and frustration he thought of his enormous expense of spirit these last few weeks, of the mounting hope that he had indulged and fostered in spite of his judgment and of their frequently violent disagreements; but the flame died, leaving not so much an active sorrow as a black and wordless desolation.

When he was walking down the street to the coffee-house, his eye, long accustomed to such things, had automatically taken notice of the two men following him. They were still there when he came out, but he was utterly indifferent to their presence. They preserved him, however, from an ugly encounter in the Green Park, where he wandered among the trees in a deep abstraction, his feet slowly guiding him eastwards to his inn, where he sank straight into a sleep as dull and deep as lead.

He was spared the slow waking and reconstruction of the day before by Abel, the boots, thundering at the door with the news that there was a messenger who would take no denial, an official messenger who must put his letter into the Doctor's hands.

'Let him come up,' said Stephen.

It was the briefest note, requesting or rather requiring Stephen's presence at the Admiralty at half past eight o'clock rather than at the appointed time of four. The tone was unusual.

'Is there an answer, sir?' asked the messenger.

'There is,' said Stephen, and he wrote it with an equally cold formality: 'Dr Maturin presents his compliments to Admiral Sieve-wright, and will wait upon him at half past eight this morning.'

At a quarter to nine the Admiral was still waiting for Dr Maturin and indeed at nine o'clock itself, for Stephen, hurrying across the parade, had met the former chief of naval intelligence, Sir Joseph Blaine, a keen entomologist and a sure friend, who had just come from an early meeting at the Cabinet Office. They had a hasty word, for Stephen was already late, contracted to meet later in the day and so parted, Stephen to keep his appointment, and Sir Joseph to walk in St James's Park.

'Hey, hey, Dr Maturin,' cried the Admiral, as he came into the room, 'what the Devil is all this? The Home Office people have picked up a couple of trollops that spend their time gathering information, and they have found your name in their papers.'

'I do not understand you, sir,' said Stephen, looking coldly at the Admiral. This was the first time he had seen him without the actual head of the department, Mr Warren.

'Well now,' said the sailor, 'I shall not beat about the bush. There are these two women, a Mrs Wogan and a Mrs Villiers: the Secretary of State's office has had its eye on them for some time, particularly on Wogan – connections with some dubious characters among the royalist Frenchmen over here and with American agents. At last they decided to act, and upon my word it was high time: in Wogan's house they found some very surprising papers indeed, many of them sent under cover to Villiers and passed on by her; and in Villiers' lodgings they found a number of letters, including these.' He opened a folder, and Stephen saw his own handwriting. 'Well, there you are,' said the Admiral, having waited in vain for Stephen to speak. 'I have laid all my cards on the table, fair and square. The Home Office insist upon an explanation. What am I to tell them?'

'One card is missing,' said Stephen. 'How does it come about that the Home Office should apply to you for information? Am I to under-stand that my character, that the nature of my activities has been divulged to a third party without my knowledge? Against my express understanding with this department? Against all the laws of sound intelligence?' Stephen's intelligence work was of prime importance to him: he hated the entire Napoleonic tyranny with a most passionate loathing, and he knew, quite objectively, that he had been able to give it some of the shrewdest blows it had ever received in this line of combat. He also knew the strange diversity of the various British intelligence services and the shocking, amateurish permeability of some of them – an insecurity that might only too easily put an end to his usefulness and his life. What he did not know, however, for his mind was dull that morning, was that the Admiral was lying: Mrs Wogan had possessed herself, among other things, of some naval papers through a junior civil lord of the Admiralty; the Home Office had therefore sent the evidence to the Admiral, and the Admiral it was who required the explanation. His bluff, frank approach had imposed upon the diminished Maturin, who felt a red glow of anger burning up his apathy – rage at the apparent betrayal of his identity. 'Upon my soul,' said Stephen in a stronger voice, 'it is I who must do the insisting. I desire you to tell me directly how it happens that the Secretary of State's people come to take notice of my name to you.'

The Admiral was puzzled to come off handsomely, and in the hope of drowning the question he adopted a more mollifying tone and said, 'First let me tell you of the steps that have been taken. All the leaks have been plugged, you may be sure of that. We interrogated the women separately, and Warren soon extracted enough to hang Wogan out of hand. But she has some very respectable, or at least some very influential protectors – she is a remarkably fine woman – and in view of that, and the undesirability of a trial, and her voluntary production of some useful names, we struck a bargain: she pleads guilty to a charge that will mean her being sent over the water, no more. We could have brought any number of capital charges, including attempted murder, since she shot the wig off the messenger's head, but we decided to play it quiet. As for Villiers, the other one, we have decided not to proceed: her explanation that she regarded the passing-on of the letters as a mere friendly act – that she looked

upon 'em as an intrigue on the part of Wogan with a married man –
was hard to break down; and then her having become an American
citizen raised grave legal difficulties. Government wants no further
complications with the Americans at this stage of the war: our pressing of men out of their ships is bad enough, without our pressing
their women too. And in fact she may have been innocent. Looking
at her, it seemed to me that her plea of helping in an amour was very
likely, very much in character. She stood up for herself amazingly, an
even finer woman than Wogan, straight as an arrow, glaring at us like
a wild cat, flushed with anger, blackguarding the Home Office man
like a trooper – lovely bosom trembling, ha, ha! I came in for a couple
of broad-sides – wish there had been more – amorous intrigues, ha,
ha, ha!'

'You are impertinent, sir. You forget yourself. I insist upon your
answering my question, instead of indulging yourself in this blackguardly manner.'

In the pleasures of his warm and luscious imagination the Admiral had indeed forgotten himself, but these words brought him vio-
lently back to the present. He turned pale, and half rising from his
seat he cried, 'Let me remind you, Dr Maturin, that there is such a
thing as discipline in this service.'

'And let me remind you, sir,' said Stephen, 'that there is such a
thing as respect for one's word. And furthermore, I have to observe
that your manner of speaking of this lady would be gross in a libidinous pot-boy. In your mouth it is offensive to the highest degree.
Bread and blood, sir, I have pulled a man's nose for less. Good day to
you, sir: you know where to find me.' He walked out of the room, col-
lided with a clerk who was in the act of opening the door, and thrust
past him into the corridor.

'Send for a file of Marines,' roared the Admiral, now scarlet in
the face.

'Yes, sir,' said the clerk. 'Here is Sir Joseph, to know whether Dr
Maturin is still within. The Marines directly, sir.'

Leaving by the little green confidential door that gave on to the park, Stephen felt his anger die away as weariness came down on him like a pall, extinguishing the fire and with it all concern. Yet he had not walked eastwards a quarter of a mile before he became aware that his knees and hands were trembling, and that his nerves jangled intolerably, as though they had been flayed: he walked faster, towards the Grapes and the square bottle on his mantelshelf.

Mrs Broad, taking the sun at her door, saw him at the far end of the street; she read his face when he was still quite a long way off, and as he turned in she called out in her fat, cheerful voice, 'You are just in time for a late breakfast, sir. Now pray go in and sit in the parlour; there is a pure fire, drawing sweet. Your letters are upon the table; Lucy will fetch you the paper; and the coffee will be up this directly minute. You could do with your breakfast today, sir, I am sure, going out so early on an empty stomach, and the streets so damp.'

He made some objection: but no, he might not go upstairs – his room was being turned out – there were pails and brooms that he might trip on in the dark – so there he sat staring at the fire, until the scent of fresh-brewed coffee filled the room, and he turned his chair to the table.

His post consisted of *The Syphilitic Preceptor*, with the author's compliments, and the *Philosophical Transactions*. After two strong cups that quelled the trembling, he automatically ate what Lucy set before him, the whole of his attention being set upon a paper by Humphry Davy on the electricity of the torpedo-fish. 'How I honour that man,' he murmured, taking up another chop. And there was that quacksalver Mellowes again, with his pernicious theory that consumption was caused by an excess of oxygen. He read the specious nonsense through, to confound the arguments one by one. 'Have I not already ate a chop?' he asked, seeing the chafing-dish renewed.

'It was only a little one, sir,' said Lucy, laying another upon his plate. 'Mrs Broad says there is nothing like a chop for strengthening the blood. But it must be ate up while it's hot.' She spoke kindly but firmly, as to one who was not quite exactly: Mrs Broad and she knew that he had eaten nothing on his journey, that he had taken neither supper nor breakfast, and that he had lain in his damp shirt.

Deep in toast and marmalade, he demolished Mellowes root and branch; and noticing the indignation with which his hand had underlined the whole claptrap peroration, he observed, 'I am not dead.'

'Sir Joseph Blaine to see you, sir, if you are at leisure,' said Mrs Broad, pleased that Dr Maturin should have such a respectable friend.

Stephen rose, set a chair at the fireside for Sir Joseph, offered him a cup of coffee, and said, 'You are come from the Admiral, I collect?'

'Yes,' said Sir Joseph. 'But as a peacemaker, I hope and trust. My dear Maturin, you handled him very severely, did you not?'

'I did,' said Stephen. 'And it will give me all the pleasure in the world to handle him more severely still, whenever he chooses, and on whatever ground. I have been expecting to receive his friends ever since I returned: but perhaps he is such a poltroon as to intend placing me under arrest. It would not surprise me. I heard him call out something to that effect.'

'In his heated state he might have done anything. He is perhaps more suited for the physical than for the intellectual side of these duties; and as you know, it was never contemplated that he should exercise . . .'

'What was Mr Warren thinking of, to leave such an affair to him? I beg pardon for interrupting you.'

'He is sick! He is most surprisingly sick: you would not recognize him.'

'What ails Mr Warren?'

'A most shocking stroke of the palsy. His laundress – he has chambers in the Temple – found him at the bottom of the stairs: no speech left, and his right arm and leg quite paralysed. He was let blood; but they say it was too late, and hold out little hope.'

They were both heartily grieved for Mr Warren, their sound though humdrum colleague: in this immediate context, however, it

was apparent to both that his stroke must result in greater power for
Admiral Sievewright.

After a pause Sir Joseph said, 'It was a mercy that I stepped into the
Admiralty when I did: I had forgotten to tell you that the Entomolo-
gists hold an extraordinary meeting tonight. I found the Admiral in a
high-wrought state of passion. I left him quiet, uneasy, and as near to
admitting himself in the wrong as it is possible for a man of his rank
in the service. I represented to him that in the first place you were a
purely voluntary ally, our most valuable ally, and in no way his sub-
ordinate in our department; that your entirely unremunerated work,
carried out at very great risk to yourself, had enabled us to accomplish wonders – I enumerated a few of 'em, together with some of the
injuries you have received. I stated that Mrs Villiers was a lady of the
most respectable family and connections, the object of your . . .' He
hesitated and looked anxiously at Stephen's expressionless face before
continuing, 'of your respectful admiration for a considerable number
of years, and no new acquaintance, as he supposed; that Lord Melville
had described you as being worth a ship of the line to us any day of
the week, a figure that I had ventured to dispute, on the grounds that
no single ship of the line, no, not even a first-rate, could have dealt
with the Spanish treasure-frigates in the year four; and that if by his
handling of this admittedly difficult affair Sievewright had offended
you to such a pitch that we were to be deprived of your services, then
I made no sort of doubt that the First Lord would call for a report,
and that this report would pass through my hands. For in confidence,
I may tell you that my retirement has proved somewhat hypothetical:
I attend certain meetings in an advisory capacity, almost every week,
and there have been flattering proposals that I should accept an office
with remarkably extensive powers: Sievewright is aware of this. He
will apologize, if you so desire.'

'No, no. I have no wish to humiliate him at all: it is always a
wretched policy, in any case. But it will be difficult for us to meet
with any great appearance of cordiality.'

'So you do not fly off? You do not abandon us?' said Sir Joseph, shaking Stephen by the hand. 'Well, I am heartily glad of it. It is like you, Maturin.'

'I do not,' said Stephen. 'Yet as you know very well, without there is a perfect understanding, our work cannot be done. How much longer is the Admiral to be with us?'

'For the best part of a year,' said Sir Joseph, with the unuttered addition, 'If I don't sink him first.'

Stephen nodded, and after a while he said, 'Certainly I was vexed by his blundering attempt at manipulating me: the guileless sea-dog lulling a suspected double agent by telling him what steps have been taken, for all love! That I should be attempted to be gulled with such sad archaic stuff: it would not have deceived a child of moderate intelligence. He spoke of his own mere motion, did he not? The alleged Home Office was so much primitive naval cunning?'

Sir Joseph sighed and nodded.

'Of course,' said Stephen, 'a moment's reflection would have told me that. I cannot conceive how my wits came to desert me so. But the Dear knows they have been wandering these many days . . . that unpardonable error with Gomez's reports.'

Stephen had left them in a hackney-coach, as Sir Joseph knew very well: the classic lapse of an over-tired, over-worked agent. 'They were recovered within twenty-four hours, the seals unbroken,' he said. 'No harm was done. But it is true that you are not in form. I told poor Warren that the Vigo trip was too much for any man, immediately after Paris. My dear Maturin, you are knocked up: you must forgive me for saying so, but you are quite knocked up. As a friend I see you better than you see yourself. Your face has fallen away; your eyes are sunk; you are a wretched colour. I do beg you will seek advice.'

'Certainly my health is but indifferent,' said Stephen, tapping his liver. 'I should never have flown out upon the Admiral had I been in the full possession of my faculties. I am engaged upon a course of physic that allows me to carry on from day to day, but it is a Judas-draught, and although I can stop the moment I please, it may play me an ugly trick. I suspect it of having clouded my judgment in a case where I lost my patient, and that weighs upon me cruelly.' Stephen very rarely confided in any man, but he had a great liking and respect for Sir Joseph, and now, in his pain, he said, 'Tell me, Blaine, just how far was Diana Villiers involved in this affair? You know the importance I attach . . . you know the nature of my concern.'

'I wish with all my heart I could make a clear-cut reply; but in all honesty I can give you no more than my impression. I think Mrs Wogan did impose upon her to a large extent; but Mrs Villiers is no fool, and a clandestine correspondence rarely assumes the form of foolscap documents forty pages long. And then the precipitate departure – chaise and four all night and day to Bristol – a six-oared boat and the rowers promised twenty pounds a head to overtake the *Sans Souci* lying windbound in Lundy Roads – gives some colour to the notion of an uneasy conscience. Yet I am inclined to think that the haste was the fact of Mr Johnson, moved by a purely personal motive. Not that as an American he might not also be interested in information of value to his own country: though we have not established any connection whatsoever between him and Mrs Wogan, apart from this perhaps fortuitous common acquaintance with Mrs Villiers and, of course, a common interest in America. But at all events it is the United States that have benefited from these activities, not France. Mrs Wogan was their Aphra Behn. Their Aphra Behn,' he repeated, finding no response.

'Aphra Behn, the lewd woman that wrote plays in the last age?' said Stephen at last.

'No, no: there you are out for once, Maturin,' said Sir Joseph with great satisfaction. 'You have fallen into the vulgar error. As to her morals, I have nothing to say, but she was first and foremost an intelligence agent. I had some of her Antwerp reports in my hands not a week since, when we were looking through the Privy Council files, and they were brilliant, Maturin, brilliant. For intelligence, there is nothing like a keen-witted, handsome woman. She told us that De Ruyter was coming to burn our ships. It is true that we did nothing about it, and that the ships were burnt; but the report itself was a masterpiece of precision. Yes, yes.'

In the long pause that followed Stephen considered Sir Joseph as he sat there musing by the fire, his fine, kindly face, more like that of a country gentleman than of an official who had spent most of his life behind a desk, set in an amiable expression; and it occurred to him that somewhere in that keen, capacious mind a thought was forming: 'If Maturin is in fact reaching the end of his usefulness, we had better get him out of the way before he makes some costly mistake.' The thought would no doubt be tempered with genuine regard, friendship, and humanity, even by gratitude; it would probably contain a clause to the effect that Maturin might yet recover, and that in his powers, his connections, and his unrivalled knowledge of the situation in his own particular sphere might be put to service; but as things stood, with regard to many factors, including the position of the Admiralty, the thought even without any qualification, would be a reasonable and indeed proper thought in the official part of Sir Joseph's mind. A well-run intelligence service must have its system of dealing with those who were past their best or who had fallen by the wayside and who yet knew too much: a knacker's yard run with more or less brutality according to the nature of the chief; or at least a temporary limbo.

Sir Joseph felt the pale eye upon him, and it was with a certain uneasiness that he returned to Aphra Behn. 'Yes. She was a brilliant agent, brilliant. And we might call Mrs Wogan the Behn of Philadelphia. She too turns an elegant verse, and she writes a pretty play; letters are as good a shield as natural philosophy, perhaps even better. But unlike Mrs Behn she has been caught, and she is to be packed off on the first ship bound for New Holland, lucky not to be hanged. I never like to see a woman hanged, do you, Maturin? But I was forgetting – all is grist to your grisly mill, and you have your female subjects too. She is not to be hanged, because the D of C, as our Admiral would put it, has made interest for her: it seems they were bed-fellows not long since. For the same reason she is to be treated with certain égards – a corner to herself aboard, perhaps a woman, and no servitude when she arrives at Botany Bay, there to spend the rest of her days. Botany Bay! What a goal for a naturalist, if not for an adventuress! Maturin, you need, you deserve, a break, a holiday to set you up. Why do not you accompany this ship? To keep your hand in, you can plumb the lady's mind; it contains a vast deal more than was revealed to us, of that I am very sure, and what she has to say may resolve your doubts about Mrs Villiers. To make my suggestion more tempting, I may observe that the ship in question is to be commanded by your friend Aubrey, though he don't yet know this part of his duty. The *Leopard*, for the *Leopard* is her name, was already under orders for Botany Bay to deal with the unfortunate Mr Bligh, of whose predicament you are aware; when she has done this, and has delivered Mrs Wogan, together with some people we shall add as a blind, she is to join our force in the East Indies, where, with your spirits quite recovered, you will be of the utmost service. Pray do consider of it, Maturin.'

Stephen's longing, temporarily allayed by food, had returned with even greater force. He left the parlour for his bedroom and his draught, and returning he said, 'Your Mrs Wogan, now: you speak of her as a second Aphra Behn, and therefore as a woman of shining parts.'

'Perhaps I was going a little far: I should have added qualifications for time and place: The Americans' intelligence is but an infant plant – you will remember the ingenuous young man that came with their Mr Jay – and native shrewdness, even where it exists, is no substitute for some hundred years of practice. Yet even so, this young woman had been well tutored; she knew what questions to ask, and she learnt many of the answers. I was surprised to find that there was no French connection: none, at least, that we could fix upon. But my comparison really does not hold, for whereas the Mrs Behn I meet in our files shows a most remarkable sagacity, and a grasp of the situation that would do honour to any politician, Mrs Wogan seems to me a somewhat simple lady at bottom, relying upon intuition and dash whenever she is required to go beyond her plain instruction, rather than upon any considerable fund of knowledge.'

'Please to describe her.'

'She is between twenty-five and thirty, but she still retains her bloom: black hair, blue eyes: about five foot eight, but looks taller, since she stands so straight – magnificent carriage of her head. A slight but undeniable figure; though these things, you know, can be improved by stuffing. A thoroughly genteel air, nothing bold or flaunting. Writes like a cat, with every third word underlined, and cannot spell. Speaks excellent French, however, and sits a horse to admiration: no other education that can be detected.'

'You might almost be describing Mrs Villiers,' said Stephen, with a painful smile.

'Yes, indeed. I was so struck by the likeness that I wondered whether there might be some relationship; but it appears there is none. The details of her birth escape my mind for the moment, but they are all in the files and I shall see that you have them. No relationship, I believe; yet there is indeed a striking resemblance.' He might have added that in Mrs Wogan's case too there was a hopeless lover, a young man who hung on the borders of her life; a young man so peripheral that he had been set free. Those who took him up found no hint of guilty knowledge, and it was thought better to let him go: Sir Joseph retained only a recollection of the deep unhappiness and the somewhat unusual name of Michael Herapath. 'Yet when I speak of her apparent simplicity,' he went on, 'I may be one of that numerous company of men who have been deceived by women. There is more in this than we know at present, and the skein is well worth the untangling. As I say, it would keep your hand in, Maturin, and it might even yield a jewel. Pray do consider of it.'

During his journey down to Hampshire Stephen turned it over in his mind, but only with the surface of his mind, the rest being taken up with longing, with a continuous, painful evocation of Diana's person, voice, and movement, a statement of her moral imperfections, her levity and her extravagance; then with a keener longing still, and an absurd tenderness. As for Sir Joseph's proposition, he did not care one way or another and in any case he knew that there was little choice – virtually none for him. He would go, and if past experience were still a guide, the naturalist within would revive in time. He would make vast collections; huge areas would open to his view; his heart would beat again at the sight of new species, new genera of plants, birds, and quadrupeds; and the Indies might provide some of those encounters with the enemy that wiped out everything but the extreme excitement of the contest. But was past experience still a guide? The stimulation of London and of all his meetings there died away as he travelled, and it was succeeded by an indifference greater than he had ever known.

In this grey state of mind he arrived at Ashgrove Cottage, and there, since his indifference did not extend to his friends' concerns, he was instantly aware that something was amiss. His welcome was as kind as ever he could have wished, but Jack's weather- and war-beaten face was even redder than usual; he was rather larger than life and taller, and there were traces of recent storms in their constrained behaviour to one another. Stephen was not very much surprised to learn that the new filly had shown a strange inability to run faster than others after the first three furlongs, and that she was given to crib-biting, jibbing, kicking, rearing, and windsucking; nor that a gang of Kimber's workmen had stoned his buzzard's nest; nor that Kimber himself was in disfavour for having made an unexpected and very costly revision of his estimates; but he was quite startled when Jack took him aside and told him that he was in a most hellfire rage with the Admiralty – was about to throw up the service – his flag be damned. He was used to their blackguardly ways – had suffered from them ever since he had first worn the curse of God – but had never supposed they would presume to use him so – had never supposed they could be such —s as to tell him, without a moment's warning, that *Leopard* was to be used for transportation.

'To a landsman,' said Stephen, 'this might seem a ship's prime function, its true *raison d'être*.'

'No, no; what I mean is transportation – ' cried Jack.

'So I had understood.'

' – the transportion of convicts. Convicts, Stephen! God's my life! I am sent a letter in a damned crabbed hand, telling me that I am to expect a tender from the hulks – the hulks, in the name of all that's pure – with a score or so of assorted murderers that I am to receive aboard and carry to Botany Bay. Orders are sending to the Yard for the building of a cage in the forepeak, and accommodation for their keepers. By God, Stephen, to expect an officer of my seniority to turn his ship into a transport, and to play the turnkey! I am writing them such a letter! You must help me to some epithets, Stephen. And what really angers me is, that Sophie doesn't seem able to grasp how monstrous their conduct is. I tell her it is a most improper proposal, but I wonder at their effrontery, and that I shall stick to *Ajax*, the new seventy-four, a fine ship, with no flash Newgate cullies lurking in the hold. But no. She sighs; says I know best, of course; and then five minutes later there she is, crying up the *Leopard*, and what a delightful, interesting voyage it would be, and so comfortable, with all my old shipmates and followers. Anyone would think she wished me away – out of the country as soon as possible. For *Leopard*'s orders are advanced, and she sails on Saturday sennight.'

'To an impartial mind, it is a little strange to see your dignity so offended by a score of prisoners. You, who have so willingly stuffed your holds with French and Spanish prisoners, to take such exception to a few of your own countrymen, whom you have always rated much higher than any foreigner, and who in any case would never be brought into contact with you, being under the conduct of proper persons.'

'They are completely different. Prisoners of war and gaolbirds are completely different.'

'The deprivation of liberty is still the same: the subhuman almost servile status. We have both been prisoners of war, and prisoners for debt. We have both sailed with a number of men guilty of the most atrocious crimes. For my part, I have not found my dignity much

DESOLATION ISLAND   53

affected. You, however, are to be the only judge of that; yet I will observe, Jack, that a bird in the hand waits for no man, as you so often say yourself, and that the *Ajax* is at present little more than a naked keel. Who knows, by the time she floats her occupation may be gone. She may sail on mere visits of courtesy, saluting the French colours with a blank discharge and a friendly cheer?'

'You do not mean there is danger of peace?' cried Jack, turning quick. 'That is to say, I mean the blessings of peace are very capital, nothing finer – but one likes to be warned.'

'I do not. I know nothing about it. I only put it to you that the *Ajax* will not swim for another six months at the least; that there is something to be said for making hay when no clouds obscure the sun; and that it is your rolling stone that gets the worm.'

'Yes, yes; very true,' said Jack gravely. 'But that brings me to another point. Six months would be very useful to me in the mining line, to get things in train, you understand. But far more important than that . . . you remember warning me about the Wrays?'

Stephen nodded.

'I could hardly credit it at the time, but you were right. I went to Craddock's while you were away: the judge was standing by, and only Andrew Wray, Carroll, Jenyns, and a couple of their friends from Winchester sat down. I watched very close, after what you had said, and although I could not make out what they were at, I saw that every time Wray drummed his fingers that way he has, I lost. I waited half a dozen times to make sure: the sixth time round there was a very pretty penny on the table, and the signals were uncommon clear. I imitated them, by way of taking notice of it to Wray, and told him I did not choose to play on those terms. 'I do not understand you, sir,' says he, and I believe he was on the point of making some fling about fellows that did not love to lose, but thought better of it. I told him I should explain more clearly whenever he wished: though upon my word I should have been hard put to it to tell who was receiving his signals. It might have been any man there. I should be sorry if it had been Carroll: I like him. But I must say he looked tolerably green about the gills. They all looked tolerably green about the gills, if it comes to that; but not a man jack of 'em spoke up when I asked whether any other gentleman wished to make an observation. It was an unpleasant moment, and I took it very friendly in Heneage Dundas to come quick across the room and stand by me. A damned unpleasant moment.'

So Stephen Maturin imagined: but his imagination, though lively, fell far short of the full unpleasantness – Jack Aubrey's furious anger at finding himself a flat, a cony, a pigeon to be plucked, not to mention his honest rage at losing a very large sum of money: the silence in that big room, filled with men of considerable rank and standing, when one of the most influential among them was openly, and in a very powerful voice, accused of cheating at cards. The silence in which many, having taken in the whole gravity of the situation, looked discreetly away; and which was broken by artificial conversation as Jack and Dundas walked out.

'Now Wray is on a tour of the dockyards, looking into corrupt practices, and he will not be back for some considerable time. I did not hear from him before he left, which is strange; but he cannot possibly sit down under this, and I do not wish to be out of the country when he returns. I do not wish to have the look of running off.'

'Wray will not fight you,' said Stephen. 'If he let twelve hours go by after such an affront, he will not fight. He will have his satisfaction some other way.'

'I am of your way of thinking: but I do not choose to let him whitewash himself by saying that I am not to be found.'

'Oh come, now, Jack, this is carrying it too far by a very long way, so it is. The world in general knows that service orders take precedence over everything else: such an affair may certainly stand over for a year or more. We both know cases of the kind, and the absent man in no way reflected upon at all.'

'Even so, I had much rather give him all the time he needs for his tour and his . . .'

The arrival of Admiral Snape and Captain Hallowell to eat their mutton with the Aubreys cut the conversation short, but it was not a great while before Stephen was on the subject once again. Sophie had whispered him to join her early, and as the three sailors were intent upon fighting St Vincent over again, shot by shot, it was not at all difficult for him to come away to the drawing-room while they were setting nutshells up in line of battle, and to come away with the certainty of a long, quiet interval before him.

Sophie began by declaring that there was nothing on earth so wicked, barbarous, and unChristian as the fighting of duels; and they would be just as wicked even if the man who was in the wrong always lost, which was not the case. She spoke of young Mr Butler of the *Calliope*, who was entirely innocent by all accounts, and who died of his wounds not a twelvemonth since; and Jane Butler, who had nursed him with all the love in the world, was left with two small children, and not a penny to feed them with. Nothing, *nothing*, she said, clasping her hands and gazing at Stephen with huge liquid eyes, could prevent Jack from standing up and being shot at or stabbed; so it was their absolute duty to make him go away in the *Leopard*. The ship could not be back for a great while, and in that time the whole thing would have blown over; or that wretched Mr Wray would have been brought to a better state of mind; or perhaps . . . She hesitated, and Stephen said, 'Or someone might knock him on the head first. It is not impossible; he frequents horse-racing men and card-players and he lives far above his income. The salary attached to his posts does not exceed six or seven hundred pounds a year and it does not appear that he has any estate, yet his turn-out is that of a wealthy man. But after this, no one will feel inclined to play cards with him for anything but love, which makes such an event more unlikely than I could wish. On the other hand, I am intimately persuaded that Wray is not a fighting man. A fellow who will stomach such words for twelve hours will stomach them for twelve years, and digest them at last in his unlovely tomb. Honey, you have no need to trouble your mind, upon my soul.'

Sophie could not share Stephen's intimate persuasion. 'Why did

Jack have to say those words?' she cried. 'Why could he not just have walked away? He ought to have thought of his children.' And once again she urged her arguments against duelling, this time with an even greater vehemence, as though Stephen, in spite of his steady assurance that he was of the same opinion entirely, needed convincing; as though convincing Stephen would in some way help her cause. With any other person he would have been sadly bored, since for want of fresh arguments on this well-handled theme she was obliged to reiterate those that had served abler minds this last hundred years; but he loved her much, her beauty and her real distress moved him deeply, and he listened without the least impatience, nodding gravely. Then, after a pause for breath (for she habitually spoke with a charming volubility, like a swallow in a barn, and now her words tumbled upon one another in a most surprising flow) she threw him out by saying, 'Then, dear Stephen, since you are of the same mind with me, you must persuade him. You are so very much cleverer than I am, that you will find arguments quite out of my reach – you will certainly persuade him. He thinks the world of your intelligence.'

'Alas, my dear,' said Stephen, sighing, 'even if he did, which I must beg leave to doubt, in this matter intelligence is neither here nor there. Jack is no more of a fighting man than' – he was on the point of saying 'than I', but having a regard for truth when he was speaking to Sophie he said, 'than your parson here. He has too much sense. But since men have agreed, this past age and more, to exclude from their society those who refuse a challenge, his views have nothing to do with it. His hands are tied. Custom is everything, above all in the Army and the Navy. If he were to refuse, that would be the end of his career; and he could never live in comfort with himself.'

'So to live comfortably, he must let himself be killed. Oh, what a world you men have made of it, Stephen,' she said, groping for her handkerchief.

'Sophie, treasure, you are being womanish; you are being a blockhead. You will allow yourself to weep presently, at this foolish rate of going on. You are to consider, that very few rencounters result in so much as a scratch, if that. No, no: a great many of them are made up by a trifling redefinition of the words exchanged, or so managed by the seconds that they end with a few passes in the empty air, or a pistol barely charged at all. Yet still, I do think that Jack should be out of the way. I do think that he should go aboard this *Leopard*, sail off to the far side of the world, and stay there for a considerable time.'

'Do you, Stephen?' said Sophie, eagerly searching his face.

'I do so. He is behaving as I have seen so many sailors behave when they are ashore with a pocket full of guineas; and presently he too will be on his scuppers, as we say in the Navy. Running-horses, cards, building, and even God forbid silver-mining. All that lacks is a navigation-canal at ten thousand pound a mile, and the perpetual motion.'

'Oh, how glad I am that you have said this,' cried Sophie. 'I have been longing and longing to open my mind to you, but how can a woman possibly say anything about her husband's conduct, even to his best friend? But now you have spoken, I may reply, may I not, without being disloyal? I am not disloyal, Stephen, not in my least, most secret thought, but it breaks my heart to see him flinging his fortune to the winds, earned so hard, with such dreadful wounds – to see his dear open confiding trustful nature imposed upon by vulgar card-sharpers and horse-racing men and projectors – it is like deceiving a child. And I hope it is not mercenary or interested in me when I say I must think of my babies. The girls have their portions, but how long they will last I cannot tell; and as for George . . . One thing that Mama did teach me was keeping accounts, and when we were poor I kept them to the farthing, so proud and happy when we could round the quarter clear of debt. Now it is very hard to see plain, with so many vast payments in and out and with so many strange gaps, but at least I do know that there is much, much more out than in, and it cannot go on. I am quite terrified, sometimes. And sometimes,' she added in a low voice, 'I have an even more terrifying thought: that he is not really happy on shore, and that he plunges into one wild extravagant scheme after another to escape from a dull life in the country;

and from a dull wife too, perhaps. I do so want him to be happy. I have tried to learn astronomy, like that Miss Herschel he is always talking about, and who treats me as though I were a child; but it is no use – I still cannot understand why Venus changes shape.'

'These are mere whimsies, my dear, vapours, megrims,' said Stephen, darting a covert glance at her, 'and I see you must be let an ounce or two of blood. But for the rest, I believe you are right: Jack must go away, grow used to himself as a man of means, and learn to swim on an even keel when he is ashore again.'

There was no hint of unhappiness in the voice that came booming along the passage as Jack shepherded his flushed and vinous guests through the builders' ladders towards the drawing-room; but there was a touch of petulance and even doggedness to be heard some hours later when, pulling his nightcap firmly over his ears and tying the tapes, he replied, 'Sweetheart, nothing on earth will induce me to accept the *Leopard* on those terms, so you might as well save your breath to cool your porridge.'

'What porridge?'

'Why, porridge – burgoo. It is what people say, when they mean to give you a hint that it is no use carping on the same string. Besides, there is a parcel of women to be sent into her, and you know very well that I have always abhorred women. Women aboard, that is to say. They cause nothing but trouble and strife. Sophie, do you mean to blow out the candle? Moths are coming in.'

'I am sure you are right, my dear, and I shall never for a moment presume to set my opinion against yours, above all in anything to do with the service.' Sophie was well acquainted with her husband's power of going instantly to sleep and of staying asleep whatever the circumstances, and at this point, taking particular care of the carpet, she flung down the candlestick, sconce, and extinguisher. Jack leapt out of bed, put all to rights, and she continued, 'But there is just one thing that I must say, because with all this hurry and unpleasantness, and the Fencibles, and the builders, you may not have seen it quite as I do. There is Stephen to be considered, and his sad disappointment.'

'But Stephen cried off in the first place. Heart-broken, said he, but he almost certainly could not come: and never a word has he said since he returned.'

'Heart-broken he is, I am very sure: he does not say so, but it is as clear as the day that Diana has wounded him again. You had but to look at his poor face when he came back from town. My dear, we owe Stephen a great deal. A voyage to Botany Bay would do him all the good in the world. The peace and the quiet and all those new creatures to keep his mind from dwelling on her. Do but imagine him brooding for months and months in some horrid lodgings, until the *Ajax* is launched – he would mope away, and eat himself up with misery.'

'Lord, Sophie, perhaps there may be something in what you say. I was so taken up with this damned business of Kimber and the *Leopard* and my letter to the Admiralty that I hardly considered – of course, I saw he looked hipped, and I supposed she had played him some vile trick. But he never gave me so much as a hint of it; he never said, "My affairs don't run as smooth as I could wish, in a certain quarter, so I will go with you in the *Leopard*", or "Jack, I could do with a change of climate, I could do with a *tropical* climate". I should have smoked that instantly.'

'Stephen is far too delicate. Once he had seen that you had changed your mind about the ship, he would never mention his own concerns. But if you had heard him speak of wombats – oh, just in passing, and not with any sense of ill-usage – it would have brought tears to your eyes. Oh, Jack, he is so very low.'

CHAPTER THREE

The north-westerly gale had built up a wicked sea in the Bay of Biscay, and for two nights and a day the *Leopard* had been lying to under a close-reefed maintopsail and no more, her topgallant masts struck long since and her foretopsail yard on deck, her head to the north. Every time a tall sea struck her larboard bow, its white head racing towards her in the pitch-black night, solid water poured over her waist, tearing at the double-lashed boats and spars and forcing her head off to the north-north-east; but every time she came up again to within four points of the wind, the water pouring from her scuppers. She laboured, she wallowed heavy – and as every seaman knew, the ironbound coast of Spain was no great way off in the leeward darkness – black reefs, black cliffs, and the huge waves breaking to an enormous height upon them. Just how far off, no one could tell, for no observation had been possible in this low racing murk for three days past; but they felt the loom of the land, and many an anxious eye peered south.

She had had a rough time of it, rough even for the Bay; she had been tossed and bucketed about like a skiff, particularly in the early part of the blow, when the north-wester came shrieking across the western swell, cutting up a steep, confused, tumbling cross-sea that heaved her in all directions until she groaned again, and her working brought so much water through her sides that the pumps had been going watch and watch: a good sea-boat, a weatherly ship, always attentive to her helm; yet even her commander could not maintain that she was a dry one.

But her trials were coming to an end: the howl of the wind in her rigging had dropped half an octave, losing the hysterical edge of malignance, and there were a few breaks in the cloud. Captain Aubrey had been standing in streaming oilskins under the break of the poop these twelve hours past, learning the ways of his new charge; and at this point he held his sextant under his arm. The sextant was already set to something near the position of Antares, in the hope of a fleeting glimpse through the rifts: and an hour after the first break the noble star appeared, racing madly northwards through a long thin gap, showing just long enough for him to fix it and bring it down to the horizon. To be sure, his horizon was very far from perfect, more closely resembling a mountain range than an ideal line, but even so the reading was better than he had hoped – the *Leopard* still had sea-room in plenty. He returned to the wheel, the figures turning smoothly in his mind, checked and rechecked with the same satisfying result. Then, having stepped to the lee-rail, there to throw up the aged Bath bun and the glass of Marsala that he had just swallowed, committing them to the sea with long-accustomed ease, he addressed the officer of the watch: 'Mr Babbington,' he said, 'I believe you may bear up. She will wear foretopmast- and main-staysails. Course southwest a half west.' As he spoke he saw the quartermaster's hairy face move into the glow of the binnacle-light as he stared at the half-hour glass: the last grains of sand ran out, the quartermaster murmured, 'Shove off, Bill', and a tarpaulined figure, bent low against the driving rain and spray, hurried forward, holding tight to a lifeline stretched fore and aft, to strike seven bells in the middle watch – half past three in the morning. Babbington reached for his speaking-trumpet to call all hands to wear ship. 'Stay,' said Jack. 'Half an hour will make no odds. Wear her at eight bells – there is no point in turning the larbowlines up.'

He was strongly tempted to stay until the change in the watch, to see the manoeuvre carried out: but he had a thoroughly competent lieutenant in Babbington, a young man he had formed himself, and his remaining on deck would show a want of confidence, would diminish Babbington's authority. He stayed another ten minutes and then went below, hanging his oilskin over a tub and wiping the mixture of salt sea and rain-water from his face with a towel placed there for that purpose: in the sleeping-cabin a very cross Killick, torn from the arms of his delight after little more than a week, was busy resling-ing the cot, which a leak overhead had soaked through and through. 'Those bleeding caulkers at the Yard,' he muttered, 'don't know their fucking business . . . I'd caulk 'em . . . oh, I'd caulk 'em, and with a red-hot caulking iron in their . . .' The fancy pleased him; his face grew less surly; and with something approaching amenity he said aloud, 'There you are, sir: you can turn in now. Which you ain't dried your hair.' The last severely; and in fact Jack's hair was hanging in long yellow streamers down his back. Killick wrung it out like a cloth, remarked that it worn't so thick nor it was once upon a day, whipped it into a tight plait, and so took his leave.

Ordinarily Jack would have gone straight to sleep with an equal lack of ceremony, like an extinguished candle, but now from his wav-ing cot he kept his eye on the tell-tale compass overhead. He had not been staring for long before a deeper thunder joined the roaring of the storm, the crash of the seas on the *Leopard*'s side, and the song of the innumerable taut ropes and lines that communicated their gen-eral voice to her hull, where, resounding, it took on a deeper note: this was the rush of the larboard watch, racing through the after hatchway – the fore and main were battened down – to take up their duties after four hours' sleep. Almost at once the card began to turn against the lubber's point as the *Leopard* fell off: north-north-east, north-east by north, north-east, then faster to south of east, where the wind's voice almost died away, and round slower and slower to south-west and south-west and a half west, where it steadied. The *Leopard* had worn: she was on the starboard tack, flanking across the seas with a fine lively corkscrew motion. Jack's eyes closed: his mouth opened, and from it (for he was lying on his back, with no wife to pinch or turn him round) came a deep, rasping, guttural snore of prodigious volume.

The screeching, hallooing, piping, and running about on the poop a few feet from the sleeper's head never disturbed him for a moment; his face remained blankly unconscious, though sometimes a smile crossed it, and once, in a dream, he laughed; yet some area of the sailor's mind was still at work, for at two bells in the forenoon watch the waking Captain Aubrey was aware that the sea had steadily diminished throughout the remainder of the night, that the wind had hauled southwards, and that the *Leopard* was making a comfortable five knots.

'This coffee has been heated up. Boiled,' he said, looking at his purplish brew. Killick's face assumed a mean, pinched expression, and the thought 'If people lay in their cots till all hours while others is toiling and moiling, they gets what they deserve' very nearly found expression; but in fact the coffee had been boiled, a crime not far short of hanging at this time of the Captain's day, and Killick contented himself with a disobliging sniff and the words, 'There's another pot coming up.'

'Where is the Doctor? And take your thumb out of the butter.'

'At work since six bells in the morning watch, your honour,' said Killick, with intent; and in a very low voice, 'It worn't in it: nowhere near.'

'Then jump forward and tell him there is some vile boiled coffee, if he can bear it. And my compliments to Mr Pullings: I should be happy to see him.'

'Good morning, Tom,' he cried, as his first lieutenant appeared. 'Sit down and take a cup. You look as though you could do with it.'

'Good morning, sir. It would go down very welcome.'

'You have a pretty bad report, I collect?' looking at Pullings's careworn, worried face.

'Yes, sir, that I have,' said Thomas Pullings, shaking his head.

'No masts sprung, I hope?'

'Not as bad as that, sir; but the convicts have scragged their superintendent; and their surgeon, he pitched down into the hold and broke his neck. All the convicts are more or less dead, so seasick, and one of the women is in a screeching fit. And the filth down there, you would not credit. I posted some Marines over 'em, just in case, but there is not one of 'em could harm a fly now – flat as pancakes, and hardly strength enough to groan. But apart from that, sir, and the forward chain-pump choked, foretop halliards badly chafed, and bowsprit gammoning not what it might be, everything is shipshape, tolerably shipshape.'

'Scragged him, did they?' said Jack, whistling. 'Is he dead?'

'As a doornail, sir. His brains all over the deck. They must have done it with their irons.'

'Their surgeon dead too?'

'As to that, sir, I cannot rightly say: the Doctor has him in the sick-bay.'

'Ah, the Doctor will set him to rights. You remember him sawing the gunner's head, in *Sophie*, and setting his brains – why, there you are, Stephen! A good morning to you. Here is an elegant kettle of fish, hey, hey? But I dare say you have set their surgeon to rights?'

'I have not,' said Stephen. 'I cannot mend a severed spinal cord. The man was as dead as a rabbit before ever they picked him up.'

They looked at him in silence; he was clearly upset, and they had very rarely seen him upset, rarely moved beyond a certain peevishness – certainly not for a couple of civilians, who (though nobody chose to say so at this time, with the men unburied) were as disagreeable a pair of scrubs as they had set eyes upon. They could not tell that his whole person was shrieking for its usual dose, but they did know that he was in need of something, and having no more than kindness, coffee, toast, and orange marmalade, they offered these, together with tobacco. None of these things satisfied the specific craving, but the combination did have a soothing effect, and when Pullings said: 'Oh, sir, I was forgetting: while we were rousing their surgeon out of the hold, we found a stowaway.' Stephen cried, 'A stowaway in a man-of-war? I never heard of such a thing,' looking keen and attentive. There were a great many things in a man-of-war that Dr Maturin had never heard of, but he had of late made some groping attempts at learning the difference between a slab-line and a selvagee – had been heard to say, not without complacency, 'I am become tolerably amphibious' – and this pleased them. They agreed heartily: a stowaway was most uncommon, indeed unheard of; and with a bow to Stephen Jack said, 'Before we tackle the ugly business in the forepeak, let us have this – this *rara avis in mara, maro*, in.'

The stowaway, a slight young man, was led aft by a Marine sergeant, holding him up rather than holding him in. He was very pale where the dirt and a week-old beard did not obscure his skin: dressed in a shirt and a torn pair of breeches. He made a leg, and said, 'Good morning, sir.'

'Don't speak to the Captain,' cried the sergeant, in a sergeant's voice, shaking him by the elbow and then hauling him up as he fell.

'Sergeant,' said Jack, 'set him on the locker there, and then you may go. Now, sir, what is your name?'

'Herapath, sir: Michael Herapath, at your service.'

'Well, Mr Herapath, and what do you mean by concealing yourself aboard this ship?'

Here the *Leopard* gave a lee-lurch, and the sea, a light green now, swept up beyond the scuttle with sickening deliberation: Herapath turned greener still, clapped his hand to his mouth to stifle a dry, vain retching; and between the spasms that shook his whole frame he brought out the words, 'I beg pardon, sir. I beg pardon. I am not quite well.'

'Killick,' called Jack. 'Stow this man in a hammock on the orlop.'

Killick, a wiry, ape-like creature, picked Herapath up with no apparent effort and carried him bodily away, saying, 'Mind your 'ed on the door-jamb, mate.'

'I have seen him before,' said Pullings. 'He came aboard just after the convicts were sent down, and wanted to join. Well, I saw he was no seaman – he said as much himself – so I told him we had no room for landsmen, and turned him away – advised him to list for a soldier.'

At that time it was true that the *Leopard* had no landsmen on her books apart from those in her original draft. A captain of Jack Aubrey's reputation, a taut captain, even a tartar at times, but a fair one and no flogger, and above all a lucky one in the article of prize-money, had no great difficulty in manning his ship: that is to say, no great difficulty in bringing the meagre draft up to its full comple-ment by volunteers, so long as the news had time to circulate. He had only to print a few handbills, set up rendezvous in suitable public houses, and the *Leopard*'s crew was complete. Men who had sailed with him before, prime seamen who by means known to themselves alone had eluded the press-gangs and the crimps, turned up grin-ning, often bringing a couple of friends, and expecting their names and former ratings to be remembered – rarely expecting in vain. His only difficulty with this crew of man-of-war's men, in which even the waisters could hand, reef and steer, was preserving it from the port-admiral. He succeeded up to the very last day, when the port-admiral, receiving orders to send out the *Dolphin* instantly, what-ever the cost, stripped the *Leopard* of one hundred seamen, replacing them by sixty-four objects from the receiving-ship, quota-men, and people who preferred the sea to a county gaol.

'And then, sir,' continued Pullings, 'seeing he looked so very down, I told him it would never answer, an educated man on the lower deck – he would never stand the labour, his hands would be flayed in no time at all, he would be started and cobbed by the bosun's mates, might even be brought to the gangway and flogged, and he would never get along kindly with his messmates. But no, he longed to go to sea, he said, and would prove very willing. So I gave him a chit to Warner, of *Eurydice*, who is a hundred and twenty hands short, and he thanked me very civil indeed.'

Stephen had also seen the young man. He was nearing the Parade Coffee-House when Herapath spoke to him, asked him the way, asked him the time, and was very earnest to enter into conversation; but Stephen was a cautious soul; many people had been set upon him before this, some in even stranger form, and although the approach was almost certainly too pitifully naive to be anything in that line, he did not choose to go into the matter, above all in his present state of apathy. He bade Herapath good day, and walked into the coffee-house.

He did not mention this now, however, partly because of his secretive nature, and partly because he was thinking about Mrs Wogan, whom he had not yet seen. He attached no great importance to her, and there was time and to spare in a voyage that might last nine months; but even so, it was worth taking care. Had Diana mentioned his name to her? His entire approach would depend on that.

Jack drained his last cup and said, 'We had best get under way.'

They came out into the brilliant daylight of the quarterdeck, the sun well up on the larboard quarter, high white clouds moving in a steady procession north-westwards across a pale blue sky, the washed air sparkling and transparent, a strong but even swell, the waves themselves a deep perfection. The *Leopard* had recovered from her battering with the most surprising speed: she was close-hauled on the larboard tack, and she was making a good seven knots, not, perhaps, with the lithe grace of a well-trimmed frigate – the image of a play-ful cart-horse crossed Stephen's mind – but with a creditable gait in a two-decker. Her topgallantmasts were still on deck; the bosun had a party out on the head, busy with the bowsprit and getting uncom-monly wet as they passed the gammoning-turns; and there were a good many forecastle hands creeping about like great net-bearing spiders, repairing the damaged rigging; yet from her general clean, trim, orderly appearance, no landsman and few sailors would have believed that she had emerged, not five hours since, from as nasty a blow as the Bay could provide.

Jack took this in with a quick, professional glance; but then his brow clouded. Two midshipmen were leaning on the rail, gazing at the remote hint of Finisterre dark on the horizon as the ship lifted to the swell. Young gentlemen were not encouraged to lean on the rail in any ship commanded by Captain Aubrey. 'Mr Wetherby,' he said, 'Mr Sommers: if you wish to view the geography of Spain, you will find the masthead a more convenient place, a more extensive vista. You will take a spy-glass with you, if you please. Mr Grant, the other young gentleman will join the bosun on the bowsprit.'

The battens and tarpaulins had already been taken from the

hatches, and Jack walked forward along the gangway, down the forecastle ladder and so to the main hatchway; then, adjuring Stephen
to 'clap on to the rail, there', for the sea was still running high and
skittish, he plunged below, turning quick at the bottom of the ladder, just in time to see Stephen hanging by his coat-tails, suspended
in Pullings's powerful grasp, and extending his limbs like a tortoise.
'You really must learn to clap on, Doctor,' he said, receiving him in his
arms and setting him down on the lower deck. 'We cannot have you
breaking your neck too. Come now, one hand for yourself and one for
the ship.' Aft along the shadowy lower deck, with its massive twenty-
four-pounders bowsed up against the tight-shut ports; down again to
the orlop and the cable tiers, where Jack called for a hold-lantern: only
a very dim light came down through the gratings overhead, and since
this part of the ship had been fitted up for the convicts he no longer
knew just how things lay. He paused at the head of the ladder leading
down to the forepeak, and considered.

Although he was sole captain, under God, aboard the *Leopard*,
this was another world, a living-space inconveniently cut out of his
kingdom, and one that was to be transported to New Holland with
the utmost dispatch, there to be emptied and restored to its true
function as part of a man-of-war. A self-sufficient world, with its own
stores, its own immediate authorities; one with which he came into
contact only through the superintendent, who, with his subordinates,
dealt with all problems that might arise. A numerous world, however, for although it had at first been considered that half a dozen
convicts would serve as a sufficient blind to cover Mrs Wogan's
transportation – to make it seem something other than the most
exceptional measure that in fact it was – some of the other bodies or
departments concerned had been unable to resist adding to the number, so that it had grown to well above a score, with a superintendent, a
surgeon, and a chaplain, besides the usual guards or turnkeys, to look
after them. And all these people, the convicted and the unconvicted,
inhabited the forward part of the orlop and the forepeak, under the
waterline, where they could not get in the way of the working or the

fighting of the ship, and where, he had hoped, they could be forgotten. The chaplain and the surgeon were allowed to walk the quarterdeck, but the remaining free men, including the furiously indignant superintendent, were obliged to take the air on the forecastle; while they also messed together in what had been the bosun's cabin.

'That is where the women are stowed,' he observed, nodding towards the carpenter's store.

'Are there many?' asked Stephen.

'Three,' said Jack, 'and another farther aft. Mrs Wogan is her name.' He collected himself, cried, 'Below there! Show a glim,' set his foot on the ladder and ran down. Forward of the bitt-pins stretched a curving, triangular space, whitened, barred with iron across its after end, and lit with three dim lanterns. Underfoot lay a mass of straw, floating a foot deep in bilge and liquid filth that heaved with the heaving of the ship, and all about it lay men in the various attitudes of extreme prostration; some few squatted against the step of the foremast; many were still uttering the hoarse sounds of seasickness; all were beyond caring where they lay or crouched; and all were wearing irons. The stench was appalling, and the air so foul that when Jack lowered his lantern the flame guttered, burning faint and blue. The Marines were lined up outside the cage: inside, near the door, stood their sergeant and a couple of guards, standing over the body of the superintendent. The man's head had been battered to a pulp and it was clear to Stephen that he had been dead some time, probably since the beginning of the storm.

'Sergeant,' said Jack, 'jump aft – Mr Larkin and the mate of the hold. Mr Pullings, twenty swabbers immediately. The channels and pump-dales are choked with all this straw: they must be cleared. Sailcloth and the sailmaker for the body. Do you wish to examine it, Doctor?'

'No further, sir,' said Stephen, bending low and rolling back an eyelid. 'I know all I need to know. But may I suggest that these men should be carried up at once, and that a wind-sail should be installed? This air is mortal.'

'Make it so, Mr Pullings,' said Jack. 'And let a hose be shipped in the head, to lead down through the manger-scuttle: that will give us a clear run to the forward well. Tell the carpenter to leave everything and repair the forward chain-pump.' Turning to the civilians, he said, 'Do you know who did this?'

No, they said, they did not: they had looked at all the irons, as far as they could, what with being hardly able to move themselves and having no orders, like, but in all this wet and filth, why, one pair of irons was much the same as another. In a low voice, jerking his head towards a huge raw-boned man who lay almost naked, utterly indifferent as the lapping surge turned his body from side to side, one of them said, 'I think it was him, sir. The big 'un. And his mates.'

Mr Larkin, the master of the *Leopard*, came running down the ladder, followed by the mate. Jack cut their exclamations very short, gave a number of sharp, clear orders, and turning to the hatchway roared, 'Swabbers, bear a hand there, swabbers. Bear a hand, God damn you all,' in a voice that could be heard on the poop.

As soon as the sickening work was well in hand, he told the senior turnkey to follow him, and propelled Stephen up the ladder into the comparative light and purity of the cable-tier. Here there was much less water, but on the other hand many more rats were to be seen; for as usual during a really heavy blow, the hold rats had moved up a stage or two, and the *Leopard*'s motion being still so brisk, they had not yet seen fit to go down again. Jack gave one an expert kick as he stopped at the door of the carpenter's store-room and bade the turnkey open it. Here again was something like the same mess of straw, but the women's pallets had disintegrated less, and it was drier by far: two of the women were barely conscious, but a third, a girl with a broad, simple face, sat up, blinking in the light, and asked 'was it nearly over yet?' adding, 'We ain't had no food, gentleman, not for days and days.'

Jack told her it would be seen to, and said, 'You must put on your frock.'

'I ain't got no clothes left,' she replied. 'They stole my blue and the yellow cambric with muslin sleeves my lady gave me. Where's my lady, gentleman?'

'God help us,' he muttered as they made their way aft, past the huge cables, still smelling of Portsmouth mud – plenty of rats among the tiers – past the carpenter's crew working on the forward chain-pump, and towards the after-cockpit.

'This is where we put the other one,' he said, 'the Mrs Wogan that was to berth alone.' He rapped on the door and called out, 'Is all well there?'

A sound within, but indistinct. The man opened the door and Jack walked in. He saw a young lady sitting in a trim cabin, eating Naples biscuits from the top of a locker by the light of a candle. She was looking indignantly, even fiercely, at the door; but when he said, 'Good morning, ma'am. I trust I see you well?' she rose, curtsied, and replied, 'Thank you, sir. I am quite recovered.'

An awkward pause followed: physically awkward, because the beam of the lower deck that traversed the little cabin, or rather the large cupboard, obliged Jack to adopt a hangdog stoop as he stood there just inside the door, blocking it entirely – the space was so small that he could scarcely advance another yard without coming into direct contact with Mrs Wogan; and morally awkward because he could not think of what to say, could not think how to tell this obviously well-bred young woman, who stood there, looking modestly down, and who had come through so rough a time so creditably – neat bunk, neat counter-pane, all dunnage stowed away – that her candle, her only light, could not possibly be countenanced, that showing a naked light, above all a naked light no very great way from the powder-room, was the most criminal act aboard a ship. He gazed earnestly at the flame, and said, 'However.' But this led to nothing, and after a moment Mrs Wogan said, 'Will not you sit down, sir? I am sorry that I have no more than a stool to offer you.'

'You are very good, ma'am,' said Jack, 'but I fear I am not at leisure. A lantern, however – just so, a lantern slung from the beam. You would be much better, with a lantern slung from the beam. For

I must tell you, ma'am, that a naked – that a bare – that is to say, an unprotected flame cannot possibly be countenanced aboard. A flame is little more – little less – than a crime.' Even as he spoke, the word crime, addressed to a female convict, a criminal, seemed to him unfortunate; but Mrs Wogan only said, in a low, penitent voice, that she was much concerned to hear it: she begged pardon, and never would offend again.

'A lantern will be sent below at once,' he said. 'Is there anything else that you could wish?'

'If enquiries might be made for the young woman that attends me, sir, it would be a great comfort; I am afraid the poor creature may have come to harm. And if I might have liberty to take a little air . . . perhaps the request is improper. But if someone would have the goodness to take the rat away, I should be most infinitely obliged.'

'The rat, ma'am?'

'Yes, sir: in the corner there. I knocked him on the head at last, with my shoe – it was quite a battle.'

Jack kicked it out of the door, said that these things should be attended to, that the lantern should be sent directly, bade her good day, and withdrew. Sending the turnkey forward to deal with Mrs Wogan's servant, he joined Stephen under the light of the breadroom grating, where he was holding the rat by the tail, examining it with close attention: a gravid rat, near her term, very much infested with fleas, a rat with some anomalous lesions apart from those inflicted by the heel of a shoe.

'That was Mrs Wogan,' said Jack. 'I had a curiosity to see her, after what the messenger let fall. What did you make of the lady?'

'The door so narrow, and your vast bulk filling it,' said Stephen, 'I saw nothing of her at all.'

'A dangerous woman, they say. It seems she offered to pistol the prime minister or blow up the Houses of Parliament – something very shocking, that was obliged to be played pianissimo; so I had a curiosity to see her. A rare plucked 'un, of that I am very sure: an ugly four days' blow, and her cabin as neat as a pin! Lord, Stephen,' he said, when he had changed his filthy clothes and they were sitting in the stern-gallery, watching the *Leopard*'s wake race from them, pure white in living blue, 'did you ever see such a Godforsaken shambles as the forepeak?' He was extremely depressed: he was conscious of having failed in his duty as far as the forepeak was concerned. He should never have allowed the cage to be so built that it would flood: the deep bottom bar, upon which the uprights rested, had acted as a dam – that was obvious to him now, as obvious as the simple remedy. And he should have sent for a report from the superintendent. Although the man was not required to report to him more than once a week, and although the man had fallen foul of him before they weighed from Spithead, he should certainly have sent. Now the unfortunate, pompous, brutal, pretentious fellow was dead, and that meant that Jack would either have to shuffle the responsibility for the convicts off on to the useless half-witted illiterate turnkeys or assume it himself; and if anything went wrong he would have not only the Admiralty down on him like a hundred of bricks, but also the Navy Office, the Transport Board, the Victualling Office, the Secretary of State for War and the Colonies, the Home Office, and no doubt half a dozen other bodies, each better than the last at calling for accounts, dockets and vouchers, at handing down reprimands, at holding officers liable for extraordinary sums, and at involving them in endless official correspondence.

'No,' said Stephen, having considered the prisons he had known. 'I have not.' They had been quite as filthy particularly in Spain; they had been even wetter, in the underground vaults of Lisbon; but at least they had been stable. In them it had been possible to die of starvation and a large variety of diseases, but not of mere seasickness, the most ignominious end of all. 'No. I have not. And it occurs to me that now their surgeon is so dead I shall have to look after their health. I quite regret my second mate.' As surgeon of a fourth-rate, Stephen was entitled to two assistants. Several well-qualified men, including some former shipmates, had applied to him, for Dr Maturin was much caressed in the physical world: his *Suggestions for the Amelioration of Sick-Bays*; his *Thoughts on the Prevention of the Diseases most usual among Seamen*; his *New Operation for Suprapubic Cystotomy*; and his *Tractatus de Novae Febris Ingressu* were read throughout the thinking part of the Navy; a cruise with him meant an accession of professional knowledge, the likelihood of advancement, and, since he generally sailed with Lucky Jack Aubrey, the possibility of large sums of prize-money – the assistant surgeon of the *Boadicea*, for example, had retired from the service on his share, had bought a practice in Bath, and had already set up his carriage. But true to that principle of isolation which prevented him from having a confidential servant, Stephen never sailed twice with the same colleague; and this time he not only declined the offers of those he knew but he also limited himself to a single man, Paul Martin, a brilliant anatomist from the Channel Islands, recommended to him by his friend Dupuytren of the Hôtel Dieu: for although Martin was a British subject, or to be more exact a subject of the Duke of Normandy, who also happened to rule over the British Isles, he had spent much of his life in France, where he had recently published his *De Ossibus*, a work that had caused a considerable sensation on both sides of the Channel, among those who delighted much in bones. On both sides of the Channel, for science flowed freely in spite of the war: indeed, earlier in the year Stephen had been invited to address the learned of Paris at the *Institut*, a journey that he might have made, with the consent of both governments, had it not been for the presence of Diana Villiers and of certain scruples that were still unconquered by the time the *Leopard* sailed.

'The chaplain,' he said. 'The chaplain might perhaps, as you would say, *lend a hand*. I have known parsons study physic with a not inconsiderable success; they have been known to be of great help to the surgeon in the cockpit during an action. Apart from their spiritual and their pedagogical functions, they may surely be considered – since even surgeons are not immortal – as potentially useful members of a ship's company, and I have often wondered at your unwillingness to have them aboard. I do not advert to the barbarous prejudice that some untutored minds are weak enough to entertain, with regard to cats, corpses, and clergymen in a ship; for that could never have any influence with you.'

'I will tell you what,' said Jack heavily. 'I respect the cloth, of course, and learning; but I cannot feel that a man-of-war is the proper place for a parson. Just take this morning . . . On Sunday, when we rig church, I dare say he will tell us to treat one another like brethren, and to do unto others, you know. We will all say Amen, and the *Leopard* will sail on with all those people in irons in that filthy hole forward, just the same. But that is only what occurred to me this morning: in a larger way, it seems to me uncommon odd, and precious near to cant, to tell the ship's company of a man-of-war with loaded guns to love your enemy and to turn the other cheek, when you know damned well that the ship and every man jack aboard her is there to blow the enemy out of the water if he possibly can. Either the hands believe it, and then where is your discipline? Or they don't, and then it seems to me to come hellfire close to mockery of holy things. I prefer reading them the Articles of War or giving them a piece about their duty: coming from me, with no bands or surplice on, why, it has another effect.'

He thought of mentioning the lamentable quality of most of the naval chaplains he had seen, and of telling the well-worn anecdote of Lord Cloncarty, who, on being informed by his first lieutenant that the chaplain had been carried off by the yellow fever, and had died a Roman Catholic, replied, 'Well, so much the better.' First lieutenant: 'Hoot awa, my lord, how can you say that of a British clergyman?' Lord Cloncarty: 'Why, because I believe I am the first captain of a man-of-war that could boast of a chaplain who had any religion at all.' But reflecting that Stephen was himself a Papist, and might be hurt, and that in any case the anecdote had something of the air of letting down his own side, he remained silent, inwardly observing, 'You was precious near being brought by the lee again, Jack.'

'Sure,' said Stephen, 'this is a question that has troubled many a candid mind: far be it from me to propose any solution. I believe I shall step forward and look at these new patients. They will have been carried up to the forecastle, I suppose, the creatures? And then there is your Mrs Wogan: when is she to be indulged in air? For I must tell you, that I will not answer for their health if they are not aired at least an hour a day, at twice, in fine weather.'

'Lord, Stephen, I had quite forgot. Mr Needham,' he cried in a strong voice, addressing his clerk in the fore-cabin, 'pass the word for the first lieutenant.' And a moment later, when Pullings hurried in with a sheaf of papers, 'No, Tom, it is not the watchbills, for the moment. Pray have a lantern sent into the little cabin abaft the tiers – the female prisoner that berths alone.' Pullings was also to find out what arrangements the late superintendent had made for victualling the convicts, their rations, the stores available, and the practice, in common transports, for prisoners' exercise.

'Aye aye, sir,' said Pullings, in his competent, cheerful way. 'And there is this stowaway, sir. What am I to do with him?'

'The stowaway? Oh, yes, that half-starved fellow this morning. Well, now, since he is so very eager to go to sea, and since, after all, he *is* at sea, I think you may enter him as a supernumerary landsman. God knows what romantic notions he has in his head . . . the lower deck will soon knock them out again.'

'He is probably running from a wench, sir. Twenty young fellows in the starboard watch are in the same case.'

'It is often those slim young men who procreate so freely,' said Stephen, 'whereas your village champion, for all his parading like the parish bull, in fact remains comparatively chaste. For lack of opportunity? Who can tell? Is the flame more ardent in a lighter form? Does a more insinuating manner count for all? But you will not set him at work until he is restored. Such emaciation! He must be fed pap from a spoon, and a small spoon too, once every watch, or you will have still another corpse upon your hands – you may readily kill him with kindness and a piece of pork.'

He considered for a while, and when Pullings had gone about his innumerable duties, he said, 'Jack, have you ever known any gentlemen on the lower deck?'

'Yes: a few.'

'And how did you like it yourself, when you were a midshipman and your captain turned you before the mast for incompetence?'

'It was not for incompetence.'

'I distinctly remember that he termed you a lubber.'

'Yes, but a *lecherous* lubber: I kept a girl in the cable-tiers. It was a reflection upon my morals, not my seamanship.'

'You astonish me: but tell, how did you like it?'

'It was no bed of roses. But I was bred to the sea, and the midshipmen's berth is no bed of roses neither. For a landsman, brought up to be nice about his food and so on, it would come very hard. I knew one, a parson's son who got into trouble at college, that could not bear it, and died. On the whole I should say that if your educated man is young and healthy, if he is in a happy ship, and can stand up for himself, and can survive the first month or so, he has a fair chance. Not otherwise.'

Stephen walked forward along the weather gangway, and in spite of the unhappiness settled deep into his heart and of the craving that filled his whole being, he felt his spirits lift. The day had grown more brilliant still; the diminishing wind had backed a point and more abaft the beam, and the *Leopard* was running under courses, topsails and lower studdingsails; and being a new suit they made a splendid expanse of white against the sky. Great smooth taut curves of a whiteness so intense that their surface was rather to be apprehended than distinctly seen, and all set among the sharp, definite, clear-cut pattern of the rigging. But above all it was the warm yet vivifying, tonic air sweeping in over the side and searching deep into his lungs that made his sad face lighten and his dull eyes come to life. He was pleased to find that his assistant and the loblolly-boy had been on the forecastle for some while, and that Martin could give him an account of those convicts who were still prostrated. Most, however, had recovered by this time, at least enough to sit up or even stand and take some interest in life. The two older women were of this class (the half-wit girl was presumably with Mrs Wogan) and they stood leaning on the breastwork, looking down into the head, to the infinite annoyance of the hands; for the head, or that part of it on either side of the stem, was the seamen's privy, their only place of ease; and many of them were now hard-pressed. One was a middle-aged Gipsy, spare, dark, fierce, and aquiline; the other a quite remarkably vicious-looking woman, with such evident wickedness on her face and eye that it was a wonder she had ever been able to make a living in any occupation that brought her into contact with her fellow men. Yet from her bulk she must have done quite well: although diminished by imprisonment and continual sea-sickness so that her filthy crimson gown hung loose, she was still a flabby, swagging fifteen stone. Sparse carroty hair, the outer half dyed yellow: tiny glaucous eyes set close and deep in a vast amorphous face, an incongruous bar of eyebrow right across the two. Some few of the convict men might have been her cousins; others had more of a mere petty-larceny look; still others would have seemed quite ordinary if they had been wearing smock-frocks; and two were idiots. They all had the deathly gaol-pallor, and all, except for the idiots, wore a hopeless, downcast expression. In their revolting clothes and their inhuman irons they were a squalid, even an abject group, herded there like cattle; they were in the way; the seamen glanced at them with disapprobation, contempt, and in some cases enmity.

The big man who was suspected of having killed the superintendent was one of the worst cases: his powerful body still heaved convulsively from time to time, but otherwise he might have been a corpse. 'Here,' said Stephen to his assistant, speaking Latin, 'heroic measures are meet to be used. A funnel having been introduced into his pharynx, fifty, nay threescore drops of sulphureous ether are to be administered.' He then prescribed a decoction of orange-peel and Peruvian bark for some of the others, and said, 'These you will be pleased to take from our chest. For my part, I shall overhaul their late surgeon's stores, and see what they contain.'

They contained an extraordinary amount of Hollands gin, a very few books and instruments – cheap, dirty instruments, with rust and old blood still coating the whole length of the large saw – and the Home Office collection of drugs, by no means the same as those supplied to men-of-war by the Sick and Hurt Board. The Home Office pinned its faith more upon rhubarb, grey powder, and hartshorn than did the Sick and Hurt, upon Lucatellus's balsam, polypody of the oak, and, to Stephen's surprise, the alcoholic tincture of laudanum. Three Winchester quarts of it. '*Vade retro*,' he cried, seizing the nearest and opening the scuttle: but after the first had gone he paused, and in reasonable, false, considering voice he observed that what was left should be preserved for the use of his patients; there were many contingencies in which the tincture might be of essential consequence to them.

Then, pausing only to summon a wan and hopeless guard, he made his way aft to Mrs Wogan's cabin. It was filled with Mrs Wogan and her attendant, folding sheets, the girl still wearing no more than a blanket pinned across her bosom. In the ensuing fuss Stephen noted that Mrs Wogan at least was capable of decisive action: she placed a shift and a plain dress in the girl's arms, told the guard to take her back to where she had come from, and so dismissed them.

'Good morning, ma'am,' said Stephen, as they faded from view along the dim alleyway, both guard and prisoner screeching at the rats. He advanced into the cabin, so that Mrs Wogan, falling back, received the light from the hanging lantern full in her face. 'My name is Maturin: I am the surgeon of this ship and am come to enquire after your health.' Not the slightest flicker of awareness. Either the woman was the most consummate actress or she had never heard his name. Diana, he reflected bitterly, might not have been so proud of mentioning it. No: he would probe again, several times for conscience sake; but even now he would lay a thousand to one that she had never heard of Stephen Maturin.

Mrs Wogan apologized for the confusion, begged him to sit down, and stated, with many acknowledgements of his goodness, that she was quite well.

'Yet your face is somewhat yellower than could be wished,' said Stephen. 'Give me your hand.' Her pulse was normal: a strong confirmation indeed. 'Now show me your tongue.' No woman can look either handsome or dignified with her mouth wide open and her tongue protruding, and there appeared to be a slight struggle in Mrs Wogan's bosom; but Stephen had all the authority of a physician, and the tongue appeared. 'Well,' he admitted, ''tis a laudable tongue. I dare say you took a good hearty vomit. They may cry out against the seasickness as much as ever they please, but as an evacuation of the gross humours and crudities, it has no rival.'

'To tell you the truth, sir,' said Mrs Wogan, 'I was not sick at all; only a little indisposed. I have made several voyages to America, and I do not find the motion very troublesome.'

'Then perhaps we should contemplate a purge. Please to inform me of the state of your bowels.'

Mrs Wogan told him frankly how they did, for Stephen had not only the medical man's authority but also his un-human quality – the Hippocratic mask was second nature to him by now – and she might have been confiding in a graven image: yet she did start a little when he asked whether she had any reason to apprehend a pregnancy, and her reply, 'None at all, sir,' was uttered with considerable reserve. There was no coldness, however, in the words that followed: 'No, sir; I conceive that I am far more likely to be cribbed and cabined, than confined. And may not my yellow face,' she added with an amused, good-natured ghost of a smile, 'be connected with my cabining? I must not presume to teach a doctor physic, Heaven forbid, but if only I might have a breath of untainted air . . . I did mention it to the very large gentleman, an officer I believe, that was here earlier in the day, but . . .'

'You are to consider, madam, that the captain of a man-of-war has a great many things to occupy his mind.'

She folded her hands in her lap, looked down, and said, 'Oh yes, to be sure,' in a low, submissive voice.

Stephen walked away, quite pleased with his pompous, official tone – a good initial position from which to retreat – and reached the forepeak, now clean and as sweet as ever it could be. While he was gazing at it, the enormous pandemonium of all hands to dinner broke out overhead, a familiar pandemonium, preceded, but only just preceded, by the striking of eight bells and the bosun's pipes. Stephen detained a deeply unwilling but civil carpenter's mate for close on ten minutes with his views on the proper accommodation for convicts, and then travelled aft along the lower deck, lighter now that the larboard gun-ports were open, and tight-packed with men, three hundred and more, all sitting at their tables slung between the guns, loudly eating their two pounds of salt beef and a pound of biscuit a head (for this was a Tuesday). The mess deck at dinner time was an impossible, an inconceivable place for an officer, except on Christmas Day, and those who did not know him were worried and distressed. But many of the Leopards had either sailed with Dr Maturin or knew of his ways by the reports of friends: they regarded him as a very valuable creature, but as one unaccountable for his actions outside the sick-bay or the cockpit, being brutally ignorant of everything to do with the sea – could scarcely tell the difference between port and starboard, right and wrong – almost an innocent, as one might say. A gentleman to be boasted of, being a genuine physician as well as the boldest hand with a saw in the fleet, but to be concealed from view as much as possible, when in company with other ships. 'Do not stir, I beg,' he cried, as he paced along between the chewing faces, friendly or bemused as the case might be; he was in something of a brown study, reflecting upon the comparison between Diana Villiers and Mrs Wogan, and it was only a particularly familiar face that brought him out of it, the large, red, smiling face of Barret Bonden, Jack Aubrey's coxswain who stood there, swaying with the motion of the ship and holding up a small spoon, clearly for his edification.

'Barret Bonden,' he said, 'what are you at? Let you all sit down, for God's love.'

The mess, eight powerful man-of-war's men with pigtails to their waists, and an insubstantial, irregular ninth sat down. 'Which we are feeding Herapath, sir,' said Bonden. 'Tom Davis pounds the biscuit in the mess-kid here, Joe Plaice mixes in our juice in t'other, to make a right smooth pap, and I send it home with this little spoon, a very small spoon, like you said, your honour. A silver teaspoon Killick lent me from the cabin.'

Stephen looked at the first kid, which contained a good pound of shattered biscuit, and at the second, which held a rather greater quantity of pap: he considered Herapath (barely recognizable in his purser's slops) whose eyes were fixed with painful eagerness upon the spoon. 'Well,' said he, 'if you give him a third part of what is in the tub, and the rest at five times, say at each eighth bell, you may make a seaman of him yet, rather than a corpse; for you are to observe, that it is less the dimensions of the spoon, than the sum total, the aggregate of the pap, that counts.'

In the great cabin he found the *Leopard*'s captain sitting in the midst of a large quantity of papers: it was clear that he had a great many things to occupy his mind, but Stephen had every intention of adding more as soon as Jack should have finished with the purser's accounts. In the meantime he continued his reflection: the comparison between Diana Villiers and Mrs Wogan really would not hold. They both had black hair and blue eyes, and they were much of an age; but Mrs Wogan was a good two inches shorter, and those two inches made an extraordinary difference – the difference between a woman who was tall and one who was not. Cleopatra's nose. But above all, Mrs Wogan lacked the infinite grace that ravished Stephen's heart every time Diana walked across a room. As to her face, it was scarcely fair to judge, after what she had been through so very recently: yet in spite of the want of bloom and the yellowish complexion, there was a likeness, a superficial likeness striking enough to make even a casual observer think of some close relationship; but as far as he could judge in this short space of time, Mrs Wogan's face had been formed by a somewhat gentler habit of mind. It was resolute enough; but in spite of her dangerous calling he thought it the outward expression of a milder, less cruel and imperious, and perhaps a more naive and even affectionate nature: not that that was saying much. A leopard to Diana's tiger, perhaps. 'A poor figure,' he said, remembering the leopards he had known, none remarkable for mildness or naivety. 'But smaller in any case: on a smaller scale.'

'There, Mr Benton,' said Jack. 'All square by the lifts and braces.' And when the purser had borne his books away, 'Stephen, I am all yours.'

'Then be so good as to bring your mind to bear on my convicts. I say my convicts, because I am answerable for their health, which, let me tell you, is tolerably precarious.'

'Yes, yes, Pullings and I have dealt with that. Hammocks are to be slung in the forepeak, Navy-fashion – no more of that vile straw. The people are to be aired on the forecastle, a dozen at a time, once in the forenoon and once in the first dog-watch; your wind-sail will have been rigged before the day is out; and when you and the chaplain have reported on them, we shall see which can be let out of irons. For exercise, they can pump ship.'

'And Mrs Wogan, is she too to pump ship? As a medical man, I tell you she cannot long survive in that damp, mephitic, lightless cupboard. She too must have air.'

'Ah, there you have me, Stephen. What are we to do with her? I have found a note in the superintendent's papers: he was directed to allow her all proper indulgences consistent with security and good order – the services of a female attendant – her own stores to the extent of one and a half ton. No word about exercise.'

'What is the custom in the common transports that go to Botany Bay, when they carry privileged persons?'

'I don't know. I asked the turnkeys – God-damned half-baked whoreson lubbers – and all they could tell me was that Barrington, the pickpocket, you remember, was allowed to mess with the bosun.

But that is neither here nor there: he was only a flash kiddy, while Mrs Wogan is clearly a gentlewoman . . . By the way, Stephen, did you notice the extraordinary likeness between her and Diana?'

'I did not, sir,' said Stephen, and a brief silence followed, in which Jack regretted having mentioned a name that might have caused a wound – 'Laid by the lee again, Jack' – and at the same time he wondered how it came about that Stephen should have grown so hellfire peevish these recent days.

'I cannot very well invite her to walk the quarterdeck,' he said. 'That would certainly be improper, since she has been condemned. A very dangerous woman, it appears – blazed away right, left and centre when she was taken.'

'Certainly you would not wish to associate with a malefactor; though I believe there is an excellent precedent for doing so, as your chaplain may tell you. Then as you so rightly say, there is the danger; and I appreciate your anxiety to the full. No doubt she has a brace of pistols in her pocket. Allow me to suggest, however, that she should have the liberty of walking on the gangway at stated intervals, and occasionally, in clement weather, upon the poop. I must confess that to reach the poop she would have to traverse the holy quarterdeck, and your not unnatural apprehension – I shall not say your timidity – will no doubt require you to have a carronade, loaded with grape, trained upon her as she does so. Nevertheless, this seems to me a valid solution of the difficulty.'

Jack was well acquainted with Stephen's ferocious defence of his patients, even the most unseamanlike of them, once they were under his hands: adding to this the likeness that had so struck him, and to his friend's present unparalleled acerbity (for Stephen had not spoken with a smile: there had been a cruel edge to his voice), he checked the words that were rising in his throat. It called for a considerable effort, however, for Jack was neither the most patient nor the most long-suffering of men, and it seemed to him that on this occasion Stephen had let his tongue run away with him. Rather stiffly he said, 'I shall consider of it,' and for once he was not displeased when the

drum beat Roast Beef of Old England a moment later, summoning Dr
Maturin away to his dinner in the wardroom.

The *Leopard*'s was a fine great wardroom, with plenty of space for
all its officers and for the guests they loved to invite, in their hospitable
Navy fashion; a long room terminating in a vast stern-window right
across its breadth, and one that seemed longer still because of the
twenty-foot table running down its middle. The lieutenants' cabins
on either side: boarding-pikes, tomahawks, cutlasses, pistols, swords,
arranged in tasteful groups upon the bulkhead and the sides. And
today, almost for the first time, it had its full complement; for during
the quite exceptionally rough passage down the Channel and across
the Bay, dinner had rarely seen more than half a dozen at a time.
Now the only man missing was Turnbull, the officer of the watch;
there were blue coats in plenty, with scarlet for the Marines, black
for the chaplain, and watchet-blue purser's jackets for the boys that
waited behind the sailors' chairs, all bright and fresh at this beginning of a new commission; a pleasant sight in the brilliance of the
reflected sun, but one that had little effect on Stephen's morosity. He
had rarely felt a more general irritation nor less certainty of being able
to control it, and he plied his spoon as though salvation lay at the bottom of his soup-plate. In a way it did: the barley-broth, glutinous and
lenitive, helped to bring his inner man more nearly in harmony with
his outward appearance – so much for free-will – and by the time
they reached the first remove little effort was needed for a proper
complaisance. The conversation at the wardroom table was banal in
the extreme, commonplace and polite: a caution natural in men who
were to be messmates for the next couple of years or so and who
wished to sound their way at first, and to find out their messmates'
nature, neither giving nor receiving any offence that might rankle for
the next ten thousand miles, to break out at last in the Antipodes.

The English, Stephen knew – and most of those sitting round the
table were Englishmen – were extremely sensitive to social difference;

he was conscious of a set of ears accurately tuned to minute differences of intonation, and he was particularly pleased to hear Pullings's fine southern burr: surely it argued a steady though wholly unaggressive self-confidence, a particular kind of strength. He contemplated Pullings as the first lieutenant stood there carving the round of beef, and it occurred to him that he had been singularly unobservant. He had known Pullings so long, from the time when Pullings had been a leggy master's mate, that Pullings seemed endowed with perpetual youth: Stephen had not seen maturity come down on him. To be sure, in company with Jack, the patron he loved and admired, Pullings still seemed very young: but here, in his own wardroom, he surprised Stephen with his size and his easy authority. Clearly he had left his youth in Hampshire, perhaps quite a long time ago: he was on his way to becoming one of those strong, eminently valuable lower-deck commanders in the line of Cook or Bowen; and until now Stephen had never noticed it.

He ran his eye down the men sitting opposite him. Moore, the Marine captain, on Pullings's left; then Grant, the *Leopard*'s second lieutenant, a middle-aged, precise-looking man; Macpherson, the senior Marine lieutenant, a black Highlander with an unusual, intelligent face; Larkin, the master, a young man for the post and an able navigator, but surely that vinous appearance so early in the day boded no good; Benton, the purser, a jolly little round soul with a moist and twinkling eye, like the landlord of a lively tavern, or a prosperous bagman. His side-whiskers almost met under his chin: he wore a number of ornaments, even at sea; and he was ingenuously pleased with his own person, particularly his shapely leg – he was, he confessed, a lady's man.

On Stephen's right sat the younger subaltern, a youth who, apart from the differences in uniform, looked almost exactly like the Marine servant Stephen had chosen, the stupidest of the sixty allotted to the ship: both had the same thick, pale lips, the dense, lightless skin, the oyster-coloured protruding eyes, and in repose their faces wore the same expression of offended astonishment; and their foreheads both gave the impression of a prodigious depth of bone. Howard was the young man's name: he had been unable to engage Stephen's attention, and he was now talking to his other neighbour, a guest from the midshipmen's berth called Byron – talking about the peerage with an enthusiasm that brought a flush to his large, pallid face. Babbington, the third lieutenant, on Stephen's left, was another old shipmate; for although he still looked very boyish, Stephen had cured him of various discreditable diseases in the Mediterranean as far back as the year nought. His precocious, enduring passion for the opposite sex had stunted his growth, but this had not damped his general ardour, and he was giving a spirited account of a fox-chase when he was called away – the Newfoundland dog he had brought aboard, an animal the size of a calf, had seen fit to guard the blue cutter, in which Babbington had laid his Guernsey frock, and to forbid anyone to touch so much as its gunwale. His going revealed the black-coated figure of the Reverend Mr Fisher, sitting on Pullings's right. Stephen looked at him attentively. A tall, athletic man, fair, perhaps five and thirty, rather good-looking than otherwise, with an eager, somewhat nervous expression: he was now drinking a glass of wine with Captain Moore, and Stephen noticed that the nails of his outstretched hand were bitten to the quick, while the back of it and the exposed wrist showed an ugly eczema.

'Mr Fisher, sir,' he said a moment later. 'I do not believe I have had the honour of being introduced to you. I am Maturin, the surgeon.' And after an exchange of civilities he said, 'I am delighted to have another colleague aboard, for since the spiritual and the physical are so inseparably entwined, perhaps the chaplain and the surgeon may be so called, quite apart from their necessary collaboration in the cockpit. Pray, sir, have you read physic, at all?'

No, Mr Fisher had not: he would have done so had he been collated to a country benefice: many country clergymen did so, and he should certainly have followed their example: a knowledge of medicine would have enabled him to do good – even more good. A shepherd must know how to use his tar-box both literally and figuratively; for as Dr Maturin so rightly observed, the disorders of his sheep might partake of two natures at the least.

This statement threw a slight chill upon the atmosphere; yet on the whole the wardroom's opinion of Mr Fisher was favourable: he was eager to please and to be pleased; and although they did not care for being regarded as a parcel of sheep, a remark of that nature was excusable in a parson.

Their opinion was echoed in Stephen's diary, which he wrote in his nasty cabin on the orlop during the intervals between dinner and the burial service, after which he was to review the convicts with the chaplain and make his report. He might have had part of Jack's splendour, a spacious region of his own, as he had done before, when he was the Captain's guest; but in the *Leopard* he did not wish the surgeon to seem unduly privileged; and in any case he was singularly indifferent to his surroundings. 'I met the chaplain today,' he wrote. 'He is a conversible man, and of some reading: not perhaps very sensible, and possibly somewhat given to enthusiasm. But he may not do himself justice. He is nervous, and ill at ease; he lacks composure. Yet he may prove a valuable addition to the mess. I feel moderately drawn to him, and if I were on land I should say that I intended to continue the acquaintance. At sea there is no choice.' He continued with a description of his symptoms – the reviving appetite – the specificity of the intense yearning somewhat diminished – the crisis of the weaning perhaps behind him. 'To be so caught,' he wrote, 'and by so old a friend! The two Winchester quarts in the late Mr Simpson's chest, do they represent a danger or rather a safeguard, a standing evidence of resolution – indeed, of freedom recovered?' He pondered over this point, sinking into a deep meditation, his lips pursed, his head on one side, his eyes stretched wide, staring at his 'cello case. After having beaten on Stephen's door for some time in vain, the midshipman who had been sent to fetch him on deck opened it and said, 'I hope I do not disturb you, sir; but the Captain thought you would wish to be present at the burial.'

'Thank you, thank you, Mr – Mr Byron, is it not?' said Stephen,

holding his lantern towards the young man's face. 'I shall come
upstairs directly.'

He reached the quarterdeck in time for the last words and the four
splashes: surgeon, superintendent, and two convicts; the last being
the only cases he had ever known of actual death from seasickness.
'Though no doubt,' he observed to Mr Martin, 'partial asphyxia, near
starvation, a vicious habit of body, and a prolonged confinement were
contributory causes.'

The *Leopard*'s logbook wasted no time on causes, nor comments:
it confined itself to facts: 'Tuesday, 22d. Wind SE. Course S27W. Distance 45. Position 42°40′N 10°11′W, Cape Finisterre E by S 12 leagues.
Fresh gales, clear weather. People variously employed. At 5 committed bodies of William Simpson, John Alexander, Robert Smith, and
Edward Marno to the deep. Swifted foretopmast futtocks. Killed a
bullock weight 522 lb.' While for his part her captain, in his serial
letter to his wife, confined himself to effects: there was nothing like
a funeral for sobering the crew. This evening none of the midshipmen would go skylarking, which was just as well, since the youngsters
who had never been to sea before simply were not up to racing to the
masthead and sliding down a backstay with anything like safety if
there was a sea running. The child Boyle had brought Jack's heart into
his mouth in the chops of the Channel by trying to reach the main-
truck, with the ship pitching like a young horse being broke. 'There
are ten of them altogether,' he said, 'and I am responsible to their
parents: it makes me feel like an anxious hen. Not that some of them
are in much danger, except of a beating. The boy I rated captain's servant for Harding's sake, is an odious little villain – I have already had
to stop his grog – and there are a couple more among the oldsters,
nephews of men who were kind to me, that are more like vermin
than anything I like to see on my quarterdeck. But to go back to the
funeral. Mr Fisher, the chaplain, read the service in a very proper
manner, which pleased all hands; and although I do not care for parsons aboard, it seems to me that we could have done much worse.
He is a gentlemanlike fellow; he seems to understand his duty; and at

present he is about to sort out the convicts in the forepeak with Stephen, poor unfortunate creatures. As for Stephen, he is grown devilish crabbed, and I am afraid he is far, far from being happy. There is a female convict aboard, the very spit of Diana, and it seems to me that the reminder wounds him: said there was no likeness at all – rapped it out sharp and brought me up all standing. A most striking young woman, and no doubt a person of some consequence, since she berths alone and has her servant, while the others, God help them, live and mess in a hole where we would not keep our pigs. But we have fine weather now, after our blow, and the south-easter I had been praying for. The dear *Leopard* proves remarkably stiff, and weatherly as well. As I write, we have the wind one point free, and she has been tearing off her nine miles in the hour ever since this morning. At this rate (for I believe the wind is settled in that quarter) we may raise the Island in a fortnight, in spite of our lying-to, and Stephen will have sun and swimming and curious spiders to cheer his heart again. Sweetheart, in the night I was thinking of the stable drains, and I beg you will desire Mr Horridge to make sure they are *really deep*, and brick-lined . . .'

Jack was right about the gravity that the burial-service induced; and about the verminous nature of some of his young gentlemen; but as to the survey of the convicts he was mistaken. The sight of the Atlantic rising, rising, and slowly falling had undone Mr Fisher, and although by a noble effort he got through his duty, he was obliged to excuse himself immediately afterwards, and retire; Stephen had made his tour alone, and he was now standing immediately above Jack's head, on the poop, talking to the first lieutenant, and smoking a cigar.

'That young man at dinner, Byron. Is he related to the poet?'

'The poet, Doctor?'

'Aye. The famous Lord Byron.'

'Oh, you mean the admiral. Yes, I believe he is a grandson, or maybe a great-nephew.'

'The admiral, Tom?'

'Why, yes. The famous Lord Byron. They still call him Foul-weather Jack: the whole Navy knows about him. There's fame for you! My grandad sailed with him when he was only a midshipman, and then again when he was an admiral, bosun of the *Indefatigable*; and many a crack they had about their days on Chile after the *Wager* came to grief. How the Admiral did relish a blow! Almost as much as our Captain Jack. Would crack on regardless, laughing ha, ha, ha; but I don't recall he was ever much of a hand in the poetry line. It was hearing about him that first made me long to go to sea: and my grandad's tales of the wreck.'

Stephen had read an account of the loss of the *Wager* in the cold, stormy, uncharted waters of the Chiloe archipelago: he said, 'Yet surely it was but a dismal wreck? No Cytherea, with coral strands, palm-trees, and dusky maidens to fill the horn of plenty? No Crusoe stores at hand? As I recall, they ate a drowned seaman's liver.'

'Very true, sir; it was an uncomfortable time, as my grandad remarked; but he loved to look back, and contemplate on it. He was a contemplative man, although he had no schooling beyond the horn-book and the rule of three; and he liked to contemplate on wrecks. Seven he went through, in his time, and he used to say you never knew a man, till you had seen him in a wreck. It still amazed him, he said, to see some hold fast, but the most part run all to pieces – discipline goes by the board, even in a right good crew, steady old forecastle hands and even warrant-officers break into the spirit-room and get beastly drunk, refuse orders, pillage cabins, dress like Jack in the Green, fight, blackguard their officers, jump into boats and swamp 'em like a parcel of frightened landsmen . . . There's an old belief on the lower deck that once the ship's aground, or once she can't steer, then the captain's authority is gone: that's the law, they say, and nothing will get it out of their stupid heads.'

Four bells struck. Stephen tossed his cigar into the *Leopard*'s wake, and took leave of Pullings, observing that he must make his report.

'Jack,' he said, when he was in the great cabin, 'I spoke intemperately to you before dinner. I ask your pardon.' Jack flushed, said that he

had not noticed it, and Stephen continued. 'I am abandoning a course
of physic, an injudicious course, perhaps; the effect is not unlike that
produced in your confirmed tobacco-smoker when his pipe is taken
from him, and sometimes, alas, I yield to fits of petulance.'

'You have enough to make you petulant, with these convicts on
your hands,' said Jack. 'By the way, I believe you were right about Mrs
Wogan: by all means let her take the air upon the poop.'

'Very well. Now as to the rest of them. Two I find to be idiots,
sensu stricto; three, including the big fellow that is thought to have
killed his keeper, are hard men. In another I recognized a resurrector,
and when there is a brisk demand for corpses, the resurrection-men
sometimes have an expeditious way of satisfying it; so perhaps he
should be included among my men of blood. Five are little silly creatures, weak and flabby, taken up for repeated stealing from shops and
stalls; and all the rest are country-men who were too fond of taking
a pheasant or a hare. No great wickedness there, I believe; and you
could well exchange them for some of the objects that came from the
receiving-ship. Two of them, brothers called Adam, won me entirely:
they know everything that moves in the woods, and it called for five
keepers and three constables to take them at the last. Here is my list.
I recommend no irons at all, since in our floating prison there is no
escape; but the men marked with a cross might be exercised separately for a while, merely to avoid a bout of folly.'

'But the murderer, he must be kept in irons until I hand him over.'

'Sure, it was a joint venture. The superintendent abused them to
the height of his power, and from what I hear he had already extorted
most of their money and their small provision for the voyage: I believe
they fell on him spontaneously, in a confused heap in the dark, he
having dropped his lantern: no one man, shackled, could have
inflicted such injuries. Of course, for half a guinea and their neck
preserved, many of them are willing and eager to inform; but what
does it amount to? Let the civilians settle their own dirty business in
New Holland, and in the meantime take the irons away: they can only
serve as weapons.'

'Well. And what about the women?'

'The Mrs Hoath, the procuress and abortionist, seems to me to have thrown off what little humanity she may have been born with, and by long perseverance to have reached a depth of iniquity that I have rarely seen equalled, never surpassed. She will not trouble us long, however: her liver alone, to say nothing of the ascites and a whole complication of morbid states, will look to that before we pass the tropic line: nevertheless, I shall see what quicksilver, digitalis, and a stout, sharp-pointed trocar will do. Salubrity Boswell, the Gipsy woman, on the other hand, is a female worthy of a nobler age. Her husband having been bitchadey pawdle, as she puts it, or sent across the water, she contrived to be bitchadey pawdle herself, in order to join him. She made his brother get her with child – a practice reminiscent of the ancient Jews – so that she might plead her belly and so avoid the gallows, and then she savaged the judge in broad daylight, the judge that sentenced him. We are to expect the child in five months' time, presumably between the Cape and Botany Bay.'

'Oh, oh,' said Jack, in a low tone, 'here's a pretty kettle of fish. In a King's ship, too. I have always set my face against women aboard, and now look what they are at.'

'One swallow does not make a summer, Jack, as you frequently observe. She also told me my fortune: should you like to hear it?'

'If you please.'

'I am to have a prosperous voyage, and not too long, and all my heart's desire.'

'A prosperous voyage, eh?' said Jack, brightening. 'Well, I am heartily glad of it, and I give you joy. There is always something in what these women say, however you may wag your head, Stephen. There was a Gipsy on Epsom Downs that told me I should have trouble with women, early and late; and you can't say fairer than that. Come, Stephen, sup with me – Killick shall toast you the Parmesan cheese – and we will have some music at last. I have not touched my fiddle since the evening we weighed.'

Stephen and Martin made their afternoon rounds: some broken ribs and collarbones, ugly contusions and crushed fingers in the *Leopard*'s sick-bay – inevitable after a violent blow, with so many landsmen aboard – together with the usual array of poxes. These, though the most familiar of disorders to the naval surgeon, were somewhat outside Martin's practical experience, and Stephen urged him to 'ply his mercurials, even to the extremity of salivation; to eradicate the noxious principle at the earliest possible moment; to dose, drench, and spare not, though it made vast inroads on their stock of venereals, for once the ship was well clear of the land, there would be no call for them, no reinfection to be feared.' But Mr Martin was to take care to note down each dose against the patient's name, since the foolish libidinous creatures must pay for their folly not only in suffering but also in coin, the value of their physic being stopped out of their pay. They moved on to the convicts' quarters, where two men exhibited symptoms of a curious nature that puzzled both Stephen and Martin; symptoms that had nothing to do with seasickness. Martin put on first one pair of spectacles and then another to look at them as he auscultated, turned, and palpated; and once again Stephen wondered whether he had made such a very wise choice in his assistant. The man had a capital brain, no doubt, but he seemed entirely devoid of bowels. He handled his patients as though they were anatomical specimens, not fellow beings at all: an inhuman, mechanical medicine. 'In this case, colleague Martin,' he said, 'our diagnosis must attend the event: in the meantime, blue pill and black draught, if you please.'

Then, taking the late Mr Simpson's bundle of keys, he walked aft to Mrs Wogan's cabin, jangling as he went: there were fewer rats in the cable-tier, he noticed, and as a ship's rat was a good weather-prophet, it looked as though the Gipsy's tale might come true, at least for the coming days; yet among those few, two rats, male rats this time, were obviously indisposed.

He knocked, unlocked, and found Mrs Wogan in tears. 'Come,

come,' he said, ignoring them, 'lose not a moment, I beg. I am come
to exercise you, ma'am; to air you for the good of your health. But
there is not a moment to be lost. As soon as they tingle on that bell, it
will be quarters, and then where shall we be? Pray put some woollen
garment on your head and shoulders; you will find the sea-air pierce
you, after this mephitis. I cannot recommend shoes of that nature:
the motion is far more violent upstairs. Half-boots, or list slippers, or
indeed bare feet, are the proper wear.'

Mrs Wogan turned, privately blew her nose, reached for a blue
cashmere shawl, kicked off her red-heeled shoes, and thanking Dr
Maturin a thousand times for his goodness, declared that she was
perfectly ready.

He led her up ladder after ladder towards the main hatchway. At
one point they both fell with a soft dump on to a heap of studdingsails, but eventually they emerged on to the quarterdeck. The afternoon was more brilliant than ever, and the steady wind swept in over
the hammock-nettings, salt and full of life. Babbington and Turnbull,
the officer of the watch, were talking by the starboard hances; three
midshipmen were busy with their sextants on the old lopsided moon,
measuring her angular distance from the sun, now well to the west
over the splendid empty sea. The talk instantly stopped; the sextants
drooped; Babbington straightened to his full five foot six and darted
an old clay pipe into his pocket; the *Leopard* came up half a point, her
headsails gave a hint of a shiver, and Turnbull roared, 'Full and by,
there, God damn your eyes. Quartermaster, mind your con. Come no
near.' Stephen led Mrs Wogan across the sloping deck to the fife-rails
and pointed out the gangway. 'That is the gangway,' he said, 'and there
you will walk in inclement weather.'

A low whistle came from a party of men at work in the waist, and
Turnbull cried, 'Clarke, take that man's name at once. You, sir, jump
up to the head and back seven times. Clarke, start him hearty.'

'And this is the quarterdeck,' continued Stephen, turning about.
'The upper level over there, is called the poop, where you may walk
today, and when it is fine. I shall conduct you by these stairs.'

The wardroom goat and Babbington's Newfoundland left the hen-coops by the wheel and paced across to meet them. 'Do not be afraid, ma'am,' cried Babbington, approaching with a smile that would have been even more winning if youthful folly had left him more in the way of teeth, 'he is as gentle as a lamb.'

Mrs Wogan made no reply other than a gentle inclination of her head. The dog smelt her proffered hand and walked after her, wagging its tail.

The poop was empty, and Mrs Wogan walked up and down it, stumbling now and then when the *Leopard* gave one of her cumbrous skips. Stephen, having watched a sheerwater until it vanished astern, leant on the taffrail and considered her. Barefooted and with that shawl, her misty eyes and a little dark hair showing, she looked wonderfully like the young Irishwomen of his youth, and sorrowful too, as he had seen so many and many after the rising of 'ninety-eight. The sadness surprised him, for although there was plenty of cause for it, with fifteen thousand miles of sea before her and a most unenviable fate at the far end, he had expected her spirits to rise when she was brought out into the sun.

'You must allow me to warn you against any indulgence in lowness,' he said. 'Were you to give way to melancholy, you would certainly pule into a decline.'

She managed a smile, and said, 'Perhaps it is no more than the effect of Naples biscuits, sir. I must have eaten a thousand, at least.'

'Unrelieved Naples biscuit? Do they not feed you at all?'

'Oh yes, and I am sure I shall come to relish it soon. Pray do not think I complain.'

'When did you last eat a square meal?'

'Why, it must have been quite a long time ago . . . in Clarges Street, I believe.'

No hint of consciousness in that Clarges Street, he observed; and he said, 'A diet of Naples biscuits alone – that would account for the yellowness.' He took a dried Catalan sausage from his pocket, skinned the end with his lancet, and said, 'Are you hungry, now?'

'Oh dear me, yes! Perhaps it is the sea air.'

He fed her slices, advising that they should be chewed very thoroughly, and he noticed that she was very near tears again – that she secretly glided some pieces to the Newfoundland, and that those she swallowed would scarcely go down. Babbington's head appeared on the larboard poop ladder: he mounted, went through the motions of looking for his dog, feigned to catch sight of it, came over, and said, 'Come, Pollux, you must not make a nuisance of yourself. I trust he has not been importuning you, ma'am?'

But Mrs Wogan said no more than 'No, sir,' in a very low voice, looking down and away; and Babbington, under the cold fire of Stephen's eye, was unable to hold his ground. Turnbull, who succeeded him, was in a better position; he had brought a quartermaster and a bosun's mate to do something to the ensign-staff. But before he had given even the first of his orders he bawled out, 'You sir! What the bloody hell do you think you are doing here?' at a young man who came running up on to the poop with a look of radiant delight on his face. The look changed; the man stopped. 'Get along forward,' shouted Turnbull. 'Atkins, start that man.' The bosun's mate darted forward, his triple rattan high; the man dodged a blow or two, and then vanished.

This kind of brutality was familiar enough to Stephen, but he turned to see what effect it would have on Mrs Wogan. To his astonishment he saw that she had flushed a bright pink: there was no yellowness in that face turned studiously away to contemplate the horizon, and when he spoke to her again he beheld an equally surprising change of expression, a brilliant eye, an evident hurry of spirits, a sudden volubility, an unavailing attempt at disguising some very strong and pleasurable emotion. Would Dr Maturin have the extreme kindness to tell her the name of that rope, the mast over there, these sails? What a great deal he knew; but then of course he was a sailor. Might she presume to beg for just one more slice, a very little slice of that delicious sausage? At times she endeavoured to stop, but after a slight pause the words would come bubbling out, in remarks that were not always perfectly coherent.

'That went down better,' he observed; and although the words were not particularly droll, Mrs Wogan laughed in reply, a gurgling laugh that went on and on, so deeply amused, so natural and so absurdly fetching, that he felt his mouth broaden, and he said to himself, 'No, no; this is no hysteria; this has none of the shrill flighty morbid ring of hysteria.' Meeting his eye she collected herself, grew grave, and said, 'I beg you will not think me impertinent, sir, but is it not a shame to put that sausage into your pocket – so very greasy, and such a handsome coat?'

Stephen looked down: yes, indeed, his idiot servant must have put out his best gold-laced coat for today's dinner; and now there was a broad grease-mark on its side. 'I was not aware,' he said, spreading the grease with his fingers. 'It is my best coat.'

'Perhaps if you were to wrap it in a handkerchief? You have no handkerchief? Here: pray hold it out by the string.' She plucked a handkerchief from her bosom, wrapped it neatly about the sausage, tied its ends, and said, with a look that could scarcely be described as anything but affectionate, 'Should you like me to carry it, sir? It would be a sad shame for the coat to grow greasier still; though to be sure a chalk-ball will soon get it out.'

'What is a chalk-ball?' asked Stephen, still looking sadly at his coat. And then, 'Come, come, there is not a moment to be lost. See the sentry going forward. In two minutes they will beat to quarters: our time is done.' He handed her to the steps, where the wind, wanton and indiscreet at the break of the poop, caught her petticoats. But every eye on the quarterdeck was fixed forward in rigid propriety, for Jack was at the windward rail; and when, having mastered her skirt at the bottom of the steps, she said, 'And the sausage, sir?' Stephen put his finger to his lips. He led her below, told her that she must never never speak on the quarterdeck when the tall gentleman, the Captain, was there; that she must eat the sausage herself, and that she must try to accustom her stomach to the ship's fare, 'which was wholesome, though rough, and which use would render palatable, to a well-thinking mind'; and hurried away to his action-station in the cockpit as the drum volleyed and thundered over his head.

The tall gentleman looked taller than usual when Stephen, carrying his 'cello, found him in the cabin. 'There you are, Stephen,' he cried, his strong, stern face lightening. 'I thought it was Turnbull. Forgive me a few minutes, will you? I must have a word with him. Take Grant's observations into the stern-gallery; they will interest you – he speaks of the birds.'

Stephen took the slim, neatly-written book and sat with it in a swinging chair out on the splendid kind of balcony that overhung the sea. It was an account of a voyage of discovery made by a sixty-ton brig, the *Lady Nelson*, which sailed from England to the Cape and then to New Holland by way of the Bass Strait, under the command of Lieutenant James Grant, R.N., in 1800, taking eleven months to do so.

From time to time he heard Jack's or rather the Captain's voice, cold, distant, and full of authority. It was not raised, but it had remarkable carrying power: remarkable crushing power, too. Mr Turnbull had not sailed with Captain Aubrey before and at first he tried to defend himself against the charge of brutality, incompetence, and ungentlemanly behaviour; but very soon his voice was heard no more, and his very large, deeply displeased Captain told him in the clearest possible manner that none but a fool started, struck, beat or abused hands for not knowing their duty when those hands could not conceivably know it, having only just gone to sea; that any officerlike man knew the names of all the people in his watch; that it was quite as easy to call out Herapath as You, sir; and that no gentleman used foul language when a lady was within earshot – any whore's bully on Portsmouth Point could outdo Mr Turnbull in that line. Discipline and a taut ship were one thing: bullying and an unhappy ship were another. The hands would always respect an officer who was a seaman, without having to be knocked about: but how could Mr Turnbull hope for their respect when they were treated to the spectacle of the headsails trimmed as Captain Aubrey had seen them trimmed this afternoon? Words on the proper trimming of headsails followed: Mr Turnbull might do well to remember the difference between a sail bowsed tight as a board and a sail with a belly in it, that could draw. It was some years since Stephen had heard Jack reprove one of his officers, and he was much struck by the remarkable advance in efficacity, by the impersonal, God-like, severe authority that could not possibly be feigned or assumed by any man who did not naturally possess it. It was the kind of wigging that Lord Keith might have delivered, or Lord Collingwood: few others had the same awful quality.

'There, Stephen,' said Jack's more familiar voice close behind his back. 'That is over and done with. Come and have a glass of grog.'

'It is indeed an interesting account,' said Stephen, waving the book. 'The writer has sailed the very waters that we are to traverse; and he is not an unobservant man, though what birds he can mean by haglets I cannot tell. Is he any kin to our Mr Grant?'

'The man himself. He had the *Lady Nelson*. That is why I was required to take him,' said Jack, with a shade of displeasure crossing his face. 'Because of his experience, you know. But he did not go as high south as I intend to go; he kept pretty close to the thirty-eighth parallel, whereas I mean to go well into the forties – you remember the dear old *Surprise*, Stephen, and the westerlies down there?'

Stephen had the clearest recollection of dear old *Surprise* in the roaring forties; and he closed his eyes: yet on the other hand, those were the albatross latitudes. 'Tell me,' he said, having thought, 'how does it come about that Mr Grant was not promoted for this feat? For feat it was, sure, with so small a ship?'

'She was a *brig*, Stephen,' said Jack. 'A brig. But a feat it was, as you say, particularly as she was one of those vile things with sliding keels; and after that wicked *Polychrest* I never wish to see another as long as I live. As for promotion,' he went on evasively, 'why, promotion is a tricky affair at the best of times, and I believe Grant contrived to get the wrong side of the civilians, both over there and at home. He fouled their hawse, and they cut his cable: perhaps he may not have all the tact in the world. I think there was some other cause of dissatisfaction too, because at one time he was put at the bottom of the lieutenants' list, and that is why I was able to have Tom Pullings as my premier, he being now senior to Grant. But be damned to all that,' he cried, reaching for his violin, his sea-going fiddle, for his precious Amati was not to be exposed to the tropical heat, the antarctic cold. 'Killick! Killick, there! Bear a hand.'

Killick's voice could be heard coming nearer: 'No peace, no bleeding peace in this barky,' and as the door opened, 'Sir?'

'Toasted cheese for the Doctor, half a dozen mutton-chops for me, and a couple of bottles of the Hermitage. D'ye hear me there? Now, Stephen, give me an A.'

They tuned their strings, that pleasant tentative wailing, and as they tuned he said, 'What do you say to our old Corelli in C major?'

'With all my heart,' said Stephen, poising his bow. He paused, and fixed Jack's eye with his own: they both nodded: he brought the bow down and the 'cello broke into its deep noble song, followed instantly by the piercing violin, dead true to the note. The music filled the great cabin, the one speaking to the other, both twining into one, the fiddle soaring alone: they were in the very heart of the intricate sound, the close lovely reasoning, and the ship and her burdens faded far, far from their minds.

CHAPTER FOUR

Every day at noon, when the sky was clear, the *Leopard* fixed her position by the sun; and every day the sun climbed higher in the south. As the crucial moment approached, the moment when it should cross the meridian, her captain, her master, all the watch-keeping officers, and all the young gentlemen would train their instruments, hold their breath, bring the sun's limb to the horizon, and record the result. The master would report, 'Noon, sir', to the officer of the watch; the officer of the watch would cross the quarterdeck to the Captain, take off his hat, and say, 'Noon, sir, if you please', and the Captain, who knew it perfectly well from his own sextant, even if he had not heard the master's voice a few yards from him, would say, 'Make it twelve, Mr Babbington' (or Grant or Turnbull, as the case might be) thus setting the boundary between one naval day and the next.

Jack's reading generally agreed with the master's and Grant's to within a few seconds, but sometimes, when Mr Larkin's morning whet had bleared his eye, there was a discrepancy, and in that case Jack preferred his own observation to appear in the log. To a knowing eye that harsh, laconic record, usually concerned with nothing but figures and the occasional disaster, betrayed something like ecstasy in its steady sequence of 'Clear weather, fresh breezes', of splendid distances run, often as much as two hundred nautical miles a day, and in the rapidly diminishing latitude. '42°5′N, 12°41′W—37°31′N, 14°49′W—34°17′N, 15°3′W—32°17′N, 15°27′W.' At this point they left Madeira broad on the starboard beam at noon, and the next day they also passed by the Dry Salvages. Stephen gazed wistfully at them from the maintop: once he would have begged Jack to stop the ship, to abandon this wild, unthinking race into the south-south-west, and to allow him a pause, if only for half a day, to look into the insect and arachnid population of these interesting rocks; but now he saved his breath. He saved it too when the loom of the Canaries crept along the eastern horizon hour after hour, the Peak of Teneriffe soaring white far over there to larboard: he knew from long, sad experience that once the steady naval routine, with its sense of unremitting urgency, had started, no plea of his would make the slightest difference.

This routine had started long before the Dry Salvages. In spite of the port-admiral's ravages an unusually high proportion of the *Leopard*'s crew were man-of-war's men; they settled into their accustomed way of life as soon as Cape Finisterre was astern, and the desk was priddied, and they drew all the raw hands after them. The glorious run, from the height of Finisterre to the tropic line, with the wind strong and steady and abaft the beam almost all the time – only a single day of calm – made all things easier, and church had not been rigged twice before the dank mists of Portsmouth belonged to another world. Before the bright dawn the decks were washed, holystoned and dried; hammocks were piped up; Jack breakfasted with Stephen, and often with the officer of the morning watch and one of the midshipmen, and then led the youngsters through *Mackay on the Longitude*; Stephen and Martin made their rounds; the convicts were exercised; the half-hour glass turned again and again and again, the bell struck, the watches changed, four dinners in succession made their appearance, the hands', the convicts', the wardroom's, and the cabin's; the afternoon wore on until the first dog-watch, quarters, and then, before the hammocks were piped down again, the evening guns: for Jack was a comparatively wealthy commander; he had supplemented the official hundred rounds a gun and the official supply of powder, and it was rare that the *Leopard* ended the day without a savage roar or two, spitting orange flames into the twilight. He had started the voyage with good captains for almost every gun and good crews for more than half, and he meant to cross the equator with excellent full teams for all fifty, being profoundly convinced that all the seamanship in the world, all the skill in manoeuvring a ship to within range of an enemy, was of little use if the great guns could not hit him hard and fast.

Very soon life became so regular that those whose duty did not require them to record the day could remember it only by church, washing-day (when the *Leopard* rigged lines fore and aft, and the clean clothes hung out to dry, presenting a strangely unwarlike appearance, particularly since some of the garments were female), or by the grim pipe of *All hands to witness punishment*, which meant that it was Saturday, for the *Leopard* punished only once a week. Day after day Mrs Wogan walked on the poop, sometimes with her maid, often with Dr Maturin, always with the dog and goat; but she might have been a ghost, passing across the quarterdeck unseen, for all the disturbance that she caused at present; for not only had Captain Aubrey given particularly stringent orders on the subject of leering, and of dumb or verbal communication, but it had come to be thought in the wardroom, the gunroom, and indeed throughout the ship, that Mrs Wogan was the Doctor's private property, and no one wished to quarrel with him. Yet unseen is too strong a word: as the distance from land increased, so the general desire for women strengthened; and an unusually handsome woman, her looks much improved since her first appearance, could not but attract many a covert look, many a longing sigh.

The days were not uneventful, however. In a ship racing through the sea under a captain who loved cracking on just this side of rash-ness, there was a continual tension; some dockyard inadequacy might reveal itself at any moment, and once, in fact, a nave-line parted without a word of warning, while on another occasion the ill-coaked fishes of the maintopsailyard sprang, so that the yard had to be struck down on deck in a hurry. And although they had seen nothing but a distant xebec, far to windward, since they left sound-ings, it was always possible that an enemy might heave in sight at any moment, a battle if she were a man-of-war, a potential fortune if she were a merchantship. And even on their one day of calm there was a pleasurable excitement.

It happened to be a Saturday, judgment day, and at six bells in the forenoon watch the bosun and his mates uttered their dismal pipe; all hands flocked aft, where each watch gathered in an amorphous heap on its respective side of the quarterdeck; nothing could induce them to form in an orderly group, except at divisions, nor to take their hands from their pockets, and they stood in dégagé attitudes, gazing at the Marines, drawn up in scarlet perfection on the poop with fixed bayonets, at the grating rigged against the break, and at the officers and young gentlemen assembled behind their Captain, all wearing their gold-laced hats and swords or dirks. The master-at-arms brought up his prisoners: three cases of drunkenness – grog stopped for a week, and ordered to pump ship for four, six, and eight hours during their watches below: a Turk, caught stealing four pounds of tobacco and a silver watch, the property of Jacob Styles, yeoman of the sheets: the goods produced, sworn to, the case proved, the prisoner mute.

'Have his officers anything to say for him?' asked Jack. Mr Byron put forward the plea that the man was a eunuch, and that the watch would not go. 'That will not do,' said Jack. 'His – his matrimonial prospects are neither here nor there; nor is the condition of the watch.' To the Turk, 'Strip.' To the quartermaster, 'Seize him up.'

'Seized up, sir,' said the quartermaster, the Turk spread-eagled on the grating.

Jack and all the officers took off their hats; the clerk passed the book, and Jack read out the thirtieth Article of War: 'All robbery committed by any person in the fleet shall be punished by death' – an awful pause – 'or otherwise, as a court-martial, upon consideration of the circumstances, shall find.' He put on his hat again, and said, 'Nine strokes. Skelton, do your duty.'

The bosun's mate brought the cat out of its red baize bag: nine hearty strokes, nine appalling falsetto screams of a shrillness and a volume enough to mark the day as quite uncommon, and to gratify that part of the ship's company which took pleasure in bull-baiting, bear-baiting, prize-fighting, pillories, and executions – perhaps nine-

tenths of those present. Next came Herapath, foretopman, starboard
watch, guilty of absence from the muster when the watch was set
on Friday night: he was pale, as well he might be, for ever since the
offence his messmates had been exercising their wit – it was the
worst crime in a ship, they told him, looking grave, and the punishment was five hundred lashes, followed by a keel-hauling if you were
lucky. What is more, for the first time in his life (since Jack rarely
flogged except for theft) he had just seen and heard the spectacular
effects of the cat.

'What have you to say for yourself?' asked the Captain.

'Nothing, sir, except that I regret my absence extremely.'

'Have his officers anything to say for him?' Babbington stated that
Herapath had not offended before, was willing and obedient, though
unhandy; would no doubt apply himself in future. Jack then represented to Herapath the folly and wickedness of his conduct, observed
that if everybody were to imitate it, the ship would be in a pretty state
of anarchy, told him to mind Mr Babbington's words and apply himself, and so dismissed him.

Later in the day, when the *Leopard* was ghosting along over a
glassy sea with only enough high moving air to fill her royals, Jack
ordered the jolly-boat away, to pull round the ship and observe her
trim, and to have a bathe. At much the same time Michael Herapath,
in the relief of his heart, decided to apply himself and to learn the
rudiments of his trade. Being slim and light he had been allotted to
the foretop, that is to say, to the upper yards above that point, but
hitherto One-eyed Miller, the captain of the foretop, had never sent
him above the top itself, there to haul on the rope put into his hand
at the word of command; now he approached Miller as he sat there
on the forecastle making himself a pair of duck trousers, surrounded
by others doing the same or weaving sennit hats or combing out their
pigtails in readiness for divisions and church tomorrow, this being
their watch below, and said, 'Mr Miller, with your leave, I should like
to go up to the royal yard.'

Miller was Bonden's cousin, and Herapath had Bonden's good

word as 'a poor unfortunate bugger, that means no harm.' In any case, he was a good-natured man: he turned his hideous face, deeply pocked with powder from an exploding cartridge-box, and his one brilliant eye upon Herapath with a look of kindly contempt, and said, 'Well mate, I'll find someone to carry you up. You couldn't a chose a sweeter day, so still up there. I doubt even a new-born lamb could fall off of the truck. You want to take care of your hands, though: the premier don't like blood on the standing rigging.' Herapath's soft palms were in fact deeply scored from hauling on bristly ropes, and there was a danger of his leaving criminal stains. Miller looked about among the tie-for-tie pairs busy plaiting each other, and his eye fell upon a young fellow who followed the new fashion, his hair cut short. 'Joe,' he said, 'just you carry Herapath aloft. Show him where to put his feet, like. Show him how to run out on a yard. Don't you come it any of your fucking bum-boy capers,' he added mildly, 'and I dare say you will see some of his evening grog.'

Up and up they went, beyond the top to the crosstrees and higher still, the horizon spreading enormously as they climbed, Joe moving easy, and, as he said with a chuckle, 'showing Herapath the ropes.' They paused for a while out on the yardarm to let a couple of skylarking youngsters hurtle past, and Joe showed him how to run out on the yard. 'Now for the jack,' said Joe, 'You want to look out here, mate; there ain't no ratlines.'

The fore royal yard itself, six inches across at the slings and fine footing; an incredible expanse of sea on either hand, of sky above and of canvas below. 'This is magnificent,' cried Herapath, 'I had no conception . . .'

'Watch me shin up to the truck,' said Joe.

'I shall run out on the yard,' said Herapath. This he did, and Joe, reaching the truck, looked down in time to see him miss his hold. He saw Herapath's face, diminishing with hideous speed, staring up at him in total horror: Herapath struck the starboard topgallant lift a glancing blow that bounced him well clear of the foretopsail, and he plunged into the sea with an enormous splash. Joe let out a shrill, broken-voiced screech of 'Man overboard', and instantly the cry was taken up on deck. Seamen milled about the forecastle, their long hair flying loose: a Marine flung a swab and a bucket somewhere near the splash.

Jack was already mother-naked when he heard the cry and saw the splash. He slipped from the gunwale into the clear water, made out the vague form at a surprising depth, dived, fished it up, swam to the ship, now a hundred yards away, roared for a line, passed the inanimate Herapath up the side, and followed himself. 'Mr Pullings,' he cried, very angry. 'Put an end to this infernal hallooing instantly. Always the same God-damned foolery, every time a man goes overboard. Damn you all for a mob of mad lunatics. Get along forward. Silence fore and aft.' Then, in an ordinary tone, 'Pass the word for the Doctor.'

Stephen had been standing with Mrs Wogan on the poop, and Jack, glancing round to see whether he were on his way, caught Mrs Wogan's astonished gaze full in the eye. He blushed like a boy, seized the fully-clothed Pullings as a shield, and darted down the main hatchway. The event caused a certain amount of ribaldry and a fair number of sentences depriving men of their grog for playing the God-damned fool, an offence that came under Article Thirty-six: 'All other crimes not capital, committed by any person or persons in the fleet, which are not mentioned in this act, or for which no punishment is hereby directed to be inflicted, shall be punished according to the laws and customs in such cases used at sea', also known as the captain's cloak, or cover-all. Otherwise it was taken as a matter of course that Captain Aubrey should rescue a drowning man; it was perfectly well known in the service that he had already saved a score or so, most of them, as he freely admitted, quite worthless. Two were aboard the *Leopard* at this very moment, the one a monoglot Finn and the other a harsh, deeply stupid man called Bolton; the Finn said nothing, but Bolton conceived a mortal jealousy of Herapath, and spoke of his foolhardy presumption, infamous character, and contemptible physique in very shocking terms. 'He'll live, mark my words,' he said. 'He'll live, until they hang him by the — neck: he would have been a gallows deal better off, left where he was, the toad.'

'Of course he'll live,' said his messmates. 'Ain't the Doctor pumped him dry, and blown out his gaff with physic?' For it was just as much part of the natural order of things that Dr Maturin should preserve those who came under his hands: he was a physician, not one of your common surgeons – had cured Prince Billy of the marthambles, the larynx, the strong fives – had wormed Admiral Keith and had clapped a stopper over his gout – would not look at you under a guinea, five guineas, ten guineas, a head, by land.

The incident caused no great stir; it never appeared in the log; and Jack did not mention it when he continued his letter to Sophie.

'*Leopard*
in the harbour of Porto Praya

'Here we are, my dearest soul, not at Madeira, nor at the Grand Canary, but at St Jago in the Cape Verdes! That will make you stare, I believe. The wind stood so fair and steady from the moment we cleared the Bay, that I could not bear not to make the most of it, and indeed we picked up the north-east Trades far higher than I expected and so cut the tropic of Cancer in twenty-six days, counting our tedious time in the Channel and our lying-to. The *Leopard*, apart from her new-fangled stern-post and pintles, which give us some little concern, pleases me extremely; she reaches almost as well as the *Surprise*, is brisk in stays, steers easy, and once we have ate up a few more tons of our provisions, she will veer as well as any ship in the fleet – at present she is by the stern, which makes her a trifle sluggish. In a word, she is more than I had hoped; and I had hoped for much. Most of the new hands are shaping well, and my old shipmates are

what they have always been, thorough-going seamen, attentive to their duty, and only rather too inclined to get drunk
whenever they can. There is a distillery on this island, alas;
but I am doing all I can to keep them out of it.

'Tom Pullings keeps the ship in capital order. He relieves
me of almost all the work; I grow fat and idle, and Stephen
and I have had many a fine concert together. Stephen seems
more settled in his mind, and this heat suits him: it nearly
killed me, when I put on full dress and made my call on the
Governor, sweating up a vile path cut in the cliff with droves
of lizards gasping in the sun, "What kind of lizards, Jack?"
says he. "Lizardi percalidi," said I, by which I meant, d—d hot
lizards. I think I was mistaken, when I said our female convict was the dead spit of Diana. Stephen smoked the difference right away, no doubt; and now it is plain to me. Though
on the other hand, she is very like the woman we saw with
Lady Conyngham's party at the races, whose clothes you
remarked; and perhaps she is the same. Diana in the colouring, but not otherwise. She is not so tall, for one thing; and
for another, she does not come down on you so uncommon
sharp; and for another, she has such a laugh – it starts low,
and goes on and on, so that I have seen the whole quarterdeck on the grin and have been obliged to stare out to windward to hide my own. Not that she has much cause for mirth,
poor soul; yet when Stephen is up there on the poop with her,
she laughs away so that even Stephen makes that odd creaking noise of his: I never heard Diana laugh, that I recall. At
least, not wholeheartedly, like Mrs Wogan. So I take it he is
not kept too much in mind of her. Just at present, however,
he is tolerably fretful, being torn between his longing to walk
about St Jago and the other islands, one of which rejoices in
a peculiar sort of puffin, and his duty to these unhappy creatures we are obliged to transport. Some of them continue
sick, and he cannot make out what it is that ails them.

'He does not miss much by staying aboard, however, for these islands really are most uncommon black and desolate, having been volcanoes and having a strong inclination to be volcanoes again. As we stood in, we saw Fogo, which is a little to the south of west and some twenty leagues from here, sending up a fine cloud of smoke. I went ashore yesterday to stretch my legs and to see whether I could knock over a few quails for the table and perhaps some curious birds or monkeys for Stephen, and I took Grant with me, in the hope of getting on better terms. But I am afraid I did more harm than good. We fagged over miles and miles of pumice and lava with scarcely a blade of green, but never a thing did we bring home, except for two ill humours; we grew very hot and dusty and tired and thirsty – never a drop in the dried-up streams – and all the way he kept pointing out places where he had seen bustards and guinea-fowl last time he was here. He perpetually proposed fresh paths, as though he owned the island, and in passing he observed that in my place he would have anchored the ship nearer the watering-place: yet in spite of all his local knowledge we lost ourselves in the end, and had to come down to the shore and creep along among the blazing boulders to find the village. He dropped his gun and hurt the lock, and grew pretty sullen with the heat; but I did my best to bear with him. You would have applauded me, Sophie. He is an older man than I by ten or fifteen years, a very fine navigator, and has been badly used. But from our first meeting aboard the flagship, I was sure it would never answer: you cannot have two captains in a ship, and his long independent command, his remarkable voyage in the *Lady Nelson*, and his knowledge of those waters, have set him above subordination. He might make a good commander, but he is too old and too high to be a second lieutenant. Oh, if only the Admiralty had attended to my plea for Richardson or Ned Summerhayes – but if only

pigs had wings, we should have no need for tinkers' hands,
as they say. Stephen is of much the same opinion with me, I
believe, though of course I cannot discuss my officers with
him, seeing that he is their messmate. Indeed, I cannot discuss them with anyone but you, my dear: and in your private
ear, I will tell you that I shall be glad to see Turnbull leave
the ship at the Cape, and to receive young Mowett again. But
good Lord, what an ungrateful fellow I am: I may have a couple of lieutenants, a master, and a bosun I do not much care
for, but on the other hand I have Pullings and Babbington,
two good master's mates, four or five decent midshipmen, a
prime carpenter and gunner, and close on half of a crew of
the kind of men I love. Not many captains can say as much,
in a fresh commission. And then again, this is such a rest,
after having been a commodore, with awkward captains to
manage, each more like Beelzebub than the last – a positive
sea-going picnic.

'Sweetheart, since I wrote those words, *Phoebe* has come
in, homeward bound from the Cape, and precious short of
water. I shall give these letters to Frank Geary, who has her
now (poor Deering and half his ship's company died of the
yellow jack when she was on the Leeward Islands station)
and you will have them, with my dear love, far earlier than I
had hoped. Before I forget it, here is the power of attorney, so
that you will get my pay; and here is a letter for Kimber – you
will read it, if you please: he is to confine himself to the strict
minimum, as we agreed – and another for Collins, about the
horses. Do not let him forget to buy Wilcox's hay, and let it
be stacked, and very well thatched (Carey is the man to do it)
in the angle between the new stables and the coach-house.

'God bless you, Sophie, and kiss the dear children for me.
When I think that George will be breached before I see him
again, it makes my heart quite low: but if we go on at the
present rate, I shall be home early enough to set him on a

pony for his first time out, perhaps to see Mr Stanhope's hounds.

'In haste, my dear, for my bosun is fuming at the cabin door. I dare say he has already sold our cables to some rogue on shore, and wants me to slip so that they may be delivered: he really carries corruption far too high, and I shall have to bring him up.

'So with my fondest love once more,

Yours ever faithfully and affectionately

Jno Aubrey.'

While Jack was writing this, Stephen was ashore with Mr Fisher. They visited the church, and there, meeting with the priest, they fell into conversation with him. Father Gomes was his name, a short, fat, elderly half-caste with a dark face – his white hair made his tonsure look almost black. He was a man who radiated goodness, and he was obviously much loved and respected by his parishioners: at his desire one of them undertook to find Stephen three sacks of physic-nuts, which the island produced in rare perfection, new-season nuts which had not yet reached the open market, while another offered to lead him to a cousin's house, where he had often seen the bird the Doctor described: the cousin sold young Branco puffins by the barrel – salted nestlings, permissible in Lent – and had an adult bird nailed to his door by way of a sign.

Stephen left the chaplain and the priest in the cool of the porch: Fisher's English pronunciation of Latin made some part of what he said incomprehensible to a Portuguese, and Father Gomes's piety so far exceeded his learning that he was often at a loss for a word, but they certainly communicated, talking away at a great rate. It appeared to Stephen that they did so less by language than by sympathy and intuition.

The physic-nuts proved of excellent quality, the puffin the true Branco puffin and not, as Stephen had feared, a cormorant or gull. A splendid acquisition, though in so advanced a state of decomposition that it was obliged to be hurried back to the ship before it should fall apart. After a brief tour of his patients and a word with Martin, he took the bird into his cabin, wrote an exact description of its plumage and outward members in his journal, and then, gasping from the stench, clapped it into spirits of wine for a later dissection.

He lit a cigar, considered for a while, and continued: 'Thanks to that dear priest, I can now renounce the Ilheu Branco without vexing my heart. It did me great good to see him, perhaps the third saintly man I have met. How it shines out, that rarest of qualities! Fisher was strongly aware of it. Poor man, he is in the sad way, I perceive; but where the trouble may lie, I cannot tell at all. I should be sorry if it were anything so commonplace as a hidden pox: though the Dear knows I have seen that often enough, and in all ranks and orders, old Adam being so strong and untimely. Quaere: would a man like Grant be moved by Fr Gomes? If time permit, I shall make the experiment. A profoundly embittered man, with long, painful service unrewarded, hopes disappointed for perhaps five and twenty years on end. How he resents JA! He has seen no action, as I understand, whereas Jack's body is pierced and criss-crossed with the evidence of battle: Macpherson pointed this out when Jack was stripped for his swim, the young gentlemen gazing with awe, and Grant cried in a passion "'twas all luck, all luck – no man was wounded from choice – a man might have all the courage and conduct in the world, and no wound to show for it". He puts his lack of promotion down to a general plot in Whitehall and elsewhere; to jealousy; and to the fact that his birth is obscure. "Had my father been a country gentleman, a general and a member of Parliament (a palpable fling at JA) I might have been a post-captain fifteen years ago and more". Though the imbecility of this argument must be apparent to him, since he served under Admiral Troubridge, a baker's boy. Like most sailors, he is widely ignorant outside his own profession; he has indeed read a certain amount, more than most of his kind, but late reading, useless as a foundation; he is convinced that no one else has ever done so, and he is a fountain of gratuitous instruction. A want of modesty: a fine fund of self-complacence. He certainly made a most admirable voyage, but to hear him relate it, one might suppose that he had discovered both New Holland and Van Diemen's Land single-handed: which is not the case. Yet even JA, whose standard is very high, confesses that he is a capital seaman. He is a most conscientious man too, and dutiful: keeps an ancient mother and two unmarried sisters on his lieutenant's pay, eight guineas a month. Talks no bawdy, and endeavours to repress loose talk among the Marine officers. A precise and formal man, destitute of the graces. He is at his best with Fisher, who hears his remarks on the Pelagian heresy with a wonderful forbearance; and he appears to know his Bible as well as he knows the Articles of War. I am no theologian and I know little of the tenets of these recent sects, except that they reject what they are pleased to call the abominable superstition of the Mass, but as far as my experience goes, they are primarily concerned with ethics: mysticism and the ancient pieties seem alien to them and to their respectable and sometimes splendid modern buildings. How, then, would one of their more rigid members perceive Fr Gomes?

'I cannot tell. Nor can I tell what the next few days in the convicts' sick-bay will show me: the prodromi are such that I should be clear in my mind – only too clear alas – if it were not for this period of latency, contrary to all my authorities from the ancients until today.

'After so much that I do not know, it is pleasant to record that I have plumbed the unhappy Herapath. He stowed away for love of Mrs Wogan. And when I consider his latibule, the minute space between two casks in which he held out for a week, and the fate to which he has condemned himself, I know not which I most admire, his devotion, his fortitude, or his temerity; and it would be indecent in me to condemn his fatal obstination, although I may deplore it. Herself is by no means unmoved by this strong evidence of attachment, which explains the curious scene when first I led her to the poop, a scene that for long I could not reconcile with reason.

'The answer was beginning to form in my mind when I perceived him in the half darkness of the corridor that runs by Mrs Wogan's cabin; he was kneeling and (a second Pyramus) conversing with her through the hole by which her necessaries pass. I stepped behind a bulkhead, or temporary wall, to make sure of my man: others have attempted to enter into illicit communication with her, and the midshipmen of the after-cockpit have bored eyelets to survey her charms; but this was Herapath. On his side the conversation consisted of endearments for the most part, none particularly original, but quite touching in their evident sincerity, and of ejaculations; on her side I distinguished little apart from that absurd purling laugh – exceptional happiness in the mirth this time – but it was clear that their acquaintance was of long standing, their relationship close, and that she was happy to have a friend in this desolation. They were so deeply engaged – hands clasped in the aperture – that he did not hear a midshipman come hurrying from the cockpit. I coughed to give him warning, but in vain. He was discovered. Asked what he was doing there, replied in sad confusion that he had meant to wash his hands downstairs, and had lost his way. The midshipman, young Byron, was not unkind: he told him he must mind his duty: did he not know the watch was set, and that even if he ran, he must surely miss the muster?

'Mrs Wogan's conscious looks when I visited her directly after were full confirmation, if confirmation had been called for. She disguised her exultation moderately well, but her pulse betrayed her: yet even without her ungovernable pulse, she is but an indifferent agent, I find. Gifted, no doubt, for the obtaining of information from certain sources; determined and resolute; but pitifully at a stand when deprived of a directing intelligence. No one has taught her the immense value of silence; she will be prattling (partly from good manners), and sometimes her invention is little better than poor Herapath's.

'Our acquaintance comes along quite well. She knows that I am an Irishman, who would wish to see my country independent; and that I abhor all domination, all planting of colonies. And when I spoke of my indignation at the act of this very *Leopard* in attacking the neutral

American frigate *Chesapeake* in the year seven, killing some of her people, and taking American seamen of Irish origin out of her – an act that very nearly brought about what I should have termed a justifiable declaration of war – I believe she was on the point of breaking out into an indiscretion. Her eye flashed; she threw up her head; but I moved on to banalities. *Festino lento*, as dear Jack would say. I doubt whether she can tell me any more than the name of her chief, her directing intelligence, but that is well worth waiting for. Even if there is no French connection, the gentleman and his friends must be watched. And if the British government, by its inept, inimical, treatment of the Americans, stifling their trade, stopping their ships, and pressing their men, forces them into a war, so that this connection almost necessarily comes into being, then this chief must certainly be laid by the heels. Slowly, slowly: and it may well be that I can make good use of Herapath. Mine is an odious trade, at times. And at times I am obliged to reflect upon the monstrous, inhuman tyranny by which Buonaparte is destroying Europe, to keep myself in countenance, and to justify myself to the ingenuous young man I was.

'Louisa Wogan: I was made aware (so little do I know myself) of a certain tenderness shall I say, or warmth, that had grown up in our relationship, by its extinction after the appearance of her lover. Nothing harsh, oh not at all; only an absence of something that is hardly to be defined. When she had no ally whatsoever in this grim floating self-contained and noisome world, she naturally clung to what offered, and tried by very pretty ways to improve her hold. The extinction is only temporary, I believe, since she can see but little of her lover, little of anyone except her maid (and Mrs Wogan has no more use for women's company than had Diana Villiers): I must therefore pay attention. There are intolerably fatuous coxcombs who protest that women pursue them: they meet with nothing but deserved contempt and disbelief. Yet something not wholly dissimilar may occur and for some time past I have been aware that an advance on my part would not be too cruelly resented. Furthermore, deep stirrings within my own person are by no means absent: a consequence of my

abstention, opium in all its forms being an antaphrodisiac, counter-
acting venereal desire. Does not duty require that I should resume? In
moderation of course and by no means as an indulgence, but rather as
part of a process of inquiry, in which a clear, chaste mind is essential.
A very devilish suggestion.

'In these cases, we read, a man causes mortal offence by refus-
ing. It may be so, but it is outside my experience; and I am bound to
remember that all tales of this nature are told by men, who love to
impute a masculine appetite and urgency to the other sex. Myself I
doubt it: did the dark-haired Sappho hate her Phaon? In any event,
none of this can apply to me. I am no Phaon, no golden youth, but
a potentially useful ally, a source of present material comfort, some
slight guarantee for the future; at the highest, a not disagreeable companion where no other can be found. Yet there is, I flatter myself, a
certain real liking: of no vast magnitude, to be sure, but enough for
me to feel that she would not have to put too much constraint upon
herself, would not betray her principles, in admitting me to her bed.
For it seems to me that she is a woman to whom these sports are of
no great consequence, but may be indulged in for pleasure, for friendship or kindness, and even, where a minimum of liking is present,
for interest. With such women sexual fidelity has as little meaning
as the act has significance: one might as well require them to drink
wine with one man alone. This attitude is much condemned, I know;
they are called whores, and other ill-sounding names; in this case I
do not find it affects my liking.' He paused, looking at the folder Sir
Joseph had sent after him, and continued: 'She has had three principal liaisons, I see: one with G. Hammond, the member for Halton,
a friend of Horne Tooke and himself a literary man; one with the
wealthy Burdett; and another with the even wealthier Breadalbane,
apart from that with the lay lord of the Admiralty which led to the
present situation. At one point a certain Michael is mentioned as a
secretary: presumably Herapath. The liaisons tolerably well known,
but her reputation preserved, at least to the extent of her continuing to frequent Lady Conynghame and Lady Jersey, to whom she no

doubt owed her acquaintance with Diana. At one time there was a somewhat nebulous Mr Wogan, of Baltimore, attached first to Mr Jay's mission and then to another in St Petersburg, where he may yet remain. Has published a comedy, *The Distressed Lovers*, under the name of John Doe, and a volume of poems, *Thoughts on Liberty, by a Lady*. Why, why did Blaine not find me copies? Nothing betrays a man like his book. Means of support unknown: irregular remittances from Philadelphia: considered an unsound risk by Morgan and Levy and the principal London money-lenders: presumably combines the higher prostitution with intelligence.'

A more than usually thunderous din made his ink-horn tremble. He thrust his balls of wax still deeper into his ears, but it was no use. The *Leopard*'s last boat-loads of water were coming aboard, the great casks plunging from the main-hatch into her bowels and there rolling to their place, growling as they went, ton after ton ranged in the echoing hold, bung up and bilge free. At the same time her people prepared to unmoor, and shortly after the last boat had been hoisted in, her eighteen-inch cables began to fill the tiers, bringing with them a great deal of water and the distinctive smell of Porto Praya ooze, which at least made a change in the stagnant fetor of the orlop. Few naval operations are carried out in silence, and now the tierers worked with a rhythmic howl, interspersed with oaths, while the fifer on the capstan-head blew with all his might, and the hands at the bar were encouraged to 'stamp and go, stamp and go' by men with brazen lungs: orders echoed from the quarterdeck and the forecastle, and above all an enormous voice cried passionately, 'Will you light along those — nippers, there?' There was indeed far more noise than usual, since all Jack's care had not kept the hands from the distillery; and while many of them were partly dazed, others were so elevated that they grew jocose, tripping their mates, adopting antic postures, affecting lameness or even palsy, and laughing immoderately.

Yet eventually the clamour died away, and when Stephen came on deck he found all the visible Leopards but six busy coiling down, fishing the anchors, and clearing away: the six lay in the lee gangway, and a swabber phlegmatically directed a hose upon them, while his companions worked the head-pump. The sober Leopards had made sail; the topgallants had been sheets home an hour ago and the little town was far astern: overhead white clouds moved steadily south-west across a deep blue sky; the air was warm but brisk, most gratefully fresh after the sheltered anchorage; and as he gazed about he saw the first tropic-bird of their voyage, gleaming white in the sun: the yellow-billed tropic-bird, clipping fast away to the south with strong quick strokes, its long tail stiff behind. He watched it out of sight, and walked forward to the convicts' sick-bay.

It smelt strongly of the vinegar with which he had had it washed; the fresh white paint made it fairly light; it was as clean as the swabber's art could make it; and pure sea-air came down through the wind-sail. The patients were still much the same: three men in a low fever, with grave prostration, a weak thready intermittent pulse, fetid breath, severe headache, contracted pupils. The same disease was on all three: but what disease? Its course was following no description that he or Martin or the *Phoebe*'s two surgeons had ever read. Yet as he leant over them, watching intently, he felt that the fever would soon declare itself, that the crisis was not far distant, and that in a little while he would not only know his enemy but have the power of bringing all his allies into action. 'Carry on with the slime-draughts, Soames,' he said to the attendant, and stepped aft to the other bay. The only man there, apart from Herapath, was his old shipmate Jackruski, a Pole, in a deep alcoholic coma once again. 'How their bodies stand it,' he said, 'I cannot tell. I can but suppose that sea-air, one solid meal a day, more or less continual damp, heavy labour, no more than four hours of uninterrupted sleep at a time, and that taken in such a tight-packed crowd of unwashed sweating bodies as would be thought severe in a Dublin doss-house, must be what the human frame in fact requires to keep it thoroughly robust; and that our notions of hygiene are quite fallacious. Herapath, how do you do?'

'Far better, sir, I thank you,' said Herapath.

Stephen peered into his eyes, felt his head and took his pulse,

and said, 'Show me your hands. Still more raw flesh than undam-
aged skin, I see. You will have to wear mittens, when you hale upon
a rope again: canvas mittens, until the horny integument shall have
had time to grow. Will you take off your shirt, now? You are strangely
emaciated, Herapath, and must put on some flesh before you return
to your labours: our diet may not be delicate, but it is wholesome, and
as you see, men may thrive with nothing else. It will never do, to be
over-nice. A proud stomach will not answer, Herapath.'

'No, sir,' said Herapath, and he murmured something about 'biscuit excellent – he ate any amount of biscuit, when off duty' before
saying, 'Might I beg you to advise me, sir?' Stephen gave him a questioning, noncommittal look, and he went on, 'I should like to thank
the Captain for taking me from the water. But I do not know whether
I should address him through my immediate superior, nor whether it
would be proper at all – I am at a loss.'

'In service matters, the first lieutenant, Mr Pullings, would be the
intermediary, I believe: yet since your relationship with the Captain
was in the ocean, rather than aboard, and was therefore that of one
private person with another, it seems to me that a direct acknowledgement on your part would be perfectly proper. And if, as I suppose, that note is intended for the Captain, I will undertake to be your
messenger.'

Carrying the note, Stephen unlocked Mrs Wogan, and, roaring
above the din of the carpenter's crew nailing sheet-tin to the outside
of her cabin, stated that if she were at leisure, he proposed attending her to the poop. He noticed that she looked less composed than
usual, and that there was a singular tension on the silent quarterdeck
as they made their way across it. A small awning had been rigged for
her, and as its shade fell amidships, there she took her paces walking
round and round the cabin skylight. After a while she said hesitantly,
'I hope your patient is doing well, sir?'

'Which patient, ma'am?'

'The young man with long curling hair; the young man the Captain saved so heroically when he fell into the sea.'

'Young Icarus? I never noticed that his hair curled. Oh, he comes along, sure: only a few ribs stove, and what are a few ribs? We all have four and twenty, whatever Genesis may say. We shall pull him through this awkward pass; but sometimes I fear that we shall do so only to see him deperish from mere inanition and want of nourishment – such a waste of all our effort. That reminds me, I have a note from him to the Captain. Pray forgive me.'

He walked down the poop ladder to the cabin door, but there the Marine sentry stopped him: only Captain Moore could be received at present. He returned in time to point out another tropic-bird, and he was speaking with some warmth of their nesting-habits when below them the sentry clashed his musket, opened the door, and cried, 'Captain Moore, sir.'

'Captain Moore,' said Jack, 'I have sent for you because it has come to my knowledge that certain officers have seen fit to disobey my express orders, and to attempt to enter into communication with the female prisoner abaft the cable-tiers.'

Moore's face flushed as red as his coat and then turned whitey-yellow. 'Sir,' he said.

'You are aware of the consequences of disobedience to orders, Captain Moore, I believe . . .'

'Perhaps we had better move away,' said Mrs Wogan. But it was no use: Jack Aubrey's strong voice, though inaudible on the quarter-deck because of the intervening sleeping and dining cabins, came up through the skylight and pervaded the whole poop.

'. . . furthermore,' the awful voice went on, 'one of your subalterns has endeavoured to bribe the armourer to make him a key to her cabin.'

'Oh!' cried Mrs Wogan.

'. . . if this criminal state of affairs is the result of one month's sailing with that infernal woman, what will it be like by the end of a voyage of half a year or more? What have you to say, Captain Moore?'

Very diffidently, very tentatively, Captain Moore mentioned the sudden warmth of the tropics – they would soon get used to it – and the very large quantities of fresh meat, and lobsters, at St Jago.

'I am weighing in my mind,' said Captain Aubrey, dismissing the heat, the beef, and the lobsters with a wave of his hand, 'whether it may not be my duty to return to St Jago, to set these unreliable people ashore, and continue the voyage with those who can exercise some mastery over their passions.'

'Such as your Turk, for example,' murmured Stephen, aside.

'There is no shadow of a doubt that any court-martial, upon the view of my order-book, signed by all the officers in question, would break them instantly: there is no possible defence – a plain order has been given, and it has been disobeyed. Still, I am unwilling to break men for what may have been a lunatic whim. But I tell you, Captain Moore,' said Jack with a shocking cold ferocity, 'that I will not have my ship run like a bawdy-house: I will have a taut ship. I will have my orders obeyed. And if there is the least hint of recurrence, by God I shall break them without mercy. Now, sir, if there are any of your men who understand what orders mean, after this disgraceful exhibition on the part of their officers, be so good as to have a sentry posted at the lady's door. And pray tell Mr Howard that I wish to see him at once.'

Howard did not last long. Having got wind of this affair long before the sleeping Captain Moore, he had been preparing for the interview for an hour at least: he was double-shaved, his uniform was speckless, his stock as tight as a stock can be; and he had swallowed four glasses of brandy and water. What he had to say did not reach the poop, but its nature could be surmised from Jack's explosive 'Contemptible, sir, contemptible! The most disgraceful mean shuffling ungentlemanly defence I have ever heard in my life. The most infernal sneaking scrub ever whelped in a gutter would be ashamed . . . Killick, Killick there,' pealing on his bell, 'Call the sentry and carry Mr Howard away. He is took ill. And pass the word for Mr Babbington.'

Babbington received the expected summons, cast a pitiful look at

Pullings, licked his lips, looking absurdly like his anxious, apprehensive dog, and stepped aft, quite bowed.

But Babbington was executed in the stern-gallery, where the overhang muted the sound; and the *Leopard* being close-hauled to weather Fogo, even those muted notes were borne away by the wind.

'The smoke over there,' said Stephen, 'is Fogo, the volcano.'

'Dear me,' said Mrs Wogan, 'how very shocking.' She paused, and said, 'So now I have seen a volcano, as well as having heard one.' This reference was contrary to their tacitly agreed rules of intercourse, but Mrs Wogan was clearly upset, and she showed this a moment later by the ineptitude of her return to Herapath. 'So your patient can read and write? Surely that is unusual in a common sailor?'

Stephen considered for a while. Although she had uttered this with a creditable air of detached curiosity, its timing was wretchedly ill-judged, and he was inclined to make her pay for her want of professional skill. Yet he was feeling benign, and she had just been called that infernal woman, together with several other disobliging names, so he replied, 'He is not a common sailor. He appears to be a young man of good family and of a certain education who has run away to sea because of some misfortune or distress, presumably of an erotical nature. Perhaps he has run from an unkind mistress.'

'What a romantic thought. But if he is shot of the lady, why should he perish away? People do not die of love, you know.'

'Do they not, ma'am? I have known them brought pretty low, however, and to take to mighty strange courses, ruin their happiness, career, prospects, reputation, honour, estate, and wits, break with their families and their friends, run mad. But in this case, I fear he may perish away not so much from a wounded heart, as from an empty belly. You cannot conceive the promiscuity of the seaman's life, nor its total lack of privacy. The seamen, upon the whole, are a very decent set of men; but to one bred up in a different way of life, their company can be strangely burdensome. What they eat, for example, and their way of eating it – the noise, the open-mouthed champing, the primitive gestures, the borborygms, the belching, the

roaring jocularity, the – I will spare you many aspects, but I assure
you that to an educated man, who has no very robust vital principle,
who knows nothing of the sea except perhaps the Dover packet, who
has lived retired, and who has been much reduced by unhappiness,
all these things together can bring about a morbid state, an anorexy;
and he may literally starve in the midst of plenty. Poor Herapath – for
Herapath is his name – is already skin and bone. I feed him up with
my portable soup, and the Captain sent him a chicken from his table;
but I look to see him buried, bone alone, before he can come to relish . . . The bell! The bell! Come, there is not a moment to be lost.'

The Marine sentry was already on the door, and it was therefore
in a very low voice that Mrs Wogan said, 'Having been present at the
young man's rescue, I feel a certain interest in him. I have vast quantities of stores. May I beg you to be so humane as to allow me to send
him this canister of Naples biscuits, and a tongue?'

Stephen returned to the cabin, and this time he was admitted. He
found Jack looking old and tired. 'I have had a damned unpleasant
afternoon, Stephen,' he said. 'How it does take it out of you, being
angry. Those lecherous sodomites have been sending Mrs Wogan bil-
lets doux, bribing people right, left and centre – cannot keep their
breeches on, the hounds. And this evening I shall beat the oldsters,
the whole after-cockpit. No dry flogging, neither. Seized to that gun,
and a hearty score or so on the bare breech. God rot them all. Would
you believe it, Stephen? They bored holes in the bulkhead of her
cabin, and stood there in rows, to see her in her shift. Oh, the odious
wench. How I wish I were rid of her. I have always loathed women,
from clew to earing; hook, line and sinker; root and branch. I always
said this would happen, you remember; I was against it from the start.
Damn her for a flibbertigibbet, the hussy. Without her we would be
sailing along as sweet as – ' for the moment nothing typically sweet
occurred to his mind, so he added 'swans' in an angry growl. 'God-
damned swans.'

'Here is a note for you from Herapath.'

'Eh? Oh, Herapath: yes. Thankee. Forgive me.' He read it, smiled and said, 'Very prettily put. Could not have put it prettier myself. The civilest line I ever had from anyone I pulled out: wrote pretty, too; an elegant hand. Well, I take that very kindly. He shall have another fowl. Killick! God damn that stone-deaf Beelzebub. Killick, there's a cold fowl left, ain't there? Send it along to Herapath, in the sick-bay. Can he take a little wine, Stephen? No wine, Killick: but rouse out a bottle of sherry for us.'

'Listen now, will you,' said Stephen, when the bottle was half out. 'In the matter of this lady, you are excessive; you are unjust. She shares in the sin of Eve, sure; but otherwise she is blameless. Not a leer, not a wink, not a handkerchief dropped. And I am to tell you, joy, that I require a free hand with Mrs Wogan.'

'You too, Stephen?' cried Jack, colouring. 'By God, I – '

'Do not mistake me, Jack, I beg,' said Stephen, drawing his chair close and speaking into his ear. 'These are not carnal words. I will say no more than this: her arrest was in fact connected with intelligence. That is the meaning of the words you found on the superintendent's instruction "all facilities will be afforded to Dr Maturin, without question". I did not explain them at the time, because the least said in these matters the better. But you will now permit me to observe that the Marine would be better marching up and down the passage, not listening at the door: he would also find it less dull. And in time he might be withdrawn entirely.'

'The least said the better,' said Jack. 'Just so. It shall be as you direct.' He paced to and fro, his hands behind his back. He had boundless confidence in Stephen, but deep in his mind there was a sense of having been – not tricked, not quite manoeuvred: perhaps *managed* was the word. He did not care for it at all. It wounded him. He took up his fiddle, and standing there facing the open stern-window and looking out on to the wake, he stroked a deep note from the G string and so played on, an improvisation that expressed what he felt as no words could have done. But when Stephen behind him, speaking over the sound, said, 'Forgive me, Jack: sometimes I am compelled to be devious. I do not do it from choice,' the music changed, ended in an abrupt, cheerful pizzicato, and he sat down again. As they finished their bottle, they talked about tropic-birds, the flying-fish they had eaten for breakfast, the very curious phenomenon of a high haze moving in the same direction as the much lower cumulus – something that Jack had never seen in the Trades, where the upper and the lower winds were always contrary – and about the unusual aspect of the sea itself.

'You know I am to dine with you tomorrow,' said Jack, after a pause. 'I have been wondering, after today's wretched business, whether not to cry off.'

'It would disappoint Pullings,' said Stephen. 'And Macpherson, who sees to the catering: he has laid on a haggis and some uncommon claret. It would also disappoint Fisher, and no doubt the midshipman Holles, who is also to be our guest.'

'Holles will eat standing, if I have anything to do with it,' said Jack. 'But perhaps I should come: it might look shabby else, and resentful. Though I doubt it will be such a jovial feast as Tom Pullings might wish in his heart.'

The wardroom's dinner to the Captain was indeed heavy going at the start, although the *Leopard* had just run one of her finest distances in this or any other of her voyages, tearing along, topgallants just holding in the splendid breeze on her quarter, the log racing astern glass after glass, reeling off ten and eleven knots at every cast, and filling all hands with pleasurable excitement. Perhaps haggis was not quite the dish for the occasion: perhaps it was not possible to make a total divorce between service and social matters. Howard was still too shocked to attempt much in that line, but Babbington and Moore did their utmost, drinking with Jack in the most sociable manner, and the purser's droll stories were a very great resource, while the chaplain told them of an unusually well authenticated ghost; the Captain himself produced a creditable flow of small but convivial talk; and when the flaccid remains of the haggis had given way to Jack's favourite dish, soused hog's face, the proper sound of naval gaiety was beginning to build up to its full volume. But now Grant struck in with a singularly misplaced disquisition on the right place to cross the equator. He maintained that twelve degrees west was the only proper longitude; anything more would bring you on to St Roque, anything less into the adverse currents, the swell, and the treacherous winds of Africa. Since Jack had clearly stated his intention of crossing in twenty-one or twenty-two degrees, it was clear to all that these words were untimely; but when Macpherson attempted to start a fresh hare, Grant held up his hand and said, 'Hush, I am speaking,' and his harsh didactic voice went on and on haranguing his restless audience until at last Pullings said, 'How often have you crossed the line, Mr Grant?'

'Why, twice, as I told you,' said Grant, put out of his stride.

'I believe Captain Aubrey must have crossed a score of times. Ain't that so, sir?'

'Why, no,' said Jack. 'Not exactly. Not above eighteen, for I don't count cruising off the mouth of the Amazon. Mr Holles, a glass of wine with you.'

'Nevertheless,' said Larkin the master, who had drunk a good deal in the forenoon watch and whose fuddled mind was still at the beginning of Grant's observations, 'there is a great deal to be said for even less than twelve degrees.'

'Oh, clap a stopper over it,' whispered his neighbour, and a dead silence fell, a silence broken by a messenger – 'Mr Martin begged the Doctor's pardon, but could wish to see him as soon as might be convenient.'

'You will excuse me, gentlemen,' said Stephen, folding his napkin. 'I hope to join you again before the cheese, the St Jago goat's milk cheese. Now, sir?' he said to Martin, in the convicts' sick-bay. Martin made no reply, but pointed. 'Jesus, Mary, and Joseph,' whispered Stephen. All three patients had broken out in a mulberry-coloured rash, extraordinarily widespread and most ominously dark: there was no possible doubt – this was gaol-fever, and gaol-fever of the most virulent kind. He was certain the moment he saw it, but for conscience's sake he checked the other signs – petechiae, a palpable spleen, brown dry tongue, sordes, raging heat: not one was absent.

'Now we know what we are about,' he said, straightening up. 'Mr Martin, you have kept the most scrupulous notes, I am sure: when we combine our observations I have no doubt that we shall add materially to the literature on this disease. A most interesting set of anomalies hitherto, and now so convincingly resolved. Some cantharides if you please: let Soames prepare three turpentine enemata; and pray pass the shears.' And to the patients, who were feeling rather better now, he said in English, 'Now we are about to attack the root of the malady: be of good heart.'

They smiled: the strongest of the three said they would see England again, and that he would like to take another hare on Mr Wilson's land. They looked at him gratefully.

He and Martin plied all the remedies they possessed, all the forms of alleviation they knew – sponging, cold affusions, shaving of the head – but the progress of the disease, from having been extraordinarily slow, now became extraordinarily rapid. As the day wore on to quarters Stephen sent a note aft, asking that the guns might not be fired, although by this time two of the men were in the coma vigil, their eyes were staring wide, but their beings so very far below the surface that no guns would ever rouse them. When hammocks were piped down, the third man entered into a muttering delirium; and at lights out he too passed into coma.

The lights burned on in the sick-bay, and in his patients' gleaming eyes Stephen read ultimate disappointment, loss of trust, and deep reproach. Between two and four in the morning they all died. He and Martin closed their eyes, told the loblolly boy to send for the sail maker as soon as it was day, and went to bed. As he walked aft to his cabin Stephen noticed that the way had come off the ship: the innumerable sounds that spoke of her movement had fallen silent, and the voice of the water, usually slipping by just above his head, had died away.

CHAPTER FIVE

The *Leopard* had lost the north-east trades in 12´30°N, far earlier than Jack had expected: he resisted the notion of total loss as long as he could, but presently he was forced to admit that it was so, that this year the doldrums had moved farther north than usual, and that his ship was in them, well in, having carried the declining breath of the true breeze right down to its last expiring waft. Day after day she lay there with her head all round the compass, inanimate, her sails hanging limp, sometimes rolling so that most hands were sick all over again, rolling so heavy that he struck her topgallantmasts before she should send them overboard, sometimes motionless; and all day long the heat beat down from a veiled sun. The air was thick, with no refreshment even in the morning watch; lightning flickered all round the night horizon; and sometimes by night but more often by day, warm rain came down so hard and thick that the men on deck could hardly breathe and the scuppers on either side spurted water as though from a powerful hose.

Sometimes, after these blinding downpours, a breeze would spring up, and he would have the *Leopard*'s head towed round to make something of it. But it was rare that the breeze was on the ship herself; far more often it ruffled the sea half a mile or more away, and then the boats would labour, double-banked, to get her there before it died – vain, exhausting labour, nine times out of ten. And these breezes, such as they were, might come from any quarter; they were as likely to push her back as to help her on. Almost all the time she lay in much the same few square miles of sea, surrounded by her own filth, with empty casks, and floating bottles from the wardroom. Yet this stretch of sea was itself in motion. Whenever he could take a good noon observation or a double amplitude, Jack fixed his position: a perfect sight of the moon and Altair proved that the chro-

nometers he had indulged in – a superlative pair, the pride of their
maker – were still within seconds of Greenwich time, and that this
sea in which the *Leopard* wallowed was very slowly drifting west and
a little south in a circular motion that would require so great a time
for its completion that he looked away from his reckoning. Like every
other sailor he had heard of ships in the doldrums lying helpless for
weeks and even months, eating their stores and accumulating weed;
he had had severe experience of it himself; and as he examined the
sky, the sea, the drifting weed, the birds and fishes, the feel of the air,
and all those minute differences that mean so much to a man bred
to the sea, it appeared to him that the *Leopard* was in for a very ugly
bout. A gloomy ship now, oppressed by heat, and disease, and dread
of the future.

At one time a school of whales passed by, sperm whales on either
side, spouting, moving steadily along the surface, half awash, diving,
reappearing farther on: some fifty huge calm dark forms travelling
fast, some so close to the ship that he could see their blow-holes open.
One was a female with a calf no longer than the *Leopard*'s launch.
Although the ship had half a dozen whalers among her people, there
was not a sound as the school moved past: the crew, frightened by
the gaol-fever, dispirited, worn out by towing, merely looked over the
side – an apathetic stare, no more. At another time, a great deal of
weed appeared, perhaps some slow streamer from the remote Sar-
gasso Sea, and with it a number of birds that he had never seen before.

It was no use sending for Stephen, however. Stephen was shut into
the fore part of the ship: it had been transformed into one vast sick-
bay, sealed off by bulkheads, forbidden territory from which he never
emerged except for the daily burials. Very early in the epidemic he
had fumigated the whole ship, section by section, with great quantities of brimstone while the hands were sent into the boats or the
tops; then he had retired with all his patients, desiring Jack to have
the bulkheads caulked and tarred, in the hope of stopping the spread
of the infection.

A vain hope. During the first week the log had recorded the burial of fourteen convicts, the two remaining turnkeys, and a loblolly boy, all of whom had lived or worked forward, and it had recorded them in Needham's fine copperplate: now it was Jack's far rougher hand that wrote the daily list, for his clerk had gone over the side with two cannon-balls to carry him down and his hammock for a shroud, the first of those abaft the mast to die of the disease.

Apart from the perpetual supply of fresh rain-water, the circumstances were as bad as they could be, with the enormous oppressive heat, the dispirited vitiated atmosphere, the excessive dread and general despondence that had come over all the crew; and when the disease struck the lower-deck it killed men faster than the plague. They gave up hope, and sometimes it seemed to Stephen that they would almost as soon not take his draughts, but would rather have it over as soon as might be: and soon it was, in many cases – headache, languor, a moderate rise in temperature, and despair at once, even before the rash and the appalling fever, far worse in this stifling heat, and so onwards to what he often believed an unnecessary death. He believed this all the more since his heroic exhibitions of bark and antimony had begun to have effect. There were now eleven convalescents, men who had survived their crises; yet in spite of this clear evidence, there were those who would die, who resigned themselves almost thankfully to death the moment they were brought in.

'I believe,' he said to Martin, 'that if only a French ship could be seen approaching, if only we could hear the drum beat and the sound of guns in earnest, several of our cases would cure themselves, and the admissions would fall off to a wonderful degree.'

'You are in the right,' said Martin, taking up his book. 'Spirit is three-quarters of the remedy, as Rhazes observes. But who can dose or measure spirit?' He pressed his hands to his eyes, and went on, 'Now in the case of Roberts, you did say twenty drachms, did you not? I must note it down.'

'Twenty drachms it was: I am persuaded he can bear it. And pray

do note it down. Our notes will be of capital importance. You have
kept them very fully, I am sure?'

'I have indeed,' said Martin wearily.

'Mr Pullings, sir,' said the new loblolly boy.

'Bring him in. Well now, Lieutenant Pullings, my dear, you have
a vile headache, you feel cold, a distinct rigor about the midriff and
in the limbs? Just so. You have come to the right shop,' said Stephen,
smiling. 'You are slightly affected, and we can take you in hand in
time. We have a prime physic that will suit your case, and belay it
with all nines: and you are to observe, Tom, that I will lay a hundred to one upon your hoisting your flag in time. Pullings never yet
said die.'

An hour later Martin asked Dr Maturin to take his pulse: he did
so: they looked at one another, and Stephen said, 'I am not sure. There
are many other possible causes – you have eaten nothing since yesterday evening. Take some soup and stay below. I shall go on deck
this time.'

He took his best coat off the cleat and put it on, for the *Leopard*
still did these things in the proper manner. He walked along the
gangway towards the range of bodies sewn into their hammocks, as
Fisher's white surplice showed on the quarterdeck. Stephen did not
go farther aft than the maintack block, but stood there with his hat
off while the service was read and the dead seamen moved down the
slide into the viscid water.

After this he conversed with Jack at a distance of some ten yards –
easy enough in that still air and that silent ship – and paced for a
while on the forecastle. By the time he returned to the sick-bay there
was no doubt remaining as to Martin's state.

'You will take our twenty drachms?' he said.

'I will even adventure upon twenty-five,' said Martin, 'and my
notes will show its progress from within.'

From that day onwards Stephen was alone. He had two literate
assistants, Herapath and to some degree Fisher, but neither was

a medical man, neither could compound his drugs nor judge their administration, and in neither could he confide when the enormous demand exhausted his medicine-chest, so that he was obliged to turn to placebos, mostly of powdered chalk, coloured blue or red. Day and night ran into one, separated only by those pauses when Fisher put on his surplice and followed the dead on deck to bury them. Although even before Martin's death the physic was no more than nominal, the immediate bodily and spiritual care, the nursing of the patients still remained, and to this he applied himself, teaching Herapath all he could; for as he remarked, nursing was quite half the battle. It had saved Martin, who in fact died from a pneumonia that struck him days after the favourable termination of the crisis and after he had written an exact description of the disease from the onset to the first stage of convalescence, the Latin faultless to the last.

It seemed an endless battle, yet by the calendar only twenty-three days passed before an even more violent deluge than usual brought a northerly breeze in the morning watch that wafted the *Leopard* down, just to the very outside limit of the region where the south-east trade-wind blew.

From the sick-bay he noticed the deafening downpour, water knee-deep on the decks and cascading into the head, and he heard all hands piped to make sail in the ensuing quietness; but this had happened so often that he paid little attention. Even when he felt her heavy, deeply-weeded bulk surge on and heard the growing hiss of her cutwater shearing through the swell, he was too utterly weary to be pleased, just as he had taken no real satisfaction in the diminishing mortality of these last few days and the absence of fresh cases.

He slept where he sat, occasionally waking for some call for water or to help a half-seen assistant lash a delirious man into his cot. Yet when he woke in the morning he knew that the ship was in a different world, that she was herself a different world. True, clean, breathable air was gushing down the wind-sail; his whole being was recharged with life.

These confused waking motions were confirmed on deck. The

Leopard had sent up her topgallantmasts – it had taken the reduced crew three-quarters of an hour instead of the usual seventeen minutes and forty seconds – and she was running west-south-west at five or six knots under a cloud of sail. A new and brilliant day, a new and healthy sea, transparent tonic air, the ship alive. Killick had been on the watch, and now he ran forward with coffee-pot and biscuit, laid them carefully in a coil of rope at the appointed place, the limit of the forbidden ground, retreated, and called out, 'Good morning, sir. This is what we have been praying for.' Stephen nodded, took a draught, and asked how the Captain did. 'Which he's just turned in,' said Killick, 'a-laughing like a boy. Says we've cleared the doldrums: the true blessed trade, he says, and never will he touch a stitch till we're at the Cape.'

Stephen drank his coffee and soaked his biscuit standing by the rail. An extraordinary change had come over the ship: men ran, talked in low cheerful voices, looked like different beings; and there was laughter out on the bowsprit. All this time the routine of the ship had been carried on, but as though the hands were already at least half-dead; orders had been obeyed, but by slow and listless automata. Now the *Leopard* might have been sailing fresh from Porto Praya, apart from the fact that her decks were so thinly peopled.

The change in the sick-bay was more surprising still. Men who had been on the point of death the evening before were now straining their heads up from their cots, talking eagerly in their weak thin voices. One very feeble convalescent had actually reached the ladder, and was attempting to creep up. The eyes, the expressions, the words that he encountered as he made his rounds possessed a vitality that he had not seen for weeks, and one whose existence had almost passed from his mind.

'I doubt whether we have many fresh cases today,' he said to Herapath. He was not mistaken: no more new admissions and only three more deaths, all cases where the coma had been abnormally prolonged.

Nevertheless, it was a full week before he opened his plague-house,

allowed his stronger convalescents to come up to the forecastle or
return to the lower-deck, and moved aft again.

'Jack,' said he, 'I am come to sit with you a while; and then, if I
may, I will beg the use of one of your little cabins. I long for a day and
a night of uninterrupted sleep in luxury, swinging in an ample cot
under an open skylight. You need not be afraid: I have been pumped
in fresh rain-water and soaped from head to foot, and I believe the
epidemic is over. Should anything untoward occur, Herapath will
wake me. Herapath knows all the symptoms now, as very few men
know them. Herapath will not be deceived. Now, sir!' he cried, frowning sternly at a stranger whose face was reflected in a small looking-
glass. 'Jesus, 'tis myself, behind that beard.' A three-weeks' beard:
with his sunken, emaciated face, it gave him the look of an El Greco,
without the length. 'Beard,' he said, pulling it. 'Maybe I shall retain
this beard – the torment of the razor a mere memory, no more. The
Roman emperors retained their beards, in war.'

At any other time Jack would have pointed out the chasm separating a Roman emperor from a surgeon in the Royal Navy, but now he
only said, 'Herapath behaved very well, I collect?'

'Very well indeed: a good, quiet, intelligent young man, that can
be relied upon. And since I am now alone, I desire you will make him
my mate. True, he has not studied physic, nor surgery; but he can
read the Latin and French in which most of my books are wrote, and
he will have nothing to unlearn, which is not the case with most of
the pitiable quackeens who come aboard with nothing more valuable
than a piece of paper from Surgeons' Hall, a set of old wives' tales, and
a secondhand saw.'

'I cannot possibly make a man an assistant-surgeon. What are you
thinking of, Stephen? The Sick and Hurt would never countenance it
for a moment. But I will tell you what I can do: I can rate him midshipman, since I have three vacancies, alas, and then he can be your
acting mate.' He went on to explain the metaphysics of acting and
substantive rank, but finding that Stephen had fallen fast asleep, his
chin on his chest, his mouth open among the beard, and no more

than a thin crescent of yellowish white showing under his eyelids, he tiptoed away.

The dawn broke clear and sudden, a brilliant sun rising at exactly six o'clock, the south-eastern wind blowing fresh; and at the beginning of the forenoon watch the *Leopard* crossed the line: crossed without the least ceremony however, nothing to mark the event apart from pork on what would have been a dried peas banyan day, and plum duff.

At six bells Herapath brought the sick-bay papers, and reported uninterrupted progress forward. Before settling to their grim accounts, Jack said, 'Herapath, Dr Maturin speaks in high terms of your conduct, and he wishes you to continue as his assistant. The rules of the service do not allow me to enter you on the ship's books as assistant-surgeon without the proper certificates, so I propose rating you midshipman. This will enable you to act as his assistant, to live with the oldsters in the after-cockpit, and to walk the quarterdeck. Is that agreeable to you?'

'I am very much beholden to Dr Maturin for his good opinion,' said Herapath, 'and to you, sir, for your most obliging offer. But perhaps I should observe that I am an American citizen, in case that should be a bar.'

'Are you, though?' said Jack. He looked at the muster, which he had opened to change Herapath's rating. 'So you are. Born in Cambridge, Massachusetts. Well, I am afraid that is a bar to your ever becoming a commissioned officer in the Royal Navy. I am very sorry to have to tell you, that advancement beyond master's mate is closed to you.'

'Sir,' said Herapath, 'I must endeavour to bear it.'

Jack looked at him sharply. No one but Stephen could make game of Captain Aubrey with impunity: but was Herapath in fact guilty of impertinence? The young man's face was calm and grave. There was no hint of a smile on Stephen's face, either. 'You have no dislike to fighting the French, I take it?' he went on. 'Nor any of the other nations England is at war with?'

'None in the least, sir. In 'ninety-eight, when I was quite a boy, I

was in arms against the French, under General Washington. And I am
happy to do what I can against any of your other enemies; unless, of
course, England should go to war with the States, which God forbid.'

'Amen,' said Jack. 'Well, I shall be glad to welcome you to my quarterdeck. Mr Grant will introduce you to the young gentlemen: here
is a note for him. And since poor Stokes was just about your size, you
may wish to buy his uniforms when they are sold at the mainmast.'

Herapath withdrew: they arranged their papers, and checking with
the log-book, Jack wrote DD, discharged dead, against the names of
one hundred and sixteen men, ranging from William Macpherson,
lieutenant, Royal Marines, and James Stokes, master's mate, down to
Jacob Hawley, boy, third class. It was a painful task, for again and
again the name was that of some former shipmate who had sailed
with them in the Mediterranean, the Channel, the Atlantic or the
Indian Ocean – sometimes in all – and whose qualities they knew
intimately well. 'One of the saddest things about this tally,' said Jack,
'is that it hits our volunteers so much harder than the rest. Once I
knew a good third of the men aboard. Now it is nothing like. Yet a
surprising number of the quota men have come through: how do you
account for that, Stephen?'

'I hazard a guess, no more. A slight attack of smallpox gives immunity; so these men, many of whom have been in prison, may have
been infected with an attenuated form of gaol-fever, thus acquiring
a resistance the others lacked. Yet I must confess that my reasoning
is very loose, because of our convicts no more than three men have
survived, and one of them will never make old bones. The women I
reckon apart, for not only do they possess the singular toughness of
their sex, but one at least is pregnant, a state that seems to confer
immunity from so many ills.'

Jack shook his head, looked through the remaining papers, and
said, 'These are your convalescents, I take it? How soon do you expect
them to be fit for duty?'

'Alas, I cannot hold out any hope of a prompt return except in the case of the few boys. The sequelae are very troublesome in this disease, I am afraid, troublesome and lingering. Of the sixty-five in my list, perhaps in other circumstances you might have a score tolerably brisk in a month; another score might take far longer; while the remaining twenty-five, who only just came through, should not be on a ship at all, whatever the circumstances, but in a well-appointed hospital.'

Jack wrote his sums, and whistled at the result. 'So at the best,' he said, 'I have about two hundred men. I can watch perhaps a hundred and twenty or so. Sixty hands to a watch: God help us! Sixty hands to a watch, in a fifty-gun ship!'

'Yet we hear of merchantmen taking their goods to the ends of the earth, with no more to sail their vessel.'

'To sail her, yes. But to fight her, that is quite another thing. We reckon the gun-crews can handle five hundredweight a man. Now our long twenty-fours weigh just over fifty hundredweight, and our twelves thirty-four. So to fight the ship one side we need a hundred and ten men on the lower deck and seventy-seven on the upper, to say nothing of the other side or the carronades and the long nines; and as you know very well, Stephen, a great many people are needed to work her, while she is being fought. This is a damned unpleasant kettle of fish.'

'It is worse than you suppose, Jack. Things are always worse than you suppose. For you are speaking as though my convalescents, my sixty-five convalescents, were presently to be restored: you did not notice that I spoke of other, of favourable circumstances. Now the present circumstances are not favourable: for I must tell you that my medicine-chest is bare. I have no bark, no electuaries, no antimony, no – in short, I have nothing but my venereals and a little alba mistura, or eye-wash – a very little alba mistura – and therefore cannot answer for my three-score convalescents, at all. Unless they have physic and a diet that the ship cannot possibly provide in mid-ocean, a whole series of ailments may carry them away. This applies with the greatest force to my first list, the list on your right, headed by the name of Thomas Pullings, the list of those that require immediate relief.'

'Cannot they hold out until the Cape?'

'No, sir. Even in this clement weather, we already have the typical swollen leg by the dozen, the very dangerous debility, the severe nervous symptoms. In the cold winds and the boisterous weather south of Capricorn, without a drop of physic, my convalescents, or the greater part of them, would be condemned. And even if my chest were full, those on the first list would stand very little chance of seeing Africa.'

Jack did not reply at once: his mind was dealing with the advantages and disadvantages of touching at a Brazilian port – the loss of the trade-wind inshore, the way the south-easter would often hang in the east for weeks on end just under the tropic, so that a ship might have to beat into it, tack upon tack, for very little gain, or else run far south for the westerlies: a whole mass of considerations. His face was already sad; now it grew stern and cold; and when he did speak it was not to tell Stephen what he intended to do but to ask whether Pullings and the people in the sick-bay might be allowed wine yet. He was going to see how they did, and would like to take a couple of dozen with him.

Just when he reached his decision did not appear, but it must have been before the first dog-watch. Stephen brought Mrs Wogan on to the poop, where he was obliged to repel a dangerous attack from Pollux, Babbington's Newfoundland; Pollux did not recognize him in his beard, and being attached to Mrs Wogan, defended her as a matter of duty. Even when she seized its ear, pulled it away, and told it not to be a damned fool – the gentleman was a friend – the animal distrusted him, and kept just behind his hams, uttering an organ-like growl, both with the inspiration and the outward breath. Babbington was below, so when she had reproached the dog and even thumped its loving head in vain, she tied a signal-halliard round its neck and attached it to the fife-rail: they moved aft to stare at the wake, and standing there they heard the aged carpenter, busy at the larboard stern-lantern, say to one of his mates, 'What's the buzz, Bob?'

Mr Gray was somewhat deaf, and his mate was obliged to whisper 'We're bearing up for Recife' in a louder tone than he could have wished.

'Eh?' said the carpenter. 'Don't mumble, God pound you alive. Articulate, Bob, ar-ticulate.'

'Recife. But only touch and go. No watering; no cattle. Greenstuff, belike.'

'I hope there will be time to get Mrs Gray a poll-parrot,' said the carpenter. 'She grieved after her last poll-parrot something cruel. Look at this here thorough-piece, Bob. Would you ever of believed that even the Dockyard could pass such a rotten bit of wood? And the whole bleeding stern-post is the same. Punk. Incest is nothing to them, nor Sunday travel, so they get us to sea in an ancient sieve, the fucking bastards.'

Bob coughed significantly, gave Mr Gray a great jerk with his elbow, and said, 'Company, company, Alfred.'

The rumour about the *Leopard*'s destination, like most ship's rumours, was quite accurate: her head pointed farther west, away from Africa; she brought the wind well abaft the beam, and began to set her upper and lower studdingsails. But just as she moved much more heavily through the water, now that she had a vast beard of doldrum-weed to drag along, so the diminished watch spent a far longer time in sheeting home; indeed, they had scarcely coiled all down before the drum beat for quarters; and after that ceremony her thin, hesitant gunfire was very different from the full-throated roar of a month ago.

In the evening Jack told Stephen that he had decided to put into the nearest Brazilian port, and asked him to prepare his list of drugs. 'We are well found in stores and water,' he said, 'and I mean only to lie in the outer road, just long enough to get your physic, and, if you tell me that it is of the first necessity, to put those invalids you name on shore. If this wind holds, we should raise St Roque tomorrow, and if it don't come foul inshore, Recife very shortly afterwards. The moment I have finished working out the new watch-lists with Grant, I shall start writing home. Have you any messages?'

'Love, of course,' said Stephen.

The next day, having made his rounds, he said, 'Mr Herapath, the Captain tells me that we are to stop at Recife, in Brazil, where we may replenish our medicine-chest. I shall spend much of my time drawing up a statement of our requirements, and writing letters. May I therefore beg you to attend Mrs Wogan to the poop, the unfortunate lady who is confined in the orlop abaft the tiers?'

'Sir?'

'You are not yet quite familiar with our sea-terms, I find,' said Stephen with great complacency. 'I mean the floor below this, in about the middle; and the door is on your right-hand side. Or, as we say, the *starboard*. No, the larboard, since you will be going backwards. Well, never mind: let us not be pedantic, for all love. It is a small little door with a square hole in the bottom of it – a scuttle – along the passage where there was a Marine for ever walking up and down at one time. But perhaps you will never find it. I remember, years ago, before I became so amphibious an animal, that I wandered in the depths of a vessel much smaller than this, my mind strangely perplexed. Come, I will show you the way, and present you to the lady.'

'Do not trouble, sir. Oh pray do not trouble,' cried Herapath, suddenly bursting out of his silence. 'I know the door perfectly. I have often – I have often remarked that particular door. It is on the way from here to the after-cockpit, where I now sling my hammock. Pray do not give yourself the trouble.'

'Here is the key,' said Stephen. 'You will make my compliments, if you please.'

Mrs Wogan's appearance under the conduct of the surgeon's mate excited a certain amount of discreet curiosity on the quarterdeck, and much more envy. The older midshipmen still ached for her – their Captain did not beat for the sport of it – but even so, more than one of them found it necessary to visit the poop, to make sure that the

ensign-staff was still there, and the taffrail. She was observed to be
in remarkable looks, and although she was decently subdued, as the
Leopard's circumstances required, she and her companion seemed
to have a great deal to say to one another. Three times her absurd
gurgling laugh was heard, and three times the whole quarterdeck,
from the officer of the watch to the grim old quartermaster at the
con, smiled like fools.

The third time the sound of the cabin door wiped the smile off
their faces. They moved over to the leeward side, with sober looks; for
the Captain was among them. The Captain glanced at the sky, the set
of the sails, the binnacle, and began his habitual pacing fore and aft,
cocking an eye at the masthead every turn, in expectation of a hail.
Again the laugh began, low but quite near, by the poop rail: it went on
and on, swelling, rolling in pure amusement, and for the life of him
he could not resist: disagreeable though his situation was, and heavy
his mind, he felt an answering catch in the region of his stomach,
and turned square to windward. 'Though why in God's name I have
to come it the grim old Stoic, would be hard to say,' he remarked to
himself: then finding that the inward heave would not be quiet, he
stepped forward to the shrouds of the mainmast, laid his coat on a
gun, swung himself over the bulwark, over the hammocks in their
netting, and walked composedly up the ratlines. 'Lord,' he said as he
mounted, 'I have scarcely been aloft this commission. That is how
captains get fat and ill-conditioned – ill-tempered, bilious, Jupiter
Tonans.' He was old enough not to have to hurry, not to have to outdo
a twenty-year-old upper-yardsman; and that was just as well, for as
he paused in the top he found that he was already puffing hard. He
glanced at his paunch, shook his head, and then looked down at the
quarterdeck. 'Mr Forshaw,' he called, picking out his youngest midshipman, a first-voyager, a slow, stupid, unhappy child, 'bring me up
my glass.'

He waited, nothing loth, until the boy's anxious head appeared:
with a violent, perilous writhe, Forshaw brought his short legs over
the rim, landed in the top, and mutely offered the telescope. It was

clear to Jack that for the moment the boy could not bring out a steady word, in spite of his studied calm. 'Now I come to think of it, Mr Forshaw,' he said, 'I have not seen you sky-larking with the other reefers. Do you find the height disturbs you?'

He spoke quite kindly, in a tone of conversation, but even so Forshaw's face turned scarlet, and he gave a hopelessly confused answer: 'it was terrible, sir; he did not mind it at all.'

'Nelson could do this sort of thing,' thought Jack, 'but I doubt that I can.' Nevertheless he went on. 'The great point is not to look down, until you have the knack of it; and to hold on to the shrouds with both hands, not the ratlines. Now, come along with me to the topgallant crosstrees. We will take it easy.'

Up and up towards the sky. 'You will find it much like the stairs at home, presently – look up all the time – don't hang on too hard – breathe easy – handsomely round the futtocks, now, always take the outer topgallant shrouds – there now, put your arm round the heel of the royal – that's the royal mast, you see: sometimes we step it abaft the topgallant, running right down to the cap; but that means more weight aloft – and sit on the jacks; they serve to spread the royal shrouds. There, ain't that prime?' He stared over the enormous expanse of ocean at the western horizon, and there, exactly where it should be, lay a dark mass, firmer than any cloud. He unslung his telescope, and in the glass Cape St Roque assumed its well-remembered form: the perfect landfall. 'There,' he said, nodding towards it, 'that is America. You may go down now, and tell Mr Turnbull. It is much easier going down, because of gravity: but you must look up all the time.'

Now and then he glanced down at the round face gazing religiously up, and beyond the face to the deck, long, thin, and wonderfully remote, a white-rimmed sliver in the sea with little figures moving on it; but most of the time he stared at the cape. 'How I hope to God that Stephen will let Pullings stay,' he said aloud. 'A year or so with that fellow Grant as my first would be . . .'

The lookout's hail broke his train of thought, for by now the cape was visible from the yardarm below him, and he heard the cry, 'On deck, there. Land two points on the starboard bow.'

From this time on the more loving family Leopards took to pen and ink, and those who could not write dictated to their learned friends, sometimes in plain English but more often in terms as stilted and official as they could contrive, and those uttered in a hieratic tone. According to his promise, Stephen passed on Mrs Wogan's request that she might add a letter to the rapidly filling bay. 'I shall be interested to see what it contains,' he said; and as he expected, Jack turned away – turned fast, but not quite fast enough to hide his expression of extreme distaste, and of something very near contempt.

Captain Aubrey would do his utmost to deceive an enemy by the use of false colours and false signals, by making him believe that the ship was a harmless merchantman, a neutral, or a compatriot, and by any other ruse that might occur to his fertile mind. All was fair in war: all, except for opening letters and listening behind doors. If Stephen, on the other hand, could bring Buonaparte one inch nearer to the brink of Hell by opening letters, he would happily violate a whole mail-coach full. 'You will read captured dispatches with open glee and exultation,' he said, 'for you concede that they are public papers. If you value candour, you must therefore admit that any document bearing on the war is also a public paper: you are to rid your mind of these weak prejudices.'

In his heart Jack remained unconvinced; but Stephen received the letter. He sat there with it in his hands in the guarded privacy of the great cabin as the *Leopard* lay off Recife early in the morning, well out in the roadstead, with the reef that guarded the inner anchorage the best part of a mile away. The first sight of it struck him with a wholly unexpected force, for it was addressed to Diana: he had never thought of this possibility – had supposed their acquaintance to be slight – and it was some minutes before he could compose himself, and set about the seal. Seals and their attendant pitfalls had few mysteries for him, and this one required no more than a thin hot knife:

yet even so he had to break off twice, because of the trembling of his hands. If the letter contained proof of Diana's guilty mind, he thought it would kill him.

At first reading it contained nothing of the sort. Mrs Wogan exceedingly lamented the sudden parting from her dearest Mrs Villiers – the event itself too dreadful and distressing to recall – and at one moment she had thought they were to be separated by the distance between this world and the next, for in her distraction at the sight of those odious ruffians, Mrs Wogan had fired off a pistol, or even two, and another had exploded of its own accord; and that, it appeared, turned a dispute over a harmless piece of gallantry into a capital crime – but, however, her lawyers had handled the matter very cleverly, and kind friends had come to her support, so that they were to be separated only by the distance of half this present world, and that, perhaps, not for very long. Mrs Villiers would remember her kindly to all their friends in Baltimore, particularly to Kitty van Buren and Mrs Taft, and she would be so obliging as to tell Mr Johnson that all was well, and that as he would hear from Mr Coulson in more detail, no irreparable harm had been done. The voyage had begun in the most shocking manner, and they had had the plague aboard; but for some time now things had been going better. The weather was delightful: her stores were holding out to admiration; and she had made friends with the surgeon. He was an ill-looking little man, and perhaps he was aware of it, for he had now allowed a horrid beard to overspread his countenance, quite frightful to behold; but one could grow used to anything, and his conversation was an agreeable break in the day. He was polite and generally kind; yet he could be snappish – he could give a short answer – although hitherto she had not dared to be impertinent, nor anything but most perfectly meek. He did not need 'fending off' as sailors would say; far from it; and she believed he must have a wounded heart. He was not married, that she could find. A learned man, but like some others she had known, quite preposterously thoughtless in many of the common things of life: he had put to sea for a twelve months' voyage without a single pocket-handkerchief! She was hemming him a dozen out of a piece of cambric she had by her. She believed she must have a *tendre* for the man. Certainly she was disappointed when the knock was followed not by the doctor but by the chaplain, a man with Judas-coloured hair and two left legs who had been paying her a great deal of the most unwelcome attention, sitting with her and reading good works aloud. For her part, Mrs Wogan perfectly loathed the combination of incipient gallantry and the Bible; she had seen too much, far too much, of that in the States: Mrs Wogan was not a bread-and-butter miss fresh from the schoolroom, and she knew what he would be at. Otherwise her life was not too disagreeable: monotonous, of course, but it was not the insufferable tedium of her last years in the convent. Her maid had amusing tales of the very lowest conceivable or rather inconceivable life in London; there was a dear fool of a dog that marched up and down the poop with her, and a nanny-goat that sometimes condescended to say good day: she had a good store of books, and she had actually read right through Clarissa Harlowe without hanging herself (though that was sometimes only for want of a convenient hook), without looking to see how the ninny would escape that vile coxcomb Lovelace – how Mrs Wogan despised conscious good looks in a man – and without skipping a line: a feat surely unparalleled in the female world. Indeed, were dear Mrs Villiers ever in the same unfortunate predicament, Mrs Wogan could advise nothing better than Richardson's works entire, together with Voltaire's as an antidote, and an unlimited supply of Naples biscuits; but Mrs Villiers was to believe that for her the very opposite – a life of total freedom, in the company of a well-bred intelligent man – was the constant wish of her most affectionate friend, Louisa Wogan.

The first reading showed no guilt in Diana: rather the reverse. The letter was obviously designed to keep her in the dark. His heart had already absolved her, but his mind insisted upon a second reading, much slower, and a third, very carefully analysing the words and searching for those minute marks and repetitions that might betray a code. Nothing.

He leant back, quite satisfied. The letter was not candid, of course; and the most obviously uncandid thing about it, the absence of Hera-path, pleased him extremely. Mrs Wogan knew that there was some risk of the letter's being read by the Captain (she certainly did not share his weak prejudices) and if she had any delicate information to convey, she meant to do so by means of Herapath. It was very prob-able that she should wish to enlarge upon the 'no irreparable harm' and to tell her chief just how much she had been obliged to give away to save her neck. Any agent worth a straw would do the same: any agent, that is to say, who had not been bought; and Mrs Wogan had not been bought. Furthermore, he had given her plenty of time to pre-pare her lover. He copied the letter for Sir Joseph, whose cryptogra-phers might find a code where his close inspection, his heating of the paper, and his chemicals had detected none: then he replaced the seal and put the letter back in the bag, at the same time looking through the recent additions for a cover addressed in Herapath's distinctive hand. There was nothing.

'Jack,' he said, 'is there to be any shore leave?'

'No,' said Jack. 'I shall call on the Governor, of course, and do the civil; and I shall see whether I can get a few hands in the port. Oth-erwise the only people to go ashore will be you and whatever invalids you absolutely insist on landing.' He looked earnestly into Stephen's face at this point, and then went on, 'I do not mean to lose a minute; and I do not mean to lose a single man by desertion. You know how they run, if they are given half a chance.'

'Here are the names of those that must go,' said Stephen. 'I exam-ined them with great care not an hour ago.'

'How I shall tell Pullings, I do not know,' said Jack, looking at the list. 'It will fairly break his heart.'

Heart-broken he seemed, as he was handed down the side in a can-vas bag to join the others in the hired tender; he was too weak even to sit up, and that was a comfort to him, because he could lie with his face concealed. Few others were quite so reduced, but all were pitiable sights and many were as fractious as ill-conditioned children. One

Ayliffe, as Stephen eased him into the sling, called out, 'Handsomely, handsomely, you bearded piss-cat: handsomely, can't you?' Stephen might have saved his life; but the surgeon's fell shears had also sliced off a pigtail of ten years patient growth and cultivation, and now, with the sun beating down on his bald white pate, the loss was very present to Ayliffe's peevish mind.

'Take that man's name,' cried the new first lieutenant.

'Take it yourself, you old French fart,' said the seaman. 'And stuff it up. There ain't no flogging here.'

The other invalids went down the side in disapproving silence; for although in extreme illness, unexpected, unusual emergency, or drunkenness they too might throw discipline aside, this was coming it pretty high, higher than the state of things allowed – after all, the ship was not on fire, nor had she struck, nor was Ayliffe roaring drunk. Stephen was about to follow them when Herapath said, 'May I come with you, sir?'

'You may not, Mr Herapath,' said Stephen. 'It was stated that there was to be no shore leave; and the transcription of our records calls for all your time, all your powers. You miss nothing: Recife is a most uninteresting port.'

'In that case, may I beg you to be so kind as to leave this with the consul of the United States?' He produced a letter: Stephen put it in his pocket.

Late, late that night, with no sound in the ship but the trade-wind singing quietly in the rigging, the occasional movement of the anchor-watch, the bells and the cry of All's well from the sentries that followed each half-hourly stroke, Stephen snuffed his candle, pressed his hands to his aching, red-rimmed eyes, took up his diary, and wrote, 'I have seen Jack glow with pleasure when he has made a perfect landfall: when he has calculated his tides, his currents, and his shifting winds, and the event proves him right; and for this once my prediction too has been as exact as I could wish. Poor lady, how she must have laboured with her coding; and how heartily she must have cursed Fisher when he would be reading her South on Resig-

nation. Judging from what she had not time to encode, I believe Sir
Joseph's experts will extract a remarkably complete picture from the
rest, and that he will be gratified by the spectacle of a nascent system
of intelligence: infant steps, perhaps, but surely those of a promising,
even of a prodigious infant. I feel for her, with that good man pros-
ing on and on, and her precious moments racing by. Her seal, though
artful enough with its double guard of hair, showed evident marks
of impatience. When we meet tomorrow I have little doubt that our
eyes will match, like those of a pair of albino ferrets; for although my
copies and my letters to Sir Joseph in duplicate may have been longer,
I am more accustomed to the act than she. I do not have to count on
my fingers for my code, blot and write again, with little calculations
in the margin; nor did I have to contend with extreme vexation of
spirit. I must keep the triumph from my glowing eye, however: perhaps I shall wear green spectacles.'

He closed his book, itself a monument of cryptography, and lay
down in his cot. Sleep was welling up to dowse his mind, but for a
while it still burned clear, reflecting both upon the satisfactions of
his trade and upon its very dirty sides – the constant dissimulation,
the long-lived lie soaking into the liar's deepest fibre, however justified the lie – the sacrifice, in some cases he had known, not only of
the agent's life but also of his private essence – upon whales – upon
the curious division of the wardroom into two parties, Grant, Turnbull, and Larkin on the one side, and Babbington, Captain Moore,
and Byron, the new acting fourth lieutenant, on the other, with the
purser Benton and the insignificant Marine lieutenant Howard in
between. Perhaps Fisher too; although of recent days his friendship
with Grant had increased. An odd creature, the chaplain, perhaps
somewhat shallow, unsteady; his conduct during the height of the
epidemic had disappointed Stephen, as far as he had had time to be
disappointed; more promise than performance: too much taken up
with his own troubles? More willing to receive comfort than to give
it? Certainly most reluctant to handle filth. And this marked concern for Mrs Wogan's welfare . . . They were not parties opposed by

any animosity, however, at least not evident animosity; they rather represented different attitudes and they were probably to be found throughout the ship, with Jack's old shipmates and volunteers on the one hand and the rest of the crew on the other. 'Will he find any more men?' was the last of these thoughts that had coherent form.

The next day brought the answer: twelve black Portuguese, and Jack was to try again in the afternoon, his last chance before the *Leopard* sailed on the evening tide. 'But,' observed Bonden, rowing Stephen to the apothecary's for his final lading, 'I doubt he'll find another soul.'

'May not he press some from the English ship that has just come in?'

'Oh no, sir,' said Bonden, laughing, 'not in a foreign port, he can't. Besides, she's a whaler for the South Sea, so most of her men will have protections, even if we meet her far out in the offing. Nor he won't get no volunteers out of her, neither, not for the old *Leopard*, if they haven't sailed with him before. No, no, they won't go into the *Leopard* of their own free will, not an old wessel of her unlikely rep.'

'But surely she is a very fine ship? Better than new, the Captain said.'

'Well, now,' said Bonden, 'I don't go for to set myself up as a King Solomon, but I know what the common chap that has used the sea for some time says to himself. He says, this here old *Leopard* may have a good skipper, no preachee-floggee hard-horse, as we say, but she is wery old, and cruel short-handed: we shall be worked to the bone, so damn the *Leopard*. For why? Because she is a floating coffin, and unlucky at that.'

'Nay, Bonden, the Captain told me distinctly, and I recall his very words, that she had been thoroughly overhauled, with Snodgrass's diagonal braces, and Roberts's iron-plate knees, so that she was now the finest fifty-gun ship afloat.'

'As to her being the finest fifty-gun ship afloat, why, fair enough. Because why? Because there's only *Grampus* in the ring, bar two or three more we call the Baltic Hearses. But as for them knees and braces . . . Well now, sir,' said Bonden, glancing over his shoulder and shooting the boat through a gap between a mob of smallcraft and the outer buoy. He did not speak again for some while, and when he did it was to say in an obstinate, contentious voice, 'They can talk to me about Captain Seymour and Lord Cochrane and Captain Hoste and all the rest of them, but I say our skipper's the finest fighting captain in the fleet; and I served under Lord Viscount Nelson, didn't I? I'd like to see the man that denies it. Who wiped a Spanish frigate's eye in a fourteen-gun brig, and made her strike? Who fought the *Polychrest* till she sunk under him, and swapped her for a corvette cut out from right under their guns?'

'I know, Bonden,' said Stephen mildly. 'I was there.'

'Who set about a French seventy-four in a twenty-eight-gun frigate?' cried Bonden, angrier still. 'But then,' he went on in quite another tone, low and confidential, 'when we're ashore, sometimes we're a little at sea, if you understand me, sir. Which, being as straight as a die, we sometimes believe them quick-talking coves are dead honest too, with their patent knees and braces and goddam silver-mines, pardon the expression, sir. Now 'tis natural for any captain to think his command the finest ship that ever was: but sometimes, being stuffed up with knees and braces, we might perhaps think her finer than is quite reason, and believe it and say it too, without a lie.'

'*Leopard*,' called the master of that fine American bark the *Asa Foulkes*, who recognized the boat.

'*Asa Foulkes*,' replied Bonden, with an offensive variation of the name and a scornful laugh.

'Do you lack for any hands? We got three Liverpool Irishmen aboard, and a quartermaster that ran from the *Melampus*. Why don't you come and press them?' Merriment aboard the bark, and cries of 'Bloody old *Leopard*.'

'From the look of your topsides and your harbour stow,' said Bonden, now abreast of the *Asa Foulkes*, 'you ain't got a single seaman in the barky for us to take. My advice to you, old Boston Bean, is to go right back to Sodom, Massachusetts, by foot, and try to find a real sailorman or two.' A general roar from the *Asa Foulkes*, a bucket of slush thrown in the direction of the boat, and Bonden, who had never at any time looked at the American, said, 'That settled his hash. Now where to first, sir?'

'I must go to the apothecary, the hospital, and the American consul. Pray choose the point most nearly equidistant from all three.'

To this point, no later than Bonden, from long experience, had expected him to be, Stephen returned, bearing a parrot for the carpenter. He was followed by two slaves carrying drugs enough to dose the whole ship's company for eighteen months, and by two nuns with an iced pudding wrapped in wool. 'Ten thousand thanks again, dear mothers,' he said. 'This is for your poor; and pray for the soul of Stephen Maturin, I beg.' To the slaves, 'Gentlemen, here is for your trouble: commend me to the esteemed apothecary.' To Bonden, 'Now homewards, if you please, and ply your oars like Nelson at the Nile.'

When they cleared the inner harbour and the roadstead came into sight, he said, 'Now there is the odd boat quite close to our *Leopard.*' Bonden replied with an amiable grunt, no more: and after a quarter of a mile Stephen went on: 'In all my sea-going experience, I have never seen so odd a boat.' At the thought of all Dr Maturin's sea-going experience, Bonden gave a secret smile, and said, 'Is that so, sir?'

'It is like a brig, with two masts, you understand. But they are arsy-versy.'

Bonden looked over his shoulder. His expression changed. He took two powerful strokes, and as the boat glided along he stared again. 'She's one of our frigates, and she's lost her foremast at the partners: jury bowsprit; and her head's all ahoo. *Nymph*, thirty-two, if I do not mistake: a fine sailer.'

He did not mistake. The *Nymph*, Captain Fielding, from the Cape for Jamaica with dispatches and so home, had run into a Dutch seventy-four, the *Waakzaamheid*, in a blinding rainstorm just north of the line. There had been a brief action in which the *Nymph*'s foremast had been wounded; but by carrying all the sail she dared she had clean outrun her much heavier opponent in a two days' chase. By the time the Dutchman hauled his wind and gave over, the *Nymph* was close in with the shore, and a little later a freakish gust off Cape Branco took her aback, bringing her foremast by the board. Fortunately the Dutchman was quite out of sight, last seen steering south, chasing no more; and Captain Fielding had brought his ship down to Recife to refit before continuing his journey.

Fielding was senior to Jack. In his opinion no good purpose could be served by whipping up a jury foremast and putting to sea in company with the *Leopard* to search for the *Waakzaamheid*. Apart from the fact that the *Nymph* was carrying dispatches, which prohibited her from going in chase of wild geese, the Dutchman sailed faster than the *Leopard*, though not so fast as the *Nymph*, and Fielding had no wish to lie there being clawed by a seventy-four while the *Leopard* came lumbering up; particularly as she was so short-handed as to be little use when she got there. Nor could he spare the *Leopard* any hands: Aubrey would find plenty at the Cape. And were he in Aubrey's place, he would give the *Waakzaamheid* a wide berth; she was a fair sailer, commanded by a determined fellow who understood his business, and she was well-manned – she had given the *Nymph* three broadsides in little over five minutes. Their parting was rather cold, although Jack did regale him with the greater part of Stephen's pudding, an act, which as Jack himself observed, had few equals in the course of naval history, the present heat and all circumstances being borne in mind.

'For my part, I rejoice,' said Stephen, as the *Leopard* fished her best bower and America faded on the western sky. 'I had messages of some consequence, and that swift-sailing, cautious *Nymph* will carry my duplicates much faster than the originals.'

K nowing of the presence of a hostile ship of the line in the same ocean, the *Leopard* redoubled her attention to gunnery. Although the presence was remote and almost entirely theoretical, since from the *Nymph*'s account the *Waakzaamheid* must be something in the nature of five hundred miles to the south and west, the *Leopard*'s guns rattled in and out every evening after quarters, and often in the forenoon watch as well.

'For, do you see,' said the commander, 'now that we have cleaned up the Mauritius and La Réunion, a Dutch ship in these waters can mean only one thing: she must be intended to reinforce Van Daendels in the Spice Islands. And to get there, she must steer much the same course with ours, at least to the height of the Cape.' He had not the slightest wish to meet her. In the course of his career he had taken on greater odds, but the *Waakzaamheid* was a Dutchman, and Jack Aubrey had been present at Camperdown, a midshipman stationed on the lower deck of the *Ardent*, sixty-four, when the *Vrijheid* killed or wounded one hundred and forty-nine of his shipmates out of four hundred and twenty-one and reduced the *Ardent* to something very near a wreck: this, and all that he had heard of the Dutch, filled him with respect for their seamanship and their fighting qualities. 'You may call them Butterboxes,' he said, 'but they thumped us most cruelly not so very long ago, and burnt the Chatham yard and God knows how many ships in the Medway.' He would have been circumspect, where a Dutchman was concerned, had the odds been even: as they stood, they were as seventy-four to fifty-two against him in guns, and far more in men. He did his best to lessen the disparity by improving the speed and accuracy of the *Leopard*'s fire; but he could not hope to fight all his guns and manoeuvre her at the same time until the Cape should furnish him with a hundred and thirty hands, far less board and carry a determined enemy of the size of the *Waakzaamheid*. Of the prime seamen who had served with him before and who were used to his notions of how a gun should be handled, he had enough to provide captains and crews for one full upper-deck broadside: for the moment the lower deck had to do as best it could with the rest, with thin crews so supplemented with Marines that no soldiers would be available for small-arms fire until the invalids should recover; and these crews were so disposed that the least efficient were amidships, in what was known as the slaughterhouse because in action most of the enemy's fire was concentrated upon it. The weaker crews on the lower deck: for although her twenty-four-pounders could bite hard, sending a ball through two feet of solid oak at seven hundred yards, the *Leopard* carried her lower gun-ports no higher from the water than the other ships of her class, and if she were brought to action with much of a sea running, they would necessarily be closed on the leeward side, and perhaps on the windward too.

He had a good gunner in Mr Burton, one who thoroughly agreed with his Captain's practice of firing live, rather than confining himself to the dumb-show of running the pieces in and out. He had a dozen excellent captains, and he was perfectly seconded by Babbington on the lower deck, and by Moore the Marine; while the older midshipmen, who loved this kind of exercise, with its bang and briskness and excitement and competition, paid great attention to their divisions. But Grant was a dead weight. His service had been limited to transports, harbour duties, and exploration, and through no fault of his own he had never been in battle; he was a good navigator, but he could not know the inward nature of a fight at sea: nor did he seem willing to learn. It was as though he did not really believe in the possibility of action or the need for anything but formal preparation for it; and his attitude, his tolerably obvious attitude, infected many of those whose idea of battle was as hazy as his own – a general smoke and thunder at close quarters, with the Royal Navy winning as a matter of course.

After one or two private interviews with Grant which did not succeed in shaking the older man's obstinate self-complacency, in spite of his perfectly correct 'Yes, sir' at every pregnant pause, Jack wrote him down as just one more burden to be borne, by no means inconsiderable, but far less important than the herd of landsmen on the lower deck; and he carried on with the task of turning the *Leopard* into a fighting-machine as efficient as his means would allow, entirely changing his methods, suiting them to his strange little crew and, as he put it himself, 'cutting his coat according to his cloth.'

The forenoon sessions took place in the great cabin itself. Here there stood Jack's own brass nine-pounders, ordinarily housed fore and aft, to take up less room. They were part of the spoils of Mauritius, light, beautiful guns, and he had had them carefully rebored to take English nine-pound shot: he had also had them painted a dull chocolate-brown, to do away with some of the incessant polishing that took up so much time in a ship – time that could be far better spent. But this humane, sensible move ran counter to some deep naval instinct: Killick and his mates, taking advantage of a few small chips in the paint round the lock and the touch-hole, had gradually increased the area of visible brass until the guns now blazed from muzzle to pomellion. Now Jack spoilt the beauty of the great cabin by causing Mr Gray to build the equivalent of a deep wing-transom, with the corresponding knees, massive enough to withstand the recoil of his brass nine-pounders, so that by removing the stern-windows as though to ship deadlights, together with some of the gingerbread-work from the gallery, he could use them as chasers, firing from a higher station than the more usual gunroom ports. And this he did almost every day under his own immediate supervision, bringing in different teams, sometimes of officers alone, led by himself – how he loved pointing the gun – sometimes of midshipmen, but more often of the two extremes of the lower deck, the first and second captains on the one hand, and the boobies, the downright creeping lubbers on the other, in the hope that the best might grow better and the worst learn the exercise at least well enough to be of some use to the ship. This firing of the stern-chase had the great advantage of allowing him to shoot at empty casks bobbing away in the wake, so that those who aimed them could see the results of their aiming at various ranges; and all this without heaving the ship to for the boats to tow out a target.

On the other hand, it made a shambles of the cabin. Most Captain's stewards would have cried out at seeing their housekeeping blasted to every wind that blew, their cherished brass, paintwork, checkered sailcloth, deck, windows, desecrated as though by battle; and Killick, old in insubordination and dumb insolence, indulged for old times' sake and grown tyrannical, was perhaps the most crabbed steward in any rated ship, an Attila to the swabbers and ship's boys under his sway, and a source of anxiety to his Captain. But Jack was happily inspired to invite him to touch off the first discharge, and after that the glory of the cabin might go hang – deck-rings and metal slides might wreck the checkered cloth, garlands of hammered shot, wet swabs, and sooty worms might ruin the unvarying symmetry of this drawing-room, adorned with swords on one hand and with telescopes on the other, the pistols forming a tasteful sunburst in between and the chairs and tables always just so, taking their bearings from the mahogany wine-cooler by the starboard quarter-gallery door, and the whole place might reek of powder-smoke – Killick was there, eyeing the slow-match that was to fire the gun, much as a terrier might eye a rat or a groom his bride. A single shot would make him civil, and even obliging, for a week.

Apart from this banging and belching of morning fire, life aboard quickly resumed the agreeable monotony of a man-of-war on passage. Jack and Stephen returned to their music, sometimes playing out on the stern-gallery in the warm night, with the wake ploughing a line of phosphorescence far behind them in the velvety sea, flecked with the distorted images of the southern stars, while the steady trade sang overhead. Sometimes birds, rarely to be identified, would dart at the stern-lanterns, and sometimes a whole acre of the surface would erupt in a brief firework-display as a school of flying-fish escaped from some unseen enemy. The daily routine went on, and although the decks looked rather thin, this thinness, and the presence of so many bald-headed languid invalids, soon began to seem the natural order of things: what is more, the bald heads, shaved in the fever, grew first a bristly cap, and then a dense upright fur, so that they looked less abnormal. Stephen became intimately acquainted with the first lieutenant's carious teeth and indifferent digestion, and with the bosun's ague, first caught at Walcheren; and he wormed the entire midshipmen's berth.

In this same resumption of their former days, he returned to his walks with Mrs Wogan, while the surviving convicts exercised upon the forecastle. Now they did so with far less restraint than in the early days; the men voluntarily heaved at the pumps and lent a hand with the simpler tasks – they no longer belonged to an entirely foreign, reprobated world, and sometimes they received illicit gifts of tobacco.

The slight stock of fresh provisions from Recife soon disappeared; iced puddings were an insubstantial dream; the wardroom went back to its ordinary fare – less monotonous than that of the lower deck, but still pretty tedious, with the inept catering of young Mr Byron, whose notion of pudding varied only from figgy-dowdy to plum-duff and back again. And in the wardroom Grant began to assert his authority as president of the mess, doing his utmost to abolish oaths and bawdy and to discourage cards, thereby coming into conflict with Moore, a jovial soul, who feared he must be reduced to total silence and inactivity.

Throughout the unsleeping four and twenty hours the watches changed, the log was heaved, the winds, the course, and the distance run recorded: none of the distances was spectacular, since the breezes, though in general steady, hung so far to the east of south that the *Leopard* was perpetually as close-hauled as she could be, her bowlines twanging taut; and still she trailed her mass of doldrum weed.

An uneventful series of days, an ordered monotony spaced by bells, among them that which the loblolly boy pealed daily at the foremast, when those who felt pale reported to the surgeon.

'At this present rate, we shall exhaust our venereals as well,' he said, washing his hands. 'How many does that make, Mr Herapath?'

'Howlands is the seventh, sir,' replied his assistant.

'The gaol-fever might fox me,' said Stephen, 'but the *lues venerea* never can: pox in all its forms is as familiar to the seafaring medical man as the common cold to his colleague by land. These are all recent infections, Mr Herapath; and since our Gipsy woman is continence itself, sure the only source is Mrs Wogan's servant Peg. For you are to observe that although a protracted voyage may bring about a wonderful increase in sodomitical practices, these are the wounds of Venus herself. A fireship is among us, and her unlucky name is Peggy Barnes.'

Stephen brushed this aside. 'How do they get at her? and how can she be rendered chaste? A serricunnium, a belt for that purpose, is not provided in ships of the fourth rate; nor, perhaps, in others. And this, when you reflect upon the number of women to be found in some vessels with captains of a different humour, is a strange lacuna. Our captain, however, obeys the letter of the law, happy to do so, since he maintains that women are a source of discord in a ship. Perhaps the sailmaker, or the armourer, that ingenious man . . . I shall speak to the Captain.'

Stephen did indeed speak to the Captain, and it so happened that he did so at a moment when Jack was particularly inflamed against the sex. 'They make a sorry heart, an heavy countenance, a wounded mind, weak hands, and feeble knees,' he said, to Stephen's unspeakable astonishment. 'And that is in the Bible: I read it myself. Damn them all. There are only three women aboard, but they might as well be a troop of basilisks.'

'Basilisks, joy?'

'Yes. You must know all about basilisks: they spread pests by glaring at people. There is this Peggy of yours, that will reduce the whole ship's company to a parcel of noseless, toothless, bald paralytics unless she is headed up in a barrel with no bunghole. There is your vile witch of a Gipsy, that has told one of the Portuguese hands the ship is unlucky, so unlucky that the two-headed fetch of a murdered sheriff's man haunts the bowsprit netting: all the people have heard

the tale, and the morning watch saw this ghostly bum sitting on the
spritsail yard, mopping and mowing at them – every hand on the
forecastle came racing aft, tumbling over one another like a herd of
calves, never stopping until they reached the break of the quarterdeck, and Turnbull could not get the headsails trimmed. And then
there is your Mrs Wogan. Mr Fisher was with me just before you
came. He thinks it would be far more proper for the chaplain to walk
her on the poop rather than the surgeon or the surgeon's young man.
His admonition would have more weight if he had the sole control
of her movements; her reputation would no longer suffer from certain rumours that are current; and most of the other officers were of
his opinion. How do you like that, Stephen, eh?' Stephen spread his
hands. 'Now I may not see much farther through a brick wall than
the next man,' Jack went on, 'but I know damned well that for all his
black coat, that man wants to come to her bed – I only speak to you
like this, Stephen, because you are directly called in question. Since I
have a respect for the cloth, all I said was, that I did not relish having
my orders canvassed in the wardroom or anywhere else, that it was
not customary in the service to dispute a captain's decisions nor to
carry dirty rumours to the cabin, and that I expected my directions
to be promptly obeyed.'

'Man is born to trouble, as the sparks fly upward: that too is in the
Bible, Jack,' said Stephen. 'I shall do what I can to lay the pox and the
ghost. I also bring you some consolation, brother. The young Marine,
Lieutenant Howard: he plays the flute.'

'The German flute has been the bane of the Navy ever since I was a
youngster,' said Jack. 'Every midshipmen's berth, every gunroom, and
every wardroom I have ever lived in has had half a dozen blockheads
squeaking away at the first half of Richmond Hill. And after what he
said about Mrs Wogan, Howard is not a man I should ever willingly
entertain, or admit to my table other than in the service way.'

'When I say he plays, I mean that he plays to calm the billows
and to still brute-beasts in their fury. Such control! Such modula-
tion! Such legato arpeggios! Albini could do no better – nay, not so

well. The man I cannot heartily commend: his lungs and lips alone I praise. When he plays, that brutish military face, the staring oyster eye, the – but I must not speak unkindly – all disappear behind this pure stream of sound. He is possessed. When he puts down his flute, the glow departs; the eye is dead once more; the vulgar face returns.'

'I am sure it is as you say, Stephen; but you must forgive me – I could take no pleasure in playing with a man who could speak so ill of women.'

'Women are not without defence, however,' reflected Stephen, passing forward along the orlop to remonstrate with Peggy and Mrs Boswell for their thoughtless conduct. Herapath had recently led Louisa Wogan down from the poop, and through the scuttle in her cabin door came the painfully familiar sound of a man being passed under the harrow.

Though passionate, the voice was low; in the most fluent French it told Herapath that he was a fool, that he understood nothing, nothing at all – he had never understood anything, at any time. He had not the least notion of tact, discretion, delicacy, or sense of timing. He abused his position most odiously. Who did he think he was?

Stephen shrugged and walked on. 'Salubrity Boswell,' he said, 'what are you about? How comes a woman of your sound judgment to act so thoughtlessly as to tell a mariner he is in an unlucky ship? Do not you know, ma'am, that your mariner is the most superstitious soul that ever breathed? That by telling him his vessel is unlucky, even haunted, you cause him to neglect his duty, to hide away in the dark when he should adjust the sails and pull the ropes? That in consequence the ship becomes indeed unlucky – it turns upon the unseen rock, it bursts, it is taken all aback. And then where are *you*, ma'am? Where is your baby, tell?'

He was told that if people crossed her palm with false silver, they must expect a dark fortune for their pains: he left her sullen and remote, muttering crossly at her pack of cards, but he knew that his words had gone home, and that what little she could do to remove the phantom bailiff would be done. It would not be enough, however: the ghostly bum would probably resist all common exorcism.

'Bonden,' he said, 'pray remind me: where is the bowsprit netting?'

'Why, sir,' said Bonden, smiling, ''tis where we stow the foretopmast staysail and the jib.'

'I shall desire you to carry me there, after quarters and the exercise.'

Bonden smiled no more. 'Oh sir, it will be dark by then,' he said.

'Never mind. You will procure a little lantern. Mr Benton will be happy to lend you a little lantern.'

'I doubt it would ever do, sir. 'Tis right out there, beyond the head, right plumb over the sea, if you understand me, with nothing to clap on to, bar the horses. It would be far too dangerous for you, sir: you would surely slip. The most dangerous place in the barky, with all them old sharks, a-ravening just below.'

'Stuff, Bonden. I am an old sea-hand, a quadrimane. We shall meet here, by this – what is its name?'

'The knighthead, sir,' said Bonden, in a low, despondent voice.

'Exactly so – the knighthead. Do not forget the lantern, if you please. I must rejoin my colleague.'

In fact neither Bonden nor Dr Maturin was at the rendezvous, let alone the lantern. The coxswain sent his respectful duty by a boy: the state of the Captain's gig was such that Bonden could not be allowed the least liberty. And Stephen's interview with his colleague Herapath lasted far into the night.

'Mr Herapath,' he began, 'the Captain invites us both to dine with him tomorrow, to meet Mr Byron and Captain Moore – come, we must run. There is not a minute to be lost.'

The urgent beating of the drum for quarters made him utter the last words in a shriek, and they hurried aft to their action station in the cockpit. There they sat while the ritual went on far above their heads, and they sat in silence. Herapath made one or two attempts at a remark, but affected nothing. Stephen looked at him from behind a shading hand; even by the light of the single purser's dip, the young man was very pale: pale and woebegone. His hair lank and dispirited, his eyes quite sunk.

'There go the great guns,' said Stephen at last. 'I believe we may walk off. Come and take a glass in my abode: I have some whiskey from my own country.'

He sat Herapath in one corner of his triangular cabin, among the jars of squids in alcohol, and observed, 'Littleton, the hernia in the starboard watch, caught a fine coryphene this afternoon; I mean to spend all the daylight hours dissecting it, so that the flesh may still be palatable when I am done. I will therefore beg you to look after our fair prisoner again.'

Stephen had his own curious limits. He had had no intention of inviting the young man in order to loosen his tongue with drink, nor of provoking his confidence. Yet had that been his design, he could not have succeeded better. Having choked over the unaccustomed drink – 'it was very good – as grateful as the finest Cognac – but if he might be allowed a little water, he would find it even better' – Herapath said, 'Dr Maturin, quite apart from my regard and esteem, I am under great obligations to you, and I find it painful to be uncandid – systematically disingenuous. I must tell you that I have long been acquainted with Mrs Wogan. I stowed away to follow her.'

'Did you so? I am happy to learn that she has a friend aboard: it would be a dismal voyage, all alone; and a more dismal landing, too. But, Mr Herapath, is it wise to tell the world of your connection? Does it not perhaps compromise the lady, and risk making her position more difficult still?'

Herapath entirely agreed: Mrs Wogan herself had urged him to take the utmost care that it should not be known, and she would be furious if she knew he had told Dr Maturin. Dr Maturin, however, was the only person in the ship in whom he would ever confide; and he did so now, partly because the continual dissimulation sickened him, and partly because he wished to be excused from attending her at present; they had had a very painful disagreement, and she thought he was forcing himself upon her, using his position to that end. 'And yet at first,' he said, 'she was so very glad to see me. It was like our first days together, long, long ago.'

'So yours is an acquaintance of some standing, I collect?'

'Oh yes, indeed. We first met during the peace, aboard the Dover packet from Calais. I had finished my work with the Père Bourgeois – '

'Père Bourgeois the sinologist? The China missionary?'

'Yes, sir. And I was returning to England, meaning to take ship for the States after a week or two in Oxford. I saw that she was alone and in some distress – impertinent fellows all about her – and she was so good as to accept my protection. Very soon we found that we were both Americans, and that we knew several of the same families; that we had both been educated mainly in France and England, and that we were neither of us rich. She had recently disagreed with Mr Wogan – I believe he had gone to bed to her maid – and she was travelling with no very clear end in mind, a few jewels, and very little money. Fortunately my half-yearly allowance was waiting for me at my father's agent in London, so we set up house in a cottage some way out of the town, at Chelsea. Those were days of a happiness I cannot hope to describe, nor shall I attempt to do so, for fear of spoiling it. The cottage had a garden, and we calculated that if we were to plant it, we could hold out, in spite of the cost of the furniture, at least until we heard from my father, in whose generosity I placed all my hopes. My books followed me from Paris, and in the evenings, after my gardening, I taught Louisa the elements of literary Chinese. But our calculations proved mistaken, for although the market-gardeners all around the cottage were very kind, giving us plants and even showing me the right way to dig, we had not harvested our first crop of beans, and Louisa had not learnt about a hundred radicals, before men came and took away her small spinet. I do not know how it was, but money seemed to vanish away, in spite of all our care. Mr Wogan had been an expansive man, in the lavish southern way and perhaps Louisa had never learnt to keep house on very little: she too was born in Maryland, with a troop of blacks about her; and in those states they do not look upon a shilling as we do in Massachusetts, and there is not the same almost religious dread of debt. Then again, having some friends in London, both English and American, she was obliged to have clothes to receive them in – she had left everything behind. They came more and more often, and they brought their friends to what they called our bower; interesting men like the Coulsons, and Mr Lodge of Boston, and Horne Tooke, whose conversation was a delight. But even a simple dinner is a costly affair in England, compared with France or America, and our difficulties grew and grew.

'And I am afraid I was a dull companion. I had seen very little of the world; my life had always been very quiet; and although she was sensible of the beauty of my poets' work, she could not share my pleasure in the China of the T'ang emperors. Nor could I share her passionate eagerness for republican doctrines. My father was a Loyalist during the War of Independence, while my mother took the other side, being kin to General Washington; they lived uneasily together, each trying to convince the other, and I heard so much talk of politics when I was a child, that being unable to reconcile their views, I dismissed both. It seemed to me that a king and a president were equally disagreeble and remote and unimportant and I conceived an aversion for all political discourse. At all events, she took to seeing more and more of her radical friends in London: some of them were wealthy and high-placed, and she told me candidly that she loved their train of life.

'By the time I heard from my father our affairs were very near their crisis: I could not have withstood the tradesmen's importunities another week, and indeed, if it had not been for the good forbearing baker, we must have gone hungrier than in fact we did. But my father's letter brought no more than a draught on his agent to bear my charges to America, and a direct order to return at once. I had laid the position fairly before him, and he replied with a frankness equal to my own. I had flattered myself that my description of the feelings I entertained for Louisa, and their everlasting nature, might overcome the rigour of his Episcopalian principles: I was mistaken. He disapproved the whole connection: first on moral grounds; secondly

because the lady was a Romanist; and thirdly because of her political views, which were abhorrent to him. He was surprisingly well
informed by his London correspondents, and he had made enquiries
in Baltimore among our common friends. Even if the lady were not
married, he would never consent to such a match. Upon the duty I
owed him, I was to return at once. And in a postscript he added that
when I called upon his agent to present the draught, the agent would
hand me a packet that I was to bring to the States with me, taking the
utmost care of it.

'I knew what the packet would contain. As a Loyalist, my father
had suffered heavy losses through his support of King George: he
had been obliged to retire to Canada for some years, and it was only
because of my mother's convictions and her connection with General Washington that he was allowed to return. The British government had undertaken to indemnify the Loyalists, and after very, very
long delays my father's claim was, in part, admitted. From time to
time I had heard of the progress of the case from his agent; and now
the payment was become due. I opened the packet, discounted the
bills, and we removed to London itself, taking furnished apartments
in Bolton Street.

'My father's money lasted little more than half a year: we lived very
cheerfully in the style that Louisa liked, and we entertained. Louisa's
circle of acquaintance grew wider still. When no more than a hundred pounds was left, she wrote two pieces and some verse, which
I copied for the playhouses and the booksellers. She had a pretty
turn that way, and they had some success. At the time I had hopes of
being admitted to a mission to Canton as interpreter: a knowledge of
Chinese was my only qualification for earning a living, yet it was an
unusual one, and I was told that I should be highly paid. But the mission was abandoned and literary success scarcely finds a couple in the
necessities of life; our last guinea melted; and Louisa vanished. She
had often told me that for literary and political reasons it was necessary for her to cultivate and indeed to visit some men whom neither
she nor I particularly esteemed: she had often paid these visits, some-

times of a week or more; and now I heard that she was living under
the protection of one of these men, a Mr Hammond.

'I did not attempt to describe my happiness; nor shall I say anything of my extreme distress. But she was not unkind; settled unkind-
ness or rancour is not in Louisa's nature. After some time she learnt
where I was living, and she sent me money. During that year and the
next she travelled a great deal, but when she was in London she would
find me out and sometimes give me a meeting in the park, or even in
my room. She told me of her various liaisons with the candour of a
friend – she always, except at that moment of parting, treated me as
a friend, and we were very well together. On one of these occasions,
when she found me extremely ill, she said I might accompany her as
a secretary: I was, however, to say nothing of our intimacy. She was
then living in a small, discreet, but perfectly elegant house behind
Berkeley Street, and she had a salon where I saw numbers of men
remarkable for their understanding, their rank, or their wealth, or
sometimes all three. The conversation was sprightly, more nearly in
the French manner than anything I had heard in England: it was rarely
improper, but upon the whole they were, I gathered, a loose-living set.
Mr Burdett, I recall; a fat melancholy duke; Lord Breadalbane. But
there were others: I remember Mr Coleridge and Mr Godwin – they
were outside the usual set, however. It was not only men that came,
for Mrs Standish used often to be there, and Lady Jersey, with quite a
band of her friends. Yet men predominated, and it was in her boudoir
that she used to receive those who were closest to her such as John
Harrod, the banker, John Aspen of Philadelphia, whom Mr Jay had
left behind, and the elder Coulson – he was their chief. They used to
come in through a door from another house beyond the garden.'

'You are the most wretched companion for a conspirator that ever
yet was seen,' thought Stephen, pouring out more whiskey, 'unless,
indeed, you are a prodigy of depth and cunning.' Aloud he said, 'I
knew a Mr Joseph Coulson, an American, in London. He talked to
me of politics, and of Irish feelings on independence, of the Irish in

the States, and of Irish officers serving the British crown. But mostly of politics, of European politics.'

'That is the man, and he had a much younger brother Zachary, who was at school with me. Joseph would perpetually be talking politics: I could not listen. And he often asked me too about the state of feeling in the country; he said it affected stocks and shares. But I could never tell him, although he asked me to pay attention to what people said. A most intelligent man, apart from his politics: I came to know him very well, because he gave me endless papers to copy, and letters to carry about the town. From his airs of mystery, and from his telling me to make sure I was not followed, I assumed he must be a man of pleasure, like so many who frequented the house.'

He stared into his glass, and Stephen said, 'I am afraid that your position must have been painful beyond expression.'

'It had its distressing sides. But my chief purpose was accomplished: I was often in the same room with Louisa, and I asked little more. What is called possession was not unimportant to me, but her friendship was of infinitely more account. Her friendship and her presence. I sometimes wondered that she should choose such protectors as those I saw about her, but apart from a few rare exceptions in the early days, I never hated them; nor could I ever find it in my heart to condemn her, whatever she might do. Perhaps it was base in me: I think I should despise it in another man. Yet I have little doubt that if still further baseness were required of me, I should commit it.'

Stephen said, 'I should rather speak of fortitude. May I take it, then, that you are not disturbed by the rumours connecting Mrs Wogan and myself? You must have heard them, in the midshipmen's berth.'

'No. Partly because I do not believe them, but even more because the word possession is so very foolish when it is applied to a woman as entire as Louisa. As for fortitude . . . yes, it did call for some fortitude at first, in spite of all my reasoning: but I had a friend with – with heavier guns, shall I say, than philosophy. Early in my study of Chinese, I met a man who introduced me to the pleasures of opium, to the pleasure and the consolation of opium. I was thoroughly acquainted with its powers before I met Louisa, and when my distress pressed very heavily upon me, I had but to smoke two or three pipes for it to grow much lighter, for my troubled mind to admit philosophy, and for a calm, comprehensive understanding to pervade my being. My opium also allayed both sexual and physical hunger: with my pipe and lamp at hand, it was easy for me to be a Stoic.'

'Did not you find any inconvenience? We read of loss of appetite, emaciation, want of the vital spark, habituation, and even a most degrading slavery.'

'In general I did not; but then in general I indulged no more than once or twice a week, like my initiator and most practiced smokers I have known – once or twice a week, as a man might go to a concert or the play, except that I believe my concerts and my plays were richer, deeper by far, and more various than any that are to be found in objective life: dreams, phantasms, and such an accession of apparent wisdom as no words of mine can encompass. As for the vital spark, I would work twelve or fourteen hours at a stretch without inconvenience; and as for want of virility, why, sir, if it were not disrespectful to you, I should laugh. Yet on the other hand, in the extremity of my unhappiness I abused my pipe, and then all that you have spoken of falls far below the truth, for in addition to the slavery and the degradation the whole of life becomes a waking horror. The dreams invade the day, and from enchanting, they turn horrible: they do so by some minute, subtle variation in tone that appalls one's mind. And the same happens to the colours – for I should have told you that my dreams were infinitely full of colour, and colour also invested the characters that I read or wrote, filling them with a far greater significance, one that I could apprehend but could not name. Yet now these colours, by a quarter-tone of difference, grew more and more sinister, threatening, and evil. They terrified me. For instance, my window looked out on to a blank wall, and on the cracked plaster a little flicker of violet would grow and glow with such a hellish significance that I cowered on the floor. I was in this state of lucid

horror when Louisa took me home to be her secretary. There, with
her at hand almost every day, I recovered. That did call for a certain
constancy: for a while my need seemed almost intolerably great. But
happily there were at that time no exacerbating circumstances, and I
held firm. At present I can look upon my pipe with a mild, affectionate regard; it is no longer the malignant, evil, necessary monster that
once it was; and I take it – or should I say I took it, since it is now some
five thousand miles away – from its place perhaps once a week, like
the mechanic with his beer-can, for mere pleasure, or when I needed
strong waking endurance for some unusual task or relief in a rare
emergency.'

'Do you tell me, Mr Herapath, that having broke the habit you
were able to return to a moderate, and pleasurable, use of the drug?'

'Yes, sir.'

'And in the intervals, did not you crave? The craving did not
return?'

'No, sir, after the clean break it did not. The opium was my old
accustomed friend again. I could address myself to it when I chose, or
refrain. Had I a supply at present, I should use it as a Sunday indulgence and to endure the tedium of Mr Fisher's sermons; they would
pass in an agreeable and coloured waft, for as no doubt you are aware,
opium plays the strangest tricks with time, or rather with one's per-
ception of its passage. I should also use it at this present juncture, to
mitigate my distress at the misunderstanding between Louisa and
myself. It gives me very great pain to think she should suspect me of
such indelicacy of mind, as to force myself upon her; and it gives me
even greater pain to remember that in a sudden heat I broke out with
vehement reproaches, accusing her, quite falsely, of want of common
kindness and affection, and that I left her in tears. How she will ever
be brought to endure my company again, I cannot tell.'

'Perhaps, Mr Herapath,' said Stephen, 'if you were presently to
return, to make a full acknowledgement of your fault, and to throw
yourself upon her magnanimity, you might yet, in the privacy of her
cabin, find forgiveness. Here is the key. Pray do not forget to return

it tomorrow: you will account for your possession of it however you choose. And you may think it wise, Mr Herapath, never in any circumstances whatsoever to speak of this conversation. Nothing could vex a woman more, no, not the worst, the most patent infidelity. I never shall.'

In his diary he wrote: 'I was most struck by what M. Herapath told me, about his resumption of the drug. He is a most intelligent and, I am persuaded, a most truthful man, and I believe I may follow his example. Mrs Wogan's beauty, her pretty ways, and above all that infinitely diverting laugh, have stirred my amorous propensities these last many days. I have caught myself peering at her bosom, her ear, the nape of her neck, too frequently by far; and I am convinced that in naked fact my beard fell sacrifice to her charms. There is no doubt that duty directs me to my laudanum and thus to chastity. I am pleased with Herapath: he and I are to dine with Jack tomorrow. What will he make of the young man?'

Captain Aubrey did not make much of the young man at all. He told Stephen quite frankly, 'I do not wish to crab your young man, Stephen, but do not you think that you should keep him from the bottle? He cannot hold his wine; he has no head for it. Why, on no more than three glasses, for I absolutely poured him out no more, he was on the point of singing Yankee Doodle. Yankee Doodle, in a King's ship, upon my sacred honour!'

Stephen could not reply. It was true that Herapath, though pale, drawn, and even haggard, as though from prolonged and violent labour, had behaved strangely, laughing for no apparent cause, snapping his fingers, smiling secretly, and answering very much at random and even speaking when he was not spoken to – untimely mirth, facetious expressions, a tendency to sing unasked. He changed the subject: 'These boomkin knottings, Jack: just where may they be?'

'The bowsprit netting, where the ghost is?'

'There is nothing more illiberal than the ostentatious correction of an obvious *lapsus linguae*: of course I meant the bowsprit netting.'

'I will show you,' said Jack, and he led Stephen forward to the head, out on to the bowsprit, to the cap, and set him on the spritsail yard.

'Oh, oh, this is the noble place of the world,' cried he, when he had been carefully turned about: he found himself sitting there, poised high but not too high above the sea, well outside the ship, well beyond her splendid bow-wave, looking back at her from a distance, the *Leopard* perpetually advancing, a gleaming pyramid of sail, and himself as perpetually fleeing backwards over the unbroken water. 'I am enraptured. I could gaze upon this for ever!'

When he could be brought to attend, Jack pointed out the horses – 'A spirited team, indeed!' – and the netting that hung from them.

'So that is the ghost's abode,' said Stephen. 'Had you said a nymph's or even a dryad's, it would have been more appropriate. Now tonight, brother, you must bring me here again, with a couple of blue Bengal lights. I myself have a bottle of holy water. With these I shall lay the ghost: for since the whole thing is stark raving lunacy, it evidently falls within the province of the medical man.'

'At night?' said Jack.

'As soon as it is quite dark,' said Stephen. He glanced at Jack, and said, 'Surely, my dear, you are not so weak as to believe in ghosts?'

'Not at all. I wonder you should make such an uncalled-for suggestion. But it so happens that tonight my time is much taken up; and in any case it occurs to me that since this is a medical matter, as you say yourself, Herapath would be far more suitable in every way.'

When Jack sprang from his cot at dawn, in answer to the rapping on the door, his mind, snatched from a dream of a soft, consenting Mrs Wogan, told him that since the wind had not changed, and since the *Leopard* had not varied from her course nor touched a sail, it must be that God-damned ghost playing off its humours again. But in a flash, in the two strides that separated his cot from the door, his recollection corrected this, presenting a vivid image of Stephen, his blue

lights and his holy water, dowsing the phantom to the satisfaction of
all hands, particularly the papists among them (a good third of the
crew) – Mr Fisher's angry cry of Mumbo-Jumbo, Stephen's perhaps
unfortunate reply of Venus-Wenus – the untroubled demeanour of
the hands sent into the bowsprit netting a few moments later. 'Good
morning, Mr Holles,' he said to the midshipman.

'Good morning, sir. Mr Grant's duty, and there is a ship fine on the
larboard bow.'

'Thank you, Mr Holles. I shall be on deck directly.'

Directly it was: trousers alone, and his long hair streaming. He
leant far out over the windward rail, and there she lay, almost stern-
on, but her masts sufficiently out of line to show all three, her topsails
nicking the red rim of the sun as it rose.

'Topgallant halliards,' he cried. 'Windward braces. Clew up, clew
up, there. Clap on to the buntlines.' And in an angry aside to the lieutenant, 'For God's sake, Mr Grant, don't you know enough to take in
your topgallants in such a case?' Then aloud, very much aloud, 'All
hands, all hands to wear ship.'

'The cursed old woman,' he said, as he thrust through the hurrying
seamen, the swabs, holystones, and buckets that littered the deck, and
ran up to the maintop like a boy. 'A matter of minutes, and he sends
to wake me.'

The first thing a cruising captain knew was that if he possibly
could he must see and not be seen, or at least see first. That was why
there were standing orders aboard the *Leopard* to double the lookouts
and send them aloft before dawn, to take advantage of that precious
morning glimpse. If those topgallants had vanished at the moment of
the hail, the *Leopard* might have passed unnoticed. Even as it was the
strange sail might not have picked her up, the *Leopard* being far to
the west, where the night still lingered, and a certain haze.

He climbed higher as the *Leopard* wore smoothly round and
steadied – Grant could be trusted to do that, at all events – and he
stared at the remote stranger, fading fast as the *Leopard* stood from
her, until he was blinded by the sun. On deck once more he held his

hand to his eye, seeing nothing but a blazing orange ball, and said, 'Who first saw her?'

A young able seaman came running aft, looking nervous, and touched his knuckle to his forehead. 'Well done, Dukes,' said Jack. 'You have damned good eyes.'

He went below to put on more clothes. The morning was brisk, as was to be expected, since the *Leopard* was now well south of Capricorn and within a day of the cold currents and the vast chilly zone before the westerlies. And as he dressed the thoughts streamed through his mind. By way of data, he had very little: she was a ship, that was certain, though of what force or nature he could not tell. He was almost sure that she had been in the act of shaking a reef out of her topsails: Indiamen and Dutchmen and some Royal Navy captains had a comfortable way of reefing them at sunset. But this year's Indiamen should have reached or passed the Cape two months ago, and any stray or extra ship was most unlikely to have crossed the line so far west as to bring her here. She was not a whaler, of that he was sure. She might be an American for the far east; she might possibly belong to the Royal Navy; but the strongest likelihood was that he had just seen the *Waakzaamheid*.

'Forewarned is forearmed,' he said to Stephen at breakfast.

'That is a very fine thought,' said Stephen, 'and strikingly original: pray, when did it come to you?'

'Oh very well, very well. But if you had said it in Latin or Greek or Hebrew you would triumph for half an hour together, crowing over those who can only express themselves like plain honest Christians: and yet it would be all one, you know. Should you like to be explained the position to?'

'If you please: the moment I have finished this piece of toast.'

'Here we are, now,' said Jack, pointing to a spot on the chart about two-thirds of the way from South America to the tip of Africa, 'not far from the pitch of the Cape. We shall still have the trade for some time, but very soon, probably today, we shall come into the cold current setting west, where the trade grows weaker – you might find

some of your albatrosses even before we get to the variable breezes
this side of the true westerlies.'

'I saw a pintado just before I came below.'

'Give you joy, Stephen. And here is the stranger, to windward, as
you see. Now if he is the Dutchman, and I am bound to reckon on
the worst, he is likely to make all the southing he can, to reach the
forties as soon as possible, run well clear of the Cape, and so north
and east for the Indies. Even if he were an enterprising fellow, with a
well-found, clean ship full of seamen, he would scarcely attempt the
Mozambique channel, not with our cruisers off the Mauritius; yet on
the other hand . . .' Jack went on thinking aloud, much as Dr Maturin
might have worked out a diagnosis on the person of a mute colleague,
and Stephen's attention wandered. He had a perfect confidence in
Jack's ability to solve these problems: if Jack Aubrey could not solve
them, nobody could, least of all Stephen Maturin. He secretly read
the obituary in an ancient *Naval Chronicle* that protruded from
under the chart – 'On the 19th of July last, on board the *Theseus*, at
Port Royal, Jamaica, Francis Walwin Eves, midshipman. At St Mary's
Isle, on the 25th of August, Miss Home, eldest daughter of the late
Vice-Admiral Sir George Home, Bart. On the 25th September, at
Richmond, the Hon. Captain Carpenter, of the Royal Navy. Suddenly,
on the 14th of September, Mr Wm Murray, surgeon of His Majesty's dock-yard, Woolwich' – he remembered Murray, a left-handed
man, very able with his knife – 'On the 21st of September, at Rother-
hithe, Lieutenant John Griffiths, of the Royal Navy, aged 67.' Yet at
the same time he heard Jack musing on the duty of this hypothetical Dutch captain to carry his ship to the Indies unscathed, without
dilly-dallying on the way – the wisdom of reefing topsails by night in
such circumstances – the advantages of other modes of conduct –
and suddenly he was brought up with a guilty start by being told,
quite sharply, that 'these neat diagrams of the winds were all very fine
and large, but he must not run away with the idea that nature copied
books, or that as soon as the trades left off, the westerlies set in: above
all in a year like this, when the south-easter did not reach nearly as

far beyond the line as they had had a right to expect – there was no telling just what winds they should find a little farther east or south.'

He said, 'No, Jack: certainly not,' and drifted away again – the melancholy fate of the sixty-seven-year-old lieutenant – until he heard the question, 'But is he the Dutchman at all? That is the whole point.'

'Might you not go and look?' he asked.

'You are forgetting that he has the weather-gage of us, and was I to close him now, he would have a good chance of bringing on an action just as he chose.'

'You do not mean to fight the Dutchman, so?'

'Good heavens, no! What a fellow you are, Stephen. Wantonly tackle a seventy-four, with thirty-two and twenty-four-pounders and six hundred men aboard? If the *Leopard*, half manned and with half the Dutchman's weight of metal, can slip past him to the Cape, then she must do so, with her tail between her legs. Ignominious flight is the order of the day. After the Cape, with a full complement, why, that might be another matter: though it would still be risky, risky . . . Still, after dinner, with only a few hours of daylight left, I shall edge away and see what I can make of him. He was ten miles off at dawn: he will be fourteen by now, with our wearing and standing on. If I close to within four or five, by crowding sail, in the afternoon watch, then even if he sails eight knots to our seven, he cannot get within range before dark: and there is no moon tonight.' After a long, considering pause he went on, 'Lord, Stephen, how often I think of Tom Pullings. It is not only that I could leave everything to him, action or no action, knowing he would do what we have always thought right, but I so often wonder how he does.'

'Aye: it is much the same with me. But I believe our solicitude is misplaced. We landed him in a Catholic country.'

'You mean he might be saved?'

'My concern is with his mortal part. What I mean is, that he will be nursed not by the hags of Haslar, but by Franciscans. Nursing is almost everything in these cases, and there is a world of difference between the mercenary and the religious. The good nuns will bear

with Tom's nervous, fractious symptoms; he will thrive there, where
a common hospital might kill him; and if he should be infected with a
slight touch of genuflexion, sure it will do him no great harm in a service where the sense of rank is carried to such Byzantine extremes.'

This should have been the *Leopard*'s washing day, but no clothes-
lines were rigged. Instead all hands were turned to chipping shot:
the guns, apart from some honeycombing in the upper-deck number
seven, were in an order as perfect as very close attention could make
them, and Mr Burton had filled large quantities of powder; but deep
in their lockers at the bottom of the hold, some of the round-shot had
corroded, as usual. They were roused up by the hundred, so many to
each gun, and the ship clicked and ticked from stem to stern as the
crews carefully tapped off the bosses and flakes of rust, making the
balls as round as they could be and then brushing them lightly with
galley slush.

It was this noise that Stephen explained to Mrs Wogan as he exercised her in the afternoon watch, she wearing a warm spencer and
half-boots, and looking remarkably pink and well, brimming with
high spirits. 'Oh, indeed,' said she, 'I imagined the whole ship had run
mad, and turned tinker to a man. But pray, sir, why are they so eager
to make them round?'

'So that they may fly straight and true, and strike the enemy in his
vital parts.'

'Heavens! Is there an enemy about?' cried Mrs Wogan. 'We shall all
be murdered in our beds.' She began to laugh, low, and then, unable to
contain her mirth, fuller and rounder still. It was not loud, but it carried; and Jack, fixed in the main topgallant crosstrees these last hours,
caught its ghost and smiled. He had had the strange sail in his glass
much of this time, and he was as nearly certain as could be that she was
the *Waakzaamheid*: the broad-sterned, Dutch-built hull was unmistakable. There was just a chance that she might be one of the captured
Dutch men-of-war, but it was most unlikely, since she was making
as much southing as ever she could, whereas a British ship would be
three points off the wind, heading for the Cape. Close-hauled for her

southing under a fair spread of canvas; yet for all her topgallants she was not making much above six knots. Something of a slug, therefore, and slower than the *Leopard* on a wind. Unless ... unless those bowlines were not as taut as they seemed, and her captain was something of a fox, happy to have the *Leopard* come up hand over hand.

'On deck, there,' he hailed.

'Sir?' replied Babbington.

'Heave the log, and send me up a pea-jacket, my flask, and a bite.'

'Oh, please, sir, please may I take it up?' whispered Forshaw.

'Silence,' cried Babbington, cracking him on the head with his speaking-trumpet. 'Seven knots and three fathoms, sir.' And then, 'Mr Forshaw, jump to the cabin, tell Killick pea-jacket, flask and bite, and run up to the crosstrees without taking breath, d'ye hear me?'

'Is it the Captain high up there?' asked Mrs Wogan.

'It is, child; and he has been viewing this strange, perhaps this wicked sail, for a great while now.'

'He sounds like the voice of God,' said Mrs Wogan. Her laugh began again, but she choked it back, and went on, 'I must not be disrespectful, however. Is there really going to be a battle?'

'Never in life, ma'am. This is only what we term a reconnaissance. There will be no battle, at all.'

'Oh,' said she, rather disappointed: and after a while, 'Do not you find it very cold, with only a cotton jacket on? My spencer is lined, but I protest it scarcely keeps me from shivering.'

'This jacket is silk, ma'am. The finest Recife silk, and impervious to the blast.'

'There I must undeceive you, sir. It is cotton, twilled cotton, the kind we call jean; I am afraid the shopman of Recife had no conscience, the dog.'

'It was a woman,' said Stephen, in a low voice, looking at his sleeve.

'I shall knit you a comforter. Is that the ship out in front there? We were looking in the wrong direction.'

There she lay, four or five miles off, hull-up from the *Leopard*'s poop.

'Just so,' said Stephen. 'Exactly where the Captain and I expected it.'

'It looks very small, and a great way off. I wonder that they should make such a coil, hammering away like Gipsies. Tell me, how far are we from the Cape?'

'Something in the nature of a thousand miles, I take it.'

'Lord, a thousand miles! You will certainly have your comforter before that.'

Stephen thanked her, handed her below into the now not unwelcome fug, and returned to the quarterdeck. Everyone was quiet, and all eyes but the helmsman's were fixed on the strange sail, by no means so distant now. She was certainly a two-decker, certainly Dutch, and probably a seventy-four. She held steadily to her course, steering south-south-west with the wind at south-east by east a half east, not pointing up very close for her trim therefore, and sailing rather heavy.

Six knots to the *Leopard*'s seven or rather better; though it was true that the *Leopard* had more sail abroad. At this rate a considerable time must pass before there was much likelihood of communication, unless the Dutchman heaved to or shortened sail. At present he showed no sign of doing either: ploughed steadily on, his bluff bows shouldering the swell, as though the *Leopard* did not exist. Combermere, a signal midshipman, had had little opportunity of exercising his still this voyage; and he was now studying his book with frantic zeal by the open flag-locker, hoping that the yeoman at his side might know more than himself. Most of the other people on the leeward side of the quarterdeck were calm enough: they conversed in low voices, not to disturb the Captain over there, with his telescope poised on the hammocks in their netting. The ship was cleared for action, but this, or something very like it, happened every day at quarters, and there was little sense of extreme urgency. Those who had been in battle, particularly under Captain Aubrey, were rather quiet; those who had not were somewhat talkative. 'Look, look,' cried Mr Fisher, pointing to a fork-tailed petrel, 'there is a swallow. What a good omen! And so far from land.'

'It is a Mother Cary's chicken,' said Grant. 'Procellaria pelagica.'

'Surely it is a fork-tailed petrel,' said Stephen.

'I think not. The fork-tailed petrel is not to be found in these lati-tudes. That is Procellaria pelagica, one of what we call the turbinares.' He went on to tell Stephen a number of facts about birds in general, in a didactic tone that was but too familiar to the wardroom.

'Mr Combermere,' said Jack at last. 'Pennant and colours. Mr Larkin' – to the master by the wheel – 'give her a point and a half.'

The *Leopard* stated that she was a British man-of-war in commis-sion, and fell off a little so that the message should be unmistakable. Half a minute passed, and then the Dutchman stated that he too was a British man-of-war in commission: he backed his foretopsail, hauled up his courses, and lay to, presenting his broadside.

'Private signal,' said Jack. 'And make our number.'

The private signal soared up and broke out. Jack's glass was trained upon the Dutchman's quarterdeck: he saw the answering hoist prepared – rather slow – he saw it move up the signal halliard – rather slow again, with the distance between the ships lessening all this time – and then come down from half way. 'Stand by to start the bowlines,' he said, without removing his eye from the glass. The Dutchman's hoist was moving up again, apparently corrected: up and up, and it broke out. The wrong reply: a mere nonsense of flags heaved out in the hope of a lucky chance. 'Hard over,' he said, and the helms-man spun the wheel. 'Mr Combermere, *enemy of superior force in sight: general chase to south-south-west.* Two guns to leeward, and keep it flying. And let us hope he understands it.'

At the same time the blue ensign vanished from the *Waakzaam-heid*'s peak, her own colours raced up, her side disappeared behind a cloud of smoke, and she put before the wind. A few heart-beats later the deep roar of her guns reached the *Leopard*, and before it had died, close on half a ton of shot, fired at extreme range, tore up the sea. The shots were admirably well grouped, but they fell short at first graze: several carried on, skipping over the swell in long bounds, and three reached their mark, a hole appeared in the maincourse; the tight-packed hammocks just by Mr Fisher's head lurched inwards; and there was a ringing thump somewhere forward.

The *Leopard* had already brought the wind abaft the beam: now it was on her quarter, and she was running fast towards the setting sun. 'Royals and weather studdingsails,' said Jack, and he walked on to the poop to watch the *Waakzaamheid*. She had lost way, lying-to, and although she dropped her courses and sheeted home so briskly that he nodded with approval, and although she too set royals and stud- dingsails, it was long before she began to make up the distance lost. And even then, with this light breeze, she did not gain.

'Mr Grant,' he said, 'come up the fore and main topsail sheets half a fathom: the pitch-barrel to the stern-davits: and pass the word for Mr Burton.'

In the bare, stripped cabin he said to the gunner, 'Now, Mr Bur- ton, we shall have some fun.' The *Leopard*'s speed was lessening, in answer to Jack's order, and with it the distance between the ships. Their pieces, the brass nine-pounders, were already loaded and run out: they stared along the gleaming barrels at the *Waakzaamheid* coming slowly up and throwing a fine bow-wave. The gun-crews crouched on either side; the slow-match smouldered in its tubs; the powder-men stood well behind, holding their cartridges.

'Whenever you please, Mr Burton,' said Jack: and as he spoke there was a flash on the Dutchman's forecastle – his bow-chaser trying the range. 'Handspike, Bill,' murmured the gunner: he eased his quoin to give a slightly greater elevation, paused for the *Leopard*'s pitch, and pulled the lanyard. The gun roared and leaped back under his arched body: the wet swab was already down its throat as the crew hauled the gun inboard, and Burton craned out to see the fall of his shot. A little short, but straight and true.

Jack fired: much the same result. He sent to check the *Leopard*'s way a trifle more, and some minutes later, when the *Waakzaamheid* was nearer by a hundred yards, the gunner made a hole in her foresail with a ricochet. From then on the nine-pounders fired as fast as they could load, bawling away in the rapidly fading light until they were too hot to touch and they jumped clear of the deck at each recoil. They did no great damage, although Jack was almost certain he had got home three times, before the sudden darkness hid their target altogether. The last thing they saw of the *Waakzaamheid* that night was a distant blaze as she yawed and let fly with her full broadsides, firing at the *Leopard*'s flashes, but firing quite in vain.

'House your guns,' said Jack: and raising his voice, 'Let go the barrel. Handsomely now.'

The barrel of burning pitch, with crackers artfully disposed about it, gently touched the sea and floated off, emitting quite lifelike spurts of flame, as though from cannon, as it went.

Out on the quarterdeck he gave the order for the sheets to be hauled aft. He was soaking with sweat, tired, and happy. 'Well, Mr Grant,' he said, 'I do not think we need beat to quarters today. What have you to report?'

'Just the hole in the mainsail, sir, and a little rigging cut; but I am afraid their first broadside damaged our scrollwork: knocked off the larboard leopard's nose.'

'The *Leopard*'s lost her nose,' said Jack to Stephen some time later, when the ship could be allowed a glim behind her deadlights and the dark-lanterns were put out. 'If I were not so fagged, I believe I could make a joke about that, with so much pox aboard,' and he laughed very heartily at the thought of his near approach to wit.

'When am I to be given my supper?' asked Stephen. 'You invited me to partake of toasted cheese, in luxury. I find no luxury, but a shambles: I find no toasted cheese, but a host groping for jocosity about what is in fact a grave and painful disease. Yet stay, I think I do perceive the smell of cheese above the powder-reek and the stench of that vile dark-lantern. Killick, belay there; are you now about the cheese?'

'Which it's just coming up, ain't it?' said Killick angrily. He had not been allowed to fire a single shot, and he muttered something about 'those that worshipped their bellies . . . blowing out their gaffs by day and by night . . . never satisfied.'

'In the interval,' said Stephen, 'might I hope to be told the outcome of all this hurry and banging and disturbance?'

'Why, it is clear enough,' said Jack. 'In half a glass we shall haul our wind, cross the Dutchman's wake, get to windward of him, crowd all the sail we can, and so say farewell. Old Butterbox did everything he could; he very nearly made us uncomfortable, and if there had been a heavier sea he might have succeeded, because a bigger ship has a greater advantage when the sea runs high; and now all that remains to him is to make up the southing he has lost, cracking on regardless if he believes the signal I threw out to our imaginary friends, while we stand on for the Cape, having, I trust, bleared the honest burgher's eye, each of us peacefully carrying on our occasions, diverging farther and farther every watch all through the night, so that by dawn we may well be a hundred miles apart.'

Dawn broke, and once again Jack was knocked up; once again he was torn from the arms of an ideal Mrs Wogan with the news of a ship fine on the larboard bow. This time the *Leopard*'s topgallants had already vanished, but it was little more than a gesture to the conventions of war, because this time the *Waakzaamheid* was a good three miles nearer, perfectly recognizable in spite of the mist hanging over the cold milky sea – hanging and parting in the light air from the east, so that sometimes she almost entirely vanished and sometimes she looked spectral, unnaturally large, as she bore up, spread her wings, and headed for the *Leopard*.

They were already at the edge of the westerly current, and the breeze chopped up the pale surface; but there was nothing of a sea, nothing resembling the great rollers with the hills and dales that so favoured a heavier ship, and by noon the *Leopard*, setting all she could carry and steering south-west, had run the *Waakzaamheid* out of sight.

'May we cry *Io triumphe*?' asked Stephen at dinner. 'It is two hours since she vanished, wallowing in impotent rage.'

'I am not going to cry Io anything at all until we pick up our moorings in Simon's Bay,' cried Jack. 'With Turnbull and Holles here, I did not like to say anything at breakfast, but I do not know that I have ever seen anything so shocking in all my life as that Dutchman at dawn, sitting there to the windward, between us and the Cape. It was exactly as though he had been leaning over my shoulder last night, while I worked out our course. And I am by no means easy in my mind about this morning's performance, neither. It was too far off to be certain, with the haze, but I had an ugly feeling he was not chasing wholehearted. No skysails, as I dare say you remarked. Maybe his pole topgallantmasts will not bear 'em; but it seemed to me he was not so much eager to catch us as to drive us south, away to the leeward. In his place, and with his advantage in men, I should try to carry the ship by boarding, rather than batter her into matchwood and maybe have her sink on me: what a triumph to carry a sound fifty-gun ship with him to the Indies! And he may be waiting for his opportunity. However, I shall do all I can to cross his wake tonight, and if only I can get the weather-gage, with the wind anywhere east of south, I shall try a luffing match with him. We can lie closer to the wind, and those broad-bottomed ships always sag to leeward more than we do. So in any sea where *Leopard* can stay, I believe we could leave him a great way astern by beating up, leave him for good and all; and I hope to be windward of him tomorrow.'

A vain hope. Jack's plan of crossing the Dutchman's wake in the night was frustrated by a dead calm; and in the afternoon of the next day, while all hands were bending a fresh suit of heavy-weather sails, the *Waakzaamheid* was seen in the north-east, bringing up the breeze. She was a noble sight, with studdingsails aloft and alow, gleaming under the clouded sky – towering canvas that gleamed with a more than ordinary and as it were inward glow, for she too had shifted her suit in preparation for the winds to be expected farther south – but the Leopards could not admire her. They had all seen the spent ball that damaged the figurehead, and they all knew that behind the lower-deck ports of the approaching *Waakzaamheid* lay a long tier of Dutch thirty-two-pounders, throwing metal nearly half as heavy again as their own guns. The best part of the *Leopard*'s hull was heart of oak, so was the best part of her crew; but there was not a man aboard who concealed his delight when the breeze reached the *Leopard* too, filled her stout new canvas, and caused the water to gurgle under her counter as she gathered way. A little later the capricious air began to fail the *Waakzaamheid*: she put down her helm and opened a distant cannonade that effectually killed what little wind there was.

Slow, deliberate fire, gun by gun from her upper tier: single shot with a heavy charge of powder; almost always short, but remarkably good practice; and some of the ricochets came aboard. He could not hope to accomplish a great deal at this distance – his twelve-pound upperdeck shot could not do half as much harm after the first graze as the Dutchman's twenty-four-pounders – but there was always the chance of carrying away a spar or cutting up the rigging, which would be all to the good with the *Waakzaamheid* five or six thousand miles from her nearest source of supply. And then a stray shot might hit a cartridge-box or a lantern between decks, starting a fire and even blowing up the magazine: it was long, long odds, but he had known it happen. Yet there were other, far more important considerations. Since her captain delighted in gunnery, and since he was well-to-do, the *Leopard* was exceptionally rich in powder and shot; and if Jack, by provoking the *Waakzaamheid*, could induce her to fire shot for shot, sending most of it into the sea, he would be relatively the gainer. Then he knew very well that even the most intrepid heroes did not much relish sitting mute, waiting to be fired at; and many of the *Leopard*'s landsmen were not heroic at all. Furthermore, experience had taught him that no target on earth could excite such a zeal, such careful, deliberate aiming, as one's fellow men: this was a perfect opportunity for getting the best into his gun-crews; the *Leopard* made the fullest use of it, and occasionally the fall of her shot would send water over the Dutchman's side, while twice, to rapturous cheers, the well-served number seven gun struck home, whereas the *Waakzaamheid* did nothing but send one spent ball into the *Leopard*'s hammock-netting. Yet Jack had a growing, disagreeable conviction that his colleague over the water had exactly the same thing in mind, that he too was profiting from the situation to work up his crew, his horribly numerous crew, to an even higher state of perfection. Jack could see him clearly through his telescope, a tall man in a light-blue coat with brass buttons, sometimes standing on his quarterdeck, smoking a short pipe at intervals of scrutinizing the *Leopard*, sometimes walking about among the upper-deck guns; and in spite of the cheering and pleasant spirit aboard, Jack was heartily pleased when another light air, neglecting the *Waakzaamheid*, enabled him to run out of range.

That night, the night of the new moon, they lay with very little movement until the morning watch, when cold rain came sweeping from the west, and a moderate swell made the *Leopard* pitch as she stood for the distant Cape, now considerably to the north as well as east.

No one had to wake the Captain this time. He was on the quarterdeck well before sunrise, muffled in a pilot jacket by the lee-rail; as he had expected, the first light showed him the *Waakzaamheid*, far over between him and Africa, steering a course that would cut his own in a few hours' time. Jack brought the wind upon his starboard beam; the Dutchman did the same, but no more – he did not attempt to close. And so they ran all day through the rain, running parallel courses, south and south. Now and then a squall would hide one from the other, but every time it cleared, there was the *Waakzaamheid*, keeping station as faithfully as if she were the *Leopard*'s consort, attending to her signals. Sometimes one would gain a mile or two, sometimes the other, but by nightfall they were at much the same distance apart, having run off a hundred and thirty miles by dead reckoning – no sight of the sun at noon, with all that driving cloud. After dark Jack began beating up, tack upon tack, both watches on deck, hoping to shake off the *Waakzaamheid*, which was not such a windward ship, and then to fetch a wide cast northwards, to cross her wake far out of sight. And so he might have done, had not the wind failed him, leaving the *Leopard* with little more than steerage-way, drifting westward on the current, so that once again the morning sun showed her that odiously familiar shape, exact to the rendezvous.

It was that night, after a day of manoeuvring in light airs that boxed the compass, that the *Waakzaamheid* made her attempt at boarding. The sun set clear in a sky that promised a true breeze in the morning; there was a fair amount of starlight before the young moon rose, and it showed the Dutchman ghosting nearer under skysails, although there was not a ripple on the long oily swell. The movement was scarcely perceptible at first, and only the successive disappearance of the lowest stars betrayed it to the lookout's watchful eye: the seventy-four must have picked up the first whisper of the air as it was born, and when it brought her within gunshot she heaved to and opened up with a most spectacular series of rippling broadsides. The *Leopard* was already at action-stations; the battle-lanterns gleamed behind her open larboard ports; both tiers of guns peered out; the smell of burning match drifted along the decks; but until the ships were closer Jack would not give the order to fire. He stood on the poop, staring across the water with his night-glass; he did not wholly believe in this attack, and he was searching for the boats he would himself have launched. No sign, no sign at all: but then, when he had almost given up, he caught the flash of oars, very much farther from the ship than he had reckoned on. The Dutch captain had launched them on his blind side in the dark, and had sent them off, crammed with men, at least half an hour ago. They were pulling fast in a wide arc to take the *Leopard* on the starboard side while the *Waakzaamheid* engaged her with distant gunfire on the other. 'The fox,' said Jack, and he gave orders for boarding-netting, for the guns to be drawn and reloaded with grape, and for all the Marines to leave the guns for their muskets.

The attempt failed because a slant of wind wafted the *Leopard* southward faster than the boats could pull, so that she caught the leaders, cutting them up most dreadfully with grape-shot at two hundred yards; and because the *Waakzaamheid* lost too much time picking up the surviving boats and men to take advantage of the breeze. But it might very well have succeeded: Jack's ship could not fight both sides at once, and the men in the boats outnumbered his crew.

'I shall not run that risk again,' he said. 'Whatever wind we have, I shall beat up, even if it means going directly away from the Cape for days on end. By every sign, and by all the rules, it should come from the south, and so much the better. With luck,' he said, touching the wooden handle of his sextant, 'a southerly breeze should let us work up well into the forties, where we can be sure of no calms. He has to have a calm night for that kind of frolic.'

True to the rules for once, the morning's wind backed right round into the south. It was neither a steady nor a convincing breeze, but several mollymawks and one great albatross were seen, sure signs of stronger winds not far away; and it did allow the *Leopard* to work well ahead, tacking like clockwork every other glass and staying perfectly each time. The seventy-four did her best, whipping her heavy yards round like wands, but she could not lie so close; on every leg she lost several hundred yards, and once she was obliged to wear, which cost her the best part of a mile. A long, anxious day, with the surest helmsmen at the wheel, the leeward guns run in, the windward out, to make her stiffer still, every possible device to wring a little extra thrust from the breeze, and the clumsier hands nearly murdered by their mates for the slightest blunder; but a day that left the *Waakzaamheid* hull down in the north, so that after the drum had beat the retreat, Jack ordered hammocks to be piped down, in order to allow the exhausted larboard watch some sleep.

'Luff and touch her,' was the order of the night, as the *Leopard* held steady on the starboard tack, with the westerly current, now much stronger, to ease her way. In the morning the *Waakzaamheid* was no more than a pale wink against the dark clouds on the horizon; she had reduced sail, and she seemed discouraged.

More albatrosses appeared during the forenoon watch, and a more normal life began again. The wardroom was no longer part of a naked gun-deck; its cabins were set up once more, and the usual quite civilized dining-room had reappeared, decorations and all. The meal itself, glutinous soup, sea-pie, and duff, was no Lord Mayor's banquet, but it was hot, and Stephen, chilled through and through from watching albatrosses in the maintop, ate it eagerly. Between courses he gnawed a biscuit, tapping the weevils out in what was by now an automatic gesture, and he contemplated his messmates. In the article of clothes, the sailors were not a very creditable lot, being dressed in a disagreeable mixture of uniform and old warm garments, sometimes wool and sometimes cloth. Babbington wore a knitted Guernsey frock, inherited from Macpherson, that hung in folds upon his little form; Byron had on two waistcoats, one black, the other brown; Turnbull

had come out in a tweed shooting-coat; and although Grant and Larkin were somewhat more presentable, on the whole they made a sad
contrast to the neat Marines. Stephen had contemplated them from
time to time since the beginning of this tension, and sometimes their
reactions had surprised him. Benton the purser, for instance, never
showed the least anxiety about being taken, sunk, burnt or destroyed,
but the *Leopard*'s vast consumption of candles in the battle-lanterns
and elsewhere rendered him gloomy, silent, irresponsive. Grant too
was rather silent, and had been ever since the first shots were fired
with intent to kill: silent, that is to say, when Stephen or Babbington were present. When they were not, as Stephen gathered from the
chaplain's remarks, he spoke at length about the measures he would
have adopted, had he been in command: the *Leopard* should either
have attacked at once, relying on the effect of surprise, or have sailed
north directly. Fisher was altogether of his mind, though he admitted
that his opinion was of no great value: there was a growing sympathy
between the two men, some underlying similarity. In other respects
the chaplain was quite changed; he no longer visited Mrs Wogan, and
he even asked Dr Maturin to carry her the books she had been promised. 'Ever since my near escape from death in battle,' he said, 'I have
been thinking very seriously.'

'To what battle do you refer?' asked Stephen.

'To the first. A cannon-ball struck within inches of my head. Ever
since then I have reflected upon the old adage about never allowing fire
near inflammable material, and about the dangers of concupiscence.'

He was obviously willing to be questioned and to open his secret
mind – but Stephen did not wish to hear. Since the gaol-fever he had
lost interest in Mr Fisher, who seemed to him a commonplace man,
too much concerned with himself and his own salvation, one whose
attraction faded on acquaintance. He only bowed, and accepted
the books.

He had the impression that both Grant and Fisher were in a state
of powerful fear. There were no evident, direct signs of it, but both
complained very often: a stream of blame and disapproval of the

modern state of mind, the present generation, their useless, idle servants, the ill conduct of the government, of the political parties, and
of those about the King: a general denigration, a frequent imputation
of motives, always discreditable. They reminded him of his maternal
grandmother in her last years, when, from being a strong, sensible,
courageous woman, she grew weak and querulous, her expression of
general discontent increasing with her vulnerability. He did not know
how either of them would behave in a really bloody fight: whether
their manliness would reassert itself in an obvious crisis. As for the
others, he had little doubt. Babbington he had known since the lieutenant was a boy: as brave as a terrier. And Byron was of the same
familiar naval genus. Turnbull would probably do well enough, for all
his loud-mouthed hectoring. Moore had seen a great deal of service;
he would shoot and be shot at with great good humour, as a matter of
course – it was his profession. And Howard, the other lobster, would
surely follow, in his phlegmatic military way: as far as Stephen could
make out, there was almost no connection between the flute-playing
Howard and the stuffed Marine lieutenant. He did have reservations
about Larkin, however: the master's courage and professional ability
might be very well, but by now he was fairly pickled in alcohol and
unless Stephen's judgment were much at fault, his body was very near
the limit of its resistance.

They drank the King; Stephen pushed back his chair, not choos-
ing to stay with the execrable wine, tripped over Babbington's Newfoundland for the hundredth time, and stepped on to the quarterdeck
for another glance at his albatross, a noble bird that had been sailing along with the ship since breakfast. Herapath was there, talking to the midshipman of the watch, and they gave him news of the
Waakzaamheid, out of sight these two hours past, even from the
jacks. 'Long may she stay so,' said Stephen, and returned to work in
his cabin.

This cabin, being on the orlop, did not disappear when the ship
cleared for action, and at intervals, even during these trying days, he
had carried on with a task begun shortly after Herapath had confided

in him. It consisted of drawing up a statement, in French, describing
the British intelligence network in France and some other parts of
western Europe, together with passing references to the United States
and allusions to a separate document dealing with the situation in the
Dutch East Indies; with its details of double agents, bribes offered and
accepted, and treason in the ministries themselves, it was designed to
cause disruption in Paris if there were in fact a connection between
Mrs Wogan's chiefs and the French; and it was intended to be con-
veyed to those chiefs by Mrs Wogan herself, by means of Herapath.
This statement was to have been found among the papers of a dead
officer bound for the East Indies. The officer was not named, though
of course Martin, who had spent half his life in France and whose
mother-tongue was French, was clearly indicated. Copies of the document were to be made for the authorities, and Dr Maturin, knowing
that Mr Herapath was fluent in that language, was to ask him to be
so good as to help with the work. Stephen was certain that the artless
young man would tell his Louisa, and that Mrs Wogan would soon
get transcripts out of him, whatever honourable resistance he might
put up at first. That she would then laboriously encode them, poor
dear, and oblige Herapath to send them from the Cape. Stephen had
poisoned many sources of intelligence in his time; but if all went well,
this promised to be the prettiest piece of intoxication ever that he
had brought about. Such a wealth of material at his disposition! Such
utterly convincing details known only to himself, to Sir Joseph, and
to a few men in Paris!

'What now?' he said, angrily.

'Come quick, sir,' cried a ghastly Marine. 'Mr Larkin's murdered
our lieutenant.'

Stephen caught up his bag, locked his door, and ran to the wardroom. Three officers had pinned Larkin down, and they were tying
his arms and legs. A bloody half-pike on the table. Howard lay back
in his chair, his mouth and eyes wide open in his white astonished
face. Larkin was still jerking and writhing with convulsive force in
delirium tremens, making a hoarse, animal roaring. They overcame

his violence and carried him away. Stephen probed the wound, found the aorta severed at the crest of the arch, and observed that death had been almost instantaneous.

The master had got up from the table, they told him, just as Howard began to screw his flute together, had taken a half-pike from the bulkhead, had said, 'There's for you, you flute-playing bugger', lunging straight across between Moore and Benton, and had then fallen roaring on the deck.

'You are strangely quiet,' said Mrs Wogan, as they walked upon the gangway an hour or two later. 'I have made at least two witty observations, and you have not replied. Surely, Dr Maturin, you should wrap up a little more, in this damp and horrid cold?'

'I am sorry, child, to seem so low,' he said, 'but a little while ago one of the officers killed another in a drunken fit, the sweetest flute I ever heard. Sometimes I feel that this is indeed an unlucky ship. Many of the men say there is a Jonah aboard.'

Some days later (for the Marines insisted upon a proper coffin and a plate for their lieutenant) they buried Howard in 41°15′S, 15°17′E, the *Leopard* heaving to the strong west wind for the purpose. Once again the log-book recorded 'committed the body of John Condom Howard to the deep' and once again Jack wrote Discharged Dead against his name.

After a melancholy, sober dinner at which Stephen was the only guest, Jack said, 'Tomorrow I think we may head north. With common luck we should raise the Table Mountain in three or four days, and then we can get rid of that poor raving maniac.'

They had been south of forty degrees since Thursday, and although at this season, the beginning of the austral summer, even the westerlies were not quite to be relied on north of forty-five or even forty-six, they had proved true enough for the *Leopard*, and together with the current they had carried her over two hundred nautical miles between one noon observation and the next day after day, with never a glimpse of the *Waakzaamheid*.

'Do you know, I wonder, whether the Americans have a consul at the Cape?' asked Stephen. His document was done; Herapath was copying it; the train was laid.

'I would not swear to it, but most probably they have: any number of their far eastern ships touch there, to say nothing of sealers and the like. Why do you – ' He choked his question short, and said, 'What do you say to a turn on deck? The heat of that stove is killing me.'

On deck Stephen pointed out one particular albatross among the half dozen following the ship. 'That dark fowl is, I conceive, a non-descript species, and not *exulans* at all: see his cuneate tail. How I should love to visit his breeding-grounds! There, you may see his tail again.' Jack gazed politely and said, 'Upon my word,' but Stephen saw that the creature's tail was of no very great consequence to him, and said, 'So you think we have shaken off the Dutchman? What a persistent fellow he was, to be sure.'

'And devilish sly, too. I believe he was in league with the Devil, unless – ' He had been about to say 'Unless we have a witch aboard that communicates with him by a familiar spirit, as many of the hands believe: they say it is your Gipsy' but he disliked being called superstitious and in any case he did not really give much credit to the tale, so he continued, 'That is to say, unless he could read my thoughts, and have private notice of the winds into the bargain. Still, this time I like to think we have lurched him good and hearty. By my reckoning he should only go north somewhere about seventy-five or eighty east, for the south-west monsoon. Indeed, I should be quite confident of it, but for one thing.'

'What thing is that, tell?'

'Why, the fact that he knows where we are bound; and that we did claw his boats most cruelly.'

'I beg your pardon, sir,' said Grant, walking across the deck, 'but they send to tell the Doctor that Larkin is at it again.'

They need scarcely have sent. The howling welled up from the master's cabin, where he lay bound, filling the quarterdeck in spite of the strong voice of the wind. 'I shall be with him directly,' said Stephen.

Jack paced on with a melancholy shake of his head. Ten minutes later the lookout hailed. 'Sail ho. On deck there: sail ho.'

'Where away?' called Jack, all thoughts of Larkin gone.

'Broad on the larboard beam, sir. Topsails on the rise.'

Jack nodded to Babbington, who raced up to the masthead with a glass: some moments later his voice came down, spreading relief throughout the attentive, silent ship. 'On deck, sir. A whaler. Steering south and east.'

The wardroom steward, pinned to the half-deck by the first awful hail, continued his course; and passing the Marine sentry outside the master's cabin he said, 'It's not the Dutchman, mate: only a whaler, God be praised.'

On the other side of the door, Stephen said to Herapath, 'There. That should calm him. Pray put up the tundish and come along. We will have a dish of tea in my cabin: we have certainly deserved a dish of tea.'

Herapath came along, but he would not linger, nor would he drink his tea. He had a great deal of work to do, he said, avoiding Stephen's eye, and must beg to be excused.

'Poor Michael Herapath,' wrote Stephen in his book, 'he suffers much. I know the harrow's mark too well ever to mistake it, the harrow directed by a determined woman. Perhaps I shall give him a little of my laudanum, to tide him over till the Cape.'

Since her hands were protected from impressment, the whaler was not unwilling to be spoken by a British man-of-war: she was the *Three Brothers* from London river for the Great South Sea, she said, in answer to the *Leopard*'s 'What ship? What ship is that?' Last from the Cape: no, she had not seen a single sail since she cleared False Bay.

'Come aboard and crack a bottle,' called Jack over the wind and the grey heaving water. The whaler's words were balm to him; they did away with the lingering, almost superstitious doubt that had kept his eye perpetually turning to the windward for that white fleck on the horizon that, in spite of all his calculations, would prove to be the devilish *Waakzaamheid*. It was notorious that whalers had the sharpest eyes of any men afloat: their livelihood depended on seeing the distant spout, often in a torn, tormented, cloud-covered waste of sea, and they always had men up there in their crow's nests, watching with the most constant eagerness: the remotest gleam of topsails could not escape them by day, nor yet by these late moonlit nights.

The master of the *Three Brothers* came and cracked his bottle and talked about the pursuit of the whale in these largely unknown waters: he knew them as well as most men, having made three voyages, and he gave Jack some particularly valuable information about South Georgia, correcting his chart of the anchorages in that remote, inhospitable island, in case the *Leopard* should ever find herself in 54°S, 37°W, and about the few other specks of land in that vast far southern ocean. But presently, as the full bottles came in and the empty were carried away, his accounts became wilder; he spoke of the great continent that must lie round the pole, of the gold that was certainly there, and of how he should ballast his ship with the ore. Sailors rarely feel that they have done their duty if their guests leave them sober: but Jack was perfectly satisfied as he saw the whaler plunge into his boat. He bade the *Three Brothers* farewell and a happy return and worked out his course for the Cape: the *Leopard* brought the wind a little abaft the larboard beam in a fine fierce curve – white water sweeping over her waist – and began to run northwards under courses and reefed topsails, her deck sloping like a moderately pitched roof and her lee chains buried in the foam that came racing from her bows. She was heading for dirty weather, for a low bank of cloud with rain-squalls drifting across its face and hidden lightning within the mass; it was precious cold, and spray, whipping across the deck in the eddy of the mainsail, kept wetting the Captain's face. But he was warm within: not only had he a comfortable coat of blubber as well as his pilot-jacket, but he also had a glow of satisfaction. He continued his pacing, counting the number of turns on the fingers clasped behind his back. One thousand he would take before he went below. At each turn he glanced up at the sky and out over the sea: a mottled sky, blue and white to the south with a steely gleam on the farthest rim, grey, high-piled storm-breeders in the west, darkness north and east; and of course a mottled sea, though in quite different tones, running from middle blue through every shade of glaucous grey to black, and the whole streaked with a white that owed nothing to the sky but all to the broken water and the spindrift of former storms. The long, even fairly heavy swell lifted him and set him down at a measured pace, so that sometimes his horizon was no more than three miles away, and sometimes he saw an enormous disk of ocean, a cold, uneasy sea, endless miles of desolation, the comfortless element in which he was at home.

The surface of his mind was concerned with that unhappy man the master: his books had proved to be hopelessly confused, neglected these many weeks. One of Larkin's duties was to keep tally of the *Leopard*'s water, but from the scrawled, haphazard notes Jack could not make out the present state: he and the mate of the hold would have to creep about in the depths, thumping casks and starting bungs. He would not ask Grant to do it, now that the first lieutenant had to keep a watch: a cantankerous, unwilling dog, with no desire to please, no goodwill – careful never to commit himself by a hasty word, but always ready with some objection, with general blame and discontent. A miserable sod. A good seaman, though: that must always be admitted. He thought of Breadfruit Bligh, and his nasty reputation: 'Before you judge a commander,' he said, on his seven hundredth turn, 'you must know just what he had to command.' Jack himself had had to speak to Grant in terms that might have earned him the name of a rough-tongued Turk; he had not lost his temper, but in the matter of Grant's interference with his orders about the storm-trysail he had spoken very plain.

He turned aft, seven hundred and fifty-one: he heard exclamations, saw faces staring, pointing hands. 'Sir, sir!' cried Turnbull,

Holles and the quartermaster all at once; and from the masthead 'Sail ho,' with extreme urgency. 'On deck, on deck there . . .'

He whipped round, and there in the west-north-west, directly to windward, emerging from a black squall with lurid light behind, he saw the *Waakzaamheid*, no hanging threat on the far horizon but hull up, not three miles away.

'Port your helm,' he said. 'In driver. Out reefs. Fore topgallantsail.' The *Leopard* turned round on her heel so fast that Babbington's dog was flung outwards, colliding with a carronade. Hands raced for the brails, braces, sheets and tacks, and the ship steadied on her course, right before the wind.

The *Waakzaamheid* and the *Leopard* had seen one another at much the same moment, and aboard both ships the sails came flashing out as quickly as the hands could move. The *Waakzaamheid* carried away a maintopgallant the minute it was sheeted home, and the cloths streamed forward, fouling her stays. 'He is in earnest this time,' thought Jack. 'We must crack on.' But the *Leopard*'s masts would not stand another stitch of canvas without going by the board. He felt the backstays and shook his head, gazed up at the tall topgallantmasts and shook it again – no question of striking them down on deck at this juncture. 'Pass the word for the bosun,' he said. The bosun came running aft. 'Mr Lane, get warps and light hawsers to the mastheads.'

The bosun, a dark fellow in a perpetual ill-temper, opened his mouth: but the look on the Captain's face turned his remark to an 'Aye aye, sir,' and he plunged below, piping for his mates as he went.

'Let us try the main topgallantsail, Mr Babbington,' said Jack, when the ship had taken the full thrust of the wind right aft and all her way was on her. The upperyardsmen lay aloft, ran out on the yard, let fall. The yard rose, the mast complained, the backstays grew tauter still; but the good canvas held and the *Leopard*'s speed increased perceptibly. Jack looked aft, over the tearing wake: the seventy-four was a little farther off. 'So far, so good,' he said to himself, and to Babbington, 'Clew up, however: we will try again when the bosun has done his work.'

So far so good: the *Leopard* was just gaining, just outrunning the *Waakzaamheid* with the canvas she could bear at present. She could certainly hold her own and better in this wind and in this sea. But he did not want to go any further south, where the westerlies blew harder still.

After an hour he altered course due east. Instantly the *Waakzaam-heid* steered to head him off, running the chord of the *Leopard*'s arc, gaining more than Jack liked to see, and at the same time setting a curious little triangular sail like an inverted skyscraper from the yardarms of her main topgallant to the cap.

'This is no time to jig,' reflected Jack. The *Waakzaamheid* had the masterhand as far as course was concerned, and he put the *Leopard* before the wind once more, a west-north-west wind with a distinct tendency to haul norther still. Then raising his voice to the foremast head, where Lane was toiling with his crew, clinging to what frail support there was, their pigtails streaming forward, stiff and straight, he called, 'Mr Lane, should you like your hammock sent aloft?'

If the bosun made any reply it was drowned by the striking of eight bells in the afternoon watch, followed by all the ritual gestures. The log was heaved, as clear of the huge wake as it would go; the reel whirled; the quartermaster bawled out 'Nip!'; the midshipman reported 'Just on the twelve, sir, if you please.' The officer of the watch chalked it up on the log-board. The carpenter made his report: 'Three inches in the well, sir,' and Jack said, 'Ah, Mr Gray, I was just about to pass the word for you. Deadlights in the cabin, if you please. I do not want to get my stockings wet, if a following sea should get up tonight.'

'Deadlights it is, sir; for nothing are so unwholesome as wet stock-ings.' Gray was an old old man, a master of his trade, and he might be a little chatty. 'Will it cut up rough, sir, do you reckon?' By most standards it had cut up rough long ago: the *Leopard* was pitching like a froward horse, white water over her bows, and although the wind was right aft, where in moderate weather it would be almost mute, they now conversed in a strong shout, while spray whipped off the rollers shot past them, to vanish forward. But they were in the forties, and in the forties this was not worth speaking of, not what would be called real weather at all.

'I doubt it may: look at the gleam to leeward, Mr Gray.'

The carpenter looked, and pursed his lips; glanced aft to catch the Dutchman on the rise, and pursed them again, muttering, 'What can you expect, when we got a witch aboard? Deadlights this minute, sir.'

'And hawse-bags, of course.'

So they ran another glass, and at the striking of the bell Jack moved to the poop: there, crouching with his telescope behind the taffrail, he inspected the *Waakzaamheid*. The moment he had it focused on her forecastle he had a curious shock, for there, full in his glass, was the Dutch captain, looking straight at him. There was no doubt about his tall, burly form, the distinctive carriage of his head: Jack was familiar with the enemy. But now, instead of his usual light blue, he had a black coat on. 'I wonder,' thought Jack, 'whether it is just an odd chance, or whether we killed some relative of his? His boy, perhaps, dear God forbid.'

The seventy-four was gaining slightly now, and in the strong remaining light – for the evening was much longer down here, and the two ships had run well clear of the gloom of the north – Jack could make out the nature of those odd triangles. There was another at the foretopgallant now, and it was a storm-staysail, suspended by its tack.

'If you please, sir,' said a midshipman, young Hillier, 'the bosun says all is stretched along, and might he have a party.'

A tidy party it would have to be, for Jack's plan was to supplement the backstays with hawsers, no less, so that the immensely strength-ened masts might bear a great press of sail with a following wind, the strain being transferred to the hull; but to bowse the massive cord-age so taut that it would serve its office called for a most uncommon force. Once, when he was third of the *Theseus*, they had set the main-sail in a hurry to claw off the Penmarks, and a south-wester blew so hard that two hundred men were needed to haul the sheet right aft: he did not have two hundred valid men, but he did have a little more time than the captain of the *Theseus*, with the breakers under his lee.

None to waste, however, with the seventy-four only three miles away, and running off the mile in just five minutes: and above all, no time to make a mistake – a mast lost in this sea was sure destruction.

'A burton-tackle to the chess-tree,' he called, loud and clear. 'Lead aft to a snatch-block fast to the aftermost ring-bolts and forward free. Look alive, there, look alive. Light along that snatch-block, Craig.' Order came from apparent confusion in five minutes: the half-drowned bosun's party scrambled in from the chess-trees; and the whole ship's company crowded into the waist and along the gangways, standing by the cablets that were to act as horizontal falls, working with a threefold power.

'Silence fore and aft,' cried Jack. 'Starboard, tally on. At the word, now, and all together cheerly: like a bowline. Ho, one. Ho, two. Ho, belay. Larboard, clap on. Ho, one. Ho, two. Ho, belay.'

So it went, on either side: short sharp pulls aft from the chess-trees, forward from the snatch-blocks, and the hawsers tightened evenly, tighter and tighter yet, a most careful balancing of forces, until the wind sung the same note in each, and each pair was iron-taut, supporting its mast with extraordinary strength.

'Belay,' cried Jack for the last time. 'Well fare ye, lads. Are you ready, Mr Lane?'

'Ready, aye, ready, sir.'

'Cast off all. Maintopgallantsail, there.'

The yard rose up; the mast took the strain without a groan; the *Leopard*'s bow-wave grew higher still with her increasing speed. Now the spritsail topsail followed, while to ease her plunging they hauled up the mainsail, giving all the wind to her forecourse: she sailed easier yet, with no slackening in her pace, clearly outrunning the Dutchman, although he had shaken out his foretopsail reef.

They raced furiously over the empty, heaving sea under a clear late evening sky, both ships driven very hard; and the first to lose an important spar or sail would lose the race that night. The sun was setting; in an hour and forty minutes the moon would rise, a little past her full. With the afterglow and then the strong moonlight, there would be small chance of jigging unperceived; yet half an hour before the moon he would bring the wind a point or so on the quarter, just so that the jibs and forward staysails would stand and give him another half knot or even more. And all things being considered, hammocks might be piped down: the larboard watch would turn in with all their clothes on in case of emergency, and there was no point in keeping them at quarters, shivering behind their tight-closed ports: the crisis, if it came to that, was some way off. Perhaps a great way to the east. He had chased forty-eight hours before this.

In the darkened cabin he found Stephen with his 'cello between his knees and a soup-tureen at his side. 'Judas,' he said, lifting the lid and beholding emptiness.

'Not at all, my dear. More is on the brew; but I cannot recommend it. You would be better with a glass of water, tempered with a few drops of wine, a very few drops of wine, and a piece of biscuit.'

'What did you eat it for, then? Why did you not leave a scrap, not a single scrap?'

'It was only that I felt my need was greater than thine, my business of greater importance than your business. For whereas yours is concerned with death, mine is the bringing forth of life. Mrs Boswell is in labour, and some time tonight or tomorrow I think I may promise you an addition to your crew.'

'Ten to one another – woman,' said Jack. 'Killick! Killick, there!'

More soup appeared, chops hot and hot, a jug of coffee, and a wedge of solid duff.

'Will this last long, do you suppose?' asked Stephen, over the booming of his 'cello.

'A stern chase is a long chase,' said Jack.

'And would you consider this a really stern one?'

'It could not well be more so. The Dutchman is in our wake. He is dead astern.'

'So that is the significance of the term. I had always supposed it to mean an eager, a grim, a most determined pursuit, inspired by inveterate animosity. Well: and so this is a stern chase. Listen till I tell you something for my part: a breech-presentation is a long, long labour too. It looks to me that the both of us have an active night ahead: you will allow me to call for another pot.'

Stephen's was active enough, with no proper forceps and no great experience of midwifery; but after Jack had gone on deck to alter course – southwards, since the Dutchman expected him to go north – and had stared at his pursuer for a while by the light of the risen moon, he stretched out on his cot and went straight to sleep. The outer jib and the foretopmast staysail were standing well, the *Leopard* was steering easy, and the seventy-four was between four and five miles astern; she had not perceived Jack's smooth change of direction for some time and she had not set her own headsails until the *Leopard* was close on another mile ahead.

He woke refreshed: yet his sleeping mind had recorded the crash of water against the deadlights, and coming on deck he was not surprised to find that both wind and sea had increased. The cold, brilliant moon showed an even array of tall waves sweeping eastward, wide apart, with a deep trough between; and now their heads were curling over, streaming down the leeward side in a white cascade; and the general note of the wind in the rigging had risen half an octave.

If this grew worse, and from the look of the western sky, the feel of the air, it must grow worse, he would have to put the *Leopard* before the wind again; the ship could not stand a heavier sea upon her quarter without being thrown off her course. The *Waakzaamheid* was still at much the same distance, but that was not likely to last.

The graveyard watch wore on, bell by bell; and still they ran, starting neither sheet nor tack, an eager, grim, and most determined pursuit. At eight bells, with both watches on deck, he took in the spritsail, got the yard fore and aft, set the inner jib, and bore up another point. It might be his last chance of doing so, for the air was now filled with flying water and the ship was tearing through the sea at a rate he never would have believed possible, a rate that in fact would have been impossible without those hawsers to the mastheads. But this was no longer the exhilarating pace of a few hours ago; now there was a nightmare, breakneck quality about it; and now the wind was blowing very hard indeed.

Hour after hour towards the morning watch, and hour after hour the wind increased. Twice, just after seven bells, the *Leopard* was very nearly pooped by a freakish bursting sea: the steady progression of the rollers was losing its regularity, becoming disordered. Eight bells again, and he put the ship before the wind, taking in the staysails. It was impossible to get an accurate reading of the log, for the blast tossed the log-boat forward of her bows; and now the carpenter's mate reported two foot of water in the well. The *Leopard* had been working and straining so much that a good deal had come in through her sides, let alone that which made its way down from the decks in spite of the laid hatches and through the hawse-holes in spite of the bags.

The sun rose on a sea in labour, the crests riding ahead of the swell and breaking: creaming water from horizon to horizon except in the bottom of the troughs, much deeper now; while from every height the wind tore foam, drops and solid water, driving it forward in a grey veil that darkened and filled the air. The *Waakzaamheid* lay within two miles. And now the extreme danger of sailing in a very heavy swell became more and more apparent: in the troughs, the valleys between the waves, the *Leopard* was almost becalmed, while on the crest the full force of the wind struck her, threatening to tear her sails from their bolt-ropes or to carry away her masts: even worse, she lost some of her way at the bottom, whereas she needed all her speed to outrun the following seas, for if they were to overtake her she would be pooped, smothered in a mass of breaking water. Then ten to one she would slew round and broach to, presenting her broadside to the wind, so that the next sea would overwhelm her.

This was by no means the worst sea Jack had known; it was still far from the total chaos of a ten-days' blow – enormous waves with a

fetch of a thousand miles running into one another, rising mountain-
high, breaking, tumbling and bursting with enormous force – but it
looked as though it might build up into something of the same kind;
and already the *Waakzaamheid* was showing how much the larger
ship was favoured. Her higher masts, her greater mass, meant that
she lost less way when partially becalmed, and she was now not much
more than a mile away: yet on the other hand she had either taken in
or lost her odd triangles.

An albatross glided down the starboard side, turned on the wind
and shot across the wake, picking something from the surface as it
flew; and it was only when he saw the brilliant flash of its wings that
he realized how yellow the foam was in fact. Even at this time of great
concentration on his ship and the countless forces acting upon her he
was astonished at the bird's perfect control, at the way its gleaming
twelve-foot wings lifted it without the least effort and sent it flanking
across the oncoming sea in an easy, unhurried curve. 'I wish Stephen
could . . .' he was thinking as the *Leopard* climbed the crest ahead,
but a crack forward and the sound of threshing canvas cut him short.
The foretopsail had split. 'Clew up, clew up,' he cried – there was a
chance of saving it. 'Halliards, there. Maintopsail.' He ran forward,
calling for the bosun. No bosun, but Cullen, the captain of the foretop, was at the mast, and the bosun's mates: they secured the topsail, the yard lowered on the cap, while the ship plunged down the
long slope among the smother of the breaking crest. The close-reefed
maintopsail kept the *Leopard* ahead of the following seas after no
more than a few minutes' hesitation, but it was too far aft for the ideal
thrust – her speed was not so great, and she might steer wild.

It was still possible to bend another foretopsail. 'Pass the word
for the bosun,' he shouted, and at last the man came stumbling aft:
drunk, not dead drunk, but incapable. 'Get along forward,' said Jack
to him: and to his older mate, 'Arklow, carry on. Number two foretopsail, and the best robins in the store.'

A cruel struggle out there on the yard, cruel and long, fighting
with canvas animated by such a force, but they bent the sail at last

and came down, hands bleeding, the men looking as though they had been flogged.

'Go below,' said Jack. 'Get your hands bound up: tell purser's steward I say you are to have a tot apiece, and something warm.'

Leaning over the rail, his eyes half-shut against the driving spray, he saw that the *Waakzaamheid* was now within a thousand yards. He shrugged: no ship, no first-rate, not even a Spanish four-decker, could show her broadside in such a sea. 'Mr Grant,' he said, 'let the pumps be rigged: we are steering rather heavy.' Then, with a look at the new foretopsail, tight as a drum, he went below for a bite himself.

Like the Dutch captain, Killick seemed able to read his thoughts: coffee and a pile of ham sandwiches were carrying in as Jack hung his streaming sou'-wester on its peg and walked into the gloomy cabin, where he sat on a locker by the starboard gun. Not a gleam came in from the stern-windows, their glass replaced by solid wood; and even the skylight had a tarpaulin over it.

'Thankee, Killick,' he said, after a first ravenous gulp. 'Any news of the Doctor?'

'No, your honour. Only howls, and Mr Herapath took poorly. It must be worse before it can get better; that is what I always say.'

'No doubt, no doubt,' said Jack uneasily, and he applied himself to the sandwiches: thick cold pancake instead of bread, but welcome. Slowly champing, he mused on women, their hard lot; on the curse of Eve; on Sophie; on his daughters, growing fast. An immense crash of splintering wood, a surge of flying spray, a flood of light, and a spent cannon-ball broke in upon his thought. He peered out through the broken deadlights and saw another flash in the *Waakzaamheid*'s bows. No sound in this universal roar, and the smoke was swept instantly away, but it was clear that the seventy-four had opened up with her chasers, trained sharp forward from the bridle-ports in her bluff bows and that a lucky shot had struck right home, smashing his coffee-cup – a chance in a million.

'Killick, another cup,' he called, carrying the rest of his breakfast into the dining-cabin. 'And let Chips come aft.'

'I had never expected that today,' he said to himself. Certainly the aim of warfare was the destruction of the enemy, and he had seen French ships totally destroyed in fleet-engagements; but in single-ship actions the idea of capture usually predominated. He had expected the seventy-four to hunt him down and take him, or try to take him, when the weather moderated: in this sea there was no possibility of capture and the Dutch captain's intent could only be to kill. Any engagement must mean the total loss of the first ship to lose a mast or a vital sail and thus the control of her run: the death of every soul aboard her. 'A bloody-minded man, I see.'

He did not spend long below, but how things had changed when he next came on deck! It was not that the wind was greater – indeed, there was a slight but certain lessening – but that the sea had grown steeper still. And the ship was labouring now, heavy on the rise, although the chain-pumps were shooting a great gush of water over her side. The storm-jib would have to come in: it was pressing her down, and in any case the boom was whipping like a bow. 'Mr Grant, we will get in the storm-jib and goose-wing the maincourse.'

'Surely, sir . . .' began the older man – he looked much older now – but went no further.

With the thrust lower, the *Leopard* fairly wallowed in the deeper troughs; yet her speed was still so great that she could certainly avoid the following seas with skilful handling: Jack named a team of men to take the wheel, prime seamen, four at a time, two glasses to a trick. The danger was more the shock when the wind took her full on the crests, and ordinarily Jack would have had her under a close-reefed foretopsail alone or even less – just enough to keep her ahead. But with the *Waakzaamheid* creeping up he dared not take more in; nor could he haul up the jib again. If this went on he would have to compensate the lack of thrust by lightening the load: he would have to pump out the tons and tons of fresh water down there in the hold. The *Waakzaamheid* was half a mile away. He saw two flashes, but never the pitch of the shot, quite lost in this white turmoil.

He made a tour of the ship – long, wind-hurried strides forward, a battle against it aft – which showed him that all was as snug as it could be in such a case, and that there was no likelihood of any change of sail for some while – no voluntary change – and he called for Moore, Burton and the best gun captains in the ship.

'Sir,' said Grant, as he was leaving the quarterdeck, 'the *Waakzaamheid* has opened fire.'

'So I gather, Mr Grant,' said Jack, laughing. 'But two can play at that game, you know.'

He was surprised to see no answering smile at all, but this was not the moment for brooding over his lieutenant's moods, and he led his party into the cabin.

They cast loose the guns, removed the wing deadlights, and looked out on to a soaring green cliff of water fifty yards away with the *Leopard*'s wake trace down its side. It shut out the sky, and it was racing towards them. The *Leopard*'s stern rose, rose: the enormous wave passed smoothly under her counter, and there through the flying spume lay the *Waakzaamheid* below, running down the far slope. 'When you please, Mr Burton,' said Jack to the gunner. 'A hole in her foretopsail might make it split.' The larboard gun roared out and instantly the cabin was filled with smoke. No hole: no fall of shot either. Jack, to starboard, had the Dutchman in his dispart sight. A trifle of elevation and he pulled the lanyard. Nothing happened: flying spray had soaked the lock. 'Match,' he cried, but by the time he had the glowing end in his hand the *Waakzaamheid* was below his line of sight, below the depression of his gun. From down there in the trough she fired up, a distant wink of flame, and she got in another couple of shots before the grey-green hill of water parted them again.

'May I suggest a cigar, sir?' said Moore. 'One can hold it in one's mouth.' He was acting as sponger and second captain, and his face was six inches from Jack's: he was encased in oilskins and there was nothing of the Marine about him but his fine red face and the neat stock showing under his chin.

'A capital idea,' said Jack, and in the calm of the trough, before the *Waakzaamheid* appeared again, Moore lit him a cigar from the glowing match in its tub.

The *Leopard* began to rise, the Dutchman appeared, black in the white water of the breaking crests high up there, and both nine-pounders went off together. The guns leapt back, the crews worked furiously, grunting, no words, sponged, loaded, and ran them out again. Another shot, and this time Jack saw his ball, dark in the haze of lit water, flying at its mark: he could not follow it home, but the line was true, a little low. Now they were on the crest, and the cabin was filled with wind and water mingled, unbreathable: the gun-crews worked without the slightest pause, soaked through and through.

Down, down the slope amidst the white wreckage of the wave, the guns run out and waiting. Across the hollow and up the other side. 'I believe I caught his splash,' said Moore. 'Twenty yards short of our starboard quarter.'

'So did I,' said Burton. 'He wants to knock our rudder, range along, and give us a broadside, the bloody-minded dog.'

The *Waakzaamheid* over the crest again: Jack poured the priming into the touch-hole with his horn, guarding it with the flat of his hand, the cigar clenched between his teeth and the glow kept bright; and this bout each gun fired three times before the *Leopard* mounted too high, racing up and up, pursued by the Dutchman's shot. On and on: an enormous switchback, itself in slow, majestic motion, but traversed at a racing speed in which the least stumble meant a fall. Alternate bursts of fire, aimed and discharged with such an intensity of purpose that the men did not even see the storm of flying water that burst in upon them at each crest. On and on, the *Waakzaamheid* gaining visibly.

Here was Babbington at his side, waiting for a pause. 'Take over, Moore,' said Jack, as the gun ran in. He stepped over the train-tackle, and Babbington said, 'She's hit our mizzen-top, sir, fair and square.'

Jack nodded. She was coming far too close: point-blank range now, and the wind to help her balls. 'Start the water, all but a ton; and try the jib, one-third in.'

Back to the gun as it ran out. Now it was the *Waakzaamheid*'s turn to fire, and fire she did, striking the *Leopard*'s stern-post high up: a shrewd knock that jarred the ship as she was on the height of the wave, and a moment later a green sea swept through the deadlights.

'Good practice in this sea, Mr Burton,' said Jack.

The gunner turned his streaming face, and its fixed fierce glare broke into a smile. 'Pretty fair, sir, pretty fair. But if I did not get home two shots ago, my name is Zebedee.'

The flying *Leopard* drew a little way ahead with the thrust of her jib, a hundred yards or so; and the switchback continued, the distances the same. It was the strangest gunnery, with its furious activity and then the pause, waiting to be fired at; the soaking at the crest, the deck awash; the intervening wall of water; the repetition of the whole sequence. No orders; none of the rigid fire-discipline of the gun-deck; loud, gun-deafened conversation between the bouts. The dread of being pooped by the great seas right there in front of their noses, rising to blot out the sun with unfailing regularity, and of broaching to, hardly affected the cabin.

A savage roar from Burton's crew. 'We hit her port-lid,' cried Bonden, the second captain. 'They can't get it closed.'

'Then we are all in the same boat,' said Moore. 'Now the Dutchmen will have a wet jacket every time she digs in her bows, and I wish they may like it, ha, ha!'

A short-lived triumph. A midshipman came to report the jib carried clean away – Babbington had all in hand – was trying to set a storm-staysail – half the water was pumped out.

But although the *Leopard* was lighter she felt the loss of the jib; the *Waakzaamheid* was coming up, and now the vast hill of sea separated them only for seconds. If the *Leopard* did not gain when all her water was gone, the upper-deck guns would have to follow it: anything to draw ahead and preserve the ship. The firing was more and more continuous; the guns grew hot, kicking clear on the recoil, and first Burton and then Jack reduced the charge.

Nearer and nearer, so that they were both on the same slope, no trough between them: a hole in the Dutchman's foretopsail, but it would not split, and three shots in quick succession struck the *Leopard*'s hull, close to her rudder. Jack had smoked five cigars to the butt, and his mouth was scorched and dry. He was staring along the barrel of his gun, watching for the second when the *Waakzaamheid*'s bowsprit should rise above his sight, when he saw her starboard chaser fire. A split second later he stabbed his cigar down on the priming and there was an enormous crash, far louder than the roar of the gun.

How much later he looked up he could not tell. Nor, when he did look up, could he quite tell what was afoot. He was lying by the cabin bulkhead with Killick holding his head and Stephen sewing busily; he could feel the passage of the needle and of the thread, but no pain. He stared right and left. 'Hold still,' said Stephen. He felt the red-hot stabbing now, and everything fell into place. The gun had not burst: there was Moore fighting it. He had been dragged clear – hit – a splinter, no doubt. Stephen and Killick crouched over him as a green sea gushed in: then Stephen cut the thread, whipped a wet cloth round his ears, one eye and forehead, and said, 'Do you hear me, now?' He nodded; Stephen moved on to another man lying on the deck; Jack stood up, fell, and crawled over to the guns. Killick tried to hold him, but Jack thrust him back, clapped on to the tackle and helped run out the loaded starboard gun. Moore bent over it, cigar in hand, and from behind him Jack could see the *Waakzaamheid* twenty yards away, huge, black-hulled, throwing the water wide. As Moore's hand came down, Jack automatically stepped aside; but he was still stupid, he moved slow, and the recoiling gun flung him to the deck again. On hands and knees he felt for the train-tackle in the smoke, found it as the darkness cleared, and tallied on. But for a moment he could not understand the cheering that filled the cabin, deafening his ears: then through the shattered deadlights he saw the Dutchman's foremast lurch, lurch again, the stays part, the mast and sail carry away right over the bows.

The *Leopard* reached the crest. Green water blinded him. It cleared, and through the bloody haze running from his cloth he saw the vast breaking wave with the *Waakzaamheid* broadside on its curl, on her beam-ends, broached to. An enormous, momentary turmoil of black hull and white water, flying spars, rigging that streamed wild for a second, and then nothing at all but the great hill of green-grey with foam racing upon it.

'My God, oh my God,' he said. 'Six hundred men.'

Throughout the day the *Leopard* ran under her foretopsail alone, and throughout the day the barometer moved up. The slackening of the wind that Jack had noticed before the sinking of the *Waakzaamheid* continued, but the sea was still as high or even higher for a while, and there was no possibility of altering course more than a point, still less of heaving to.

Jack lay there in his cot in the strangest state of daze. He knew that the ship was steering well, and that she was in good hands; he knew that the pumps were gaining, and that the carpenter had dealt with the shattered deadlights, while Killick and his mates were now restoring the great cabin, where they had already set the stove to rights; and he knew there was a strong likelihood that the storm was blowing itself out – that the ship had come through, and with all her guns aboard. If the Dutchman had not foundered when he did, they must have followed her water over the side. Yet all these things were at a remove. He knew them, but they did not concern him much. The vision of the *Waakzaamheid* on her beam-ends, overwhelmed by that terrible sea, presented itself again and again to his inner eye. This was war; she had sought the battle; she had done her utmost to destroy the *Leopard*; it was the biter bit, and his ship had accomplished a feat of great value to the Royal Navy in the farther Indies. But it filled him with a kind of sorrow, a strange abiding grief.

A light appeared, and he closed his eyes. 'Well, my dear,' said Stephen, 'you do not like the light: just so.' He put it behind a book and they talked quietly for a while. It was, as Jack had supposed, a splinter that had wounded him, a two-foot piece of oak with a jagged cutting edge, sent flying by the Dutchman's shot. 'I dare say it will give you pain in your head for some days,' said Stephen. 'The wound itself is spectacular, and it will spoil your beauty; but you have had many

worse. It was Lord Nelson's wound, you know – your forehead hanging over your eye.' Jack smiled. He would almost have done without
an arm to follow Nelson. 'Yet I do not quite like the bang the flat side
gave you; there is some degree of concussion. Still, that is nothing to
what the recoiling gun might have done. But for the interposition of
St John, you were mere pulp, of little interest even to anatomy. As it is,
I have great hopes of your leg. Is there any feeling in it, now?'

'Leg? What leg? Why, it is numb! Upon my sacred honour, it is
numb.'

'Never be perturbed, my dear; I have seen far uglier limbs
preserved.'

After a silence in which Jack seemed to lose all interest in his leg,
he said, 'Stephen, what is that round your neck? You was not hurt, I
trust?'

'It is a woollen comforter against the cold, knitted by Mrs Wogan.
The lively red is designed to increase the wearer's sense of warmth, by
the association of ideas. I am much obliged to her.'

'Which Mr Grant asks can he report,' said Killick, thrusting his
head through the door, and speaking in a hoarse whisper.

Stephen stepped out and told Grant that the patient must not be
disturbed; disturbance might agitate his mind.

'Do you mean he is not right in the head?' cried Grant.

'I do not,' said Stephen. He disliked the man's eager tone extremely,
his obvious willingness to believe the worst; in any case he was on edge
from want of sleep, and when he returned to the sleeping-cabin his face
had a wicked, reptilian look. In his remoteness Jack did not notice it,
however: he said, 'After anything of any action, I always have the blue
devils. This time it is much worse. I see that ship broaching to, and all
her people, five or six hundred men. I see her over and over again. Can
you explain that, Stephen? Is it something in the physical line?'

'To some extent I think it is,' said Stephen. 'Five and twenty drops
of this' – pouring carefully from a bottle by the shaded light – 'will
rectify your humours, as far as physic can.'

'It is less disgusting than your usual dose,' said Jack. 'I forgot to ask you, how was your night? How does your Gipsy woman come along?'

'I cannot answer for Mrs Boswell: the Caesarean section is no light undertaking, even without a hurricane. But if it can be fed, the child may live, the creature. It is, as you predicted, female; and therefore hardy. I was at a loss to know what to do with it at first.'

'There is the girl that waits on Mrs Wogan.'

'There is. But you will recall that she was transported for infanticide, repeated infanticide. She is a little eccentric where babies are concerned, and I could not think her quite a proper person. However, I opened my mind to Mrs Wogan, and she very handsomely offered her services. She tends it at present in a basket, lined with wool; and begs it may be indulged with a hanging stove.'

'Christ, Stephen, how I wish Tom Pullings were here,' said Jack, and drifted off to sleep.

In the wardroom Byron and Babbington were playing chess while Moore and Benton looked on. Fisher took Stephen aside and said, 'What is all this I hear about the Captain's intellects being disturbed?'

Stephen looked at him for a moment and said, 'It is no part of my function to discuss my patients' maladies, and if the Captain's mind were in any way affected I should be the last to say so. But as it is not, I may tell you that Captain Aubrey, though weak from loss of blood, is intellectually a match for any two men here. Nay, any three or four. Bread and blood, sir,' he cried. 'What do you mean by questioning me? Your manner is as offensive as your matter. You are impertinent, sir.' He took a quick step forward and Fisher fell back, appalled. He was sorry to have offended – he had meant no harm – if a natural concern had led him into impropriety he would most willingly withdraw. With this he edged round the table and hurried from the room.

'Well done, Doctor,' said Captain Moore. 'I love a man who can bite, if vexed. Come and have a glass of grog.'

Stephen turned his cold glare on the Marine; but although he had had a wicked night of it and great responsibility, and although his anxiety for Jack had made him savage, Moore's round red good-humoured friendly face brought a smile to his own. 'Why, no,' he said. 'I was too hasty, too hasty by half.'

'To be sure,' said Moore, near the bottom of his glass, 'for a moment the Owner's wits *were* all astray, and small wonder, when you consider the knock he had. You may not believe me, but when I gave him joy of the victory, he said he could take no joy in it at all. The captain of a fifty-gun ship to take no joy in sinking a seventy-four! Clearly, for the moment he was all to seek. But from that to say his intellects are disturbed, why . . .'

The door opened, letting in a blast of freezing air, and Turnbull appeared, calling for a hot drink. He was covered with snow, which he distributed pretty liberally about the wardroom, beating it from his cloak in thick clots. 'It has come on to snow,' he said. 'Would you believe it? Half a foot on deck, and falling fast.'

'How is the wind?' asked Babbington.

'Dropping all the time; and the snow has flatted the sea amazingly. It began with rain, and then turned to snow. Would you believe it?'

Grant came out of his cabin, and Turnbull told him that it had come on to snow. At first it had been rain, but now there was half a foot of snow on deck; and both wind and sea had dropped amazingly.

'Snow?' said Grant. 'When I was in these waters I never came south of thirty-eight, and there was no snow. The forties are nothing but strong winds, storms, and pestilence: believe me, and I speak with thirty-five years' experience, a prudent commander will never go south of thirty-nine degrees. He will find no snow up there, I believe.'

Stephen found no snow in forty-three degrees either, when he came on deck early the next morning; but it was extremely cold and he did not linger more than the few minutes needed to show him that the swell, though heavy, had no breakers upon it, that the sky was low and dark, that the clouds moved evenly across it, at no great pace, and that the albatross out there on the starboard beam was a young bird, perhaps in its second or third year. He turned to walk into the cabin, and as he turned he saw Herapath's head coming up the hatchway: Herapath caught sight of him and dodged back, his face quite altered.

Stephen sighed privately. He liked Herapath; he regretted this young man's provoked and necessary betrayal, with its consequent suffering. But there was a friendlier face on the far side of the rail; an open, welcoming grin. 'Good morning, Barret Bonden,' he said. 'What are you at?'

'Good morning, sir; new puddening for the mizzen. A fine bright morning for the time of the year, sir.'

'I find it disagreeably chill; a dank and cutting air.'

'Well, perhaps it is a little parky, too. Cobb here says he can smell ice. He was a whaler, and they can smell ice a great way off.' They both looked at Cobb, and the whaler blushed, bending low over his puddening.

'Ice,' thought Stephen as he stepped into the cabin, 'and perhaps the great southern penguins, eared seals, the sea-elephant . . . How I should love to see a mountain of ice, a floating island. Killick, good morning, and how is himself?'

'Good morning, sir: passed a quiet night, and is as comfortable as can be expected.'

Comfortable, maybe, although he still seemed closed in and reserved: no doubt there was a good deal of pain in his head. Nausea for sure: he could not touch the huge breakfast that Killick provided. But Stephen was pleased with the leg, and when Jack stated his determination to be on deck for the noon observation he agreed, only insisting that there should be proper support, and wool next the skin. 'You may also receive Mr Grant if you wish,' he added. 'No doubt you are eager to learn the state of the ship. But you would be wise to speak very quietly, and to keep your mind as calm as may be.'

'Oh,' said Jack, 'I sent for him the moment I woke, and asked what the devil he meant by altering course without orders. There was the line' – with an unguarded nod at the compass hanging over his cot and a wince of pain – 'pointing north-east and then north. Anyone would have thought I had been killed in the action. I soon undeceived him. What a loud voice that fellow has: I dare say his mother was one of those bulls of Bashan. What is it?'

'Which it's Mr Byron, sir,' said Killick, 'asking may he report a mountain of ice to windward.'

Jack nodded, and winced again. As Byron came in Stephen rose, laid his finger to his lips, and left the room. The young man, quicker in wit than Mr Grant, whispered, 'A mountain of ice to windward, sir, if you please.'

'Very good, Mr Byron. How far away?'

'Two leagues, sir; bearing west-south-west a half west.'

'I see. Pray let the bell be muffled, Mr Byron. It fairly goes through my head.'

The muffled bell struck through the day, in a ship that had grown as silent as the tomb, so silent that those near the hatchways could distinctly hear the mewling of Mrs Boswell's baby on the orlop.

It quietened when it nuzzled its red, crinkled face into its mother's tawny bosom, and Mrs Wogan said, 'There, poor honey lamb: I will come back for her in an hour.'

'You are handy with these little creatures, I find,' said Stephen, leading her back to her cabin.

'I have always loved babies,' said she, and she seemed about to go on.

After a pause in which nothing emerged Stephen said, 'You must put on the warmest garments you possess before your walk, which I must ask you to take early today, with Mr Herapath. You have looked yellowish and peaked these last days, and the air is extremely raw. I recommend two pairs of stockings, two pairs of drawers, drawn well up about the belly, and a pelisse.'

'Upon my word, Dr Maturin,' said Mrs Wogan, starting to laugh.

'Upon my word, you are beyond the pale of humanity. You tell me I am not good in looks, and you name what cannot be named.'

'I am a physician, child: at times my office sets me as far beyond the human pale as the tonsure sets a priest.'

'So medical men do not look upon their patients as beings of the same race with themselves?'

'Let me put it thus: when I am called in to a lady, I see a female body, more or less deranged in its functions. You will say that it is inhabited by a mind that may partake of its distress, and I grant your position entirely. Yet for me the patient is not a woman, in the common sense. Gallantry would be out of place, and what is worse, unscientific.'

'It would grieve me to be a mere deranged female in your eyes,' said Mrs Wogan, and Stephen observed that for the first time in their acquaintance her composure was far from entire. 'Yet ... do you recall that at the beginning of this voyage you were so indiscreet as to ask whether I might be confined?' Stephen nodded. 'Well,' said she, twisting a piece of blue wool, 'were you to ask me now, I should be obliged to say yes, perhaps.'

After the usual investigation Stephen said that it was too early to be sure; that her view of the matter was probably correct; and that in any case she was to take more than common care of herself – no stays, no tight-lacing, no high-heeled shoes, no gross indulgence of any kind, no high living.

Mrs Wogan had been nervous and solemn up to this point, but the notion of high living in so desolate an ocean – half a pot of jam, three pounds of biscuits and a pound of tea all that remained of her stores – made her laugh with such amusement that Stephen was obliged to turn away, to preserve his character. 'Forgive me,' she said at last. 'I shall do everything you say, most religiously. I have always longed for a baby of my own, and although this one falls a little awkwardly perhaps, it shall have the best start that ever I can give it. And may I say,' she added, in a faltering voice, 'how much I honour your discretion? Even with Dr Maturin, I had dreaded this interview – perhaps I should say this confession – with its almost inevitable personal questions. You have been even kinder than I had hoped; I am so much obliged to you.'

Stephen said, 'Not at all, ma'am,' but the sight of her eyes brimming with tears and full of confiding affection made him deeply uneasy, and he was glad when she went on, with a gravity unusual in her, 'How I hope the rumour is not true, that the Captain is dying. I have heard that dreadful muffled bell, and all the sailors tell Peggy it tolls for him.'

'They are never in conversation with her again?' cried Stephen.

'Oh no,' said Mrs Wogan, who caught his meaning, 'they only talk through the bars. Pray, how does he do? I have heard such a tale of blood and wounds.'

'He was hurt, sure, and cruelly hurt; but with the blessing he may do well.'

'I shall say a novena for him.'

The novena had begun at noon, but Jack did not appear: it was not so much that he was unequal to the exertion, nor that low cloud made observation impossible, as that he was fast asleep. A deep, lasting, healthy sleep right round the clock and farther still, while Killick and the cook ate the enormous meals prepared for him, meals they had designed to fill him with good red blood. He woke with less pain, and although he was still somewhat removed, 'a bar or so behind' as he put it, he felt a keen interest in the welfare and the whereabouts of the ship. His leg was coming to, and a little before noon the next day he stumped out on to the quarterdeck and viewed the scene with the liveliest attention – much the same attention with which he himself was viewed, though covertly, by his officers, the young gentlemen, and all those members of the crew who were not actively employed in the head. He saw a grey and misty sea, with vapour rising from it; a smooth sea that heaved with a quiet swell; a low sky, but clearing here and there as the clouds or rather sea-fog parted, showing pale blue above; the *Leopard* neat and trim, slipping along through the smoking sea with scarcely a sign of her rough time apart from the mizzen-top, which was still repairing. On the starboard quarter, a school of whales, rising, rolling and spouting quite close, perfectly undisturbed. The quarterdeck beheld a tall, pale, strange-looking Captain with a fresh bandage over his gaunt face, silent, uncertain in his movements.

'Deck ho,' called the lookout. 'Ice island three points before the larboard beam. Maybe a league.'

Jack stared over the sea, and there in the wafting mist loomed the island, half a mile across or so, with a tall triangular peak to one side. Noon was too close for any detailed inspection: but he did see that it was surrounded by a mass of floating blocks. He made his way to his usual place, leant on the rail, gave Bonden his watch, took his sextant, and stared aloft. All the officers, all the young gentlemen did the same; if only the fog would clear in the north there was a fair chance of an observation, and it was thinning out fast. The pale sun at its height broke through: a general 'Ha' of satisfaction, and Jack wrote his reading while Bonden gave him the time by the watch. Then came the ritual of noon, the acting master to the officer of the watch, the officer to the Captain, Jack's grave 'Make it so, Mr Byron', and the hands piped to dinner. On the assumption that Jack was quite restored the order was carried out with the usual hullabaloo. He clapped his hand to his forehead, turned, stumbled on his game leg, and fell flat on the deck.

They ran to help him – small thanks for their pains – and when he was upright, clinging to the rail, he said, 'Mr Grant, when the hands have had their dinner, we will hoist out the jolly-boat and the red cutter to fetch ice from off that island.'

'I beg your pardon, sir, but it will run on to your coat,' said Grant. Indeed, the wound had opened, and the bandage was soaked already, the red blood dripping down his face.

'Well, well,' he said testily. 'Bonden, give me your arm. Mr Babbington, get that hairy thing of yours out of the fairway.' He had meant to ask Grant and the midshipman to dine with him. He was fully aware of the importance of the invulnerable, infallible commander, superior to all mortal ills, particularly with a crew like the *Leopard*'s, with some indifferent officers and what was now so large a proportion of raw hands, and he had caught the atmosphere of intense, doubting curiosity; but suddenly he felt that he could not bear an hour of Grant's loud, metallic voice, and he decided to put it off until tomorrow.

Yet before his solitary meal, Stephen, having renewed the bandage, sat with him for a while; and to Stephen he said, 'Here we are, do you see, in 42°45′E, 43°40′S. A good observation, and I checked the chronometers by a lunar only ten days ago, so we cannot be more than a minute out.'

Stephen looked at the chart and said, 'The Cape seems a great way off.'

'About thirteen hundred miles, give or take a score or so. Lord, how we did run off our easting, with the Devil at our heels.'

'It will take longer, I presume, to run it in again, and bring us back to the Cape.'

'There is little point in going back to the Cape. It is less than five thousand miles to Botany Bay, and down here in the forties, with the likelihood of fair winds all the way, we may run them off in under a month. As for hands, Mr Bligh or the Admiral are as likely to supply us as the Cape. Our stores have held out very well; so rather than beat back or run north and west, I mean to carry on, keeping to this parallel, or perhaps a little south.'

'No Cape,' said Stephen.

'No. Did you particularly wish to see the Cape again?'

'Oh, not at all,' said Stephen. And then, 'But come, you poured all the water away. What do we drink, during this month of yours?'

'Dear Stephen,' said Jack, smiling for the first time since the action, 'there is as much fresh water a few miles to leewards as ever we could wish. If you had been on deck for the observation you would have seen it, a monstrous fine great island of ice, enough to last us ten times round the world. That is why I had the ship's head kept south-

east. You always find these mountains floating about the high lati-
tudes, though I had not hoped for them quite so soon, this being what
they call summer.'

Stephen may have missed the iceberg in the forenoon, when he
was deep in Mrs Wogan's papers, she being walked by Herapath, but
he was not going to miss it now. As soon as he was free he put on his
comforter, a pilot jacket, and a woollen hat, borrowed Jack's common
telescope – much as he loved Stephen, Jack would not let him have
his best – and found a sheltered corner by the shivering hens. He sat
upon a coop and stared at the towering ice with great satisfaction: far
grander than he had imagined, a most enormous mass, fretted at its
base into fantastic shapes – deep bays, caverns, lofty pinnacles, over-
hanging cliffs. An ancient island, he presumed, decaying fast in its
northward drift. Great numbers of detached blocks floated at its foot,
and some fell from the heights as he watched. A deeply gratifying
spectacle. The Cape was a disappointment, particularly as both he
and Mrs Wogan had relied upon it: her papers were almost ready, and
only a few pages of Herapath's transcript remained to be encoded. By
now she was much quicker at her task, though she still used the inky,
often-folded key that he had copied on an earlier occasion to include
in his own letter from the Cape – such a letter from an agent put out
to grass! 'But still,' he said, shrugging, 'Cape Town or Port Jackson,
the end is much the same: though I do regret the loss of time. If the
British boobies do provoke the Americans into a declaration of war,
they may weep for these lost months.' Far over, where the boats were
busy, a dark form hauled out on to the ice. He stared more intently
still. 'A sea-leopard?' If only it would turn its head. 'God damn this
glass.' He wiped the lens, but with no good result: it was not the glass
misting, but the fog that dimmed his view. A yellowish fog that presently increased, so that the spires of the island came and went, showing like floating castles made of glass.

The ice had been coming aboard at a fine pace, hoisted up with
cam-hooks, and there was question of using the other cutter, perhaps

the launch. From what little Stephen retained of the conversation on the quarterdeck as it flowed past his inattentive ears, the officers were in disagreement. Over and over again Babbington said that when he was in *Erebus* north of the Banks he had noticed that the current always set in towards an ice island; and the larger the island the stronger the current – it was common knowledge in northern waters. Other voices maintained that this was all stuff; that everyone knew the current set eastward in these latitudes, regardless; the southern hemisphere was quite different; Babbington was only showing away, with his Newfoundland Banks; he might keep that for his Newfoundland dog, or tell it to the Marines.

The *Leopard* stood off and on for some time after Stephen had given up hope of seeing anything at a distance, and in spite of the apparently immobile fog her topgallantsails caught enough breeze up there to send her along at a comfortable pace, so that she came about easily at the end of each of her short boards. Babbington kept insisting, in an earnest voice, that something should be referred to the Captain; grant that he should not be disturbed. The Captain was far too sick to be disturbed. Eventually Babbington came over to Stephen and said, 'Doctor, do you think I can go into the cabin without doing any harm?'

'Certainly, if you talk in a reasonable tone, and not as though your interlocutor were seven miles off, and he deprived of hearing. You may find that answer in the wardroom, Mr Babbington, where people interrupt you before you have opened your lips; but it will not do in the cabin today. For you are to consider, that loss of blood renders the ears preternaturally acute.'

Two minutes later Jack came out, leaning on Babbington's shoulder. He looked at the sea and the fog and said, 'Where is the jolly-boat?'

'Between us and the island, sir, right on the larboard beam. I saw them not ten minutes ago.'

'Signal the cutter to follow, run down and pick 'em up. We do not want to lie here all day, firing guns, while they wander about in the fog looking for us. I do not like the look of this current, either. There will be plenty of ice tomorrow, and clear weather, if this breeze goes on.'

The *Leopard* ran down, heaved to within three-quarters of a mile of the island, unloaded the jolly-boat, hoisted it in, and waited a while for the cutter. During this time a thin gleam broke through the fog, and although Stephen could not distinguish anything but a single giant petrel he did have the pleasure of seeing even greater masses of ice fall from the high cliffs above the low-lying mist, masses the size of a house that either shattered at the foot of the mountain or plunged straight into the sea, sending up vast fountains of water: scores of these monstrous great blocks.

The cutter was hoisted in. Jack said, 'Spritsail, foresail, topsails and topgallants: give the island a wide berth with this damned current, then east-south-east.'

The watch changed. Turnbull came on deck, muffled like a bear; Babbington handed over: 'Here you have her; spritsail, foresail, topsails, topgallants; give the ice-island a wide berth, then east-south-east,' and Stephen, licking a piece of ice – it was quite fresh – once again meditated upon the enormous amount of repetition in the service.

Jack lingered until Turnbull had trimmed the sails and the *Leopard* was making five or six knots; then he said, 'Mr Grant, come and take a dish of tea in the cabin. You will join us, Doctor?'

'Thank you, sir,' said Grant, 'but I am sure you are not equal to company.'

Jack made no reply: he stared over the side for a while, trying to pierce the fog and see the iceberg out on the larboard beam, but it was gone. Then he led the way aft, holding Stephen's arm, and followed, rather awkwardly, by Grant.

The awkwardness persisted throughout the tea-drinking, and it caused Grant to speak in a voice louder and more brassy than usual. Stephen was glad to escape: 'I shall sit with Mrs Wogan and her stove for a while,' he said as he made his way down to the orlop.

He was on the top step of the lower ladder when he was flung bodily down to its foot. An enormous echoing crash seemed the cause, and the total arrest of the ship's forward motion. At once all the people below rushed over his body as they made their way on deck, and it was some time before he could gather his wits. He heard furious contradictory cries of 'Up with the helm' and 'Down with the helm' and a confused bellowing.

Herapath came leaping below in two bounds, with a spike in his hand. Seeing Stephen he cried, 'The key! The key! I must get her out from down there.'

'Calm yourself, Mr Herapath. There are no rending timbers, no evident leak, no immediate peril. But here is the key, and that of the forepeak. You may liberate them if the water should rise.' He spoke quietly enough, but Herapath's frantic dismay affected him to the extent of causing him to step into his cabin, make a quick, judicious selection of his papers and put them into his bosom before climbing up to the deck.

There he found an appearance of complete disorder, some men running aft, others running forward to join the vague shadowy forms on the forecastle. The ship and everything around her was shrouded deep in fog until an eddy of wind tore it apart; and there, high above the masthead, he saw a wall of ice, soaring up and up, leaning out so as to overhang the deck; and its base, with the breaking waves, was not twenty feet away.

'Haul of all,' came Jack's voice, loud and clear, doubled by the echo of the ice. The disorder vanished, the yards creaked round, the towering wall moved sideways, gently on and on until it lay abeam. Then the fog closed in and a dead silence fell.

'Fore topgallant staysail,' said Jack. 'Rig the pumps.'

The sound of running feet and hauling died away: in the silence nothing could be heard but once the thunderous crash of falling ice some way to starboard, the grinding of the pumps, and the gush of water from the side. No one spoke: all on the quarterdeck stood motionless, and their breath, condensing, joined the silent fog. Silence, and the ship dead still, quite motionless.

Then a vast rending that jarred the *Leopard* throughout her length and breadth, and she began to move.

'Helm amidships,' said Jack.

'No helm, sir,' said the quartermaster, spinning the wheel.

Babbington raced below. 'Rudder's beat off, sir,' he reported.

'We shall soon deal with that,' said Jack. 'All hands to the pumps.'

Now began a period of the most intense activity. Stephen saw sails taken in, others lowered down, and sheets let fly. Mr Gray or his mates kept running up to report the depth of water in the well, and presently Jack disappeared, hobbling with his arm round Bonden's neck. His face was firm and confident when he returned, but Stephen was persuaded that he had found a very grave state of affairs below. This impression was confirmed within the minute, for parties were taken from the pumps and set to lighten ship. Her precious guns went overboard, splashing into the quiet, misty sea through their open ports, their careful breeching slashed through with an axe. All the shot within reach. All the hard-won ice that was still on deck. The anchors, cut from the bows. The great cables followed them, and cask after cask of provisions, all that were nearest to the hatchways. Hours of furious toil.

'How well they throw up the water,' said Stephen to his neighbour on the pump-winch.

'Too bloody well, mate,' said the seaman, who did not recognize him in the growing dark. 'The scuppers can't take it all. It's swilling about the deck, and if this fucking sea gets up any more, it'll pour down the hatch every time she rises.'

'Perhaps we shall exhaust it very soon.'

'Hold your jaw and pump, you silly bugger. You don't know nothing.'

The sea mounted, the wind blew stronger; men were sent all along the lee-scuppers to keep them clear and help the water over the side. But at last the hatch had to be battened down, and the lightening of the ship grew harder still. At midnight the cleverer hands were called from the pumps, and they set to in the waist, plying needle and palm by lantern-light, sewing rolls of oakum to a studdingsail that was to be passed under the ship's bottom to stop the leak; but still the pumps whirled on and on, and in time the night assumed an everlasting quality – heaving round the winch, poising on the roll in the darkness to thrust with all one's force, was all that mattered in the world. At one point there was a general cheer at the report that the larboard chain-pump was sucking, but they did not stop for a moment: and although the report proved false – it was only a temporary blocking of the channel – the cry itself was encouraging.

Once the extreme measures had been taken the hands were relieved at regular intervals, and they trooped aft to the wardroom, where the purser and his steward had thin grog, biscuit, cheese and sausage laid out on the table. They all ate together, worn and exhausted by the toil at the heavy pump-winches and even more by the icy wind and the rain, but still hopeful, still cheerful, as though this were an unpleasant, long-lasting dream that would come to an end in time.

The slow grey morning showed a troubled, broken sea, a strong and rising wind: the *Leopard*, low and heavy, had lost her main topsail and her foretopgallant. Hands could not be spared from the pumps to furl them, and they had blown to ribbons. Shortly after, the foretopsail followed them. Yet now the studdingsail that was to stop the leak was over the side, and men with ropes on either gangway were working it along the bottom. The great question was to find the leak, for since the ship had first struck the ice stern-on and had then turned, hanging on her keel, there was no telling where it might be. Grant was right out on the jibboom in spite of the heavy sea – it very nearly killed him twice – but he could make out no damage to the bows; and in the close-packed hold, deep in water, it was of course impossible to come at her bottom or her sides.

But the likelihood was that the leak was in the stern, where the rudder had received its blow, and they cut the deck to reach the breadroom right aft, hoisting up everything that could lighten the ship and throwing it from the wardroom window; for once the breadroom was clear they could cut lower still and perhaps find the leak, down in the

Leopard's run. At the same time they worked on another fothering-sail, since the first had had little or no effect. And all through these hours the pumps worked on as strongly as ever; never a pause for a broken chain, never the least slackening of the general effort, although by now the seas were making a clean breach over the gunwale and soaking the hands as they worked. Each pump was discharging a ton a minute, a splendid gush; yet all the time the water mounted in the well. Seven feet, eight feet, ten feet.

It was when Mr Gray reported ten feet in the well that the star-board pump-chain broke and the poor old man had to turn to and unship the casing to get at the link – hours of work in the darkness after his spell at the winch. And then as soon as it was repaired the small-coal, swilling about in the water below, choked it.

Stephen had now lost count of time. It seemed to pass round him, or over him, in a perpetual muddle and hurry, or at least with so many things going on at once that he could not keep track of them, though he was aware that some guiding intelligence directed the obscure movements in the darkness. The only thing that was clear in his mind – the centre of his physical and mental activity except on those occasions when he was called away to dress a wound – was the pump, and the plain, direct, urgent task of heaving it round so that the ship should not sink.

Now, with the team standing idle while it was being repaired, he stared stupidly for a while, and then followed them aft to the ward-room. Men had now been pumping so long and so furiously in this bitter rain and sleet that the moment they had a pause in the shelter they fell asleep as soon as they had eaten, or even while they were eating.

Hours passed. The pump was repaired and the midshipman in charge of it roused them all out. Another spell, and the heaving soon became mechanical again, the wind and the rain hardly noticed. Relief: deep and apparently momentary sleep: and they were called out again.

After an indefinite period Stephen noticed that they had prepared another sail for fothering the ship, and that they were going through the same laborious motions of passing it under her bottom, a long, tedious operation with innumerable orders roaring over the grind of the pumps. Being an animate cog in the machine was hard enough, the hardest, most prolonged physical exertion he had ever performed: he did not envy the man who had to command the whole, adding extreme mental exertion to all the rest.

With great labour the sail was passed aft and bowsed taut. The leak still gained. Jack had been at the pumps all the time he could spare from the lightening of the ship and all the fothering: his leg had not allowed him to move about nearly as much as he wished and he had had to rely on Grant for much of the work and many of the instant decisions; and Grant had behaved extremely well. His heart warmed to the man: Grant knew his calling through and through – a real seaman.

He was pleased with the *Leopard*'s people too. They had worked nobly; discipline had held after the initial panic – it was true that he and his officers had taken the greatest care that they should not get at anything stronger than the thin grog in the wardroom. They had toiled on and on, soaked in the wicked cold with nothing to cheer them but one false report, in a ship that already looked very like a wreck – never had he seen pumps worked round so fast for so many hours together.

But after his last visit to the well, and the report that he heard there, he wondered how long they would hold out against the discouragement, the biting wind, and the physical exhaustion. Hitherto he had been able to tell the men at the pumps something that he at least partly believed, and that heartened them: now, returning for another spell, all he could produce was the old 'Huzzay, heave round. Heave round, huzzay!'

Grant relieved him, with the same cry, and he stumped to the wardroom for a bite. Here he found Stephen and Herapath, dressing a number of wounds – crushed fingers and the like among the men employed in getting the casks of flour up from the breadroom – and

the women. He saw the women without surprise; by now the water
was above the orlop. Above the orlop: the hold quite full: and everyone knew it.

Byron and three of the youngsters were down here too: in five
minutes they would be rousing out the men of their divisions. Most
of them had behaved well, as far as he had had time to see, carrying
messages and co-ordinating the labours of the crew, though he had
noticed some absences. One little boy was sobbing convulsively, but
this was mere exhaustion: Jack had seen him on deck five minutes
ago, running with a great load of cable-junks. Byron silently passed
him a piece of cheese. He took it, put it in his mouth, and dropped
into a sleep, if such a stupor could be called sleep. But he jerked into
consciousness when the relief was called, and returned through the
darkness to the starboard pump on Bonden's arm. There were fewer
men at their duty now – more and more were hiding – and these
worked silently, with much less strength: hope was fading, if it was
not entirely dead. He called out, 'Huzzay, heave round,' mechanically,
and as he did so he forced his mind to work out fresh ways of coming
at the leak, and of steering the ship once it was stopped; Pakenham
had made a rudder from spare topmasts . . .

How he got through that night he could not tell, but after a stretch
of darkness in which time had no meaning there was Bonden half
leading, half carrying him back to the cabin. Before they reached it,
the heat of hard pumping was all gone, and the cold reached through
to his heart. Here Stephen dressed his wound and made him lie down,
swearing to wake him within the hour.

'Sit on the locker, Bonden,' said Stephen, 'and drink some of this
coffee. Tell me, now, how much longer will they hold out?' He had
already heard much of the muttering, the frightened, exhausted men
calling for the boats, for anything but pumping for ever in a ship that
must surely sink – that might sink at any minute, drawing them all
down. He had felt the panic dread of that mortal plunge, the Dutchman's fate, and many a time he had heard the words 'unlucky ship.'

'I doubt they'll last out today,' said Bonden. 'I mean the hands that don't know the Captain. They say the boats should have been got out right away – they say Mr G knows these waters and will take 'em back to the Cape – they say the Captain's not right in the head. I crowned one bugger for that – beg pardon, sir, and in course they all know she's an unlucky ship.' Bonden's head drooped forward: from his sleep he murmured, 'They say Mr G said something to Turnbull . . .' but no more.

Jack was awake, grey but alive, with Killick's good breakfast dispelling the cold, when Grant came to him, reported the water over the top of the well and gaining fast, and the parting of the new fothering-sail at the clews. 'So there we are, sir. We have done all we can by the ship. We cannot pass a new sail before she settles. Shall I provision the boats? I presume you will go in the launch.'

'I do not intend leaving the ship, Mr Grant.'

'She is sinking under us, sir.'

'I am not sure of that. We may save her yet – fother the leak – fashion a rudder with a spare topmast.'

'Sir, the hands have wrought hard, very hard, ever since the moment we struck. We cannot in honesty give them any more hope. And if I may speak plain, I doubt they would come to their duty, with the water deep in the orlop. I doubt they would still obey orders.'

'Would you still obey orders, Mr Grant?' asked Jack with a smile.

'I will obey orders, sir,' said Grant, deadly earnest. 'No man shall ever accuse me of mutiny. All lawful orders. But, sir, is it lawful to order men to their death, with no enemy at hand, no battle? I respect your decision to stay with your ship, but I beg you to consider those of another way of thinking. I believe the ship must founder. I believe the boats can reach the Cape.'

'I hear what you say, Mr Grant,' said Jack. He reflected: the discontented men would do nothing from this moment on – they certainly knew Grant's mind; there would be no point in putting down the mutiny, if mutiny this could be called, even if he could rely on the Marines. 'I hear what you say. I think that you are probably mistaken, and that the *Leopard* will swim. But swim or not, I stay with her. Each man must do what he thinks right. If you think it right to go off in the boats, you may do so, and God speed you well. But you must see them provisioned. What now, William?' he said, looking up.

It was Babbington, looking old, yellow, and destroyed. 'The bosun has come aft with a party of men, sir. I said I thought you would see them,' he said, with a significant look. 'Shall I ask Captain Moore to step in?'

'No. I will see them.'

They wanted the boats, they said: they meant no disrespect – they believed they had done their duty – but the barky was sinking – they wanted to chance their luck in the cutters and the launch.

'Yes,' said Jack. 'You have done your duty; no man could ask more. And it is true, the ship is in a very sad way. But I believe she has a better chance than the boats. At all events, I stay with her. I tell you again, I tell you fair, I believe she may swim. If you and your mates will go back and pump, while we fother her again, I promise you I will give Mr Grant orders to prepare the boats; they will be there and ready, if there is no hope for the ship.

'There you are, Mr Grant,' he said when they were alone, 'that will give you some hours to provision them. Launch and prepare both cutters: leave the jolly-boat – it will be no use to you. Take what you need; but for God's sake do not let the hands get into the spirit-room.'

They would go: he was certain of that. Go even before he had tried a new sail. Some of these men were mad for escape, even into open boats with thirteen hundred miles of sea between them and the Cape, and soon there would be no controlling them by any means short of death; and there was nothing to be gained by killing men at this juncture. When Stephen came in he said, 'Stephen, the boat will soon be away, probably some time before nightfall. If you choose to go, pray dress up warm and take my waterproof cloak. They will take you, I know.'

'They? You do not go?'

'No. I stay with the ship. But I do not wish you to feel the least obligation to remain, if you had rather not.'

'It is a matter of principle with you?' Jack nodded. 'Listen, will you lay it plain before me, now? I speak for some papers I have, not for myself. Principles aside – for I know your views on what is right in a captain – which is the better course?'

'I may be wrong, but I still think the ship. Yet the launch may get through. Bligh took his boat farther, and Grant is an excellent seaman: he will certainly be in the launch.'

'Then I shall give him what I can copy. Forgive me now, Jack, I must work as fast as I can. The ship is all on a buzz with this talk of the boats, and there are some fellows may break out in no time at all.'

Jack hobbled out on to the quarterdeck. There was still a fair semblance of order. A man stood by the useless wheel: the glass had been turned; the pumps were working steadily. The wind had lessened, and with it the sea; the *Leopard*, strangely low in the water, moved steadily on, her trim keeping the breeze on the beam. He called for the bosun and gave orders for the launch to be hoisted out, then the cutters. The jolly-boat was not to be touched. A long task, but efficiently carried out, the men working with a will: and all the time he was conscious of furtive looks darting at him from the men and boys on the quarterdeck. When it was done he told Grant to see them provisioned and went below to write to the Admiralty and to Sophie. It was when he came to this that the shift between himself and the present broke down, vanished entirely. It had been with him ever since that remote day of the *Waakzaamheid*, this sense of observing the world from a distance, and of moving, functioning, more through duty than intimate concern; and the moment of its breaking, of his coming wholly to life, was exquisitely painful.

At the same time, below him, down on the orlop with the water washing about his shins, Stephen wrote like a man possessed: a summary that nevertheless covered page after page in close-written code.

They were both of them jerked from their writing by a bawling, hallooing, rioting din. What Jack feared most had happened: getting aft, uncontrolled, for provisions, some hands had forced the spiritroom door. Some were roaring drunk already. Others were follow-

ing their example. At much the same time the larboard chain-pump
broke down at last, choked with the coal that had washed into the
well; at once its team hurried aft; and at once the leak began gaining
faster still. This was the end.

In the event the boats' parting was not a clear-cut division between
those who wanted to go and those who, from duty or loyalty to their
captain and trust in his powers, chose to stay: it was a period of very
ugly confusion, panic in some, drunken madness in others, a period
in which cabins were looted, boxes broken open, so that waisters
appeared in laced coats and hats and two pairs of trousers, and men
were killed or drowned as they tried to crowd into the boats. Some
tried to launch the jolly-boat, but Bonden and a score of his friends
would not let them. The division had a good deal to do with men's
ability to hold drink, and some good hands who would have stayed
an hour earlier now went over the side. Yet still, roughly speaking, it
followed the line of attachment to the Captain, although there were
some surprising, sober departures.

But with the spirit-room open the final stages were so squalid, so
saddening, that Jack would not look on at all. Having shaken Grant's
hand, having given him the packets for England, and having wished
him all that a sailor could hope for, he retired to his charts and his
drawing of a jury-rudder.

Stephen stayed by the rail to the end: sometimes they called to him
to come into one boat or another, but he only shook his head. He saw
the launch hoist a lug-sail and stand away to the north: the red cutter,
unable to step its mast, rowed after it, while the blue pulled back to the
ship, catching crabs, falling about, and then ramming the side. They
had already lost their sails, and they bawled out for more. Someone
flung a bundle of canvas into the boat, and perhaps a score of men with
second thoughts or with none at all jumped from the ship's gunwale
and chains. The last the *Leopard* saw of them as they went astern was
the dark struggling mass in the icy water as those in the sea fought to
get into the boat and those in the boat fought to keep them out.

CHAPTER NINE

'Wednesday, 24 December. Course estimated E 15°S. Latitude estimated 46°30′S. Longitude 49°45′E. First part, fresh breezes at WNW, latter parts calm and fine. People employed pumping and thrumming spritsail to fother ship. Water one and a half foot above orlop beams forward, one foot amidship and aft.

'Thursday, 25 December. Course estimated E 10°S. Latitude observed 46°37′S. Longitude estimated 50°15′E. Winds light and variable with haze and rain. Sea calm with several small blocks of ice. PM hauled up foresail, veered out stop-water to check ship's way, and passed fothering-sail forward from abaft the sternpost, bowsing it taut from the fashion-pieces to the mizzen-chains. The sail answered and the pumps gained five foot in the day.'

Jack was copying his rough notes into the log-book, and when he came to this triumphant entry he smiled. He was tempted to embellish it with an epithet or two – to add something about the feeble screech by way of a cheer when the gain of the first clear foot was reported – to describe the extraordinary change of spirit, the flood of new strength that sent the winches flying round, so that from having to encourage, threaten, beat or even cajole the exhausted hands, their officers had to restrain their zeal, for fear that the pump-chains would break or choke yet again – to speak of the Christmas dinner (fresh pork and double plum-duff) eaten with such merriment in relays. But he knew that even if he could find words to describe this change, a log-book was not the place for them, and he contented himself with drawing a small pointing hand in the margin.

His earlier notes, those that dealt with the first days after the boats went off, had been lost when he and the carpenters were trying to rig some kind of a rudder, working out of the stern-window – a following sea had set the whole cabin in a swim. They had recorded the *Leopard*'s eastward course, directly before the wind for the most part, travelling on in what seemed a slow death-agony, while all her people's efforts were divided between trying to keep her afloat and trying to get her to steer. The pumps never still, except when they broke down or choked with the infernal coal: the men perpetually heaving the winches round and sometimes even baling too, when the water surged up through the scuttles and hatchways, as though the ship were settling at last.

Even now, with the leak so much reduced that the ship made no more than the pumps could throw out, the *Leopard* still could not be made to wear and stay. She was very much by the head, so that the water there did not flow back to the well; and the almost invariably western winds with following seas kept her so. The first steering-machine had been too heavy for its supports and had carried away; the remaining hawsers, towing vanes of one kind and another, had little effect when they were veered out; and none of the combinations of sails and drogues had moved her head more than a few points. Now he and Mr Gray were busy, or as busy as the poor old carpenter's failing strength would allow, with a steering-oar, an object that harked back to the earliest days of sail, now taken up on an enormous scale.

The question of steering had of course been of the first importance from the moment the *Leopard* had lost her rudder, but these last few days it was even more present to his mind than usual. At any moment now the Crozet Islands might heave in sight, and to reach them he must be able to manoeuvre the ship. Just when they might appear he could not tell: in the first place he had little confidence in the longitude laid down by their French discoverer, and in the second his chronometers had been overturned in the drunken turmoil when the boats put off, so that he had only his hack-watch for his position. However, neither he nor the Frenchman could be far out in the latitude, and he had been keeping the *Leopard* as near to 46°45′S as ever he could, though with these covered skies he could rarely make a noon observation. And for days now, in spite of the shortage of hands, the sharpest eyes in the ship had been at the masthead.

The log ran on: 'Sunday. Course E 10°N. Latitude estimated 46°50′S, longitude 50°30′E. Fresh breezes at W and WNW. Larboard pump sucked. Rigged church for shortened prayers and thanksgiving; read Articles of War. Admonished Wm Plaice, James Hole, Thos. Paine and M. Lewis for drunkenness and sleeping. People employed about steering-machine and pumps. Set the foresail and middle staysail. PM starboard pump-chain broke for the eighth time; hove up and rove again in under one hour.'

Jack had very nearly brought the book up to this day's date when the welcome drum began to beat, and he stumped out into the rain and down the hatchway to the wardroom. All the officers messed there now, and, since both the Captain's and the wardroom cook had taken to the boats, and Killick's notion of cookery went little farther than toasted cheese, their food came straight from the galley, unadorned. They still ate it in a certain style, however, and they still made a fairly creditable appearance; for with the Captain presiding this amounted to something like a cabin-invitation, and they all wore at least a uniform coat. Although the remaining oldsters had come from the drowned midshipmen's berth to fill the places left by Grant, Turnbull, Fisher and Benton, the long table looked rather sparse, particularly as there were no servants behind the chairs; but, as Jack, Babbington, Moore and Byron frequently observed, *the fewer the better fare.* Today's fare, by immemorial custom, should have been half a pint of dried peas and oatmeal, this being a banyan day; but the pumps still called for unusual exertion and the steering-oar was going to call for a great deal more, so all hands were allowed a piece of salt beef. As every officer took his full share at the winches, night and day, and as the temperature was only just above freezing, the wardroom ate up its beef with silent, barbarous avidity, relaxing only when the plates disappeared and the wine came in. A brief return to civility – the King's health – a very little conversation – and Jack said, 'Well, gentlemen . . .'

The steering-oar was a most imposing affair, a spare foresail-yard with a paddle at the seaward end: it was to pivot on the taffrail, strengthened for the purpose, and the inboard arm was to be moved from side to side by tackles to the crossjack yard and the mizzen. The rigging of such an engine called for a high degree of skill with ropes, blocks, and the marlinspike, an intuitive grasp of marine dynamics: Stephen could be of no use – indeed, he was invited to go away – and when he had finished his spell at the pump he stood at the rail, indulging himself with a view of the birds. They had increased in number quite remarkably these last days – skuas, whalebirds, alba-trosses and petrels of different kinds, sheathbills, terns – and he had noticed that they appeared to be travelling to or from some fixed point to the north. The north, however, was at present swathed in rain, and he crossed to the starboard side, where the light was better for looking down into the water, with its splendid wealth of penguins: here he had seen a seal pursuing them, so that the little creatures shot from the surface almost like flying-fish, but not so far nor so efficiently, alas. And here he had seen the seal herself pursued, hunted down and dismembered by a troop of killer-whales, so that the sea turned red. Penguins: there they were, flying nimbly under water, chasing long thin fishes that in their turn were feeding amidst an infinity of fine stout shrimps, as pink as if they had been boiled. Duty called Stephen to the side of Mrs Boswell and young Leop-ardina and to his sick-bay; humanity called upon him to visit Mrs Wogan. In vain. 'If her constitution can withstand a Caesarian deliv-ery in the midst of battle,' he observed, 'five minutes delay cannot much affect Mrs Boswell; besides, she is doing extremely well – no doubt she is asleep.' Five minutes: ten: and as the warmth of pumping was leaving him – as the wind was biting through his fourth waist-coat and comforter – he was rewarded by what appeared to be the sea-bed rising to the surface right by the ship, a vast dark area that grew clearer and clearer until it assumed the form of a whale. But a whale of unspeakable dimensions: still it rose, unhurried, and as he stared, holding his breath, the sea rounded in a smooth boil – the surface parted – the creature's streaming back appeared, dark blue-grey just flecked with white, stretching from the fore to the mizzen-chains. The head rose higher still and expired a rushing jet of air that instantly condensed in a plume as tall as the foretop and floated over the *Leopard*'s bowsprit: and at the same moment Stephen himself breathed out. He believed he heard the hissing inspiration just before the head sank and the enormous bulk slid over in an easy, leisurely motion; a dorsal fin appeared, far back; a hint of the flukes themselves, and the sea closed softly over Leviathan; but his hurry of spirits was so great that he could not be sure.

'Cobb, Cobb!' he cried, seeing the whaler and dragging him to the side. 'What is that? Tell me, what is that?' An acre or so of monstrous back could still be seen, moving slowly through the shrimps.

'Oh, he's only a blue finner,' said Cobb. 'You don't want to take any notice of him.'

'But it was a hundred feet long! It stretched from here to there!'

'I dare say,' said Cobb. 'But he's only a blue finner, a nasty, spiteful thing. You plant a harpoon in his side, and what does he do? He rushes on you like a thunder-clap and beats the boat to splinters and then runs out a thousand fathom of line. You don't want to take notice of him. Now by your leave, sir, I must go aloft. There's Moses Harvey looking down quite old-fashioned, for to be relieved.'

Chilled through and through, Stephen cast a lingering glance over the sea and went below: he looked at Mrs Boswell's stitches with great satisfaction and then made his way to the store that now served as a sick-bay. Herapath was waiting for him, and together they inspected their only patient, the Turkish eunuch. This being Ramadan, the Turk refrained from food and drink throughout the daylit hours; and as he also refrained from pork by night he was now in a very feeble state. They had tried to delude him with artificial darkness, but some inner clock frustrated them. 'The new moon alone will cure this case,' said Stephen, and they talked about the general health of the ship, most astonishingly good in spite of the long absence of fresh provisions and in spite of the incessant toil. This Stephen attributed to the great reduction in numbers, so that when the men slept, they slept with plenty of space about them, and no vitiated air; to the bracing cold;

and above all to the sense of crisis, that left no time for hypochondria. 'And to this same sense of imminent disaster,' said he, 'we no doubt owe the singular harmony, the quasi-unanimity with which the work of the ship is carried on. No harsh words, no vehement rebukes are heard; the rattan canes, the knotted ends of rope no longer encumber the lictors' hands. A cheerful compliance, even an anticipatory zeal, does away with the fretful exercise of authority; and upon this, perhaps more than upon any other factor but the Captain's skill in navigation, we may rely for our eventual salvation. And no doubt it was providential that we got rid of the discordant element, of those whom he might term the awkward sods . . .'

'We got rid of the Jonah, is all that matters,' said the Turk, to their astonishment. 'All's well, now no Jonah.'

Stephen walked over and looked down at the wasted yellow glabrous face: the Turk closed one knowing eye, and said, 'No Jonah now,' closed the other, and spoke no more.

'It is true, sir,' said Herapath, after a pause. 'I have heard it all over the ship – my former messmates – all the lower deck. They were convinced Mr Larkin was a Jonah: that was why he drank so much, they said, because he believed it himself. They were very pleased when he tried to get into the boat in the last rush, and,' he added in a whisper, 'I think some of them helped him over the side.'

Stephen nodded: likely enough. He would have offered some observations on the power of faith, had not the cry of 'Land ho' transfixed him as they formed.

On deck they followed the pumpers' staring eyes, and there, on the larboard beam, a snowy peak showed and vanished among the clouds some ten or fifteen miles to the north. Stephen, Herapath, the few remaining landsmen and convicts, were jubilant; they would have cheered, capered, tossed their hats into the air, had it not been for the reserve, the anxious questioning looks of the sailors.

To these it was clear that everything depended on the steering-oar. If it could bring the *Leopard* up to the wind so that she could stay and lie close-hauled on either tack, all was well. If it could even bring the west wind one point forward of the beam, the ship might make the land on the larboard tack alone, so long as the operation was carried out within the hour, before she had been driven still farther to the east. But if the oar could not bring her up, or if it could not bring her even half up precious soon, she was condemned to travel on and on, with nothing between her pierced bottom and the antarctic sea but a piece of worn sailcloth that could not last much longer.

Once again the ship broke into the most intense activity. Few could help in the long and complex rigging of the oar, but once the sails were so trimmed as to bring her head as far north of east as possible, they could all set to the pumps, they could all lighten the ship, so that she would answer her helm the quicker, when she had a helm to answer to.

'Huzzay, heave round,' they cried, and again the water gushed out in a stiff, prodigious jet. Stephen stood between Moore and his remaining sergeant, both of them experienced theoretical seamen, and in gasps they kept him informed of the progress aft. It was maddeningly slow: they kept glancing at the mountain, clearer now that the clouds had dissolved in rain, and saying that the ship was not to leeward, no not by a mile and more. It was plain, from their talk of preventer-guys, double-rove, and the like, that the Captain was leaving nothing to chance: that was wisdom, no doubt, yet a huge impatience welled up, a violent longing for the oar to be tried, perfectly rigged or not.

An hour passed by: the rain beat on the pumpers' steaming backs; and at last some hands were called away to the poop. Those at the pumps saw the head of the oar rise to its place just abaft the mizzenmast; they saw the tackles tighten; and after a pause in which the rain turned to sleet, they heard the cry, 'Stand by, starboard: handsomely now, handsomely, and half a fathom. Larboard ease away.' The *Leopard*'s motion changed perceptibly. Still heaving the winches round like fury, the pumpers tended their faces to the wind, felt it come full abeam, and then a little forward. They heard the familiar call of the men at the bowlines, 'Heave one, heave two, heave belay,' that meant the ship was sailing on a wind – a call they had not heard for weeks. One point free: but no farther. In spite of all the orders from the poop, all the movements of the enormous oar, the *Leopard* would not lie closer. Jack could not set the driver, and all their recent labour to get the ship by the stern so that she would wear prevented her from coming up, or at least from coming up with any headway still on her.

'Still,' said Moore, 'she will do. A near-run thing, but she will do.' And indeed Stephen, looking forward, saw that the *Leopard* was heading not straight for the island, but a very little to the windward of it.

Now began a long series of operations carried out with extraordinary speed: yards were braced, jibs hauled down, set again and flatted in, staysails flashed out, hands sent to the larboard side of the forecastle and head so that their weight might help – every conceivable manoeuvre to get the ship a few yards to windward, to overcome her natural leeway, the effect of the waves that kept knocking her head off the wind, and that of the powerful current perpetually setting east. At first Moore explained these one by one, but presently he fell silent; and as Stephen watched the island he saw it gradually move from the right of the bowsprit to a point where the bowsprit bisected the peak, and at last, when it was within a mile, well to the left. He had never seen leeway more clearly exemplified: all this time the *Leopard* had been pointing due north, yet all the time she had slipped a little sideways in a sea that was itself in motion, moving bodily away to the east, so that with the two the island itself appeared to travel west.

Although the light was fading fast by now – a growing purple low in the south-west – the rocky shores were well in sight, with clouds of sea-birds over them, and the minute forms of penguins, crowds of penguins, standing on the beaches or emerging from the sea. And what is more, there was a small sheltered bay, clear of surf, just under the lee of an outward-running spur.

More orders from the poop. 'He is going to commit all his forces now,' said Moore. 'Throw in his last reserves.'

'Half a fathom, handsomely. Half a fathom more,' said Jack, and the island moved to the right: the little bay opened wider. 'Half a fathom – Christ!'

A long rending crack and the oar broke at the head. The loom and paddle went astern, held by a guy, the *Leopard*'s head swung from the wind, the island moved to the left in a long, slow, even motion until it lay on the larboard quarter, dwindling astern, as inaccessible as the moon.

'In mizzen topsail and topgallant,' said Jack in the midst of the heavy silence.

It was within three days of this that the first cases of scurvy appeared in the sick-bay. All four of them were prime seamen, broad-shouldered, long-armed, powerfully-built, responsible men, cheerful in an emergency, valuable members of the crew. Now they were glum, listless, apathetic; and only a sense of what was right kept them from complaining or open despondency. Stephen pointed out the physical symptoms, the spongy gums, the offensive breath, the extravasated blood, and in two cases the old reopening wounds; but he insisted even more upon the gloom as the most significant part of the disease. 'I must confess, Mr Herapath,' he said, 'that nothing grieves me more than this dependence of the mind upon the body's nutriment. It points to a base necessitarianism that I rebel against with all the vehemence my spirit can engender. And here, in the particular instance, I am at a loss. These men have had their sovereign lime-juice. Perhaps we must inspect the cask: most merchants are a sort of half-rogues, and quite capable of supplying a sophisticated juice.'

'With submission, sir,' said Herapath, 'it occurs to me that these men may not have had their juice.'

'But it is mixed into their grog. With all the perverse wickedness of seamen with regard to their health, they cannot avoid taking it. We use the Devil for a righteous end: execrable in theology, but sound in medicine.'

'Yes, sir. But Faster Doudle, the tall man, was in my mess, and he often exchanged his grog for tobacco: it may be the same with the others.'

'The dogs. The wicked dogs. I shall deal with them. A spoon, ho: a spoon, there; and half a pint of juice. I shall put an end to this: they will drink their grog or be flogged. And yet, you know,' he said, pausing, 'it will look strange in me, who have always set my face against their nasty rum – who circulated a petition throughout the fleet calling for the abolition of the monstrous custom by which grog missed during sickness is made up to the patient on his discharge – if I ask the Captain to issue an order requiring each man to drink his tot. Still and all, in this case a citreous drench will answer, I believe.'

The drench answered; the physical symptoms disappeared; but the gloom remained, and not only in the former patients but throughout the ship – a perfect atmosphere for the breeding of disease, as Stephen pointed out. Apart from a score of the poor flibberty-gibberty creatures who had been left behind by the boats, the men were attentive to their duty, but the fine drive was gone. The leak gained on them as the oakum of the first successful fothering worked through the leak, and the passing of a new sail was a slow, exhausting business that had little evident result: the *Leopard* drove eastward and a little south under small sail in a rising wind, pumping day and night. At any time the weather, fairly kind for the forties these last weeks, might break: the *Leopard* might have to run before an enormous storm of wind, with the great seas building up; and the general view aboard was that she could not survive the half of it.

'Tell me, Mr Herapath,' said Stephen. 'In circumstances like these, were you supplied with a large quantity of opium, should you take a pipe?'

Herapath shied away from the renewal of their intimacy. He could not tell, he said – probably not – there was perhaps something indecent in its use against mere apprehension – but then again perhaps he might.

Except when their work required his presence, he avoided Stephen whenever he could, either pumping beyond his time or shutting himself up in the cabin he had inherited from the purser – there were many vacant cabins, both fore and aft. Now he said, 'You will excuse me, sir: I have promised to put in a spell at the pumps.'

Stephen sighed. He had hoped to engage Herapath on the subject of the Chinese poetry that seemed to be the young man's only consolation when he was deprived of his mistress's company. More than once, in earlier days, Herapath had spoken of his studies, of the language and its poets, and Stephen had listened greedily through half the night. But those days were past, and at present he would flee as he had fled now, leaving his papers on the sick-bay table. Standing there alone, Stephen looked at the sheets covered with neat characters: 'It might be directions for making tea,' he reflected, 'or the wisdom of a thousand years.' But on one of the sheets he noticed a small interlined translation, the direct word-for-word method that Herapath had explained:

> Before my bed, clear moonlight
> Frost on the floor?
> Raising head, I gaze at the moon
> Bowing head, think of my own country.

There was indeed a moon, three days from the full, riding through the sparse clouds beyond the scuttle. He sighed again. It was some time since he had eaten or sat tête-à-tête with Jack: he felt a delicacy about seeming to force his confidence at this juncture, the more so as Jack was more remote, more closed in since the failure off that far island, wholly taken up with the preservation of his ship, very often deep in the after-hold with the carpenter, trying to come at the leak. Yet Stephen missed those brief periods, and he was particularly pleased when, on his way back to his cabin, he met with the youngster Forshaw, the bearer of an invitation 'when the Doctor might have time to spare – there was nothing urgent.'

As he traversed the quarterdeck he noticed a relative kindness in the air – it was distinctly above freezing – and a peculiarly brilliant star quite near the moon.

'There you are, Stephen,' cried Jack. 'How good of you to come so soon. Do you feel in the mind for music? Just half an hour? God knows what state my fiddle will be in, but I thought we might scrape, if only for a glass.'

'I might,' said Stephen. 'But listen, will you, till I say you a poem:

> *Before my bed, clear moonlight*
> *Frost on the floor?*
> *Raising head, I gaze at the moon*
> *Bowing head, I think of my own country.'*

'That is a damned good poem,' said Jack, 'although it don't rhyme.' And after a moment in which he too bent his head he said, 'I have just been gazing at her too, with my sextant: a perfect lunar, with old Saturn there, as clear as any bell. I have my longitude to within a second. What do you say to the Mozart B minor?'

They played, not beautifully but deep, ignoring their often discordant strings and striking right into the heart of the music they knew best, the true notes acting as their milestones. On the poop above their heads, where the weary helmsmen tended the new steering-oar and Babbington stood at the con, the men listened intently; it was the first sound of human life that they had heard, apart from the brief Christmas merriment, for a time they could scarcely measure. And Bonden and Babbington, who had known Jack for many years, exchanged a glance of significance. The last movement worked up to its splendid end, to the magnificent, inevitable final chord, and Jack laid by his violin. 'I am going to tell the officers presently,' he said in a conversational tone, as though they had been talking about navigation all this time, 'but I thought you might like to know first. There is land laid down in about 49°44′S and 69°E. A Frenchman by the name of Trémarec discovered it – Desolation Island. Cook could not find it, but I think Trémarec was out by ten degrees. I am confident the place exists; the whaler off the Cape spoke of it, and he fixed the position with a lunar. At all events, I am confident enough to prefer the risk of not finding it to the risk of hauling north. I dare not carry a press of sail tonight, for fear of floating ice; but in the morning, wind and weather permitting – and there is a big word, Stephen – I mean to put the ship's head south. I have not said anything before this, partly because I could not fix our position, and partly not to raise the people's hopes; they could not stand out against another disappointment like the Crozets. But I thought you would like to know. You might choose to say a prayer or two. My old nurse always said there was nothing like Latin, for prayers.'

Prayers or no, the morning broke fair and clear. And secrecy or no, there was already a certain eagerness abroad. The pumps turned somewhat faster, and if the spirit of the crew could be measured by the jet, it had risen by some ten to twelve per cent. The lookouts mounted to the masthead not indeed at a run, but with none of the languor of the day before: almost at once one cried out for a sail far down on the southern horizon, and although this was dismissed as only another ice-mountain – there were two monsters a mile to windward, and in the night the blessed moon had allowed them to avoid two more – the hail brought a new kind of liveliness. And when with infinite care the ship's head was brought due south, and more sail set, this life increased surprisingly, overcoming the immense fatigue that weighed upon the ship's company like a pall of lead – no man or boy had had more than four hours' sleep on end between the spells of heavy pumping for as long as he could remember.

'Good day to you, ma'am,' said Stephen, opening Mrs Wogan's door. 'I believe you may take some air at last. The sky is clear, the sun shines bright with a surprising warmth, and although our poop is now the scene of strange activity, the gangway remains, the wind-ward, or weather gangway, ma'am. And we had best profit by the morning while it lasts.'

'Lord, Dr Maturin, that would be Paradise. I have not seen the sky, nor you, this age. We have been a gaggle of women all together, knitting without a moment's pause and trying to keep warm; how-ever, a baby is a great subject for conversation. Is it true we are going to the antarctic pole? Is there land at the pole? I suppose there must be, or they would not call it the pole: nor, indeed, would they want to go there. Pray try this mitten, for the size. Dear me, your hand is grown horny to a degree – the perpetual pumping, I presume. Land! Of course, we can scarcely hope for shops; but I dare say there will be the equivalent of Eskimoes, with furs for sale. How I yearn for fur, a deep, deep bed of fur, and a fur nightgown too!'

'I cannot answer for the Eskimoes, but I can guarantee the fur,' said Stephen, yawning. 'These are the seas from which the sealskin comes, the darling of our modern age. I am credibly informed, that the pole itself is ringed with seals three deep; and this morning alone I myself have seen enough to make a cargo for a ship of moderate size, or emplacement, as we say; seals of three several kinds, besides four and twenty whales, and a plethora of birds, including, to my aston-ishment, a small duck, not unlike a teal, and what may well have been a shag. I am infinitely obliged to you, ma'am, for your kind thought of mittens.'

All day they sailed, and all day the glass in Jack's cabin sank. It had foretold full gales in the Channel and the Bay, the wicked mis-tral in the Mediterranean, a hurricane off Mauritius, but rarely had it dropped so fast. When he had taken what few precautions the case would admit, he kept to the poop, watching the western sky out there on the windward beam; and all the while the sun shone bright, the deck gay with drying clothes, among them Leopardina's pink socks and caps. The *Leopard* heeled pleasantly on the fine blue swell, and Stephen walked Mrs Wogan on the gangway below, pointing out not only the kinds of seal that might make her bed, but those that would

not, and eighteen whales, together with so many birds that a less
good-humoured woman might have rebelled.

From time to time Jack looked at the masthead; he did not wish to
go up there himself, for fear of raising hopes that might be dashed,
but with all his force he willed the man to hail the deck. He was in as
high a state of tension and anxiety as he had ever experienced, and
Mrs Wogan's gurgling laugh sent a jet of anger through his mind;
however, he paced on and on and on, his hands clasped behind his
back, from the taffrail to the hances and back again, showing no emotion of any sort. And when the hail did come at last, he still paced on
for a while before taking his best telescope to the foretopgallant jacks.

Yes, there it lay, high land, black rock beneath the snow, broad on
the larboard bow. Even with the *Leopard*'s leeway and the current
setting east at what he judged to be close on two miles in the hour, he
could still fetch well to the windward of the land. Farther south and
east mountain peaks heaved up, a great way off; and in the lie of the
land he recognized the Frenchman's description of Desolation Island.
He had no doubt of it: this was the landfall that he had prayed for.

With a sober, contained triumph he climbed down, steadily packed
on sail after sail until the *Leopard*'s masts complained in spite of their
extraordinary supports. To his surprise – water being but a shifting
ballast at the best – she was astonishingly stiff, and once all her vast
mass had gathered its momentum, the *Leopard* ploughed fast across
the sea.

He called young David Allan, the remaining bosun's mate and now
the acting bosun, and with him he told over what the ship possessed
in the way of anchors and massive cordage. They had done this before
the sad day off the Crozets, and the sum was still much the same,
amounting to the kedge alone and just enough cablets and hawsers to
veer out a reasonable scope. But since then two carronades, intended
not for the *Leopard* but for the settlement of Port Jackson and therefore carried in the hold, had been located and brought within reach of
the main hatchway: these, made fast to the kedge, would give them an
anchor not far from the weight of the small bower, enough for her to

ride at single anchor, given good holding ground and a moderate tide. 'And for the rest, sir?' asked Allan.

'For the rest, as soon as we are well in with the land, we shall reduce sail. You will have the hawsers from the mastheads, splice 'em end to end, point 'em out of the gunroom port, and then we shall proceed as circumstances may require.'

Allan looked a little blank, but the Captain's placid assumption that such a task was well within his powers impressed him; and when he was told that he should have all the forecastle-men and quarter-masters in the ship, the pumps be damned, he went off cheerfully enough.

Nearer and nearer, still with the land on the larboard bow. Before dinner the most northerly shore was visible from the deck, right down to the white line where it met the sea. And after that meal had been gulped down it was clear that this land was a bold cape running northwards from the mass. Nearer still: Jack paced up and down the poop with a quicker step; and although he had a crocodile's digestion, the lumps of ancient beef that he had swallowed dwelt there, under his rigid midriff, as firm and solid as when they had left the galley cauldron. Growing cloud in the west; and in the pale sky southwards the beginnings of an aurora, a shimmering curtain that wavered high up there, over a quarter of the sky, faint prismatic streams perpetually falling yet always in the same place. Three huge ice islands to windward, one of them four miles long and perhaps two hundred feet in height, and several smaller masses scattered about the long even swell, sometimes flashing as they rolled.

When should he begin to reduce sail, to let the bosun get at the precious hawsers? Could he ask the exhausted people to strike the topgallantmasts down on deck against the expected blow, and then call upon them for unknown exertions when it came to securing the ship? How did the tides run in these uncharted waters? The threat grew stronger in the west: lightning flickered on the far horizon – far, but not so very far. The feeling of the day had changed.

These and many more were decisions that only he could take. Collective wisdom might do better, but a ship could not be a parliament: there was no time for debate. The situation was changing fast, as it often did before an action, when a whole carefully worked-out plan might have to be discarded in a moment, and new steps decided upon. This rested on him alone, and rarely had he felt more lonely, nor more fallible, as he saw the headland advancing towards him, and with it the moment of decision. The lack of sleep, the pain, the confusion of day and night for weeks on end, had told upon him; his head was thick and stupid; yet a mistake in the next hour might cost the ship her life.

The swell was increasing, and the wind. He knew very well that once it came on to blow, to blow as the wind could blow in the forties, the clouds in the west would cover the sky with extraordinary speed and this seemingly sweet day would turn into a howling darkness, full of racing water. A visit to the cabin showed him the glass lower still: sickeningly low. And back on the poop he saw that he was by no means the only one to have noticed the mounting sea – an oddly disturbed sea, as if moved by some not very distant force; white water too, and a strange green colour in the curl of the waves and in the water slipping by. He glanced north-west, and there the sun, though shining still, had a halo, with sun-dogs on either side. Ahead, the aurora had gained in strength: streamers of an unearthly splendour. Below him, the pumps churned on and on: but both down there and here on the poop he caught an atmosphere of growing apprehension. Stiff though she was, the *Leopard* was heeling now so that her larboard cathead plunged deep on the leeward swell. And now the surf was rising higher on the icebergs and on the weather face of the headland on the bow. The howl in the rigging was louder and higher by far, and growing fast: a dangerous, dangerous note.

The broad expanse of water between the *Leopard* and the cape showed far more white than green; and inshore, where there had been smooth water not half an hour ago, there was the ugly appearance of

a tide-rip, a long narrow stretch of pure white that raced eastwards
from the headland and that must grow longer, broader, and fiercer by
far as the tide reached its full flow.

The situation had changed indeed; but worse was coming, and
coming very fast. A grey haze overspread the sky with the speed of a
curtain being drawn, and it was followed by tearing cloud: the lightning increased on the starboard beam, much nearer now. And right
ahead, a white squall, the forerunner of the full almighty gale, swept
over the mile or two of the sea northward of the cape, veiling the land
entirely.

It was no longer a question of where and how he should negoti-
ate the tide-race, but of whether he should be able to approach the
cape at all, or whether he should be obliged to put the ship before the
ever-increasing wind and run before it. Speed was everything: in five
or ten minutes at this rate of increase there would be no alternative –
he would either have to put before the wind or perish. Or put before
the wind and perish: the people could not pump for ever – they were
already very near their limit even with this encouragement – and in
any case the *Leopard* would almost surely founder in the kind of seas
that would build up before nightfall.

The tide-race was cutting up higher still, as nasty a race as ever
he had seen: yet the *Leopard* must go through it, whether or not. Go
through or run; and running could only mean the end, somewhat
delayed.

'Whether or no, Tom Collins,' said Jack to himself, and raising his
voice to the full to be heard over the wind, 'Jib and forestaysail. Mr
Byron, give her half a point.'

He had made his decision: it had formed clear-cut in his mind and
now he was quite calm and lucid, somewhat detached. Speed was all,
and the only question was whether the sails and masts could drive
the waterlogged hull hard enough without giving way, whether the
Leopard could race the western gale across that mile of sea before it
reached its full force and either flung her on her beam-ends or forced
her to run due east. It was a desperate choice: if any sail abaft the fore-

mast gave, if the oar should yield, or any upper mast, then all was lost: but at least the choice was made, and he believed it was the right one. He only reproached himself for not having driven her faster, sooner: for having lost minutes earlier in the day.

With the greater speed she gave a cumbrous great leap forward, like a carthorse spurred, and ploughed on faster still. The wind was now abaft the beam and she buried her larboard bow so that green seas swept the forecastle. She was madly overpressed, but so far she could just bear it; and now she was racing through the tall waves, their white crests tearing head-high across her waist. A gust on the rise laid her over so that her lee-rail vanished in the foam. He gave her another point – he could afford it – and now she tore towards the terrible zone where the gale screamed round the headland with redoubled force and joined the tide-rip.

At this point the adverse forces reached their highest pitch: the likelihood of being dismasted was very great.

A quarter of a mile to go, the gale rising every second. 'Main topgallant,' he said, and she gave an appalling lee-lurch as it was sheeted home. A moment's pause, like the suspension of life before a fall, and then she hit the tide-rip: she staggered as though she had struck ice. All round them the roar of breaking water and an intolerable wind; bursting seas on either hand, and a knock-down blow as the counter-eddy took her full aback; a confusion of water, green and white, spray covering her entirely, and as it settled she was through, rocking in the smooth water under the lee of the high land.

The transition was unbelievably abrupt. At one moment the *Leopard* was among bursting seas, furious winds howling upon her, the next she was gliding along in silence beneath the shelter of an enormous cliff, her masts still swaying like inverted pendulums from the momentary counterblast that had knocked her captain into the scuppers.

He picked himself up, glanced aloft – the upper masts had held, though the main topgallantsail had blown from its boltropes – and then leant far out over the rail to view the land. From the cape it trended westward, westward, towards a bay whose narrow mouth was almost closed with islands.

'Bosun's party away: Allan, carry on, and look alive. Mr Byron, get the lead going, if you please,' he said.

'No ground with this line,' came the cry, strangely loud – no other sound against it, apart from the water lipping along the side and the cry of seabirds.

'Pass along the deep-sea line, and let it be armed. Pumps, there! What the bloody hell are you thinking of?' cried Jack, but quite mildly: he would have stopped heaving himself, at such a time. The long, stunned pause stretched on and on: the hands at the pumps heaving mechanically, staring about them as though amazed: the ship was still running fast of her own momentum through deep green water under the shadow of the monstrous cliff. A desolate land, black rock topped with snow to the right-hand; to the left an island-studded sea; high overhead the wrack of a full western gale, with thunder in the clouds; down here, an unnatural calm, as though the world were deaf.

'Forecastle, there,' called Jack, breaking the silence, 'how are those hawsers coming along?'

'All off of the foremast, sir, and stretched along.'

The solemn splash of the heavy deep-sea line. 'Heave away, watch, watch! Bear away, veer away,' they cried; then, 'Fifty fathom, sir,' and after a short pause, 'Grey sand and shell.'

In another mile the *Leopard* had almost lost steerage-way. The sky was now as low as the higher cliffs, and a thin drizzle floated down. Her sails hung limp, but from the mist of rain up there it was clear that a small breeze, a back-breeze, drew in with the land. They set the remaining topgallants to take it, and so she glided on.

'How are those hawsers now?' called Jack again.

'Four fore and aft, sir,' replied Allan from the break just under him, where he and Faster Doudle were long-splicing like men possessed.

The bottom shelved steadily, always with the same good shelly sand, and now, as she approached a passage through the islands that closed the mouth of the bay, the hand-lead was going fast: 'By the

mark, seventeen; by the deep sixteen; and a half sixteen; by the deep
eighteen . . .'

A clear deep-water passage, and beyond the islands they could
see right into the bay, a purse-like bay opening wide from its narrow
mouth, a deep inlet sheltered on three sides.

Jack stared intently at the nearer island; its foot rose sheer, and
from the motion of the spume and the current rounding over the
black rock it was plain that the tide was making still. 'Man the braces,'
he said, limping forward. He did not mean to run her on a shoal if
care could prevent it, and this tide was moving her uncommon fast.

'Sir, sir,' cried Babbington, running after him. 'There is a flagstaff
at the bottom of the bay.'

Jack took his eyes from the surface for a moment, saw that the bottom of the bay divided into two lobes, each with a strand at the foot
of the cliff, and that on the height above one of them there stood an
upright pole. 'Dear me,' he said, 'so there is. Allan!'

'Sir?'

'How are you come along?'

'Hawser's knit, sir, and pointed from the gunroom port.'

Nearer and still nearer in, with seals staring up on every hand,
some of monstrous size: one of the countless seabirds dropped filth
on him – oh such good luck – and with his eye fixed on a small island
near the shore and his ear following the cry of the lead, he called, 'All
hands to bring the ship to an anchor.'

A long pause while she ghosted still farther in, and then, 'Down
with the helm.' Her head came round: hands flew to the halliards,
braces, sheets and clewlines, hove the mizzen topgallantsail aback,
and he said, 'Let go.' The anchor and its carronades splashed down,
and the hawser ran out as the *Leopard* went astern.

'Stopper,' he said.

'Stopper it is, sir,' replied Allan: and indeed the *Leopard* stopped,
brought up with a mild jerk that nevertheless staggered them as they
stood. The hawser rose, and straightening took the full strain; and
this was the crucial moment. Would the anchor hold? The anchor

held, yes, yes, the anchor held; the hawser, though still taut with the tide thrusting on the ship, sank into a gentle curve, and the *Leopard*'s seamen breathed out a general sigh. Yet still, the turning tide, and God alone knew how fast it ran in these seas, could swing her, wrench the anchor from its hold, and fling her on the islands close at hand.

'Jolly-boat away,' said Jack. 'Mr Babbington, be so good as to proceed to those rocks between us and the shore, carrying out a line bent to the hawser from the gunroom port. Haul the hawser to the rock, and make all fast. You may have the spare iron horse, if you choose, and a grapnel; you will take particular care to make all fast, Mr Babbington, and then, perhaps,' he said, grasping the wooden knighthead, 'we may sleep tight tonight.'

Ａnd tight they slept indeed, so tight that Stephen, roused out at three in the morning for his spell at the starboard chain-pump, was first unable to find his way to that familiar post until the drooping midshipman whom he was to relieve led him there by hand, and then powerless to reconstitute the events of yesterday until he had been heaving for half an hour – until the exercise and the steady half-freezing rain had dispelled the fumes of that trance-like sleep.

'I believe those were sea-elephants that we saw on entering the bay,' he said to Herapath, his neighbour. 'Foster states that the sea-elephant boasts an external scrotum: or do I confuse him with the eared seal Otaria gazella?'

Herapath had no views on this or any other kind of seal. He was fast asleep, pumping as he stood. But that very night the pumps, though languid, gained five feet upon the leak: with her hull no longer worked upon by the motion of the sea nor the straining of her masts, the *Leopard* made no more water than a single watch could deal with. They pumped her dry, or at least no more than very damp – for real dryness had little meaning on Desolation, where it rained almost without a pause – and began the long task of emptying the holds to reach the leak and to ship a rudder.

At first they had nothing but the jolly-boat for all the hundreds of tons that had to be removed, but this was soon joined by a raft, worked by a system of windlasses that sent it to and fro across the still waters of the inlet, untroubled even at the beginning of their stay, when the storm blew with such shocking violence high overhead that even the albatrosses stayed within. The bay was of course affected by the tides that made their way through the many islands, but they delayed the work far less than the intense curiosity of the penguins. Most of these birds were breeding, but even so they found time to stand in dense crowds on the flagstaff strand, and to hurry to watch the unloading, getting between men's legs, sometimes bringing them down, always hindering their movements. Some of the seals were quite as bad, and harder to remove: many a privy nip and kick did they receive from exasperated seamen; but no more than this, for strict orders had been given that the landing-place was to be considered holy ground. No blood was to be shed there, whatever might happen afar off.

For the first few days Jack let the Leopards take it easy, mounting no more than an anchor-watch, so that they might take their fill of sleep, which by this time had become almost as important to them as food. Where food itself was concerned, there was no difficulty: fresh meat lay there at hand, for the taking. And taken it was, often in bloody excess, for this was almost virgin land, and the creatures did not fear the men: not quite virgin, however, for a bottle at the foot of the broken studdingsail boom they called the flagstaff contained a paper stating that the brig *General Washington* of Nantucket, Wm Hyde master, had been there, and that if Reuben should come in for cabbages, he was to tell Martha that all was well, and that Wm reckoned he might be home before the fall, with a tidy lading.

After this period of rest, with all hands recovered, fat and greasy from their four meat-meals a day, Jack set them to work, and the stores piled up on Flagstaff Beach: neatly squared arrays, covered with sailcloth, heaps so high and wide that long before even half the after hold was cleared it seemed impossible that any single ship should have contained so much. The work was steady, even quite severe upon occasion, but the summer days were long and the men had plenty of time to wander off, murdering sea-elephants, seals, albatrosses, giant petrels, small petrels, Cape pigeons, terns, any of the tame creatures that lay or nested in their path. Stephen was perfectly aware that these creatures too lived by incessant carnage, that the skuas wreaked perpetual havoc among eggs and chicks of every kind, that the sea-leopards ate anything warm-blooded they could catch, and that none of the birds showed the smallest mercy to a fish; but at least they respected a certain established hierarchy in their killing, whereas the sailors respected none, slaughtering indiscriminately. He reasoned with them; they listened gravely and carried straight on, only keeping somewhat more out of sight, rambling farther afield, up to the great albatross colonies on the higher slopes or the seal rookeries in the neighbouring cove. He knew that his words did not carry full conviction, since he himself spent all the daylit hours collecting specimens of everything from the sea-elephant to the very small wingless flies and the fresh-water tardigrades, and much of the night dissecting them or ranging eggs, bones and plants. He knew that some of the killing had real point, and that the barrels of penguins, young albatrosses, and seal-flesh could be justified; but it sickened him, and after some weeks he withdrew to an island in the bay, an island forbidden to all but the *Leopard*'s surgeon.

They made him a little canvas boat, and it was thought that if he were obliged to wear two sea-elephant's bladders, blown up and attached to his person, he could not come to harm in such a placid sea; but after an unfortunate experience in which he became involved in his umbrella and it was found that the bladders buoyed up his meagre hams alone, so that only the presence of Babbington's Newfoundland preserved him, he was forbidden to go unaccompanied.

The duty of going with him generally fell to Herapath, who was of little more use in the rummaging of a hold than Stephen himself. The common world of papers and intelligence, of people walking about the paved streets of towns, was so very far away, so nearly dream-like, that his conduct towards Dr Maturin seemed to wound him less; and so much close-packed experience lay between his copying of the poisoned documents and the antarctic present that it might have occurred in years gone by. Their former intimacy revived to some extent, and although Herapath loathed walking knee-deep in the rank sodden grass that covered much of the lower ground, and although he did not greatly care whether the huge nesting fowl upon which they pored was a royal or a wandering albatross, he did not dislike these expeditions so long as he was not too often called upon to admire a pool of algae or an infant blue-eyed shag. He had built a shelter by the water's edge, and there he sat with an angle for hours on end while Stephen walked about. It was almost always too wet to read or write, but he was a contemplative young man, and the sight of his cork bobbing away out there allowed his mind to drift far away, yet with a local attachment; and sometimes he would take a fish. When the rain was too heavy even for Dr Maturin they would sit there together, talking of Chinese poetry, or, more often, of Louisa Wogan, who at present lived on shore, and who could sometimes be seen in the distance, a straight, fur-clad figure, walking with Mrs Boswell's baby in the rare gleams of sun; for now the women's imprisonment was merely nominal.

'This is Paradise,' said Stephen as they landed.

'A little damp for Paradise, perhaps,' suggested Herapath.

'The terrestrial Paradise was no howling desiccated waste of sand, no arid desert,' said Stephen. 'Indeed, Mandeville particularly mentions its mossy walls, a sure proof of abundant moisture. I have already found fifty-three kinds of moss on this island alone; and no doubt there are more.' He gazed about the black streaming crags, the slopes between them covered with coarse matted grass, yellow viscous cabbages, many of them in a state of slow decay, or raw spewy earth, the dung of seabirds everywhere, and the whole enveloped in drifting swatches of mist or rain. 'This is very like the north-western parts of Ireland, but without the men: it reminds me of a promontory in the County Mayo where first I beheld the phalarope . . . Shall we visit the giant petrels first, or should you prefer the terns?'

'To tell the truth, sir, I believe I had rather sit in the shelter for a while. The cabbage seems to have turned my inward parts to water.'

'Nonsense,' said Stephen, 'it is the most wholesome cabbage I have ever come across in the whole of my career. I hope, Mr Herapath, that you are not going to join in the silly weak womanish unphilosophical mewling and puling about the cabbage. So it is a little yellow in certain lights, so it is a little sharp, so it smells a little strange: so much the better, say I. At least that will stop the insensate Phaeacian hogs from abusing it, as they abuse the brute creation, stuffing themselves with flesh until what little brain they have is drowned in fat. A virtuous esculent! Even its boldest detractors, ready to make the most hellish declarations and to swear through a nine-inch plank that the cabbage makes them fart and rumble, cannot deny that it cured their purpurae. Let them rumble till the heavens shake and resound again; let them fart fire and brimstone, the Gomorrhans, I will not have a single case of scurvy on my hands, the sea-surgeon's shame, while there is a cabbage to be culled.'

'No, sir,' said Herapath. He could not but agree: he had seen the cure. The Leopard's crew, having killed a sea-elephant early in their stay, ate its enormous liver by way of a change; they came out in dull blue, clearly-defined blotches, about two inches across. Stephen instantly prescribed the cabbage that he had found and that he had tried upon himself and the loblolly boy, an unattractive plant with a startling smell. It did away with the blotches: as Jack observed, 'it made the Leopards change their spots' – the first really full-hearted laugh, eyes vanishing in a face scarlet with mirth, that he had uttered in the last five thousand miles. And since the ship was short of lime-juice, and since the practice was sound even if the ship had been swimming in anti-scorbutics, Stephen insisted upon the cabbage's being mixed with dinner every day: as to its alleged laxative properties, he had not perceived any inconvenience; and if they had an existence outside a hypochondriacal high-fed cosseted fancy, it was all to the good. Men, said he, looking sharply at his Captain, men who would breakfast on two albatross eggs, weighing close on a purser's pound apiece, should be purged of their gross humours daily.

'No, sir,' said Herapath again. 'But if you will forgive me, I am a little weary, and should like to fish awhile. You will recall that last time, when the giant petrel covered me with oil, you said I might be excused.'

'It was only that you startled the poor bird by falling down, and by falling down, as you must allow me to observe, in a singularly abrupt and awkward fashion, Mr Herapath.'

'The ground was wet, and deep in the excrement of seals.'

'Petrels cannot abide the least gaucherie,' said Stephen. But it was true that Herapath was an unlucky wight; many of the petrels had shot their evil-smelling stomach-oil at him, quite unprovoked, whereas they never resented Stephen; and an albatross had given him a cruel nip, sheering quite through his inoffensive sleeve. 'Well,' he said, 'you shall do as you please. Let us share out the sandwiches, for I mean to stay until sunset.'

Stephen's Paradise was quite large, an hour's walk from the inner to the outer side, and unlike most of the islands, which were broken masses of rock, rising sheer, it possessed little in the way of cliffs except for two on the seaward side, being for the most part a smooth dome. Yet although it had a fine and park-like extent of many hundred acres, it was scarcely big enough for all the creatures that hurried to it for the breeding season, coming in from the limitless southern ocean, an ocean almost devoid of land, where they roamed for the rest of the year. The few resident birds, the curious teal, the blue-eyed shag, perhaps the sheathbill, could scarcely find room to turn, and Stephen himself had to walk very carefully not to step on eggs or plunge into the burrows made by the countless whale-birds. The top of the dome was occupied by the great albatrosses, and here it was easier to walk; the grass was not so long, and the nests were well spaced out. He knew many of the members of the colony quite well, having seen them in their courting, building, and mating, and now he recognized several as they walked about visiting other nests – the place was something like a common with white geese upon it, but gigantic geese, coming and going on wings like those of the genii in the Arabian tale, or walking, or sitting on their hollowed mounds. Most, indeed, were sitting now – few nests without an egg – and he made his way through the throng to the first nest in which he had seen a clutch, if a single egg could be called a clutch. The sitting bird was fast asleep, with its

head along its back; it was so used to him that it only opened one eye
and grunted when he pushed gently into its breast to find whether the
egg were chipping yet. It was not, and he sat on a vacant nest close by
to gaze about. A great rush of air – a distinct warmth and the smell of
fishy bird, and the albatross's mate landed by him, staggering on the
ground as it folded its enormous wings – and waddled over to address
soft mutterings to its spouse and nibble her outstretched neck. At
his feet a minute dull black petrel scrambled awkwardly among the
tussocks, and at head-height the piratical skuas planed, glaring from
side to side for an unguarded prey. The rain had stopped: he laid his
sealskin aside – he wore it as farm-hands wear a sack, over his head
and shoulders – brought out his lunch, swivelled round upon his nest,
and surveyed the part of the island he had traversed. On the right
hand, down by the sea, the sea-elephants, each weighing several tons.
Most of them were kind or at least indifferent, but there was one old
twenty-foot bull with a remarkable collection of wives that still would
not suffer him to come close to, although they had been acquainted
for such a while: it would still rear up and writhe its person, gibber-
ing, gnashing its teeth, blowing out its inflatable nose, and even roaring aloud. 'Did he but know,' reflected Stephen, 'could he but imagine
the present mildness of my carnal desires with regard to Mrs Wogan,
he would not fear for his harem.' Then came the little fur-seals with
their charming pups: he knew them well. Still farther to the left, and
straggling high up the slope, the enormous penguin rookeries, myriads upon myriads of birds. And almost beyond his view, the place
where sea-leopards bred: yet although in one sea-leopard's stomach
he had found eleven adult penguins and one small seal, by land they
were on civil terms with their prey: indeed, all the various creatures
shuffled and walked about in mingled crowds, abiding by some social
contract that dissolved in the sea. Another rush of wings, a screech,
and the biscuit with a slice of seal that he had placed upon a tuft, vanished, born off by a skua. 'Oh the thief,' he said, 'the black anarchist,'
but in fact he had already had enough, and he gazed on without the
least vexation.

There, between him and the little settlement, lay the ship, the very awkward-looking ship: once the bay had been sounded in every part, the *Leopard* had been warped across until she lay so close to a sheer-to rock that she could be partially heaved down. They had found the leak, a most terrible long gash, almost a death-wound, and it had long since been dealt with: now the great trouble was the rudder, and she lay there with staging about her stern, absurdly down in front and up behind so that they might struggle the more effectively with her stern-post, gudgeons, pintles, and the like.

And now the jolly-boat swam into his field of vision, rowed by Bonden, with Jack and the little Forshaw jammed into the stern-sheets. It stopped at a given buoy. Jack peered at various points with his sextant, calling out figures that the midshipman wrote down in his book: he was obviously carrying on with his survey, as he did whenever the tide was unsuitable for work on the *Leopard*'s hull. Stephen walked to the edge of the declivity from which the albatrosses commonly launched themselves, and here, as six of the enormous birds plunged into the breeze on either side and even over him, he called out, 'Hola.'

Jack turned, saw him, and waved: the boat pulled in. It disappeared under the land and presently Jack came toiling up the slope. It was not his leg that made him toil and puff, for the numbness had passed off some time ago, but rather his bulk. While he had only been able to stump for a hundred yards or so he had nevertheless eaten voraciously; and greed growing with its indulgence, he was now walking up the hill for his breakfast eggs.

'It seems almost sacrilegious,' said Stephen, as Jack held them out. 'When I think of how I prized mine, perhaps the only specimen in the three kingdoms, how I preserved it from the slightest shock in jeweller's cotton, the idea of deliberately breaking one . . .'

'You cannot make an omelette without breaking eggs,' said Jack quickly, before the chance should be lost for ever. 'Ha, ha, Stephen, what do you say to that?'

'I might say something about pearls before swine – the pearls

being these priceless eggs, if you follow me – were I to attempt a rep-
artee in the same order of magnitude.'

'I did not fag all the way up here to be insulted about my wit, which,
I may tell you, is more generally appreciated in the service than you
may suppose,' said Jack, 'but to bemoan my lot; to sit upon the ground
and bemoan my lot.'

Stephen looked at him sharply: in themselves the words were
cheerful, facetious, jocose, and they matched the apparent well-being
of Jack's face; but there was something very slightly false about the
note or time or emphasis. Throughout his service in the Navy, Stephen had observed the steady, almost mechanical, and as it were
obligatory facetiousness that pervaded the various gunrooms and
wardrooms he had known; the stream of small merriment, long-
established jokes, proverbial sayings and more or less droll allusions
that made up so large a part of his shipmates' daily intercourse. It
seemed to him a particularly English characteristic and he often
found it wearisome; on the other hand he admitted that it had a value
as a protection against morosity and that it encouraged fortitude. It
also protected those who had to live together from those more adult
forms of discussion in which men could commit themselves entirely,
confronting one another in strong disagreement: whether that was
its underlying purpose or whether it was no more than a manifesta-
tion of national levity and disinclination for intellectual pursuits he
could not determine; but he did know that Jack Aubrey was so much
in tune with this tradition, that he so entirely shared the notion of
there being something indecent in solemnity, that he could only with
real difficulty bring himself to speak of matters outside the running
of the ship without a smile – he would go to his death with a pun half-
formed, if he could think of nothing better.

But when this facetiousness rang false, it rang very false indeed. It
reminded Stephen of a 'cello suite that he had often tried to play, with
small success; one in which, through very slight successive changes a
simple, artless air in the adagio took on a nightmare quality. He rec-

ognized something of this nature now, and his sharp look detected an extreme weariness behind Jack's smiling eye, as though he were not far from despair. Why had he not seen this before? The fantastic wealth of Desolation must have absorbed him very deeply: indeed, it had – birds as he had always dreamed of seeing them, birds that he could touch; a whole flora and fauna almost unknown, and time for once to study them. He said, 'Why, brother, what's amiss? Is the leak broke out again?'

'No, no, the leak will do very well – better than new. No: it is the rudder.'

During this long period of clearing the hold and repairing the leak Stephen had been satisfied with a vague general view of the progress: few of those concerned had troubled him with technical details and in any case he was usually too wet, cold, tired, by the end of the day, too filled with his own fascinating discoveries to attend closely to those few descriptions he heard as he sat blinking and gaping by the seal-oil fire. He had been content to let experts carry on with their own tasks, while he carried on with his. He had seen the bright new planks entirely covering the leak inside and out; he had seen the fine new rudder, carefully sawn from spare topmasts and to his eye indistinguishable from the old; and his only fear was that the *Leopard*, dry, well-found and weatherly, should sail long before his collections were more than a skimming of the surface.

Now he heard a technical description indeed, and he learnt that the experts' darkest foreboding had been realized. The essential connection of the rudder to the hull could not be accomplished, or at any rate had not been accomplished; and Jack could not tell how to bring it about. The stern-post, constructed on new principles and a sad gimcrack affair that Jack had disliked from the beginning, had proved horribly defective, so damaged by the ice and so deeply rotten behind its sheathing that 'poor old Gray absolutely shed tears when we cut into it.' The only way of attaching the rudder was to forge new gudgeons, the massive iron braces with eyes that received the rudder's pintles, and to forge them with much longer arms so that they should reach the body of the ship, where there were solid timbers to hold them. But although the *Leopard* could be made to provide enough iron, she had no forge. It had gone overboard, together with the anvil, the sledge-hammers and all the armourer's other tools, when the guns and anchors and so many other heavy objects were sacrificed to keep the ship afloat. Almost all the coal had either been whipped up in sacks or, washing about in fragments down below, had been pumped over the side; and although seal-oil kept the huts and the 'tween-decks warm, it could not bring iron to the welding point. Even if it could, the iron could scarcely be worked without heavy hammers and an anvil.

'But what a crow I am, for God's sake,' said Jack. 'I talk as though this were the end of the world, which it ain't. I have some notion of an improved blast, blowing on bones soaked in oil, and of weighing one of the carronades and fashioning an anvil and a couple of sledges out of it – cold chisels and files can do wonders, with patience. And even if in the end it proves impossible to ship the rudder, we can build a boat, a half-decked cutter, say, and send Babbington off for help with a dozen of our best hands.'

'Could a boat ever live in these seas?'

'With a fair amount of luck, it could. Grant certainly thought he had a reasonable chance. Though to be sure, he had not much above a thousand miles to go, and we have as much again. But a boat can't be built quick, and with the ice moving north as the nights grow longer, I dare say we shall have to winter here. You may like that, Stephen, although it means knocking a good many more of your seals on the head; but nobody else will, with the rum almost gone and the tobacco running out.' He shied as an albatross passed within inches of his head, stood up, and said, 'We are not come to that yet, however: I have some other shots in my locker – a better sort of bellows, for example, and a new kind of hearth. Still, I must make preparations, and unless there is some progress before the end of the week, I shall set about drawing up plans for the boat.' Seeing Stephen's grave, concerned expression he said, 'It is a great relief to whine a little, rather than play the perpetual encouraging know-all, so I lay it on a trifle thick: don't take me too seriously, Stephen.'

The week passed, and another: all over Stephen's Paradise the albatrosses hatched, and the cabbages came into flower. But on shore parties still battered iron amidst shattered heaps of stone, with no real success; and the general plan for next year's boat began to take shape.

With the shorter days the weather had turned fine, perhaps ominously fine; on shore the killing increased, and the cooper packed cask after cask of meat and bird-flesh, cooked in seal-oil, for they had little salt, and that was needed for the barrelled cabbages. It would not be pleasant eating but it would keep them alive, they thought, over the antarctic winter, when all the seals and birds were gone. By now the rum was down to one tot to each mess of eight men, the tobacco to half an ounce a week a head. As a physician, Stephen could not but applaud this weaning from noxious substances: as a member of the ship's company, he felt the gloom that weighed upon those to whom drink and tobacco were among the few positive pleasures in life, and he spent even more of his time upon the island; the hepaticas and lycopods were coming into their own, and he was deep in the various lichens.

After a long evening among them he returned to the shelter, where Herapath had passed the day, sometimes fishing, sometimes gazing at his love upon the shore through a small telescope bought from Byron for three ounces of tobacco – money had long since ceased to have any value among them.

'I have caught five small fishes,' he said in rather a loud voice – the crab-seals had begun their evening chorus, wow, wow, wow.

'A capital omen,' said Stephen. 'More would have been superfluous. But what have you done with the boat, at all?'

'The boat?' said Herapath, smiling. 'Good God, the boat!' he cried, with a horrified look on his face. 'It is gone!'

'Perhaps we did not attend to the painter with sufficient care. It is not gone very far, however: see, it lies between the islands at the entrance of the bay.'

'Shall I swim for it?'

'Could you indeed swim so far? I could not. And even if I could, I doubt I should adventure upon it. No, Mr Herapath, put on your coat. We are very short-handed, and Captain Aubrey would never forgive me if a froward killer-whale, or a sea-leopard, or dampness next the skin were to deprive him of a man. No, let us rather hail the shore. They will launch the jolly-boat, take up the skiff, and rescue us.'

'To be sure,' said Herapath, doing up his buttons, 'I am under great obligations to the Captain: he saved my life, as you recall.'

'Sure, you have often mentioned it. Now both together: Hola, the shore.'

Hola the shore, they cried; and the crab-seals barked louder still. Presently they were joined by the sea-elephants, and the little shrill-voiced otaries. Once they thought they saw a remote figure give an answering wave in the deepening twilight; but this proved an illusion.

'They will never send,' said Herapath. 'Those on shore will suppose we are in the ship; those in the ship, on shore.'

'How well you put the case,' said Stephen. 'And now the mortal rain has begun again. Presently it will freeze, and we will think of the warm clothes, the impermeable sealskin cloaks lying in our cabins with an even greater longing.'

They sat in the mouth of the shelter, looking through the drizzle at the distant lights; and after a while Stephen said, 'How active the smaller petrels grow, at this time of the day. But come, here is a boat that will deliver us. To the right of the rock with a shag upon it. Just entering the bay.'

'It is not the jolly-boat! It is far larger than the jolly-boat!'

'What of that? Unless rowed by bears or Huns, it will deliver us. Hola the boat!'

'Ahoy!' answered the boat, resting on its oars.

'Pray be so good as to tow the little canvas skiff on your left towards us. It is out of our reach, and we are, as it were, marooned.'

Mutterings in the boat. A churning of oars, the little craft secured, the whale-boat pulling in. 'You say you're marooned?' asked a tall figure, leaping over the bows as they grounded.

'Figuratively marooned,' said Stephen. 'The rope holding our boat became untied, and we are cut off from our friends. I am very much obliged to you, sir. Have I the pleasure of addressing Mr Reuben?'

'That's him,' said the man on shore, pointing back into the whale-boat.

Mr Reuben scrambled through the rowers, sprang to the land, and lowered his face to the level of Stephen's with a look of extreme amazement. 'I reckon you are off of an English ship,' he said at last. His breath was extraordinarily offensive, his face puffy; it was clear to Stephen that he was suffering from scurvy, moderately advanced.

'Just so,' said Stephen.

'Well,' said someone in the boat, 'this beats the band.'

'For the land's sake,' said another.

'Are we at war with England yet?' asked Reuben.

'No,' said Herapath. 'Not when we quitted Portsmouth. You hail from the States, I guess?'

'Now, if you will excuse me, gentlemen,' said Stephen, bowing under a fresh sweep of rain as he stepped carefully into his fragile skiff, 'we must reassure our friends. Many thanks again, and I trust you will honour us with a visit. Come, Mr Herapath.'

'You ain't touched none of our cabbages?' called a voice after them.

'Cabbages?' said Stephen. 'Cabbages, forsooth.'

The rising sun, clear once again, swept away the darkness that hung over this encounter. It showed two vessels in the bay, the *Leopard* of course, and the brig *La Fayette* of Nantucket, Winthrop Putnam, master. The brig came right into the bay on the early tide and a little later her master, with his first mate Reuben Hyde, pulled ashore and walked up to the flagstaff. Here they met Captain Aubrey, who, although the *La Fayette* had not saluted the *Leopard*, wished them a good morning, produced a bottle, held out his hand and invited them to breakfast.

'Well, sir,' said Captain Putnam, taking the hand with no great eagerness, 'I am obliged to you, but – ' he caught the whiff of fresh-brewed coffee, coming from Jack's booth, coughed, and went on, 'You mean here on shore, I guess? Why, then, I don't mind if I do.'

He was a tall, spare, able-looking man with a blue nose and a blue, piercing eye: one side of his face much swollen. Taciturn and reserved, if not wary: from time to time he put his hand to his cheek, and his lips clamped tight with pain.

He was two and a half years out of Nantucket, had done tolerably well in whale-oil and spermaceti and sealskins, and was going home as soon as he had picked up a load of cabbages for the run: he had a good deal of scurvy aboard, he said; scurvy and a good deal of other sickness.

'You must let my surgeon look at your invalids,' said Jack.

'You have a surgeon aboard, have you?' cried Captain Putnam. 'We lost ours off South Georgia, with the griping of the guts.'

'Yes, and a rare hand he is with scurvy; while as for sawing off a leg, he can beat any surgeon in the fleet.'

Putnam made no reply for some time. 'Well, to tell you the truth, sir,' he said, with another twitch of pain, 'I do not care to ask a favour of King George's navy.'

'Ah?' said Jack.

'And I will tell you this, sir, that I should not care to set foot aboard the *Leopard* neither. We recognized her the moment we came in. I do not say this for you, sir, because she had another captain in the year seven, when she killed my cousin in the *Chesapeake*, pressing men out of her, but I had rather see the *Leopard* at the bottom of the ocean, than sailing on its surface. I reckon that is the view of most Americans.'

'Well, Captain,' said Jack, 'I am heartily sorry for it.' He was too: most heartily sorry. He was well aware of the incident that rankled in the skipper's mind: in 1807 the *Leopard*, then commanded by Buck Humphreys, had fired three broadsides into an unprepared American man-of-war, the *Chesapeake*, killing or wounding a score of her men and forcing her to strike: had he been an American he would

never have forgiven or forgotten such an insult. He too would have
wished the *Leopard* at the bottom of the sea. For his own part he
utterly condemned the whole business: he would never have gone
to such lengths to take a few deserters nor even a hundred of them.
But he could not say this to a foreigner, a pretty inimical foreigner
at that. Instead he proposed another cup of coffee – the *La Fayette*
had drunk the last of hers south of the Horn – and said something
more in praise of Dr Maturin. 'He also has an American assistant,' he
added. 'They are the gentlemen your boat rescued last night.'

'I reckoned they might not be seamen,' said Captain Putnam, with
something nearer to a smile than anything he had yet achieved. He
stood up, thanked Captain Aubrey for his hospitality, and said he
reckoned the American surgeon's mate might find himself in a tolerably awkward situation when the war broke out, if indeed it had not
already been declared.

'You think it likely, then?'

'If the English go on hampering our trade and stopping our ships
and taking whatever men they choose to consider British, how can it
be prevented? We are a proud nation, sir, and we have whipped you
before. If I had been President Jefferson, I should have declared war
right away, the minute your *Leopard* fired on the *Chesapeake*. And let
me tell you, sir, we have frigates built and building now that can whip
anything you have in the same class; so when we do declare, we shall
be able to wipe off a long, long score. Yes, sir.' He grew angrier as he
spoke; he looked Jack straight in the eye with a fiery glare, and after
the last emphatic 'Yes, sir' he stalked off to his boat, accompanied by
his mate, who had remained silent throughout the interview.

Later in the day the whaler's collective attitude became if anything
yet more apparent. Her boats came in, to what the whalers evidently
considered their own private beach, and the men made their way up
the slopes behind to gather their own eggs and their own cabbages.
Jack had taken measures to ensure that those Leopards who were
ashore should not enter into conflict with the whalers, but there was
little need. The whalers walked by without any greeting apart from an

offhand grunt, communicating only indirectly, by remarks intended to be overheard – 'That's the — old *Leopard*', 'Remember 1807', 'Stole half our — cabbages, the sods', and the like. They were a very tough-looking set of men, many so bearded that they looked like bears: yet to an attentive eye it was clear that some were not in the prime of strength; the higher slopes made them gasp and pause for breath, and though few carried more than half a hundredweight they bent under their nets of cabbages as they came down, eating the raw leaves on their way.

During this time Jack watched not only the whalers but also their brig, from whose galley chimney there poured a fine stream of black smoke, rising without a doubt from coal. What line of conduct to adopt he could not tell: any whaler, working far from land for months and even years, must have a forge; but he could not run the risk of a direct refusal to let the *Leopard* use it. In his present frame of mind, Putnam certainly would refuse, and that would be the end of negotiations. Moore was all in favour of the strong hand: the Marines seizing the whalers on shore, taking their boats and boarding the brig. 'There would be little or no resistance,' he said. 'I have seen a good many invalids creeping about her deck: and after all, it is only to borrow their forge – they would scarcely cut up rough in such a case.'

'I doubt that,' said Jack. Captain Putnam had already run out his four six-pounders and rigged boarding-netting: a natural precaution in a sperm-whaler frequenting the cannibal islands of the great South Sea, but more significant by far off Desolation. At all events, in such a time of tension, the use of force would certainly cause a diplomatic incident, if not provoke an actual war, the *Leopard* having such an unlucky name and reputation. Yet it might be the only solution: furthermore, war might already have been declared, and in that case he would be perfectly justified – the brig would be a fair prize, forge and all. It was extremely tempting. And he must act soon, for the whaler would be away as soon as she had gathered her greenstuff. 'Pass the word for Dr Maturin,' he said.

At this time Dr Maturin and his assistant were on Paradise again, grubbing up the lower mosses, Herapath in a state of extreme but suppressed excitement. He was much less concerned with botany than the likelihood of war, which he turned in all directions with a wealth of hypotheses; and he was very urgent with Stephen to intercede with the Captain to allow him to visit the *La Fayette* in spite of this morning's order.

'But since you are yourself American,' said Stephen, 'the Captain would never be able to bring you back without violating international law; and as you know, the *Leopard* is terribly short-handed.'

'It is true, then, that an American citizen, born in the States, cannot be removed from an American ship?'

'Gospel true.'

'But I leave a hostage on shore: I should never, never leave her behind, as you know.'

'I know that, but Captain Aubrey does not. Poor Mrs Wogan. It must go hard with her, to see freedom floating not half a mile away: for she too would be out of the reach of English law, once she set foot upon an American deck. Perhaps it would be as well not to mention this, however, lest she should break out in some wild, unconsidered act. She may not know it, and – hush, I hear a voice.'

He would have to have been stone deaf not to hear it. Allan had by now developed the full bosun's roar, and he was hailing the mossy slopes of Paradise with all his might from the jolly-boat – the Captain wished to see the Doctor.

'Make a lane, there,' he said, addressing the penguins as he hurried Stephen down the road that countless generations of the birds had made.

'Now, Mr Allan,' said Stephen in the boat, 'what is all this haste? Is there news of this dreadful war – do we hear that it has broken out?'

'God forbid, sir,' said Allan. 'There is my brother in the States, ran from *Hermione*, though bosun's mate and ripe for a warrant; and I don't want to point no gun at him. No: all I know is the Captain seemed mortal anxious to see you.'

The anxiety in Jack's face diminished somewhat as Stephen walked in. He laid the case before him, and after thinking for a while Stephen said, 'Perhaps the best course would be to let Herapath have his way. He very much wishes to go aboard the whaler. The visit is natural; he is under an obligation to the ship; he is a fellow-countryman. Let him go, and I believe good will come of it.'

'But would he ever come back? I cannot spare even such a landsman as Herapath – he can heave at a pump in an emergency, or haul on a rope. The whaler can sail off whenever she wishes: she will never have to winter here and maybe freeze or starve to death. She is homeward-bound, Stephen – think of that! And even if the *Leopard* were in perfect order, it would not be pleasant for him to have to serve with us, if war breaks out.'

'I will answer for his coming back, if for no other reason than that he is an honourable creature: he has a strong sense of duty, and he is very sensible of your having preserved his life and of having promoted him. He has often mentioned it in the course of the voyage, the last time only yesterday. He will certainly return.'

'Yes: he seems a very decent sort of a man,' said Jack. 'Very well: let us send for him. Killick, pass the word for Mr Herapath.'

'Mr Herapath, I understand that you wish to visit the whaler, and you have my permission to go. You are no doubt aware that there is a great deal of ill-feeling between the United States and England, and that most unhappily the *Leopard* was the cause of some of it: that is why I thought best to forbid the usual ship-visiting, to prevent quarrelling of any kind. You also know the *Leopard*'s condition: one day's use of a forge and the proper tools would enable her to put to sea rather than winter here. The whaler certainly possesses a forge, but as a gentleman you will understand that I am extremely reluctant to ask a favour of the American skipper, extremely reluctant to expose the service or myself to a rebuff. I may add that he is equally reluctant to come a-begging to me, and I honour him for it. However, on reflection he may feel inclined to exchange the use of his forge for our medical services. You may give him a view of the situation, but without committing us to any specific request – harkee, Mr Herapath, don't you expose us to an affront, whatever you do. And if it should turn out that he would like the exchange, why, I should be very much obliged to you. Very much obliged indeed, for I should be even more reluctant to use force.'

'Surely, sir, you could never do that?' cried Herapath.

'I should find it abhorrent. Anything that might increase the ill-feeling would be abhorrent to me: I utterly detest the notion of a war between the two countries. But necessity is law, and I have my duty to the ship and to the people, particularly the women who may have to winter in her otherwise, with all that wintering means. However, let us hope it don't come to that. Pray see what you can do to prevent such a state of affairs: there are almost no terms that I should refuse. And by the way, Mr Herapath, I remember your telling me that you were an American citizen: I need not say that if you had anything of the air of a rat that leaves a sinking ship, I should not allow you to go.'

Herapath left, stayed an hour, and returned. 'Sir,' he said, 'I scarcely know what to report. I found Mr Putnam confined to his bed, and at times the pain from his jaw made him incoherent. The mates are his cousins and part-owners, and they too had their say. I am sorry to have to tell you, sir, that the feeling against England is very strong indeed. They do have a forge, but Mr Putnam and Reuben swore that no Englishman should ever set foot in their ship: the other two were less violent. The one with the horribly swollen leg and his brother were in favour of an accommodation; they spoke of the health of the crew in very serious terms, and I saw some cases that shocked me. Mr Putnam wavered, and in one bout of pain he desired me to draw the tooth straight away. I told him that I had no instruments with me, and that I must return to consult with my chief.'

'Very good, Mr Herapath,' said Jack. 'I see that you have done all that is proper: well fare ye, my lad, as we say.' Herapath gave a forced smile, and Stephen, watching his strained face, with its slightly hang-dog expression, was convinced that he had not confined himself to the forge and the whalers' health. 'Well now,' said Jack, 'here is your chief. I shall leave you to talk about physic and pills.'

'Dr Maturin,' said Herapath, when they were alone, 'may I beg you to come with me, if only to give advice? There are men in the whaler far, far beyond my competence. You have taught me the symptoms and treatment of the usual diseases, but here are cases I have never seen. Frostbitten toes that their late surgeon amputated and that are now blue and green, perhaps gangrenous; a harpoon-wound that had gone bad; and what I take to be a strangury, as well as ... I could not even deal with the Captain's tooth, which he has mangled horribly with pincers. And all the time they looked at me with such confidence – indeed, they very much wished me to go with them, and offered me what they call a full doctor's share. I should never have represented myself as an assistant-surgeon; I feel extremely guilty.'

'Oh, you would do very well, once things were set in order,' said Stephen. 'I have known many young fellows who have walked the wards with far less knowledge than yourself. You are a reading man, and with Blane and Lind to refer to, and a decent medicine-chest, you would do very well. Your conscience is too nice: I have noticed this before.'

'Will you go with me, sir? I have mentioned that you come from Ireland, and that you are a friend to independence: you would be most heartily welcomed, I know. Heartily welcomed, and I am sure that Mr Putnam would agree to any fee you might choose to name, although he will never ask Captain Aubrey for your services.'

'I have never firked a fee out of any man,' said Stephen, frowning. 'Recollect yourself, Mr Herapath. All we want is the use of his forge. And Captain Aubrey will no more ask for it than Mr Putnam will ask for the *Leopard*'s surgeon. A foolish, foolish situation. Each, as an individual, would pull the other out of the water; each would succour the other, even at considerable danger to himself. But each, as the representative of his tribe, will batter the other with great guns and small; sink, burn and destroy at the drop of a hat. A foolish, foolish situation, that must be dealt with by men of sense, not by gamecocks stalking about on stilts and high horses. Come to my cabin.' There he opened his locker and said, 'Which tooth does it be?'

'This one,' said Herapath, opening his mouth and pointing.

'Hm,' said Stephen, picking out a grisly instrument and clapping its jaws. 'Still, we had better take the whole shooting-match. There are sure to be several more, with scurvy aboard. Retractors. Catlins. Perhaps a few little saws: yes, a selection of these capital Swedish-steel saws. Bone-rasp, just in case. Now physic. What is the condition of their medicine-chest, Mr Herapath?'

'They have emptied it, sir, apart from a little lint.'

'Of course. Just so. Calomel on top of physic-nuts, no doubt, with cassia and James's powders to send it down. Small wonder they are sickly.' When he had filled his bag he said, 'We must have someone to row us over. It will never do to have trembling hands, if we are to operate.'

It was a sensible precaution. As soon as he had seen what passed for the whaler's sick-bay, Stephen realized that he would have to conduct two delicate resections at once if the legs were to be saved; and there were, as he had supposed, a good many teeth that would call for a firm, steady hand, a strong wrist, when the more important work was done. He looked at Putnam's jaw, told him to stop chewing tobacco, to hold this dressing on his gum, and to sit with his feet in hot water until the surgery was over. He might have time to deal with Captain Putnam before the light failed, but he was not sure: nor would he touch it until the swelling had diminished.

'May I ask you to name your fee, Doctor? Whatever it is, I will double it and welcome, if you draw this – before sundown.'

'I am not come here for a fee, sir,' said Stephen. 'Your men asked no fee for taking me off the island: they made no stipulations, and nor do I.'

Checking his cases while the operating-table was being prepared – four chests lashed together under the roundhouse skylight – Stephen learnt at least one of the reasons that made Captain Putnam so very unwilling to have the Royal Navy aboard his brig. It was Stephen's custom to listen attentively to what his patients had to say; this was unusual in the profession, as he admitted, but he found it helped his diagnosis. Now as he listened he realized that many of them were try-ing to deceive him, not about their various ills, but about their coun-try of origin. He had heard the distinctive American dialect often enough to know that this was a poor imitation; and the particular syntax of the English spoken in Ireland could never escape his accus-tomed ear, still less the odd murmurs of Irish itself in the background. And when the strangury showed a strong reluctance to take off his shirt, Stephen told him candidly that if he was afraid of having to do with an informer rather than a physician he might keep it on and go to the Devil, for there he would be in another week's time without he was treated; and this he followed with some of the peculiarly shock-ing Gaelic oaths and blasphemies that remained from his childhood.

The shirt came off, revealing the tattooed image of a first-rate man-of-war in sail, HMS *Caledonia*, and the strangury was not the only one: quite a large proportion of the whaler's men were Irish-born and therefore liable to be pressed; and some of them were deserters, liable to be hanged or at least flogged and compelled to serve again in the Royal Navy. Jack could probably seize as much as a third of the *La Fayette*'s crew, remaining well within the law; and he was known to be short-handed. However, the tension grew far less after Stephen's remark, only to be replaced by tension of another kind when he set-tled down to his work. The *La Fayette* was a democratic brig, and faces lined the skylight, watching the long, delicate play of the knife, the brusque intervention of the saw, with a horrified fascination.

When the first resection was carried away, the tall harpooner from Cahirciveen said, 'Will you take a tint now, Doctor dear?'

'I will not,' said Stephen. 'I want my head as clear as if I had the College of Cardinals under my knife. But when I have done, I might look on a drop.'

The work was long and exacting. Fortunately he had a good light, a steady sea, sharp instruments, and a capable assistant. Herapath would make a good surgeon, with experience: Stephen, speaking always in Latin, explained each step; and he spoke of the necessary after-care as though the young man were to tend these patients for months. Stephen was in fact convinced that Herapath would leave in the whaler, if only he could get his mistress aboard; and nothing could suit Stephen better. He would miss them both – they had engaged his affections – but he could scarcely wait for them to be gone, carrying the poison, harmless to Wogan, that would play Old Harry with Buonaparte's intelligence system, and saving Wogan herself from the dreariest exile.

The evening came, and with it the drop. 'Jesus, Mary and Joseph, that went down well,' said Stephen. 'You may fill it again. Another hour like that, and I should have been killed.' He looked at his hand, quivering as it relaxed after its delicate task. 'The teeth will be for tomorrow.'

'Tomorrow?' cried Putnam. 'Why, you son of a bitch, you promised – ' He checked himself, and in terms as civil as the pain would permit he urged Stephen to 'whip it out right now' – he could not stand such another night.

'Yours is a difficult, ill-set tooth, Captain, and the swelling has not gone down. I would not touch it now, in the half-light, and with my hand unsure, if you were the Pope,' said Stephen.

'Oh — the Pope,' cried the skipper.

'Hey there, Winthrop Putnam,' said his master in a warning tone.

'Do you think I am not going to do the right thing?' said Putnam. 'I tell you, sir, that forge will be on shore at sunrise, come hell or high water, along with a dozen thirty-foot strips of five by one, an anvil, small-coal, and all that's proper.'

'I am sure of it, sir. But I could not answer it to my conscience, to touch your tooth this evening. Drink this down, keep your dressing in its place, and I give you my word you will pass a tolerable night.'

On their way back to the shore Stephen said not a word to his assistant; he felt worn and emptied, and Herapath was as mute as himself. Stephen was little more loquacious when he reported to Jack: 'I suggest that all the Irishmen and foreigners and black men the ship still contains should assemble on the strand in the morning, to help unload the forge; and that you and the officers should keep out of the way,' he said. He looked thoughtfully at Jack's shining face for some moments; then, without saying anything more, he walked off to Mrs Wogan's hut.

'I am come to drink tea with you,' he said, 'if you will indulge me so far.'

'Delighted, enchanted,' cried she. 'I had not expected you today, in the least. What a surprise. What a very pleasant surprise. Peggy, the tea-things, and then you may go.'

'What shall I do with the trousers, ma'am?' asked Peg, raising her broad innocent face from the sewing.

Mrs Wogan darted across, plucked them from her hands, and hurried her from the room. Stephen gazed at the kettle singing on the seal-oil stove, and said, 'A dish of tea, a dish of tea . . . I have been sawing up your countrymen, my dear, and mine too for that matter; and when it was done, they would ply me with whiskey, Geneva, and rum: a dish of tea would settle my spirits.'

'My spirits too have been in a strong hurry and flurry today,' said Mrs Wogan; and she was obviously speaking the truth – she could scarcely keep still, and she had quite lost the somewhat drawn, pasty look of her first weeks of pregnancy; her complexion now had an extraordinary bloom, and this, combined with the light in her eyes and the brimming life of her person, made her quite strikingly beautiful. 'A strange hurry of spirits. Let us drink a whole hogshead of tea together; and then we shall be calm – Look, Dr Maturin, I have adventured upon a pair of seamen's trousers – I hope you do not think them immodest – they are against the cold, you know. Most prodigious warm, I assure you. And see, I have finished your blue comforter. Pray, sir, have you news of the States?'

'How infinitely kind. I shall wear it about my loins; for the loins, ma'am, are the seat of animal warmth: my very best thanks. As for

news, alas, it seems that a war cannot be long delayed, if it has not
already been declared. The *La Fayette* spoke of another American off
Tristan no great while ago, and – but Herapath can tell you better
than I; he had more time to talk. As for our merely local news, they
have very kindly undertaken to lend us their forge and their anvil, so
that we may continue our voyage.'

'Will they stay here long, do you know?'

'Oh no: just to pick up greenstuff for their voyage home; a day or
so, while I see to a few more cases, and then they are homeward-
bound. Homeward-bound for Nantucket, which is in the Connecti-
cut, I believe.'

'Massa – Massachusetts,' said Mrs Wogan, and burst into tears.
'Forgive me,' she said, through her sobs, 'forgive me. It must be my
pregnancy – I have never been pregnant before. No, pray do not go.
Or if you must, send Mr Herapath: I should so like to hear what news
he may have.'

Stephen withdrew. He felt somewhat more dirty than usual – it
had been a dirtying day – but in his diary he wrote: 'Things seem to
be following their train much as I could wish; and yet I am not quite
sure. I should carry the poor simple creatures aboard the whaler
myself, only that Wogan must not suspect that I am aware of their
motions: that would destroy the credibility of her papers, at least if
her chief is as intelligent as I suppose. I am tempted to confide in Jack,
so that he may withdraw guards, leave boats lying about: anything to
facilitate their escape. But he is a wretched hand at playing a part; he
would over-act, and she would see through him directly. Yet I may be
driven to it at last. Herapath is the most unfortunate accomplice for a
conspirator that can well be imagined: true, he possesses that invalu-
able air of integrity which can so rarely be assumed once its basis is
lost; but on the other hand he can control neither his countenance
nor his memory. He observed that I was 'a friend to independence',
which is very true; but I never told him so and the information can
only have reached him through Wogan: a sad gaffe on his part. And
then this very integrity may well bring on an untimely fit of hon-

ourable feeling: I dread it. Jack's words about rats were most unhappily chosen. However, I have done all I can, and tonight I shall allow myself just twenty-five drops, which I shall drink to Herapath's felicity. I am much attached to that young man, and although I may not be doing the kindest thing by him in fact – a prolonged association with Wogan may not prove quite what he hopes – yet I wish he may enjoy what there is to be enjoyed: that he may not eat up his youth in longing and hope disappointed, as I have ate mine.'

He slept long and deep, and he was woken by the sound of hammers ringing on iron. The forge was already on shore, a white-hot blaze in its heart, and the whalers had returned to the brig.

He had rarely seen Jack happier than he was at breakfast, sitting there in the great cabin drinking coffee, with a spy-glass at hand so that he could watch the beautiful smithy between cups. 'There is good even in an American,' he said. 'And when I think of that poor skipper with his face-ache, drinking small-beer for his morning draught, I have a mind to send him a sack of coffee-beans.'

'There is a proverb in Ireland,' said Stephen, 'to the effect that there is good to be found even in an Englishman – *is minic Gall maith*. It is not often used, however.'

'Of course there is good in an American,' said Jack. 'Look at young Herapath yesterday. I told him so, when we had a word first thing this morning. In his place, I should have been strongly tempted to skip. What an amazingly handsome woman she is, upon my word: jolly too, which I love in a girl. She don't look so jolly at the moment, though: I hope he has not said anything impertinent. It looks to me as if he had said something impertinent, and she is bringing him up with a round turn – he hangs his head – ha, ha, the dog. He should not have done so in the morning – the cold dawn is no time for such capers. But I tell you what, Stephen, there are run seamen in that whaler: one I recognized for certain – Scanlan, yeoman of the signals in *Andromache*, always on the quarterdeck, so I could not mistake him. And I am sure there are others.'

'I beseech you, Jack,' said Stephen wearily, 'I beseech you to leave

them alone. With things as they now stand, you would do immeasur-
able harm by stirring it all. Pray, my dear Jack, just sit in your good
comfortable chair until they are gone. I speak in sad sober earnest.'

'Well,' said Jack, 'I will do as you say; though you cannot imagine
my hunger for men. Prime seamen, whaler's hands, good Lord! Are
you away?'

'I go to draw the skipper's teeth.'

'They are drawn already,' cried Jack. 'His forge stands there on the
beach, ha, ha, ha! What do you say to that, Stephen?'

Stephen said little to that, and less to Herapath as they rowed across
to the *La Fayette*. The whale-boats were putting off for their last few
loads of greenstuff and eggs, and their crews called out, friendly and
familiar, as Stephen went aboard. The youngest mate met him with
the news that the skipper had only just woken up – they had thought
he was dead in the night – and speaking for himself and his fellows,
the mate asked whether the Doctor wanted to trade any. Coffee-
beans for a hog, for example; a prime Marquesas hog of twelve score.

'I have no occasion for a hog, sir; but if you would like some beans,
you will find a small sack under the seat in the boat. I will attend to
the Captain directly.'

Putnam was rapidly coming to life; so was his tooth. But the swelling was less; the tooth was ripe for extraction; and with one long
firm twisting wrench Stephen delivered him, leaving him gaping,
amazed, staring at the bloody fang. He then moved on to his other
patients, and once again he observed that men who would submit to
grave surgery, even amputation, with a noble fortitude, and bear the
worst with no more than an involuntary groan, grew unaccountably
shy when sat in a chair and told to open wide. Unless the pain was
urgent, there at the moment of sitting or within the last hour, many
would change their minds altogether, grow evasive, and move silently
off. The teeth dealt with, he attended to the dressing of yesterday's
wounds, again explaining just what should be done: he did not wish
to lose any one of these men for want of a clear understanding, and
he repeated himself frequently, so frequently that he feared his aim

might show through. And it would have shown through, if Herapath
had not been so absent. 'You seem somewhat distraught, colleague,'
said Stephen. 'Be so good as to rehearse the main points I have made.'

'I beg your pardon, sir,' said Herapath, having done so moderately
well. 'I slept badly last night, and am stupid.'

'Here is a smell will revive you,' said Stephen. The whole ship was
embalmed with the roasting of coffee, or rather with the parching of
the beans in a red-hot skillet.

They finished their dressings, and Stephen made some general
observations on the drugs he had provided for the whaler's medicine-
chest: coming to the antimony, he enveighed against the custom of
calling it poison, and of frightening young practitioners: 'Certainly
antimony is a poison, when wrongly exhibited. But we must not be
the prisoners of words. There are times when it is right to use antimony, and many another thing that has an ugly name. It is very weak
to be swayed by a mere word, Mr Herapath, by a categorical impera-
tive imposed from without by those who do not know the inward
nature, the full complexity of the case.' He was still speaking of the
necessity for a clear head, free of prejudices and of notions precon-
ceived by others, for the mind that could judge for itself, and that, on
perceiving two evils, could choose the less, whatever its ugly name,
when they were invited to drink coffee with the Captain.

The absence of pain, the presence of coffee, made Mr Putnam a far
more agreeable companion; he was very complimentary about Stephen's abilities, and he blessed his stars that he had put into Desolation, though when he saw the *Leopard* in there, he had very nearly
turned about, and would have, too, but that the tide was on the make,
the breeze in his teeth, and no other sheltered harbour, with greenstuff at hand, that he knew of anywhere under his lee. He reckoned
he would sail on the ebb today, round about moonrise; and he begged
Dr Maturin to accept these sea-otter skins, ready dressed, that they
had picked up off Kamschatka, this piece of ambergris, and these
sperm-whale teeth, as a token of the *La Fayette*'s sense of his kindness and skill.

'Hear him,' said Reuben.

Stephen made a suitable reply, but said that he would not say fare-well, at this point: he would visit his patients once more, just before they sailed, to see that all was well and above all to give Captain Put-nam the fullest instructions for their subsequent care, a point of the greatest importance, since they had no surgeon aboard. At this, as he observed with deep satisfaction, Captain Putnam's face went as blank as a wall, all expression wiped out; while Reuben looked down at his feet.

'But stay,' he said, considering. 'I think I shall take my leave after all. Mr Herapath is quite as competent as myself in these matters: he will come in the evening. Yes, Mr Herapath will come in my place. And so farewell to you, gentlemen; and I wish you a most prosperous voyage home to the States.'

As they rowed back Herapath said, in a low, troubled voice, 'Dr Maturin, I should very much like to speak to you privately, if I may.'

'Perhaps when we go through the chest again, in the afternoon. We may be able to spare your countrymen some asafoetida. There is nothing more comforting to a seaman with the megrims, than asa-foetida.' The asafoetida, with examples of its various mixtures, lasted them to the *Leopard*, where Stephen went aboard, asking Herapath to carry on to the shore – a shore still filled with the clangour of ham-mers and the roar of the forge – to note what drugs remained in the hut; and, while he was there, to tell Mrs Wogan that Dr Maturin pro-posed himself the pleasure of waiting on her after dinner. Mr Hera-path still had the spare key, he believed.

In spite of the very high spirits in the wardroom – everyone talking at once, although the Captain was present, laughing, guzzling alba-tross soup, tender sea-elephant, mutton-bird fritters – dinner was a somewhat empty ceremony as far as Stephen and Herapath were con-cerned: they both of them took little on their plates, and of that little they ate less, concealing the gobbets of flesh beneath biscuit. And whenever Stephen happened to look down the table, he found Hera-path's eye fixed upon his face or the Captain's: as the meal progressed

Stephen grew more and more alarmed. If Herapath jibbed now, with
the whaler almost on the wing . . . 'Captain Moore,' he called through
the din, 'you have sailed with the Prince d'Auvergne, have you not?
Pray what kind of a man is he?' The gentleman was one of the few
French royalist officers serving as a post-captain in the Royal Navy,
and his reserve, his aloofness, was a by-word in the service.

'Why, as to that,' said Moore, his smile changing to a serious look,
'I cannot say very much. I never saw him in action, though no doubt
he would have behaved very well; and I never saw much of him out
of action either, if you follow me. He was in an awkward position,
fighting against his own country; and as far as his officers were concerned he kept himself very much to himself. I suppose he did not
care to risk hearing us crowing over the French, or – ' Babbington's
Newfoundland, excited by the merriment, interrupted with a melodi-
ous baying, and the general talk flowed on – it was of gudgeons and
braces – drowning Moore's final observations, which he delivered in
dumb-show, shaking his head in disapprobation. Stephen was quite
pleased with the result of his words, but his satisfaction disappeared
at the end of the meal, when they drank the King's health. Herapath
emptied his glass and joined in the general 'God bless him' with what
seemed an unusual emphasis; and Stephen recalled, with dismay, that
Herapath's father had been a Loyalist – a man with a deep sense of
allegiance. How much of this had he passed on?

'It seems to me,' said Stephen to himself, 'that an interview would
be fatal. Herapath would certainly open his mind to me. Unsuccess-
ful opposition on my part would confirm him in his resolve; successful opposition would expose my hand. In any case I have not the
strength to argue a decent man out of his convictions; not today. I am
sick, sick to the heart of these manipulations.'

Nevertheless, when he called upon Mrs Wogan he took with him
a soft parcel, which he laid upon the small table in the middle of the
room, a table that was usually covered with books, sewing, a variety of objects, including, at times, Stephen's stockings to be darned.
It was empty now, and indeed the whole place was curiously trim,

almost bare. 'Upon my word, ma'am,' he said, 'you are in prodigious fine looks today. I speak with never a word of flattery.' Nor did he. She might not have quite the feral grace of Diana, but Diana's complexion had suffered from the Indian sun, and Mrs Wogan's was now of a brilliance he had never seen surpassed. The drifting rain was much the same here as it was in Ireland: perhaps that was a cause. 'You are superb,' he said.

Mrs Wogan blushed and laughed, said she was happy to hear it, and wished she might believe him. But in fact this was largely mechanical: she paid little attention to his remarks. After a turn or two about the room she observed that it was a wonder how the weather held up: day after day of something almost like summer. He had never heard her reduced to the weather before: nor had he seen her so little mistress of her emotions. She asked after the state of the tide, and whether the whale-boats were still on the shore, with quite a painful edge of agitation.

'So we have a set of beautiful new gudgeons,' she said, 'and may sail away directly.'

'I believe they are all done but two,' he said. 'The wardroom is in a great state of jubilation. But I do not collect that we are to leave Desolation quite so soon. These gudgeons must first be attached, or shipped, as we say; then all the innumerable objects on the strand must be returned to the ship. In any case, Captain Aubrey could never answer for it to the Royal Society, were he to hurry me away before my collections were completed; and I am not half way through the cryptogams.'

'The cryptograms, sir?' cried Mrs Wogan.

'No, child,' said Stephen. 'Cryptogams. A cryptogram, with another r to it, is a puzzle; and the word is also used for a secret writing, I believe. Cryptogams are plants that produce offspring without any visible, apparent marriage.' Mrs Wogan blushed again, and hung her head. 'And that reminds me,' said Stephen, taking the parcel and slowly untying it. 'Your kind countrymen made me a compliment of furs. I beg you will accept them to wrap your baby in. When it arrives it will need all the warmth it can get; both figurative warmth and literal too.'

'It shall certainly have them both, poor honey-lamb,' said Mrs Wogan, and then, 'Oh, oh,' she cried, colouring again, 'sea-otters! I have always longed for a sea-otter. Maria Calvert had two – how we envied her – and here there are four! I shall wear them first, with great care, and then the baby shall have them on Sundays. What luxury! And it is my birthday too, or almost.'

'Give you joy, my dear,' said Stephen, saluting her.

'Dear Dr Maturin,' said she, returning a hearty kiss. 'How immeasurably kind. But surely, sir, there must be some lady who . . . ?'

'Alas, never a one. I have no advantages of person, nor family, nor purse; and it has always been my misfortune to aim far beyond my deserts. I am unlucky in love.'

'You must come to Baltimore. You would find plenty of girls, and good Catholics too – but what am I saying? We are bound for Botany Bay.' After a longish pause, in which she stroked the furs against her cheek, she said, almost to herself, 'It depends what you mean by love, of course.' Then, in quite another tone, 'So you do not think the *Leopard* will sail quite yet?'

'I do not.'

'Suppose it takes a week. Tell me, since you know everything about the sea, and ships, would the *Leopard* catch up with the whaler, if they went in the same direction? The *Leopard* has more masts and sails, and is a man-of-war, so much faster, I presume.'

'No, no: the *Leopard* will never catch the whaler, my dear. When the *La Fayette* sails tonight on the turn of the tide, you must say farewell to her for ever. She will never be seen again.'

Mrs Wogan wanted to understand this matter of the tide – it was dreadful to be so ignorant – and Stephen told her all that he knew, adding that Mr Herapath, who would be rowing the jolly-boat across to see the patients just before they left, would find no adverse current, but rather slack water. It would be perfectly easy for him, in spite of the darkness. There followed a number of questions of much the same kind: when would the whalers take off their forge? Would they have difficulty rowing across? Suppose the wind turned, or failed, would the tide still take the ship away? Would it, indeed? She was happy to hear it. Stephen watched her with pleasure: there was a touching mixture of ingenuousness and skill, and when she had finished he said, 'As for what is meant by love, sure there are definitions without end; but perhaps they must all include an abdication of the critical sense. I mean that the one may see the faults of the other, but utterly refuse to condemn them. But come, if I were to tell you my thoughts on the passion, I should still be here at midnight. Good day to you, ma'am.'

'Oh, must you be away? Shall you not go with Mr Herapath to the whaler?'

'I shall not see him again today. He did propose our meeting after dinner, but to tell you the truth I am very weary at present. It will have to wait till tomorrow. I mean to spend the rest of the day by myself.'

Suddenly, and à propos of nothing, Mrs Wogan said, 'I know you are a friend of America – Mr Herapath tells me that the whalers sing your praises, and I am sure they should – and when you are next in London I wish you would go to see a friend of mine, a most interesting, intelligent man: Charles Pole. He has a place under government, in the Foreign Office, but he is not the ordinary dull kind of official; and his mother came from Baltimore.' She was looking at him very hard now, not only with affection but with a particular significance.

'I should be happy to know Mr Pole,' said Stephen, rising. 'Good day to you, now, my dear.'

She held out her hand; he took it, returned the pressure, and walked off.

He called on Jack, told him that he had desired Herapath to go to the whaler tonight rather than himself, and asked for the loan of his very best glass. He was on the point of going farther, of saying that Herapath should not be stopped whatever the circumstances – even farther, perhaps, if persuasion were needed – when Jack spontaneously observed, 'He will have to go by himself, then. There will not be a soul ashore tonight, apart from the women. We are going to hoist up the rudder, and I need close on every hand that can tally on to a rope. Stephen, you will take great care of this telescope, will you not? It is the very best achromatic, with extraordinary light-gathering powers, and a truly virgin objective.'

'I will, too. But Jack, I hope you will be able to let me have Bonden, in spite of the rudder? I very much wish to be on my island.'

'Oh, one more or less don't signify. But surely, Stephen, you don't mean to miss the hoisting up of the rudder? To miss such a glorious sight?'

'Is this the definitive, final, triumphant move?'

'Oh, of course not. This is for the pintles, Stephen. The *pintles*, not the gudgeons. But it is pretty triumphant for a sailor, upon my sacred honour, it is.'

'My sacred honour,' said Stephen, closing the door. '*Tantum religio potuit saudere malorum.*' And to Bonden, 'Barret Bonden, pray be so good as to accompany me to my island in the canvas boat. I must make observations in the afternoon, and later I wish to see my chicks by the light of the moon.'

'She rises a little after dark tonight, sir,' said Bonden. 'Maybe I had best bring a bite and some furs. There will be a rare old frost, once the sun has dipped. Mr Herapath was asking for you just now, sir. He's gone off with the raft, to see if you're in the sick-bay.'

'Aye. Well, buckle to, Bonden; we must be off. Leave word that I am not at leisure today, but will see him tomorrow.'

Bonden had accompanied the Doctor on many a curious expedition. He made no comment when Stephen concealed himself on the island and trained the powerful glass on the shore, where all hands were assembled to be ferried aboard on the raft. After an hour Herapath appeared in the objective, alone on the beach. He looked thin, worn, sad and tormented. He had a large bundle wrapped up in a cloak, and he carried it across the strand, deserted but for Mrs Boswell and her baby, past the still-smoking forge, to one of the whale-boats that were waiting to carry the whole smithy away. The boat-keeper was lying with Peggy under the lee of a rock, out of his sight but within the telescope's view. Herapath hesitated, heard a hail from the cliff where Reuben and his men were gathering their last cabbages, nodded, put the bundle into the bows, and paced up and down for a while before disappearing into Mrs Wogan's hut. A sweep of the glass showed the *Leopard*, every man aboard staring intently at the massive great rudder as it mounted into the air.

From then on the glass remained fixed on the hut, as though by staring at the door and the oiled-paper window Stephen could learn something of the doubtful battle raging within. 'Surely she must overcome him,' he reflected. 'She has this baby to wield, and the war, and tears, as well as all common sense. But when it comes to honour, dear Lord . . . *I could not love thee, dear, so well, loved I not honour more*: and so on to the foot of the stake. And there is the infinitesimal fact that he owes me seven guineas for his uniforms: it might prove the ludicrous sticking-point. Who can tell just where another man will jib? All shame, all ignominies, but not this one. Which one, though? Hardest of all to tell in men that are weak; or weak in places, like Herapath. If she overcomes him, perhaps he will never forgive her: if she does not, she will certainly never forgive him. She will certainly win the day. Maturin, friend, you are protesting too much: you do not know.'

'Sun's dipping, sir,' said Bonden at last. 'You'd best put on your cape.'

Dipping already. The time had passed with extraordinary speed. Twice Herapath was seen in the twilight: but still Stephen could not tell what was in his mind, apart from conflict.

'They are having a high old time with the rudder,' observed Bonden, putting the sealskin over Stephen's shoulders. 'The Marines have hauled it into the larboard shrouds, the lubbers.'

There were lights all over the *Leopard* now: Jack did not intend to lose a minute. The stars were beginning to show, dimmed in the south by the aurora australis, waving down there towards the pole, a great arc of increasing splendour: and the frost had begun to fall.

Darkness now, and the barking of seals: the vague forms of petrels in the starlight. 'What is that you are smoking?' asked Stephen.

'The best Virginny,' said Bonden, with a contented laugh. 'There was an old shipmate of mine on shore from the whaler this morning. A bit leary at first, when Joe Plaice and me tipped him the wink, because there is an R against his name. Run, sir. But then we got talking, and he gave us a keg. It don't matter my telling now, because they're winning their anchor, and he's as safe as the Tower. Do you see how the brig's crept across? Now she's signalling. Lantern to the peak: up and down, up and down. Has she left someone on shore? Yet I never seen no boat. Now she's at single anchor, and they're shifting the messenger for t'other. Stamp and go, stamp and go: you hear 'em, sir?' In a deep rumbling undertone Bonden echoed the shanty: *Stamp and go, stamp and go, the lady comes from Mexico.* 'Now the cable's up and down: she's right over her anchor – hear the skipper call for nippers thick and dry.'

The moon rose, huge and very little past the full, flooding the sea with her pale fire. Clear of the horizon now: higher still, and somewhere on the left a battle broke out among the sea-elephants.

'Maybe they've fouled a fluke, hanging about so long,' said Bonden at last. 'No. She's loosed her foretopsail. She'll weigh any minute now. Soon be gone, with the ebbing tide; and she'll cast pretty on this breeze. Soon be gone, and so shall we, thank God. Gudgeons in and rudder shipped tomorrow, and homeward bound maybe, once the hold is stowed. The lantern again. They'll lose their tide if they keep hanging about like this: what a rum way of carrying on! Do you hear that, sir? No, not the old seal. A boat, a-pulling for the brig. There, I see 'un, coming from behind the pointed rock. Why, our jolly-boat. I dare say it is Mr Herapath to say good-bye, he pulls so awkward. Yes, so it is. But who's his mate, the black-haired boy? I don't know that phiz. Sir, sir, it's Mrs Wogan! She's skipped her bail. Shall I shove off and bring 'em back?'

'No,' said Stephen. 'Sit still and keep quiet.'

The boat came nearer still, passed within whispering distance, and the moon shone on their faces, delighted, ingenuous, and absurdly young. It passed on; swung into the black shadow of the whaler's side. Some low cries from the *La Fayette* – 'Get a good hold on the lines, ma'am, and mind your petticoats – easy, all, as she rises' – and then, as the brig swung to the breeze and gathered way, Mrs Wogan's laugh, floating clear across the water, very cheerful and amused, more amused than ever, so amused that both Stephen and Bonden chuckled aloud; and now, for the first time, it had a fine trumphant ring.